THE KISSING HOUSE

MICHAEL PERT

Published in Australia by Sid Harta Publishers Pty Ltd,
ABN: 46 119 415 842
23 Stirling Crescent, Glen Waverley, Victoria 3150 Australia
Telephone: +61 3 9560 9920, Facsimile: +61 3 9545 1742
E-mail: author@sidharta.com.au

First published in Australia 2019
This edition published 2019
Copyright © Michael Pert 2019
Cover design, typesetting: WorkingType (www.workingtype.com.au)

Pert, Michael
The Kissing House
ISBN: 978-1-925230-67-3
pp422

ABOUT THE AUTHOR

Born and raised in suburban Melbourne, Michael escaped at the earliest opportunity to pursue his dream of a military career. He worked predominantly in military intelligence and his career spanned more than thirty years. During this period, he saw service in Australia and overseas, including postings in Asia, South East Asia, Africa and the Pacific region.

Michael specialised in human intelligence operations and held multiple operational, training and leadership roles within the discipline. He was made a member of the Order of Australia in 2005 for his significant and multi-faceted contribution to Australian intelligence. In post-military life, he completed both bachelor's and master's degrees as a mature aged student and worked as a public servant in Australia and New Zealand.

Michael currently resides in Canberra with his wife Kerry, his partner of forty years. They have two adult children and one grandson. He is currently self-employed and consults to government departments, non-government organisations and business entities in Australia and overseas on specialist security and intelligence applications. In addition to writing, he lists family, people, bushwalking, travel, sport and reading among his interests and hobbies.

ACKNOWLEDGEMENT

Sincere thanks and gratitude for the exacting work of my editor, Kristen Rohde, who made my book better, and from whom I learned a great deal. She treated me, and the characters within this book, with great respect. And to Luke Harris for his friendly advice and creative drive in designing the wonderful cover of the book.

Love and appreciation to my daughter Kylie; literary critic, proof reader and plot adviser extraordinaire, and without whom this book would not have the title that it does. And to my son Ryan, who is not an avid reader but who is an enthusiastic taskmaster, and without whose energy and confidence the project could easily have stalled. And finally, to my late uncle, Geoff Olney, writer and poet, from whom I learned the love of writing and who was there with me when I took those first tentative steps.

AUTHOR'S NOTE

This book is a work of fiction, but placed within an historical context. All of the characters are fictional, as are all the events portrayed in the book, with the exception of one.

The 'Kissing House' in Balibo is a real place. It earned its sinister name as a place of rape and murder during the post-election mayhem that engulfed East Timor in 1999. This was a dark time for the East Timorese people, a time when the violent excesses of pro-Indonesian militia groups and elements of the Indonesian army went completely unchecked.

In using the Kissing House as a central theme around which a fictional story has been woven, I have taken great care in my attempt to do justice to both the events of the time, and to the women and girls who were sexually brutalized and murdered there — by men who knew better, but went on to commit appalling atrocities anyway. It is a further stain that many of them have not yet answered for their crimes.

To this end, while the narrative about the Kissing House in this book is fictionalised, I have tried not to either understate, or exaggerate events that occurred there, or at a dozen other similar places during those times. Rather, I have attempted to portray them in the context of the story and as I came to understand them; drawing on conversations during the many hours it was my great privilege to spend with some of the survivors.

I pay tribute to the personal strength, resilience and dignity of the victims and their families in a cultural and religious environment in which there are no words to describe the extent of the indignity they have suffered, or the trauma that remains. Above all, I was humbled by their capacity for forgiveness, but this is not something I am able to share with them.

To my wife Kerry, with love always.

HISTORICAL NOTE

On 30 August 1999, the people of East Timor voted in a United Nations supervised referendum to decide whether their country would be an independent nation, or an integrated province of Indonesia. With the distinct prospect of losing the pro-Indonesian vote, the Indonesian military and their supporters raised local militia groups to terrorise independence voters, de-stabilise the voting process and ultimately de-legitimise the referendum.

Nevertheless, on polling day, 78.5 per cent of the East Timor population bravely voted for independence. Notwithstanding the clear will of the people, militia groups organised and supported by the Indonesian military commenced a large-scale, scorched-earth campaign of violent and brutal retribution against the East Timorese people and the country's infrastructure.

The Indonesian military and their proxy militia groups killed approximately 1,300 Timorese, committed gross human rights abuses and other crimes including assault, torture and rape, and displaced about 300,000 people who were forced into Indonesian West Timor as refugees. Many public buildings and homes were damaged or destroyed and the majority of the country's infrastructure, by some estimates up to seventy per cent of all irrigation systems, water supply systems, schools, and almost all the country's electrical grid were rendered inoperable or damaged beyond repair.

On 20 September 1999, the Australian-led International

Force for East Timor (INTERFET) deployed to East Timor, and in a sensitive and difficult operating environment quickly brought the violence to an end, although sporadic militia attacks continued. In October 1999, the United Nations Transitional Authority for East Timor (UNTAET) was established to administer the country in preparation for self-government.

The mandate of INTERFET ceased in February 2000, and UNTAET assumed military and security responsibility for East Timor, including the continued prosecution of the counterinsurgency campaign against the remaining pro-Indonesian militia forces. On 20 May 2002, a new, free and democratic nation, the Democratic Republic of Timor-Leste, was established. The UN continued to support the country in its infancy, and provided a bulwark against any potential militia resurgence.

Viva Timor-Leste!

PROLOGUE

BALIBO

INDONESIAN PROVINCE OF EAST TIMOR

....

September 1999

Lucia da Cruz was confused. At just shy of ten years old, there was still much of a complex world that eluded her. She didn't know why the soldiers had come to Balibo or what they wanted. They were angry and gruff; they spoke Indonesian very quickly and it was a language she could barely understand. What she picked up from those around her was panicked and disjointed, and only made her more confused — and much more afraid. More afraid than she had ever been in her short life.

The soldiers had driven through the town and forced all the women and girls into their big trucks. *For protection,* they said. But Lucia knew this was a lie; she had seen her dear father and other men from her village roughly pushed away and threatened with guns when they tried to stop the soldiers.

She thought she heard what might've been gunshots away in the village but she had no idea if anyone was hurt or what was happening. She knew that somewhere there must be a fire because amidst the chaos the bitter taste of smoke caught in the back of her throat. She looked back from the truck in desperation as it pulled away from her hut, and she knew from her father's tears and the anguish on his face that he loved her, but he could do nothing. Only God could save her now.

The truck drove the short distance to the town square and then stopped. More than half a dozen other trucks were already there, all parked at different angles with the engines noisy and thumping and the smelly exhaust fumes filling the still air around them. From the back of the trucks she could hear the desperate cries of the other women and girls, captive and frightened. *Have you seen my Ermelinda? Where is my mother? Is my sister safe? What is happening?*

The haphazard pattern thrown by the trucks' headlights and the orange light that danced from the burning houses nearby illuminated the hellish scene around her. There were other men with the soldiers, and they had guns too. But they were not soldiers, they were Timorese. She recognised some as local men, but they were unnervingly different now. She could see it in their eyes; they looked crazed and angry, like they might do anything. Not like she had ever seen them before.

She saw Senhor Esposito, the shopkeeper, dragging two of her friends, each held in a vice-like grip by the wrist as they struggled and fought, screaming and kicking and finally trying to dig their feet into the dust of the square, but to no avail. Through a rip in the canvas tarpaulin of the truck, she watched transfixed, her eyes widening with horror as her friends disappeared with the shopkeeper into the old Chinese house next to the square.

Chinese merchants had once lived there, she knew, but that was long ago in the Portuguese times and not during her lifetime. She had played in the house like other children; it had no roof, but it had previously been a place of solitude and safety. Not now.

In an instant she saw her mother dragged from a nearby truck by a soldier, her long black hair tightly wrapped around his hand as he pushed her roughly towards the house. Lucia started to call to her, she wanted to tell her how much she loved her, but a woman sitting near her quickly grabbed her and held her mouth tight to keep her silent. When she looked back her mother was gone.

She wanted to run, fast and far away. Perhaps she could get up into the hills above the town; no one would find her there. But there was a man with a gun standing guard at the back of each truck, and she had no doubt what would happen to her if she jumped down and tried to get away.

Suddenly a bony hand reached out and touched the arm of the little girl sitting next to her, the long fingernails startling her and sending a shockwave through her body. The girl recoiled in fright and wet the seat and the floor around her, the warm stream of urine flowing down and splashing across her bare feet. She shrank back and held her head in her hands and cried.

Lucia put her arm around the little girl's shoulder. A woman she knew, Senhora da Alma, soothed them both and rubbed the little girl's arm as she positioned all the young girls up against the front of the truck and away from the back where they might be seen. The women warned the young ones sternly not to look backwards out of the truck or show their faces. They complied without knowing the reason, but huddled together away from the light anyway.

Meanwhile, the older women shuffled around to sit near the back and whispered amongst themselves. Lucia saw that all their faces were desperate and weary. Their eyes were vacant and she could see the life was draining from them but they were resolute, and she sensed their strength. She watched as they embraced and prayed together, some nervously fidgeting with their rosary beads and others with their heads bowed, weeping quietly. She knew they were afraid too, and she sensed they understood something she and the younger girls did not. They all sat as quietly as they could, encouraged by their collective thought that if they couldn't be heard, they might be forgotten and the danger would pass them by.

Meanwhile, the mayhem around them continued; in the square, orders were barked, men laughed loudly and shouted, and the occasional gunshot rang out and made them all jump and then cringe closer together in terror. Above it all the cries and desperate pleas of those around them could be heard as they were pulled from the trucks and dragged away to the house.

Their terrified voices begging to be spared from a fate unknown gave Lucia a feeling of dread deep in the pit of her stomach. The girl closest to Lucia vomited and the stench was immediately unbearable, causing others in the group to do likewise. The acrid mess ran among them on the smooth metal floor of the truck, sticking to their legs and gluing their clothes together. But they kept their faces turned away and huddled closer together, seeking the safety and strength they could only get from each other.

Without warning the metal tailgate on the truck was noisily uncoupled and dropped down with a resounding clang. A dark shape climbed into the truck and they all instinctively pushed up towards the cabin away from it, and against each other. The intruder kicked the older women aside viciously and punched one of them very hard in the face when she tried to impede him. Torchlight played around inside the back of the truck and Lucia looked back briefly without thinking. She took the full beam of the light in the face and although she held her hand up protectively and kept her eyes squinted against the light, it was too late. She was chosen.

She slipped in the muck as she tried desperately to avoid the muscular brown arms that now reached for her in the darkness, while other smaller hands sought to hold her back. The girls screamed and clung to each other in the agony of their uncontrollable fear, but there was nowhere to go. The man just laughed loudly. It wasn't the kind, playful laugh of her father; instead it was sinister and cruel. It was then she knew this man would hurt her, and perhaps even kill her and never care.

As soon as his hands grasped her nightshirt, she was powerless to resist and he pulled her back towards the rear of the truck. Lucia fought with every fibre of her young being, but with a final tug, her attacker prevailed and she fell heavily off the back of the truck and onto the ground.

Before she had time to recover, the man jumped off the truck and stood over her. He reached down and grabbed her violently by the hair and yanked. She screamed in pain as his hard fingernails dug into her scalp but she could do little else other than half-crawl, half-run in order to keep up with him as he propelled her violently along the ground towards the house.

Once inside the house he hurled her against the wall like a discarded doll. She cracked her head on the masonry and fell back, dazed. Bleeding above her eye and with her vision blurred, she attempted to regain her balance. Another soldier swigging from a bottle pulled her roughly to her feet; his breath stank of alcohol and cigarettes and he drunkenly laughed in her face. Animated, his eyes wide and crazed, he motioned for her to remove her clothes.

Lucia stared at him dumbly as she looked around at the growing pile of discarded clothes nearby. She recoiled at the sight of a woman who lay contorted amongst the clothing, naked and dead. Much of her face and head were missing and only a dark gory hole remained. Lucia shuddered, knowing this was the punishment for disobedience.

Ahead of her was a line of women and girls, mostly around her own age. They were all naked. Some she knew but in shame they all averted their eyes, even from each other. Some looked down and others stared ahead with vacant, unseeing eyes, already resigned to a fate they neither knew, nor understood.

The line snaked unevenly into an unseen room further up the hallway from which cries of unimaginable anguish and sudden jarring screams emanated amidst the guttural comments and drunken laughter of their tormentors. Girls in the line shook uncontrollably and held their arms tightly across their nascent breasts, leaning forward in a vain attempt to preserve their modesty. Their faces were grimy and stained with tears; their eyes wide and red-rimmed.

The girl in front of Lucia soiled herself and the sticky mess ran down and caked onto the back of her leg, but in her trance-like state she neither knew, nor cared. Lucia heard the group called forward from the unseen room and the drunken soldier flapped his arms like a huge bird, cajoling them all to get moving. Lucia's legs failed her.

As she crumpled to her knees she retched violently and collapsed. She lay there and sobbed the lament of the damned as tears flooded down her face to mix with the blood and her own vomit, which had slickened the blue cement floor. Nothing could save her now.

1

BALIBO

UNITED NATIONS ADMINISTERED EAST TIMOR

....

January 2001

Young Leonardo sat idly on the window ledge of the old police post, shaded under the spreading foliage of an ancient and gnarled banyan tree. The post had once been whitewashed but was now largely faded and the timber beneath showed through in an uneven patchwork. The window shutters were long gone and the boy leaned easily against the upright of the window frame, his skinny brown legs dangling over the edge.

His lime-green shorts were grubby and his black shirt was fastened crudely with a knot at his waist. He flicked back the fringe of his unruly dark hair and looked about as the market-place came alive around him. All the while his dirty calloused heels drummed a tattoo against the wall as he periodically cork-screwed his finger into his nostril in search of some offending matter, and then inspected the tip.

Small groups of boys had already rushed by on their way to school and yelled cheeky greetings to him, but Leonardo would not be joining them. Until his family provided a pencil and an exercise book, the seven-year-old was not welcome at the local school. The Catholic Church cried poor, and the nuns simply turned away those without their own essentials.

Leonardo watched as the marketplace began to fill with people and the hum of activity rose steadily. Occasionally, the banter of the local women, barefoot and elegant in their colourful wrap-around skirts and plain white blouses, carried to him. They laughed and chatted excitedly amongst themselves, their woven baskets brimming with corn and bananas balanced carefully on their heads. In carefully selected places, woven mats were being laid out, and it was on these that the various goods and produce would be presented for sale.

Elsewhere, traders from out of town with their nut-brown faces tired and unshaven, struggled with enormous bundles wrapped in striped plastic sheeting. One passed close to Leonardo, a small wiry man bent double under the weight of his load. A billow of bluish smoke wafted back as the man passed and it momentarily engulfed them both. The pungent mixture of tobacco and cloves from the Indonesian Kretek cigarette attacked Leonardo's senses and he snorted loudly.

He thought the man looked like an ant, trying to carry a grain of rice many times larger than him. Leonardo knew the traders had tramped through the night along the border tracks from the markets in what was now Indonesian West Timor, and that the bundles contained petrol, kerosene and cigarettes. All of these were contraband items in East Timor under the new UN law, but they were the lifeblood of the economy too. And likely to fetch a big profit.

This Leonardo knew better than most because his father drove the old bus between Balibo and far away Dili every other day. The once gaily painted yellow and red bus that sounded like a bulldozer spewed clouds of choking, black smoke at every gear change. The bus that had one of its tyres stuffed with dry grass because the inner tube had long ago perished, and which usually carried more passengers clutching frantically to the roof than could sit inside.

Tonight, market day, Leonardo would help his father unscrew the rusty metal floor plates of the old bus. Into its hungry belly they would pack the fuel and the cigarettes that his father said would one day make them all rich. It was a secret, of course, and done to avoid the periodic searches of the Australian soldiers from AUSBATT, or the foreign police officers from the UN police, CIVPOL.

It was a secret to be kept in his heart and known only to himself and his father. And others who could be trusted, he reasoned, which included the town priest Padre Alberto, who shared things only with God, and his good friend from AUSBATT Senhor Mateus, because he knew everything anyway.

Leonardo's attention was suddenly drawn to the figure of a woman running frantically into the marketplace. Others close by were alerted by her cries but Leonardo was too far away to hear exactly what was going on. As he watched, she tripped and fell, the dust marking her black skirt down one side. Another woman leaned over to help her and she quickly regained her feet and hurried on.

Leonardo watched as the crowd began to gather behind her as she headed towards the CIVPOL station. Sensing excitement, he slipped nimbly from his perch and bolted across the dusty marketplace towards her. Jostling his way to the front of the growing throng, he listened to the excited villagers around him.

'Senhor da Silva is dead!' the woman implored as she hurried on.

How? Where? Why? Who has done this? The questions fired at random from the crowd around her.

'... stabbed in his bed in the night! ... right through his body ... so much blood,' the woman ranted, almost incoherently.

Leonardo's heart leapt as he heard the shocked comments reverberating around the crowd. This was surely something that Senhor Mateus would want to know, and it was equally possible he might be rewarded for his diligence.

He struggled to free himself from the jungle of brown legs imprisoning him at ground level and watched briefly as the crowd moved on towards the CIVPOL station. He quickly turned on his heel and sprinted off towards the fort. He prayed he would be the first to bring the news that there had been a murder in the town.

2

....

January 2001

The old fort at Balibo was built sometime in the eighteenth century. The Portuguese sited it on the most prominent feature, and over time it became the focal point for the villages that grew around it to eventually comprise the town. The large stones were hand-quarried from the surrounding hills, but they had become mossy and pock-marked over time and the weather had smoothed their edges. Still, the fort stood as an imposing sentinel above the town, just as it did when it was first built.

Corporal Richards and Private Zidelowski had manned the guard position at the fort's main gate since dawn. Two and a half mindless hours later, and well into the umpteenth day, they could remember having sat in the same sandbagged sangar, their sense of humour wearing thin. Boredom had taken on a new meaning.

They relaxed on two specially designed chairs which afforded them easy visual access over the height of the sandbags and through the chicken-wire screen to the world beyond. They were shaded from the direct rays of the sun by the corrugated iron roof of the sangar but the air was already hot and steamy. Soon they would be roasting from the heat that radiated down into their position as well.

Both soldiers noted the blur of movement as Leonardo reached the top of the stone stairs leading from the marketplace and raced across towards them. Puffing heavily, the young boy leaned on the sandbag wall for a few seconds catching his breath before looking up at the familiar faces peering down at him.

'*Bon dia*, Senhor Zed. Please… to see Senhor Mateus.'

'Come on Leonardo, you know the drill. No weapons allowed in the fort,' Zed teased, pointing to the boy's slingshot, tucked into the front of his shorts. Knowing the routine well enough, Leonardo quickly passed his slingshot through the slit in the wire. The occupants were already looking around for small stones to shoot at the local workers cutting the grass nearby.

'OK Zed, take him up to see Sergeant Major Hurley. Oh, and get two brews and a refill of water on the way back, will ya?' the young NCO yawned.

Zed grunted in acknowledgment. Placing his helmet on and retrieving his rifle, the big man eased his way out the rear of the sangar and set off back through the main gateway. At first, Leonardo fell into step beside him and willed him to walk faster, but he knew he would have to wait in the sun until the sentry had spoken with Senhor Mateus anyway.

He ran forward to the waiting seat in an attempt to speed up the process. The guard was in no such hurry however, and he plodded in the growing heat, his heavy feet dragging on the gravel that edged the roughly tarmacked road inside the fort. Leonardo watched as eventually his large frame disappeared into the line of tents.

Each of the tents backed onto the forbidding stone wall of the fort and fronted the road which ran centrally inside the fort. Leonardo had visited this particular tent many times before although he had no idea the stencilled sign "FSG" was an acronym for AUSBATT's Force Security Group.

It wouldn't have mattered anyway, it meant nothing to him or anyone else who may have taken an interest. The label itself was deliberately bland. It was chosen because it smacked of the ordinary and was designed to give no hint of the secret work carried out by Hurley and his team.

When Zed reappeared a short time later, he motioned the waiting boy inside before trudging back to his post. Inside, Matt Hurley sat waiting and when he saw Leonardo he waved him to the vacant canvas chair positioned on the duck-boards. This was also part of the routine.

'*Bon dia, colega,*' Hurley greeted him, using the local language and the familiar term for a friend.

'*Bon dia,* Senhor Mateus,' the young boy answered respectfully, using the Portuguese form of Hurley's name in the accepted fashion.

'Now, what's all the fuss about?'

'Senhor da Silva is dead. We must come,' the boy blurted out excitedly, at the same time motioning a stabbing movement into his own chest.

This was certainly unexpected and Hurley noted the boy's actions carefully, knowing very well Leonardo was not prone to exaggeration. He also knew the boy's capacity to understand English was far greater than his ability to speak it.

A number of things began to run through Hurley's mind. Da Silva was a common name throughout Balibo, and there were many branches of the same extended family. Some of them were more interesting to Hurley than others.

There had also not been a murder in Balibo since the UN had arrived. If it was true, it would be very unusual. He nodded and smiled reassuringly at the youngster.

'Which Senhor da Silva is dead, *colega?*' he asked carefully.

Leonardo thought for a moment and then shrugged in response, his shoulders almost touching his ears as he did so. He should have known that Senhor Mateus would want to know that and he silently rebuked himself. At the same time, he hoped his oversight would not interfere with any benefit that might be forthcoming.

'And how did he die?' Hurley prompted, watching the boy closely.

Leonardo began making the stabbing movements again. When he looked around and spied the bayonet on Hurley's webbing underneath the nearby table, he pointed to it but seemed unable to find the word he wanted. Hurley followed his gaze.

'Knife?' Hurley queried.

'Yes, knife. Push right through the heart.'

'When did this happen?'

'In the night, Senhor.'

'And how do you know this?'

'Every people, Senhor, they is talking now.'

Hurley had heard enough for now. He stood and grabbed his light blue cap from the table.

'OK Leonardo, thank you for bringing this very important news to me.' Leonardo beamed.

'Why don't you get something from the fridge and then we'll go to CIVPOL,' Hurley suggested as he turned to the nearby filing cabinet and opened the top drawer.

Next to the filing cabinet sat an aqua camping refrigerator, the size of a small esky. Nevertheless, it was large enough to hold a small quantity of milk and fruit; and the chocolate that could not survive the heat of even the coolest Timor day. *Morale lived inside the esky,* Hurley's ops sergeant would often say, and she got no argument on that score.

When Leonardo had finished ferreting around inside, he closed the lid and turned to face Hurley with a broad grin across his face. In his hand he held a king-size Cherry Ripe. It was the biggest one on offer and the one most likely to be selected by any seven-year-old. Hurley smiled and slowly handed Leonardo the pencil and exercise book he had retrieved from the cabinet.

The boy's head immediately dropped, his eyes seeking the floor and his hands dropping limply to his side. It was not the first time that Senhor Mateus had given him a book and a pencil, and he was now ashamed that he had traded the others to his friends. Hurley knew of these illicit transactions and could plainly see the young boy's discomfort.

'I know it's easy to lose them Leonardo, but try not to this time. You need to go to school to have a good life in the new East Timor,' he said encouragingly.

'*Obrigado*, Senhor Mateus,' the young boy thanked him sheepishly.

'*Nada, colega.* Let's go.'

Leonardo skipped merrily alongside Hurley as they walked down the fort road, his discomfort quickly forgotten. He had peeled back the chocolate's wrapping and was savouring the cold dark sweetness, but the heat was already hard at work causing the first rivulets of chocolate to run down the wrapper and onto his hand.

As they passed the guard post, Leonardo collected his slingshot and continued walking with Hurley, down the stone steps and towards the marketplace and the CIVPOL station. As they descended the stone stairway to the town, Hurley could clearly see the marketplace and the large crowd gathered there.

He noticed his local interpreter, Eduardo, among the masses and waved him over. Leonardo was happy to take his cue and he wandered off to finish his chocolate, the exercise book now placed down the back of his shorts for easy carriage. The two stood together, but apart from the buzzing crowd.

Hurley met Eduardo on his initial trip to Dili. He was a small wiry young man of just twenty, and his skin was darker than most Timorese. The latter was testament to his part-African ancestry, or so he would say with a cheeky grin. His darkness certainly contrasted with his prominent white teeth. These dazzled when he smiled and he would caress them lovingly each day with the toothbrush Hurley had given him, and which he kept on a wire hook in his tent. His black woolly hair was cut short and he wore a navy-blue *Nike* t-shirt Hurley had also given him, and long khaki shorts. On his feet he wore his latest acquisition, a weathered pair of *Adidas* sandshoes tied up with green nylon cord from the Quartermaster's store.

'So tell me, Eduardo, exactly which Senhor da Silva is it?' Hurley queried.

'It is Senhor Abrio da Silva sir,' Eduardo reported, and crossed himself as he spoke. 'His body has just now been brought wrapped in a sheet by those who found him. He is inside with Padre Alberto.'

'Jesus,' Hurley said in a low voice, almost to himself. His expression did not change to those who might have been observing him, including Eduardo. The information confirmed to Hurley what he had feared most when listening to young Leonardo's story.

The fact that one of his agents was now dead, and possibly murdered, was bad enough. But he was also aware of how bitterly disappointed CIVPOL would be that the crime scene had been disturbed. In their eagerness to help, the villagers who had brought the body had almost certainly ensured no one would ever be held responsible for the crime. Hurley sighed audibly.

'What's everyone saying then, Eduardo?'

'Kopassus, sir, and the knife was so big it went in the front and came out the back.'

Hurley's eyebrows raised instinctively at the thought of such a wound but it was Eduardo's reference to the Indonesian special forces group Kopassus that he found most disconcerting. He wondered if there was a reason for that idea to have popped up so quickly. He tucked the thought away for later on.

'I think we will go and see Senhor da Silva, Eduardo.'

Eduardo had obviously been anticipating this turn of events and had prepared himself.

'No, sir. I think *you* will go and see Senhor da Silva, I will mangle and find things out.'

Hurley smiled at Eduardo's sudden assertiveness and patted the young man affectionately on the shoulder. He didn't blame him one bit.

'That's *mingle* Eduardo, and I'll see you when I come out.'

Hurley walked towards the crowd which was now pressing around the steps of the station and humming with excitement. The station door was a new addition, its core was hollow and the plywood exterior was newly painted in UN blue livery.

It was closed and there were no windows at the front of the building to afford a view inside. This was probably just as well, as the assembled masses would have been straining to peer in and see what was happening inside. Seeing Hurley approach, the crowd parted respectfully as he greeted them, their chatter easing to a whisper as he made his way towards the door. He opened it and stepped inside, deftly closing it behind him in a single movement.

3

UN CIVPOL STATION
BALIBO, UNITED NATIONS ADMINISTERED
EAST TIMOR

January 2001

The body of Abrio da Silva was wrapped in a dirty grey sheet and lay on the main conference table dominating the front room of the station. Hovering over it, resplendent in white robes with an ornate green and gold stole positioned around his neck, was Padre Alberto. He had a round, serious face and was not known for his kindness or sense of humour.

He held a Bible in one hand and with the other was making various signs while he muttered incantations in a mixture of Tetum, the local language, and Latin. Periodically, he pushed his heavy black rimmed glasses back on the bridge of his nose with the forefinger of his right hand.

The officer in charge of the station came through from the rear of the building holding two mugs brimming with hot coffee. Placing these down on a desk he turned to Hurley, his face lighting up immediately. He wore the light grey uniform of his national police force, neatly ironed as always and trimmed with a black leather belt. His boots gleamed.

'Ah! My good friend, Mr Hurley. As every time, you are here when things are happening. You take coffee, yes?'

'G'day, Stefan. Coffee would be great, thanks.'

Stefan smiled infectiously and disappeared to the back of the stationhouse. He was ever the good host and in Stefan's eyes, a small thing like a murder did not negate the need for social niceties. Hurley sat down and let Padre Alberto finish his esoteric ministrations.

The amiable Stefan — Sergeant Stefan Osmanovich of the Bosnian Police Special Services — was well known in Balibo and throughout the wider administrative district zona Bobonaro as "The Giant". He stood six feet nine inches in his socks and had a build to match. Accordingly, he commanded quite a presence. But he was like many large men Hurley had known; friendly, good-natured and cheerful. Often gentle too, as in many ways Stefan was also.

Stefan's English was stilted and heavily accented, and his grammar was only rarely correct, and then probably only by accident. The result was a strange mixture that could be both formal and childlike at the same time. Amazingly, this was interpreted by many in AUSBATT as proof that his intellect was lacking.

Consequently, Stefan was classified by most as a non-swimmer. This was the unofficial label granted to incompetent internationals, the unfortunate souls who found the depth and the speed of the current simply too much. Swimmers, on the other hand, were viewed as competent and there was no greater accolade an international could be given.

However, it was annoying to everyone that non-swimmers outnumbered swimmers in almost every UN mission around the globe. *Good luck changing that,* Hurley had often been heard to say. But labelling the Giant a non-swimmer was a grave error of judgment. He was not only an experienced policeman; he could communicate quite adequately if given the opportunity to do so.

Hurley liked to remind the critics that Stefan was working in his fourth language when he was speaking English. Hurley would often play mischievously with these critics, particularly those AUSBATT officers who tended to think themselves just a little bit better than others. He would comment on Stefan's multi-linguistic ability and then ask them casually how many languages they spoke, knowing full well that for the majority of white privileged Australians the answer was predictable — one.

It was true that language had caused the odd problem, and Hurley would recount to others with great amusement his first meeting with Stefan. Hurley had come to the station to introduce himself and Stefan had been eager to brief him on some of the local nuances he felt were important for Hurley to know.

'Important men of the town are told by the size of their cocks,' Stefan had begun in all seriousness. Outwardly, Hurley had not blinked. Inwardly he had fallen apart. In his faltering English, Stefan had gone on to explain — 'the more bigger and power to the cock, the more it is smiled on by every man, and women too,' he added enthusiastically, 'women, they are liking big cocks too.'

Hurley had quickly realised that his new friend was referring to the large colourful birds regularly brought to the marketplace to participate in the favoured Timorese pastime of cockfighting. So, he had introduced the big Bosnian to the word *rooster*, and they had talked and laughed about the complexity of the English language with its sometimes difficult, double meanings.

In the end it proved impossible for Hurley to explain why the sport had never been called rooster fighting. Ironically, the perception that Stefan was a non-swimmer helped Hurley. He quickly found that any favour he could do for the big man came back ten-fold.

Soon after their first meeting, Hurley heard of his plight in trying to re-surface the pot-holed driveway of the CIVPOL station prior to the onset of the wet season. It had been a small matter for Hurley to arrange a truckload of crushed rock from the AUSBATT engineers. Stefan was overjoyed and had worked like a dog all afternoon in the searing heat spreading the rock with a spade, much to the amusement of the local children.

Hurley's gut feeling told him that the Giant knew his real intelligence role, though neither of them ever spoke openly of it. He probably knew from his experiences at home, reasoned Hurley, and probably knew also that it was something better left alone. The truth was that they needed each other to preserve their individual spheres of influence and there were no petty jealousies between them.

Stefan for criminal matters, and Hurley for security; that was their unspoken understanding and their partnership dictated that each respect and protect the domain of the other. If Hurley needed a vehicle checkpoint, a roadblock or a house searched and did not wish to involve AUSBATT, the Giant could be relied upon to set it up and make it happen.

More importantly, he could be trusted not to ask any difficult questions and to get results. Those working for Stefan did what they were told and were happy to do so. His happy-go-lucky assistant Romeo cared little about anything and his two non-swimming counterparts from India and Bangladesh were much the same. The latter two were known locally as Laurel and Hardy, due to both their physical characteristics and their perceived level of competence.

In his turn, Stefan was more than happy to take the crumbs from Hurley's table. If it was convenient and not attributable, Hurley would pass on the location of contraband, the presence of criminal elements or information relating to criminal activity in the Balibo area. Much of this came to Hurley as a matter of course but was often of no real use in his own reporting, so he guarded it carefully and fed it to Stefan.

And sometimes there was gold dust for Stefan, hard information on crimes to be committed sometime in the future. To further secure his ally, Hurley kept a very close eye on the UN policing statistics and passed on just enough information to ensure that Stefan ran the most efficient CIVPOL station in zona Bobonaro, the largest administrative region encompassing much of the border area.

Padre Alberto completed his work and looked over the top of his glasses to acknowledge Hurley's presence. *His face has the undertaker look, Hurley thought, the look that is so often used in the company of the dead.* Hurley, of course, had adopted it too.

'*Bon dia*, Padre Alberto,' he greeted the priest, his voice somewhat lower than normal, complementing the undertaker look to perfection.

'He is with God now,' Padre Alberto said with finality, almost to himself as if he had not heard Hurley at all. At the same time, he turned and packed the well-thumbed Bible into his leather satchel on the desk, fastening the little metal buckles which tinkled as he did so.

He took up one of the mugs that Stefan had brought and turned back to face Hurley.

'A sad day, Senhor Mateus, he was a good man all of his life,' the priest continued as he took a noisy slurp of the coffee.

'Yes, Padre, he will be sadly missed,' Hurley added dutifully. *And a whole lot bloody more than you will ever know.*

Stefan returned in a flourish, the metal plates on the heels of his boots echoing with authority on the painted cement floor. It was the only sound now apart from the occasional outburst of static or the squeal of a disembodied voice from the bank of radios charging in the corner.

He handed Hurley's coffee to him, upon which Hurley nodded and winked. It was a signal they would talk when the priest had gone.

'More coffee, yes Father?' Stefan prompted politely after a few minutes had passed, knowing full well that the offer would hurry the busy priest on his way.

'No thank you, Senhor Stefan, I must be gone as there are preparations to make.'

They watched in silence as he collected his satchel and again made the sign of the cross over the body before Stefan let him out the front door. The opening brought the buzzing sound of the crowd inside momentarily, but it was cut off as quickly as it had started when Stefan closed the door.

'We drink coffee while we work, my friend.' It was more a statement by the tone, but Hurley knew he meant it as a question and nodded his agreement.

Stefan donned bright blue rubber gloves and with one deft movement removed the sheet to expose the body beneath. The small figure of Abrio da Silva lay face up on the table, resting on the remainder of the sheet beneath him. He was dressed in faded denim shorts and by his facial expression he looked as though he was asleep. Hurley hoped he had been when it had happened.

There was only one wound in the upper left side of his chest and otherwise, the body appeared unmarked. The wound was certainly large. An elongated, almost diamond shape that was at least three centimetres long and gaping at its widest point. Hurley noted that it was parallel to the breastbone and about midway between that and the shoulder joint.

'You know this man, yes?' Stefan enquired.

Hurley nodded and answered distractedly as he peered over

to inspect the wound. 'Yes, I knew Senhor da Silva, he was a good man. No trouble for me, or for you.'

'I get photo for you, with tape to show size, no problem. But first look at this,' Stefan said with obvious interest. He then placed his massive hands gently around the left arm and leg and turned the body like a rag doll onto its right side, exposing the back to Hurley. Stefan steadied the body as he pointed out the wound to the back.

A smudge of blood had discoloured the cloth below. The wound was smaller than that in the front, only a centimetre or so in length, and it had almost closed. It was barely visible due to the darkness of the skin.

'I think very amazing,' Stefan started, obviously quite intrigued by what he had seen. 'This same cut, at front and back. Very big force and very big knife, I think, to make such a cut.'

The power of the blow had forced the weapon into the diminutive man's chest so hard that it had gone through and not only broken the skin at the back but probably broken a rib or two on the way through.

The flaps of skin at the back had simply closed as the blade had been withdrawn. Hurley made a mental note that even if it had been buried to the hilt, the blade must be twenty centimetres long, or more. He shuddered at the thought.

'He just missing the heart though,' Stefan continued, as if reading Hurley's thoughts. 'I think he dead from shock of such big cut and maybe losing blood after.'

'Have you spoken to anyone yet?' inquired Hurley as he turned to prop on the nearby desk and withdrew a notebook from his trouser pocket. He quickly made some notes of his observations and jotted down things he knew he would need to remember later on. He closed his notebook and sighed.

Unfortunately, Hurley had seen more than his fair share

of the dead and this one wouldn't be the last. Hurley was also responsible to examine militia insurgents killed by AUSBATT, seeking information about the type, manufacture and condition of their clothing, weapons and equipment; details of their tattoos, scars and jewellery.

All of this was vital information which not only fuelled the insatiable intelligence machine but helped identify the victims. *Even the dead talked to Hurley,* the soldiers would often joke. But it was no joke to Hurley. His silent customers were rarely a pretty sight and there had been several to process in the past month alone.

'No, but I know who is finding him and bring him here,' Stefan said, shaking his head.

'Any idea what time this might have happened?'

'I think maybe about midnight, maybe shortly before, maybe shortly after, by condition of body,' Stefan suggested, his facial expression mirroring his uncertainty.

Hurley didn't know if such an imprecise window might help or not. At this stage he supposed it was better than nothing.

'Are you going to the scene?' he ventured, knowing that Stefan could refuse his attendance but also knowing he probably wouldn't.

'Of course, my friend. We go in shortly time when Romeo returns to watch over station and Senhor dead person,' he joked, pulling a wide-eyed face of mock horror and tilting his head in the direction of the body. Hurley smiled weakly over his coffee.

He was not offended but he was reluctant to make jokes at the expense of the dead. He also had to take care not to give Stefan any hint of the special relationship he shared with the dead man.

'What about crime scene investigation?' Hurley went on quickly, knowing there was a unit at the main CIVPOL station, just thirty kilometres away in Maliana.

'I one stepping ahead,' Stefan teased as he waved his big finger playfully at Hurley. 'They tell me on radio that they come maybe tomorrow. Their boss on leave, having wonderfully holiday time in Darwin, drinking much Australian beer and fucking with much Australian woman, I think, until next week. I send body to Maliana this afternoon. Probably they send to Dili for autopsy, but they get no more information from this I think.'

It was a statement of fact. Hurley was certainly no specialist in this field but felt inclined to agree. He had been frustrated before by the so-called specialist elements of CIVPOL. In the most recent militia attack two villagers had been shot while they slept, the woman had later died. There had not been a sober CIVPOL investigator to attend the scene and the trail was well cold by the next day. It had been New Year's Eve after all.

The door opened suddenly breaking Hurley's train of thought, and in strutted Romeo. He always reminded Hurley of a youngster playing at cowboys and Indians. Today, Romeo was the sheriff. His tailored brown polyester uniform hugged his thin boyish frame. In true Filipino style it was adorned with shiny badges of gold and silver on the front, and colourful patches including the UN badge and the Philippines flag on the sleeves.

His custom made, dimpled black leather belt with its holster and various multi-purpose pouches completed the ensemble and would have made Batman green with envy. He was always smiling and today was no exception. Hurley nodded and smiled as he came inside.

'Now you watch station and this body,' Stefan ordered sternly, pointing at the lifeless form of Abrio da Silva laying before them. 'And no let anyone in, or go away until I coming back, you understand?'

'Yes, yes, no problemo Big Boss Man, I fix,' Romeo soothed impatiently as he smiled the smile of those without a care in the world. He then began inspecting each of the coffee cups on the desk looking for a free mouthful. It was a habit and the beginning of a ritual Hurley had witnessed many times.

'And go make coffee yourself! I tell you plenty times before,' growled Stefan, his voice rising to anger as he lunged for his unlikely sidekick. Romeo yelped and quickly scooted out the back of the station like the chastised child he was.

4

AUSTRALIAN EMBASSY
DILI, UNITED NATIONS ADMINISTERED EAST TIMOR,

....

January 2001

The Australian Embassy was the cleanest building in Dili, or for that matter, probably on the entire island of Timor. This fact confronted many Australians. It was the manifestation of some kind of survivor guilt, because deep down they knew it had been prudently left untouched by the rampaging militia while the rest of the city had been burned and the population terrorised during the violence of '99.

The thick acrid palls of smoke, fuelled by petrol and debris from across the city, had not so much as marked its stucco exterior. It was known locally among the expatriate community as the palace, for it was an imposing structure with pleasing architecture and carefully manicured lawns.

Adorning the entrance from on high, the great coat of arms of the Commonwealth of Australia stared forbiddingly down to scrutinise all those who might wish to enter its pristine walls. One of those who did was Roger Sanderson.

Despite the growing heat of the morning, he strode purposefully along the path leading to the front entrance. He was neatly dressed in a lightweight grey suit, less tie, and wore his signature Akubra hat. It was an iconic accessory he had brought from home for the simple purpose of protecting his shiny bald head from the sun.

The local guards attending the outer turnstile smiled through the tinted smoky glass of the security post as he approached. They recognised him as an important person within the embassy and greeted him accordingly. Once through, he was into the small inner courtyard. He waved to them in response as he walked across and pushed open the large glass doors of the embassy foyer. Here, he flashed his security pass to the uniformed Australian guard who nodded in greeting and remotely unlocked the staff entrance door.

Sanderson quickly disappeared, the door closing and locking behind him with an audible metallic click. In a country where very little was new or clean, the interior of the palace reflected a world almost unimaginable to those who struggled to exist outside it. The finest Tasmanian hardwood panelling was complemented by the smoothest Italian marble flooring, in turn trimmed with the plushest of wool carpets. Indigenous Australian *objects-de-art* and the framed oil and watercolour paintings of other celebrated Australian artists tastefully adorned its walls.

It was all largely reminiscent of Australian missions the world over but particularly those in the Asia-Pacific region. In this sterile and air-conditioned opulence, Australia's representatives toiled for their post allowance and to advance the interests of the lucky country. But while it was physically close to home for the dozens of Australians on post, it was a world away from the lives of people there and what most of them knew or even cared about.

Sanderson bounded up the stairs two at a time until he reached the first floor where he was confronted by a heavy polished door fitted with an electronic keypad. He pinned in his personal code using the bony thumbs and forefingers of both hands and pushed the door open into his world. And it was his world.

While it was certainly true, he would never reach the dizzy heights of an ambassadorial post, success can be measured in many ways. Roger Sanderson regarded an ambassadorial position as an ambition more befitting the eager diplomatic types whom he largely considered pretentious and boring. Somewhat like their diplomatic jobs. That had never been the plan for him.

Instead, while he looked more like the amiable CEO of an insurance company, he was finally living his own dream. A dream he had nurtured throughout his long career in the Australian Secret Intelligence Service and one which had only recently come to fruition.

Approaching fifty and with service in more than half a dozen missions across Asia and the Middle East, the recently appointed Head of Station was now finally master of all he surveyed. Some of the young thrusters wanted the service to adopt the title Chief of Station, in concert with their CIA counterparts. Not Roger Sanderson. He was happy to be Head of Station, Dili — even though the title harked back to the ways of the British service MI6, from which his own service had been spawned.

This was how he measured success. Once inside his world, he heard what he liked to hear first thing in the morning; the tap-tapping of keyboards and the buzzing and whirring of printers and fax machines. In the background the droning voice of a faceless, accent-less CNN newsreader could just be heard. His world was alive, and he continued on down the carpeted corridor to his own office, invigorated by the aroma of coffee that had attacked his senses since opening the door.

Only when he arrived at the doorway of his large corner office did he take off his hat and launch it with great deliberation towards the hat stand in the far corner. He missed all the hooks as usual.

'Roger, hello. You wanted to speak with me this morning?'

Sanderson turned to face the greeting with his long-practiced smile already upon his lips. He recognised the voice of Simon Urquhart, one of his senior people, but he knew also that any engagement with him was rarely pleasurable. Certainly not for himself anyway.

'Hello Simon,' he began warmly, and with apparent genuineness. His lifetime as a chameleon had prepared him well for these early morning moments of need. 'Yes. Look, give me a few minutes to read this morning's brief and then I'll pop along to your office. Thanks.'

'Right you are,' Urquhart acknowledged casually as he waved his hand and disappeared back down the long corridor, humming some annoying tune to himself as he went.

Sanderson seated himself in his leather chair to read the morning brief, a task he usually enjoyed and about which he was normally quite deliberate and meticulous. Instead, he soon found he was distracted. He flipped through the folder of notes seeking key words he hoped might jump out and demand his attention. They chose not to and he finally admitted defeat.

With an audible sigh he closed the folder and slapped it onto the desk, knowing he would return to it later. Sitting back momentarily, he reflected that for the third time in as many months he would have to sit down with Urquhart and reject one of his operational proposals. He knew only too well it was the right decision, and he knew also it was his to make.

But he also knew Urquhart had his supporters in Canberra, and some of them were powerful and influential. People who were livid when Urquhart had not been elevated to fill Sanderson's current position, and who wasted no opportunity to lobby on his behalf and when it suited them, against Sanderson. *How anyone could ever think Urquhart could run a station, God only knew,* he thought glumly as he stared into space.

It was true Urquhart had some fine points and was rightfully regarded as an experienced officer. He was urbane and, unlike Sanderson, had attended all the right schools. He had also come to the service complete with all the right connections. When it suited him, he was personable, and could be sent to do almost anything that was asked of him. It was the other side of Urquhart that concerned Sanderson. He was a loose cannon who had too high an opinion of himself, and he needed watching.

Urquhart, on the other hand, was not big on self-awareness and believed himself a visionary. He regarded input from people such as Sanderson as the bureaucratic stifling of his not insignificant talent. And with his warped self-concept came the trait that washed all the good away, and which settled as a millstone around Sanderson's neck. Over-confidence.

It was the death knell of their secret work and Sanderson knew it. Just as all the heads before him in all the stations the world over had always known it. And he wasn't about to let it worm its way into the operational decision making of his station for the sake of Urquhart's ego. The name of the service would not be sullied during his incumbency. He had given his hand on it to the director general and it was not negotiable.

Reluctantly he unwound his long frame from the comfort of his chair and headed off to confront Urquhart. He knew his speech was well-prepared and experience told him it would roll easily off his tongue. Knocking perfunctorily on the open door as he entered, Sanderson moved to occupy one of the two easy chairs available. Urquhart abruptly closed the file he had been reading and with what Sanderson interpreted as a flash of irritation, placed it on the desk in front of him.

He made no overt move to join Sanderson and had obviously decided, for whatever reason, to seek refuge behind his desk. Sanderson took all this in at a glance, but it was unimportant to him. He came straight to the point, in keeping with his usual style.

'I won't beat around the bush, Simon. I'm afraid I shan't be able to support your latest operational proposal,' he began. 'I'm sorry, but it just doesn't meet the rigor of the risk-versus-gain equation that we're operating under at present. It's a very sensitive political environment at the moment as I'm sure you're fully aware.'

'I see,' Urquhart said evenly as Sanderson fed him his medicine.

Sanderson noted Urquhart was conflicted inwardly as his outer demeanour struggled to play its necessary part. He knew Urquhart considered him to be a meddler at best, and probably an uncreative dolt at worst; nevertheless, as usual, Urquhart would appear to accept any criticism with grace, and nod with apparent understanding at the appropriate times.

'I've made some detailed notes on your proposal, of course, which will come back to you, but I really wanted to speak to you personally first. I know how disappointed you will be, this being your third proposal I have vetoed. I'm more than happy to sit down with you at length when you've had a chance to read through my comments.'

'A bit too *creative*, eh?' Urquhart suggested, almost interjecting, his emphasis clearly showing the jaundiced view he entertained about his own ability.

'Creativity isn't a problem, Simon,' Sanderson corrected firmly, the level of warmth in his eyes dropping slightly as he held Urquhart's gaze. 'It's the harnessing of creativity to meet group needs that lies at the central issue. From my perspective, this plan is too risky and I'm not able to support it. Rather than put another plan to me per se, I should like you to channel some of your *creativity* into the work of the others in the station. You're far more experienced than most and I could see you playing a vital role with their development. As a mentor, if you like. See the team leaders, they could certainly use your input, although not at the expense of your current caseload I hasten to add,' he smiled encouragingly, the warmth returning now that the message was delivered, and he needed Urquhart's buy-in.

'Sounds good, Roger. I shall relish that, and the extra work will keep me off the streets, so to speak,' Urquhart said with a charming smile.

His easy conversion caught Sanderson a little by surprise, but it did not show as the two chatted easily and set out the broad parameters of the new assignment. As he walked back to his own office, Sanderson was almost buoyed. It was one of his better meetings with Urquhart. Perhaps he had been too hard on him in the first place. *Play it by ear,* he cautioned himself, *play it by ear.*

5

Balibo

United Nations administered East Timor

....

January 2001

The murdered man's hut was slightly set apart from the others of the village and Hurley took advantage of this when he visited Abrio late at night to talk of things he had seen and heard in the land to the west. As he approached it now, Hurley reflected bitterly the murderer had probably taken similar advantage and the previous night's events would have gone unnoticed by the nearby occupants.

It would have been a silent killing and in most of the villages people rarely ventured out after nightfall or took any interest outside their own walls. These were lessons they had learned the hard way during the long years of the Indonesian occupation. It had been dangerous to know things then, and old habits die hard.

It was a ramshackle dwelling and largely typical of those found throughout the villages of East Timor. The walls were constructed from a mixture of rusted corrugated iron, nailed inexpertly onto a jerry-built frame, and supplemented by woven palm fronds. The waterproofing of its thatched palm roof had been enhanced by the addition of a blue UNIICR tarpaulin which was visible through the palm fronds.

There were only two windows, both small and glassless, and with wooden shutters made from packing crates that still bore the Indonesian trading marks. Both were closed. The door of rusty, flattened metal which opened into the single room was already slightly ajar as the two men approached. Stefan walked in first.

Eduardo was happy to have been left to rest in the shade of a nearby banana grove and his head was already buried inside his latest book. A collection of children stood in a huddle at a discrete distance and watched the proceedings with interest, all the while whispering with excitement, their little hands held up to their faces and their eyes wide with wonder.

Once inside, Hurley's eyes struggled to adjust to the gloom. The heat was heavy and oven-like, and while it was very clichéd to suggest it smelled of death, that thought did come to Hurley as he fought an initial inclination to retch. The stench of congealing blood was layered over the general village odour of decay from foodstuffs and animal waste which was ever present.

As they entered the hut a carpet of flies rose into a dark angry cloud from the black patches of blood, and then hummed unmercifully around them. Hurley took pains to hide his familiarity with the surroundings, but truth be told, he had spent many hours inside the hut. He looked now for the differences that might tell him the story as to why and how his agent had been killed.

A rough concrete slab covered almost half the interior floor space. On it, positioned away from the walls to benefit from any breeze, was the iron cot with its striped, straw filled mattress. A single, heavy stain of blood was evident soaking into it. A faded mosquito net was collapsed across the mattress and blood soaked into this also, gluing the two together.

Hurley's eyes went automatically to its ceiling hook and he noted that the string of the mosquito net had been snapped midway, the remnants of it hanging from the hook were still in place. They stood centrally in the room, observing all around them but touching nothing. Though he was not a policeman, Hurley knew the drill well enough. Stefan spoke quickly in Serbo-Croat into a micro-cassette recorder, clicking it on and off efficiently as he recorded his observations.

Also, on the slab were the dead man's meagre possessions. Hurley eyed the old battered navy-blue suitcase, resting on its base. He knew it contained the valued items that had given Abrio a past, and a life. Inside it was his mother's wedding veil, kept for the daughter he and his wife never had, and a leather-bound Bible written in Portuguese. Abrio did not speak or read the language, but it had been presented to his grandfather by the local administrator and was inscribed accordingly on the inside cover. Hurley had run his hands over the soft leather and read the decorous but faded ink inscription.

The suitcase was also the repository of Abrio's savings, a few thousand *rupia* at most, and his much more valuable family photographs. Not the expected happy snaps known to most families of the first world, but a sterile collection of identity cards that by themselves told the story of the time before Hurley. The only photographic record available to the poor, they had been painstakingly collected and preserved over time.

Each bore the characteristic manual typewriter printing and the respective Portuguese or Indonesian script. Importantly, each card carried a neat black and white photograph of its original holder, though the very old ones were sepia brown. *This is my dear wife Emilia,* Abrio had said, *on our wedding day,* as he carefully selected a card from among the small pile held together with a dirty yellow rubber band.

Hurley had graciously accepted it and looked unexpectedly into the face of a young girl from another time. Pretty, with a wide smile and her thick black hair swept back. Not a care in the world for the girl in the photo with her whole life in front of her, he remembered thinking. With his eyes moist, the old man told him of the identity card scam.

The villagers always knew the authorities would replace the document and upgrade the photograph at the same time. It had humbled Hurley to learn that the card he held served the same purpose to the old man as his own wedding photos did for him. Hurley was subsequently introduced to them all, parents, siblings, and grandparents too. All now long dead.

Hurley knew also that Abrio's best black trousers and white shirt were neatly folded on top inside the old suitcase. *Last in and first out*, Abrio would always say, and then laugh. They had once fitted Abrio's father but had never properly fitted him. Nevertheless, they were proudly worn to church each Sunday and on every special occasion.

Hurley knew also the case was locked and would be forced open later by the Giant or other investigators, but he also knew he couldn't stop them. He could never explain how he knew the key was sitting within Stefan's reach; on top of the main roof frame and tucked up safely in the corner. Next to the case Abrio's favourite red ceramic coffee mug sat empty. Partially under the bed were his worn leather sandals as they had been left, one slightly on top of the other.

Abrio's wardrobe was a collection of rough shelves made from palm fronds and discarded wooden planks. It had no doors and contained what little of his clothing there was. Leaning against the wardrobe was the old worn broom, used to brush the dust from the slab, but not very often.

The other half of the floor space was of beaten earth and

hard as the concrete itself. It contained the cooking hearth in the rear corner with the stones neatly arranged. Abrio's prized possession, a speckled-brown enamel coffee-pot, was resting upon them. Other cooking pots, small and large, some with lids and others not, sat on the earthen floor nearby.

Three coloured china mugs, two with their handles broken, and a metal sugar container sat on a makeshift shelf. Together, he and Abrio had made the shelf on one of his visits. Baskets woven from banana leaves hung on rusty nails at the wall beside the hearth. Inside Hurley could see rice and cobs of corn, bananas and tinned food from army combat rations. The latter were commonplace throughout the villages and would attract no undue attention, though it was true these had come from Hurley.

The centrepiece of the earthen floor was the obligatory plastic table and chair set, common to almost every East Timorese home. This one was grimy and worn but had once been bright pink. They came in every conceivable colour, and Hurley often wondered where they all came from. Surprisingly, he had never seen them on sale anywhere.

On the low plastic table surrounded by its four empty chairs sat what passed locally for a kerosene lamp. It was made from an old food can and had a few centimetres of blackened wick protruding from a hole that had been fashioned in the centre at the top. There had once been electricity in Balibo, street lighting on the main routes and power to many houses, but not since the time of the burning.

Now a year after the UN's arrival, the power station on the road to Maliana still sat silent and overgrown. It had been stripped of every useful item that could be carried away, and then torched by the TNI and the militia when they withdrew into West Timor.

Hurley looked at the lamp and recalled his many hours

sitting at the table with Abrio. Talking and enjoying each other's company, but mostly Hurley listening, and asking questions. Listening and taking notes by the soft yellow glow of the lamp, the fumes mixing with the aroma of the old man's coffee.

Only the best, Abrio would say about his coffee, and he was right. A cousin brought the rich powder from the cool of the highlands far away to the north-east, and Abrio was known locally for procuring the product. Two large white calico bags sat propped against the back wall and these contained single kilogram packs of his brown gold, ready for sale.

'What you think, my friend?' inquired Stefan at last.

'Well, it certainly wasn't a robbery gone wrong,' answered Hurley, stating the obvious and choosing his words carefully. 'I mean, everything you would expect to see is here, and anything worth stealing is still here.'

'Yes, me agree. Remember also that he still wearing wedding ring,' the Giant emphasised, holding up a single finger as he turned to face Hurley. 'So, this no killer who come for money or gold.' He walked over to the suitcase and pushed against the lock with the end of his pen. 'This goody box still locked too, probably any money still in here I think.'

'What do you think, big fella?' Hurley asked, eager to deflect the inquiry and know the policeman's perspective.

'I think he know his killer, and that he big, strong man, like me,' he said smiling, returning to the centre of the room as he spoke. 'Also, he maybe let killer in. See lock on door. Only can lock from inside, so if door locked he must open when somebody comes and maybe knock or call out. Then killer left and cannot lock door when he goes. Local people come inside because door open, and they find him dead.'

Hurley nodded slowly. 'Why do you say he was a big and powerful man?' he asked finally.

'Three things, my friend. First, wound shows power and size. Killer is tall man to Senhor da Silva by how knife enter; how you say this word?' he queried, showing the slant of the imaginary weapon through his own chest with his outstretched hand.

'Angle?' Hurley prompted.

'Ah, yes, angle from up to down. Second, he stabbed right here where we are. Look down see blood marks from attack, but he picked up and thrown onto bed, through net and on mattress, breaking rope on net and die here on bed, blood then flow into net and mattress I think.'

'And the third thing?' Hurley pushed, impressed with Stefan's thought process.

'Look at legs of bed. See four new scraping marks. One for each leg all make in same direction towards corner. When body thrown on bed, bed moving about two inches with force, very strong.'

It certainly made sense to Hurley, but he didn't like where it was heading from his own perspective. There were few locals who fitted such a description and the earlier mention of Kopassus still played in the back of his mind.

'What if there was more than one killer?'

'Possible,' Stefan conceded with his usual smile, and then winked, 'but my story best.'

It certainly supported and fitted with Hurley's observations, so he took up the commentary.

'Also, the sandals are next to the bed, probably indicating that he was asleep at the time the killer came to the door. So, he answers the door and the killer enters, which means he may have been here before,' Hurley said, almost to himself.

'Why he come before?' Stefan asked quickly, his brow furrowed and his mind alert for something he may have missed.

'Well, possibly anyway,' Hurley went on, 'because it would

have been dark, and he's known the layout of the room. Villagers don't usually go to the trouble of lighting their lamps just to answer the door.'

'Maybe, maybe,' Stefan toyed with the idea and seemed, by his expression, to like it. He walked over to the lamp and carefully picked it up using his fingertips on the rim. He shook the can gently, holding it up to his ear and listening as he did so.

'OK. Still got fuel inside, so can rule out only that lamp was burning and later die. Still might be burning for murder and then killer put it out when he go, eh?'

'Yeah, you're right of course,' Hurley conceded, knowing that the flame could equally have blown out in the breeze, or that perhaps the killer had used a torch. They would probably never know.

'Maybe he wear Star Wars hat to see at night, eh?' Stefan teased, referring to the metal frame and head harness of the night vision goggles he had seen the AUSBATT troops wearing. The use of NVGs had not crossed Hurley's mind, but it was certainly valid, and compounded his earlier worries about Kopassus involvement. He nodded his acceptance of the possibility, though knew that Stefan probably thought it unlikely.

'So, we looking for big, strong, right-handed man who maybe know and get angry with Senhor da Silva, eh? Also, maybe been here before,' Stefan summed up.

Hurley nodded and knew it was certainly a big ask, particularly since the body had been moved and the crime scene examiners were still a day away. Stefan knew it too.

6

AUSBATT HEADQUARTERS, FORT BALIBO
UNITED NATIONS ADMINISTERED EAST TIMOR

January 2001

News of the murder had not officially reached the fort by the time Hurley returned. Even when the story did break, it would remain the subject of gossip only until something more interesting came along. He made a beeline for the Combat Information Centre, an underground space known within AUSBATT as the cavern.

Hurley usually tried to avoid the cavern, but he was sometimes forced to go there in search of Major Fletcher, his boss and the commander of all the intelligence, surveillance and reconnaissance activity feeding AUSBATT's intelligence machine. Hurley's team was part of this of course, but in addition there were state of the art technical collectors that together provided an unprecedented amount of information.

No expense had been spared to ensure AUSBATT's superiority on this sensitive and complex battlefield. The ramifications of failure were not only the likelihood of Australian casualties, but also dented national pride in what was proving to be a testing relationship with Indonesia.

Hurley walked the few stone steps down from ground level and drew back the hessian flap covering the doorway. Peering inside, he immediately saw the heavily set, fair-haired Major Fletcher propped against one of the many map boards that covered the walls. The walls had long ago been carved from the rock but had more recently been lined with timber.

Fletcher stood reading a report in consultation with the young and frazzled battalion intelligence officer. Around them, seated at half a dozen wooden trestle tables and staring unblinkingly into computer screens, his charges tended to the never-ending processing and analysis of all that was collected.

Fletcher looked towards the doorway and Hurley smiled ruefully, making an opening and closing motion with his hand. Fletcher smiled in return and held up one finger to which Hurley nodded his understanding. He disappeared from the doorway and headed back to his work tent.

On arrival, Hurley fired up the gas stove and the water was on the boil by the time Fletcher arrived. As he eased his bulky frame into one of the empty chairs, he was evidently pleased to temporarily escape from the cavern.

'How was Bobonaro, Matt?'

'Everything's sweet, Boss. I'm very happy with things down there, and so should you be,' he said with a grin, 'that detachment is firing on all cylinders and we've had some pretty good reporting of late too.'

'That's certainly true. The CO has said to me personally and publicly that the bulk of actionable intelligence is coming from your teams. It's a good wrap, well done.' Fletcher looked genuinely satisfied with the outcome.

Hurley was clearly pleased too and smiled widely. 'Thanks Boss, I'll pass that on to the troops. But this is really something that evolves over time; we've had a presence in the country for eighteen months now, and it's our duty to grow it for our successors. We might be here for five years or more, who knows?'

'True enough,' Fletcher agreed. 'I'd like to get some of those developing sources and liaison contacts into more targeted reporting if we can, and perhaps develop a few more agents. They'll be invaluable over the longer term.'

Hurley quickly replied. 'Believe me Boss, I'm on it, but it's a slow and deliberately incremental process as you know. That said, at my weekly conference on Sunday we will be looking at every source and reviewing their profiles for any new tasking or roles.'

Fletcher nodded. 'Mmm. OK, sounds good. So where did you get to last night? I came looking for you and you weren't around.'

'Unfortunately, we had a vehicle problem and I had to stay overnight in Maliana on the way back, which was stinking hot as always. The guys are good there too though. We got back just after breakfast this morning to be greeted with an interesting little situation.'

'Oh, problem?' Fletcher asked carefully, noting Hurley's tone and searching his mind for something that might forewarn him.

'Maybe,' said Hurley as he poured the boiling water into his own mug. He looked up. 'Tea or coffee?'

'Tea thanks.' Fletcher waited while Hurley finished the preparation. It was the time-honoured ritual that transcended all cultures.

'So, what's the rub, Matt?' he asked finally, stirring his tea slowly as he did so.

'Unfortunately, last night a local man was murdered in Balibo. His name was Abrio da Silva, but he's better known to you by his agent number, AUSBATT 01/2431B. It probably occurred within an hour either side of midnight. He was killed in his hut, where he lived alone, by a very large knife wound to the upper body. The motive is unknown, though it probably wasn't theft.

He had no known enemies, in fact, quite the contrary. He was an older man, fifty-seven and a widower for the past twelve years. He was well-liked and respected. The coffee you send home to your lovely wife comes from him.'

'Go on,' Fletcher encouraged as he sipped his tea, his mind now completely focused on Hurley's narrative.

'There's nothing to hang our hats on yet,' Hurley continued, 'but the Giant thinks it was probably a largish, well-built bloke, and there aren't many locals that fit that description. The villagers are talking Kopassus but in reality if something evil or inexplicable happens, they always blame witches, goblins or Kopassus. I can't rule it out yet, particularly with the type of weapon used, but I'm sceptical all the same. We know they are here collecting intelligence, and they have developed agents that are doing so on their behalf, but the issue of assassination is hugely different in the current political climate and would be totally out of left field.'

'OK. So, what did he report on? I mean, can we cover the loss first of all, and secondly, is there anything to connect him to us?'

All the right questions, Hurley noted and smiled inwardly. Major Fletcher was not a cold man by nature; indeed, he was amiable and pleasant, but he would leave the human side for Hurley to sort out. His immediate concerns were rightly for operational issues.

'Yeah, that's not a drama. We get overlapping reporting on some issues from two or three others, which is good for confirmation, but Abrio's trips across into West Timor to sell his coffee were pretty bloody productive and improving. The visibility issue is squared away too. Only our people knew about him. I ran him and Alan helped out, so his role was unknown to Eduardo. And I always met him at night using the normal security procedures.'

Hurley noted Fletcher's brow crinkle fleetingly in annoyance at the mention of his sergeant and he understood. Alan

Campbell was difficult and moody. He had fallen foul of many in the AUSBATT headquarters and at times had made things difficult for both Hurley and Fletcher. Campbell was ill-suited to the more delicate human intelligence collection role, or the more sensitive investigations that Hurley's team undertook. Accordingly, he was kept on a very short lead.

In taking this decision though, Hurley had not only short-changed his own team, he also had to live with the sergeant's ongoing resentment. Campbell was, however, a very capable Indonesian linguist, a language widely spoken in the border area. This enabled Hurley to utilise him in the relationships he needed to keep most discrete, while at the same time shielding his local interpreter, Eduardo, from exposure.

Hurley knew it gave both he and Fletcher a sense of relief to know that Campbell was on his way to Dili. He was returning to Australia for leave and would complicate neither of their lives for at least the next ten days.

'The drama might rest with our next move actually,' Hurley warned.

'What do you mean?' Fletcher asked, his brows knitted.

'Well, our orders say that if an agent dies in suspicious circumstances, then the counter-intelligence people must be called in as a matter of course, even if it's only for a preliminary look.'

Fletcher sat back and sighed, bracing his hands behind his head. Hurley could see he was thinking through the implications. The operational directive to which Hurley referred, was highly sensitive. Even within AUSBATT, only the CO, Fletcher and Hurley knew about it. It was signed off at the highest level of national command and governed everything Hurley and his team could, and more importantly, couldn't do. All the rules — and all the limitations.

On the issue at hand it was very specific. The unexplained

demise of an AUSBATT agent was potentially suspicious and could easily be the work of darker forces on the other side of the line. While the role of allied counter-intelligence was primarily to identify Indonesian and militia agents, turn them, and run them back to create maximum mayhem, they also worked on high pro-file war criminals with Indonesian connections, and investigated issues just like the one which had presented itself. Dangerous and complex work in a shadowy world which paralleled Hurley's.

Hurley reasoned that Fletcher was most concerned about briefing the CO. The CI operatives were unknown to them all, and they were non-Australian troops operating covertly on the AUSBATT commander's patch. That was bad enough. It added insult to injury that the CO exercised no command or control over their activities whatsoever. It was every field commander's pet hate and the job of briefing him about the recent turn of events necessarily fell to Fletcher.

'Look,' Hurley counselled earnestly, reading his mind, 'the CO's a smart cookie. He knows it isn't your fault the big head-shed decided to keep the CI presence hush-hush. It's need-to-know stuff and now he needs to know what's happened and that the CI people will need to do their work — end of story. When he knows the nature of how they work and what they're trying to achieve on our behalf, he'll be OK with it I'm sure.'

'What you say makes complete sense Matt — technically,' Fletcher conceded. 'But we also know commanders hate things like this winging in from left field, and so do I. I had hoped to get through this tour without needing them in a professional capacity at all.'

'Agreed, but let's look on the bright side,' Hurley teased as he smiled ruefully over the brim of his tin mug, all the while his eyes watching Fletcher's face playfully. 'It could have been the Yanks or…'

'Spare me… please,' Fletcher said resignedly, his hands now raised in mock horror and surrender. But he knew Hurley was right again. It was purely the luck of the draw that a British CI team had been allocated to support AUSBATT.

'And you might like to remind him if he goes too ballistic,' Hurley pushed on, 'that it was because people who should know better, and some of them quite senior, couldn't keep their damned mouths shut that the whole concept of having allied CI teams in support of deployed forces was developed in the first place.' Fletcher could find no fault in Hurley's argument.

'Yeah, I'll cut it don't worry,' Fletcher said, his eyes twinkling mischievously. 'Now, I've got one for you. Very timely it is too, I'm sure you'll agree. In the circumstances, I think it comes under the heading of "shit happens".'

'OK, hit me,' Hurley dared, never dreaming of what would follow.

'You'll be interested to know that Brian Ashby has been shipped back to the UK.'

Hurley could feel the wheels beginning to wobble on his trolley. Ashby was their contact with the very CI team they had just been discussing. Hurley met with him intermittently to brief him on his own activities and to make sure any potential joint activities would go smoothly. But Ashby was their only contact. Neither Fletcher nor Hurley knew the identities of any other team members. A new contact would mean building a new relationship, and now at such a critical time.

'What's the problem?' he asked finally, genuine concern in his voice for Ashby, whom he had come to like.

'Malaria unfortunately. He rang me from Dili about an hour ago and sounded terrible. He said the doctors had given him no option under the circumstances. But he also said not to worry, and that a good replacement has been found; some retired bloke who will take over Brian's cover job as head of World Reach. He'll be here sometime this week or next, so he'll come by as soon as he gets his feet on the ground. When he comes, give me a yell, will you? I need to meet him too. His name's Warburton apparently, Harold Warburton. Anyway, I'll touch base with you later today about the details so I can brief upwards.'

Fletcher stood and smiled down at Hurley. 'Keep this whole thing just between us for now until we know which way the wind's blowing. Not even our own blokes alright? And thanks for the brew.'

Hurley nodded and sank back into his canvas chair as he watched Fletcher amble back down the fort road towards the cavern. *Just what we bloody need, having to hook up with some out-of-touch retiree, just when a job like this pops up. God help us all.*

Never rains, it pours, he warned himself as he drained the dregs from his mug and placed it on the table. As if on cue, the real afternoon rain arrived. Big heavy drops at first, thumping singularly on the canvas overhead and splashing loudly on the hard ground outside. As the tempo increased, the sound became a thunderous roar above which it was impossible to hear, and Hurley found it hard to think.

7

Australian Embassy
Dili, United Nations administered East Timor

....

January 2001

When he was alone, Simon Urquhart retrieved the file from his desk and opened it. He slowly read the top folio over again, savouring its significance. It was a brief CIVPOL report that would normally have attracted little attention; scratchy details of a murder in the border region. But the name of the victim, Abrio da Silva, sent a tingle of excitement up his spine.

There would be time enough for briefing this little number a bit later, he reflected cunningly, as he placed the file discretely away from view in the tray to his left. When his efforts were bearing fruit and his own credit was assured, *that* would be the right time. The fact that Sanderson had vetoed the original idea would be irrelevant by then; it would be too late to switch it off.

Instead, Sanderson would be begging to get in on the game too, to wrestle some of the credit for himself. And Canberra would be falling over him as the architect, the way it should always have been. He leaned back and smiled to himself, interlocking his hands behind his head and placing his feet on the desk as he did so.

Outside the palace walls in the humid, fetid street below, he watched idly as Laurindo the petrol seller laboured on, unaware of such lofty matters. Instead, the boy was trying desperately to manoeuvre his old bicycle through the throng of humanity on the dusty footpath outside the palace.

His machine was without tires and weighed down by scores of old plastic bottles filled with petrol, dangling and bobbing from the handlebars. A machete attack had cost him his left arm below the elbow, making the task almost impossible. But still the young boy struggled on.

Urquhart's self-congratulatory daydreaming was disturbed by the arrival of yet another visitor, this one certainly welcome but completely unexpected.

'Hello Simon.'

'Well, good morning to you Gabby,' Urquhart answered charmingly as he flicked his feet from the desk and half rose from his seat. He gestured expansively with his hand to the available seat. His visitor walked across the office with an air of ownership and confidence, bringing with her just a hint of arrogance. At one glance it was evident she was a young woman accustomed to getting exactly what she wanted.

She came from money, and old money at that, or so the rumour mill within the service said. It was because of this she was held in awe by some, but bitterly resented by others. It was sometimes difficult for those toiling for a government salary to accommodate others seeking only the adrenaline rush of the secret world, and for whom a pay packet was viewed as mere pocket-money. After meeting her for the first time, few were ambivalent.

At just twenty-six, and with less than two years with the service, Dili was her first station and she had secured the post as a favour, or so the same rumour mill said. In truth, she spoke fluent Indonesian and her future would eventually be tied to the Jakarta station anyway. Dili was as good a place as any for her to learn the ropes, but the logic of this did not appease her detractors.

She sank with ease into the coolness of the black leather easy chair. It was no accident that it was positioned perfectly for Urquhart to admire her shapely legs. She knew this, of course, and smiled inwardly. It was part of the game and she had long ago learned how to play the game — and win. In return, she took just a fraction longer than necessary to cross her legs in front of him.

'I didn't expect you back until tomorrow,' Urquhart said warmly, his pleasure evident at this unexpected turn of events.

'I could have stayed a few more days in Canberra but I really wanted to get back. There are... some things I wanted to check on, so to speak,' she answered cryptically and with a knowing smile, her voice lowering as she did so.

'Speaking of *that*,' Urquhart began, his conspiratorial tone mirroring hers as he reached for the file he had earlier secreted away. 'Have a little bo-peep of this — top folio.'

She leaned forward slightly and took the offered file, readjusting her position before opening the green plastic cover across her knees. Urquhart watched her carefully as she read. She was certainly a vixen, he reflected for not the first time. From that raven black hair, long and falling loosely about her shoulders, all the way down to the elegant, heeled sandals. Her tailored suit was businesslike and immaculate. All the trimmings, perfect. The lipstick, and the matching nail polish. The jewellery, just right; expensive certainly, but classy and not over the top. They turned them out well, he thought, at whatever private school for girls it was she had attended in Sydney.

But she was dangerous too, he quickly reminded himself. Ambitious, and ruthless. Just as the report she was reading confirmed. Why else had he chosen her? He had known instinctively that she was perfect for his special project. But she was playing him too, to get what she wanted, and he would have to use all his experience to control her, show her that only he knew the answers when things got difficult.

As he watched her, he thought he detected a sharp intake of breath when she began reading; a slight rising of colour in her neck, a quickening of breath evidenced by the rise and fall of her breasts against her jacket. He did, and he liked what he saw.

He knew that she was getting her fix and that he had read her right from the start. She was excited by what *she* had caused, by what her agent in the field had done. He had killed at her bidding because she believed it necessary and had made him believe it too. The power coursed through her as she looked up at Urquhart, not trying to hide her pleasure but to accommodate it, a slight smile playing across her lips, her eyes wide and aroused.

'Well done,' he said sincerely. 'It's a significant obstacle you've overcome. If you're confident you can maintain the momentum then it'll be plain sailing for us, my girl.'

She loathed it when he called her that, but she was far too clever to show it. Not yet anyway. She would play along with Urquhart so long as it suited her and then she would tell him, once and for all. But not yet.

'Oh, *Hobbit* is primed,' she began in businesslike fashion, using the codename they had agreed for her agent. 'He understands the situation and knows what's required, although he took a bit of convincing, I have to tell you. These early results look good though, wouldn't you say?'

Urquhart acknowledged her understated point with a thoughtful nodding of his head before he continued. He knew he needed to tread delicately. Although he was her superior, the last thing he wanted was his star pupil all fired up over nothing. They had moved to the next level and things might become tricky enough.

'Do you have the requisite control over *Hobbit*, do you think? For him to see this through to the end?' he ventured.

'Yes,' she responded without hesitation. 'He believes we can give him what he wants. He's also getting respect and a real friend, something he needs and something he hasn't got at the moment. And then, of course, there's the unspoken.'

It was true. He could hear his own voice as he lectured new-comers on the subject — *for every agent there is always a cocktail of motivations. Rarely one single thing or another, instead a subtle blending of needs and desires that varies over time. One thing important today, something else tomorrow — and always monitored, the ego always stroked as required.*

'I have to say I'm a little concerned about the unspoken actually,' Urquhart admitted, casually. The result sounded as if he was guiding a conversation about the weather rather than pulling apart the emotions of another human being.

'Oh, come on Simon. *Of course* he thinks he's going to fuck me,' she cut in, a little irritated now but soothing him nevertheless. 'We always knew he would. But I didn't need any special training to know that. It's my job to make him think it might happen without ever telling him so. Hiding it behind friendship, that's what we agreed on, remember? And it's working.'

Urquhart listened and agreed but was distracted momentarily. She could have been talking about their relationship, and he wondered if she was playing games with him on that score too. Silently he kicked himself, yet again, for losing the initiative.

By coming onto her all those months ago when she first arrived, he had shown his cards too early, and hers were always kept so damned close to her chest. He pushed the thought from his mind and snapped himself back to the importance of the present.

She watched his face and knew when he was back on track,

sensing his need for reassurance. The report she cradled in her lap indicated just one thing; that there would be no turning back now. She knew it, and so did he. The pressure would be on from now and she would have to make sure he didn't lose it.

'Don't worry,' she cooed, smiling provocatively and presenting her cupped hand to illustrate her point. 'He's just a man like any other, you know? And I may as well have his balls right here. A little bit of pressure…'

Urquhart watched and felt her slim fingers tightening around his own vulnerability, her neatly manicured nails digging into his own flesh. He shifted uneasily in his chair and despite the air-conditioning, his armpits suddenly felt damp. She was playing the slut and he marvelled at how she moved in and out of role at will, wondered sometimes which was the real her.

He knew instinctively what the answer was, although he chose not to admit it. He knew also that this side of her had certainly never seen the light of day during her training and would be incomprehensible to the likes of old Sanderson. Strangely, he found it disconcerting but at the same time powerfully exciting. Which of course, she knew and relished.

'We just need to monitor it closely, that's all,' he summed up weakly, and not wishing to antagonise her further. He could think of little else to say and she sensed this also.

'Look, I really do need a cigarette Simon,' she implored dismissively, ignoring his last remark as she rose to leave. 'We can talk more later but we need to be careful.'

'Good news there, actually. Roger has tasked me to be more involved in some other work in the station. Helping with planning and mentoring the younger ones, including you. So, we shall be seeing a bit more of each other work-wise, which will be quite handy for this project. But keep that to yourself for now.'

'My lips are sealed,' she whispered playfully as she crossed the office and disappeared into the corridor. Urquhart watched her go. It wasn't the first time the thought came to him that with this one, he may have bitten off more than he could chew.

8

AUSBATT HEADQUARTERS, FORT BALIBO
UNITED NATIONS ADMINISTERED EAST TIMOR,

January 2001

Fort Balibo was a closed world to everyone outside AUSBATT, apart from the few villagers who were employed to sweep the paths, trim the bushes and cut the patchy grass that lined the road inside. They were all well-known to the AUSBATT soldiers and passed unchallenged through the gates each morning, proudly sporting their coloured security passes as they did so.

Everyone else who wanted to enter reported to the guard post while arrangements were made for them to be escorted wherever it was they needed to go. Almost a week after the murder of Abrio da Silva, a nondescript visitor strolled casually up the stone ramp to the fort gates. He spoke briefly with the guards before leaning against the sandbagged wall of the sangar, taking care to use the little shade available.

His brow was beaded with sweat in the growing heat of the morning, and he periodically removed his brimmed straw hat and wiped it with his handkerchief. All the while he smoked a cigarette he had rolled expertly from materials he carried in his pocket. He was early for his appointment with Hurley but had figured it wouldn't matter.

Inside the fort, Hurley was deep in thought. He was reading through the complexities of one of his investigations and there were maps and photos spread across the duckboards around him. He didn't consciously register the arrival of Corporal Richards and was startled when the young soldier spoke.

'That NGO bloke you're expecting from World Reach is at the gate, sir.'

Hurley looked up and rubbed his eyes with the heels of his hands. It had been another long night and to top it off, his boss had been forced to leave him with the task of meeting Brian Ashby's replacement.

'What's he like?' Hurley inquired offhandedly, as he briefly looked at his watch and then began packing away the material he had been working on.

'Oh, just another silly old bugger really. Looks like a bit of a waster to me.'

Hurley's feelings of dread were not helped by Richo's assessment. Nevertheless, he took some comfort that the perceptions of the young soldier could be very different from his own — and very different again from reality. The fact that he thought this of the visitor did not necessarily mean it was true.

'What, older than me, you mean?' he asked mockingly, knowing that those of Richo's generation found it difficult to comprehend human life after about twenty-five.

'I know it sounds hard to believe sir, but I think that's the case,' the laconic Richo countered with his usual style. 'Here, he gave me this card.'

Hurley smiled and took the offered business card. *Dr Harold Warburton*, it announced in block lettering on white, cheap card and below that in smaller script, *Research Director — Asia Pacific*

Region. It bore the embossed World Reach logo in the top right-hand corner and a mobile telephone number in the bottom left.

Hurley toyed with the card momentarily, rotating it through his fingers before he placed it on the desk. They certainly seemed to have managed that transition seamlessly, he mused to himself. He knew well it would have taken some serious string-pulling to embed Brian Ashby into World Reach in the first place as cover to protect his true role as the head of allied CI. The fact they had managed to swap him out at short notice spoke volumes for their operational reach. It was certainly impressive.

'OK. Thanks, Richo, bring him up,' he said finally.

Hurley arranged the canvas chairs and sat down, taking a long drink from the water bottle on the table. It was steaming under the green canvas and the small open window flaps served no purpose whatsoever without any breeze to blow through them.

Hearing footsteps on the gravel outside, Hurley rose from his chair to see Richo and the visitor enter the tent.

'Sir, this's Doctor Warburton from World Reach,' Richo announced.

Hurley smiled warmly and extended his hand.

'Doctor Warburton, hello and welcome to Balibo. I'm Sergeant Major Matt Hurley.'

'Thank you, Mr Hurley, it's so good to be here,' the visitor replied formally, accepting the offered handshake.

Hurley turned to Richo and nodded. 'Thanks, Richo, that's all.'

'No worries sir,' he called without enthusiasm, as he departed for whatever remained of his guard duty.

The visitor had already taken the chair offered to him and the two sat in brief silence opposite each other while the crunching of Richo's footsteps died away. Finally, it was Hurley who spoke, a smile playing at the corner of his mouth.

'Harry, what the fuck are you doing here?'

'I thought I'd surprise you,' the visitor answered with an evil glint in his eye.

They both laughed. And it was the easy, shared laughter between friends. *How long had it been?* thought Hurley, *ten years?* For Hurley, it was a lifetime ago — but it was yesterday too.

'In answer to your question, so succinctly put,' Harry went on, 'frankly I was bored at the university. The director rang and told me that poor old Brian had malaria, so they put the weights on me to stand in for him at short notice. What could I say? With Jean away nursing her sick mum on the Isle of Wight and me baching it in any case, I saddled up, yet again for another adventure.'

He had certainly achieved his surprise and Hurley smiled at the circumstances that had reunited them. It was just so typically Harry.

'But Harry, just in case you don't remember, you pulled the pin three years ago,' Hurley chided.

It was true. Harry had left the British Army and created a second career in academia. His long years of study while he had been in the army had not been wasted; he had established valuable connections and his impressive intellect had opened doors. He had been awarded his doctorate in the months leading up to his retirement from the army and a research position at a university in Sussex had quickly followed.

'I'm *reinstated*, shall we say. A contractual servant of the Crown,' he explained humbly, with a mock bow of his head as he did so.

Very few people become legends. Fewer people while they still live. Harry Faversham, his *real* name, was such a man, although only the fortunate few who had shared the shadowy world with him knew this. Harry for his part did not care. He had been born the son of a London taxi driver and, restless at school, had joined the British Army as a boy soldier.

His natural accent had almost disappeared during his long years of service. It was neutral now, but he was a brilliant mimic, much to the annoyance of his wife and the eternal amusement of his children. He could revert to his native cockney when it suited his purpose, but he could also be anything else he wanted; Scouse, Glaswegian, Texan or Afrikaner, a Catholic from South Armagh or a Protestant from the Shankill Road. Indeed, he had been all these and more at one time or another, and those who had listened had never been the wiser.

He had changed little since their paths had last crossed in Hong Kong. Hurley had thought it a stroke of luck then to be seconded to Harry's team. Later he had learned that it was Harry who had pulled the strings and made it happen. The three years that followed had been a roller coaster ride for Hurley.

First there was the harsh training regime in the UK, long days and nights of exacting work, learning the secrets of the agent runner's trade. A discrete country house in Kent, known only as *The Manor*, was their home, school and base. Rumour said it had been this way since the Second World War. London and the south coast counties had been their playground; and for testing they had travelled further afield, to Wales and Scotland, and then to France.

In those final, turbulent days of the cold war when Hong Kong's time was fast running out, it was a different game. There were different enemies too, and different rules. But only the names and faces change, Harry had always said. And Hurley had come to know it was the truth. Hurley noted that at fifty-something, Harry was perhaps a little thicker around the middle, though his hair had remained dark. It was woolly around the edges and in keeping with his moustache, which was now decidedly civilian — unkempt and lengthened at the corners.

As a young paratrooper patrolling the streets of Belfast, Harry's talents had been quickly identified by those who knew Britain faced a long and intractable terrorist war in Northern Ireland against Republicans and Loyalists alike. The eager lad had been quickly snatched up for a life in the world of Special Duties. As it turned out, it was something Harry was born to, and in the thirty years since he had carved out an envied reputation in all the secret trades.

Twice wounded and as many times decorated for gallantry, Harry sat now before Hurley, dressed in rumpled bone trousers and a faded blue denim shirt, sleeves rolled to the elbows. Hurley looked at his old friend and the new head of allied CI in East Timor, by necessity under cover as the World Reach Director of Research — and doing it with his usual aplomb. He shook his head at the fateful turn of events and smiled inwardly at Richo's earlier assessment of Harry, *silly old bugger* indeed, the young soldier would never know how far from the mark he was.

They talked easily as Hurley made the tea and scratched around in a nearby cupboard, producing an upmarket packet of shortbread biscuits. Left over from Christmas, Hurley had been saving them for a special occasion and Harry's unexpected arrival seemed apt.

They laughed and skipped merrily from one topic to another, working to fill the gaps created by the passage of time and their shared weakness as letter writers. Harry playfully bragged of his children who rightfully deserved a special place in their father's eyes. There was only one subject they avoided, as if by unspoken consent. Until Harry deemed the time right, knowing it must be broached for both their sakes.

'How's Rachel going, Matt?' he asked softly, unexpectedly.

For a moment Hurley just stopped, his eyes focused on something a long way away.

'She's never getting better Harry,' he answered in his matter of fact way, taking a deeper breath and shifting slightly in his chair as his eyes levelled to meet Harry's gaze. 'She's in permanent care now. I just couldn't give her what she needs and work too. I visit when I can, but it's much less often than I should. It just cuts me up, and in any case, it serves no purpose. She doesn't know me, just stares at me instead. Like she's annoyed really, all the time trying to remember who I am and why I'm talking to her. But the more I tell her, the more confused she gets. She can't remember, and never will,' he said finally, and tried to smile bravely. He was unsuccessful.

Harry looked into Hurley's grey eyes and could clearly see his pain, but he saw beyond it too. The accident that had taken Rachel from Hurley was just that, an accident like any other. Unfortunately, Hurley had been driving and had lost control on the wet road and blamed himself. Paradoxically, it was Hurley's greatest strength, and at the same time, his one great flaw, and always had been. His acceptance of responsibility — too readily undertaken, but once accepted, never surrendered.

He remembered fleetingly the young Rachel he had whirled recklessly around the dance floor in his alcoholic merriment when they had first met. She and Hurley on their first posting overseas. How her laughter had lifted to every corner of the mess and touched them all. He remembered too, the brain injury described in Hurley's letters following the accident and knew that any chance of recovery was remote and probably impossible.

'Ah, well then,' Harry soothed optimistically, 'there's a certain comfort in knowing that she's being well looked after, I suppose, and you never know with these things. New advances all the time and knowledge of the brain doubling every generation, or so they say.'

Hurley appeared not to have heard him.

'Do you know what I'd give to have her back, Harry?' Hurley asked pointedly, unexpectedly. But the question was rhetorical and he quickly continued on. 'Everything. Every damned thing I've ever had or done that's made me happy I'd trade in a heartbeat just to see her look at me and remember.'

Harry listened and nodded, and knew it was true. And he knew also that Hurley was on a dangerous path. Any chance of a shared life in his autumn years, or a family, would probably deny him. Divorce would probably be a betrayal in Hurley's eyes, regardless of what others might think.

'Course you would mate, and who wouldn't? Life's a prick sometimes, and it's the truth,' Harry agreed with warmth and finality.

'Yeah,' Hurley agreed. 'Another brew, mate?' he asked, taking the opportunity to change the subject. Harry knew that they would return to it when the time was right.

'Luvvly jubbly,' Harry said, animated again, leaning back in the easy chair and rubbing his hands together, 'then I suppose you'll want to talk about fucking work.'

9

AUSBATT HEADQUARTERS, FORT BALIBO
UNITED NATIONS ADMINISTERED EAST TIMOR

....

January 2001

For over an hour, Hurley talked. Harry, for his part, just sat and listened. He said nothing as he absorbed all Hurley had collected over the past week and learned over the previous months. Periodically, he sipped his tea. And while he missed nothing, he couldn't help noting the transformation the years had brought to Hurley. Sharp then, he remembered thinking back, but sharper now.

When Hurley was through, Harry placed his empty mug down and leaned forward towards him, his face cradled in his hands.

'I agree with you that while it *is* a murder, it doesn't appear to be *specifically* the murder of an agent, but we need to be very careful not to lose sight of that possibility,' Harry cautioned.

'Well, you can forget about anything extra coming from CIVPOL, I reckon,' Hurley warned, 'they didn't turn up for three days and they're not really equipped to be fair. On top of that, there are no fingerprint records and you'd have to have a red-hot suspect for comparison anyway.'

'From what you say, I don't think there were any fingerprints anyway,' Harry said wearily, 'And no suspects either. That is, except for about a thousand villagers and a couple of hundred UN workers and peacekeepers.'

'Well, that's true — if it was a murder with an obvious motive,' Hurley urged, 'but to be honest, I've found nothing to indicate the presence of any type of motive. Not hate, not greed, not theft or anything political or a lover's tryst. Nothing.'

'Which is worrying in itself,' countered Harry, 'the absence of the usual signalling the presence of the unusual.'

'And the unusual being?' Hurley prodded.

'The unusual being that he was either killed for some association with you, or there's something we don't yet know about,' Harry summed up, and then went on, 'For starters, who actually knew he was an agent?'

It was something Hurley had rolled over and over in his mind the past week. That, and looking at the motives and opportunity for those who did know. Some things were black and white, as they always were, but in this case, there was also a very thick curtain of impenetrable grey.

'Well, the CO, my boss Major Fletcher and my team here, in this location,' Hurley began, 'then of course you've got a few select staff in Dili. All the profiles and reports also go across into the civilian reporting chain, although I couldn't tell you the exact extent of access there.'

Harry closed his eyes and slowly nodded his understanding. Hurley knew Harry had long experience dealing with the civilian intelligence agencies and reckoned there had been a fair share of headaches as a result. He also knew some things would never change.

'So, from among those here in Balibo, to whom do you categorically, *factually*, give a clean bill of health?' asked Harry carefully.

It was Harry's clever way of asking Hurley the results of his enquiries over the past week, and his way of letting Hurley relate his own situation, which they both knew may need to come under closer scrutiny. It wasn't an issue of his loyalty being questioned, Hurley reminded himself, though it always smelled like it, regardless of how it was dressed up.

'Firstly, Major Fletcher. The CO had a bit of an officers' night in his tent that night. They played cards and board games, shit like that. All the officers who weren't on duty were there. I've confirmed beyond doubt that the boss was there from last light until a few minutes before one o'clock. He stayed late because there was no point getting his head down; he went straight on duty to the ops room from there and finished his shift about seven in the morning.'

Hurley sensed it was a relief to Harry that Major Fletcher could be eliminated. It could pose all kinds of problems if he could not trust Hurley's boss and indeed, the fragile relationship between AUSBATT and the CI team could be severely tested over it. Neither of them needed such a complication.

'The CO was obviously there too,' Hurley continued, 'and the last ones trickled out of his tent about two. Now to be honest, the CO would not even have known this particular guy by name, let alone what he looked like, what he reported on or most importantly, where he lived or how to get there — especially in the dark. He has access to all that information when he wants, but he has never asked that kind of stuff from me. After all, that's what I get paid for.'

Harry nodded. Everything Hurley said was consistent with his own experience. COs were rarely interested in the daily nuts and bolts; they were about product and operational viability. If you were briefing a CO about an individual human asset in such detail, something had usually gone very, very wrong.

'And myself,' Hurley said finally, with a mischievous smile and his eyes open to Harry's scrutiny. 'I was in Maliana that night… *all* night. I drove up the previous afternoon to Bobonaro and stayed overnight in Maliana on the way back, returning here about an hour before I got wind of the murder.'

'You know I hate coincidences,' Harry chided, and returned Hurley's smile. Hurley knew his story would be checked, for the record, but it was a relief this particular coincidence would take suspicion away from him with such certainty. It meant that Harry could trust him on fact, not just loyalty. Not that it really mattered — hell would freeze over before Hurley would kill one of his own agents, and Harry knew it.

'So, what's the situation with your people?' Harry inquired.

'Well, I have two sergeants and a corporal permanently with me here in Balibo. The first one, Alan Campbell, was on gun picket from midnight to two that morning here at the fort, which I can confirm. After that, nothing. At that time there's no one up to see him get into his fart sack or anything. He was seen again at the showers about six-thirty before catching his transport to Dili to go on leave. He gets back in a few days and I'll talk to him then. Certainly, no motive that I can readily identify at the moment.'

'And the other ones?'

'Jodie Masters, my ops sergeant. She doesn't sleep in the fort, but down at the female lines near the medical centre. They report seeing her getting into her mozzie-dome about midnight. This fits because as I was away she took the daily reports over the radio from my teams at 2200, 2230 and 2300 hours as normal, and I checked that happened as per schedule. She was then next seen at the showers about six the next morning. Again, no motive evident, and as we discussed, the murderer was more than likely a bloke.'

'And your corporal?'

'Ben McGreevy. Again, somewhat lucky, but not so much for him. He went on patrol the day before with one of my teams and picked up a bug — lost a lot of fluid and the medics put him in overnight on a drip. He didn't get released until lunchtime and according to the medics he was there all night and wasn't fit to be running around the scrub in any case.'

'Mmm. OK, so if you were to do the job,' Harry said, pointing his finger at Hurley, 'how long do you reckon it would take you to get there, do it and then get back without being seen?'

'I know exactly, Harry,' Hurley stated coldly. 'I did a dry run a few nights ago. About thirty minutes, a bit more depending on where you leave from.'

Harry nodded slowly. 'I was coming to that actually. The guard post at the front gate, and the others scattered around the battalion echelon area, are they all manned every night? And if so, the sentries would see anyone leaving and returning and would challenge them, and log it wouldn't they?'

'They are manned every night, but there are dozens of places that can't be observed from the guard positions. And there's something I need to show you,' Hurley said, as he rose from his chair. Leading Harry out and down the side of the tent, they entered the annex at the rear. Behind the rear wall of the tent there was additional space not immediately evident to the casual observer. A four-metre gap between the rear of the tent and the north wall of the fort had been enclosed by canvas to form a discrete annex.

Access to this area was gained through a flapped entry point on the side. Inside, space was at a premium but there was adequate room for two sleeping stations on the stone floor. There were also three comfortable chairs, video and sound recording equipment and a heavy grey safe fitted with a combination lock. The secure satellite-phone was set up on an improvised table and a small dirty pedestal fan atop another table maintained the air within the annex in perpetual motion.

The roof of the annex had been raised to about a metre above the fort wall, so stepping up from ground level onto the parapet, it was easy to look over the wall and off into the hills to the north. Six narrow stone steps lead down to an old reinforced wooden door with an iron cross-bolt — access to the world outside the fort.

'There's half a dozen of these doors in the fort, all permanently sealed up except this one,' Hurley explained. 'I've checked them all and they haven't been touched. This one opens into dead ground outside and is shielded by crops and other vegetation. We can visually check the area around from up here before we go out or bring people in. We use it to go out at night, and sometimes we bring agents in through here and debrief them in the annex. That way we can avoid unwanted questions from those who might see us come and go. We never open it in daylight hours — everyone thinks it's sealed up like all the others.'

'This is magic,' Harry remarked as he admired the view from the parapet. 'Who knows about the door then?'

'Apart from my team, just you.'

'Could anyone else?' Harry urged.

'Well, technically yes, I suppose. The work tent isn't manned twenty-four hours a day, but it's off limits and I've never seen anyone poking around inside or anything. One thing you need to know about the door is that it's a one-way operation. It can only be opened or secured from the inside. There's no bolt or latch on the outside or anything that can be operated from out there. When we use it, we have this annex manned and it's locked after us and opened for us when we return.'

'So you think the murderer couldn't have used this door unless they had someone wait for them to return?'

'Exactly,' Hurley agreed. 'And the odds tell us that a conspiracy between two people is always less likely.'

'That's true enough,' conceded Harry. 'But you're overlooking one simple possibility; that someone is prepared to leave the door unlocked, the fort vulnerable and your own stuff here for the taking, knowing that they would return in say, thirty minutes.'

'I'd like to think it wouldn't happen,' Hurley said evenly, his face grave.

'People will do anything me old mate, they just need the motive that's all, as we very well know,' Harry warned as they left the annex and walked back.

Harry sat with his head back momentarily, staring up into the apex of the tent. His hands were clasped in his lap and his thumbs rotated slowly around each other, mirroring his methodical thinking.

'Can they get any closer on the time of death, do you reckon?' he asked hopefully.

'An hour either side of midnight doesn't sound very flash, does it?' Hurley agreed. 'But it's the best we've got to date, and CIVPOL have said anything better is likely to be pure conjecture.'

'Mmm. Your local interpreter?' he asked, catching Hurley somewhat by surprise. 'Has he ever been to the hut, know this bloke's significance, or anything like that?'

'Eduardo visited with me early on, but that was when I was learning the ground and visiting twenty houses a day. At one time or another, Eduardo has been with me to every house in Balibo. Once I knew I wanted to develop this one and he would eventually be recruited as an agent, I never took Eduardo so he's unaware of any ongoing relationship. In any case, Eduardo hasn't an evil bone in his body and if he's in any way involved in this, I'll stand naked in Bourke Street.'

Harry had no idea where Bourke Street was, but the meaning of Hurley's statement was self-evident.

'Were there any AUSBATT patrols out in Balibo that night?' Harry continued, slowly ticking off items of interest to him. Hurley knew he would later sit down and pull the whole thing apart again.

'No. I had actually planned a job for that night and ended up having to change plans and go to Bobonaro instead. We always coordinate our night work with the local patrolling program. Basically, if they're out, we're not — but they have no idea about our covert activities. That way we avoid the possibility of a blue on blue contact, but also being seen by our own people with big mouths. CIVPOL normally only do roadblocks and vehicle check points in Balibo and there were none that night.'

'So, what's the feel of the town at night?'

'It's pretty grim really. There's no street or house lighting in the town. They're all still a bit edgy and like to be inside and safe soon after sunset. Occasionally now you do get groups of younger ones hanging out together a bit later, but generally it's pretty quiet. Later in the night, when we're out, we rarely see anyone. With NVGs, we see anyone long before they see us, and we just avoid them. We use all the normal security procedures and counter-surveillance as you'd expect. Do our work and come home.'

Harry nodded slightly. He had seen the ground when he drove through the village that morning, and he could visualise Hurley's team making their way stealthily through the same village in the blackness. His mind was adapting to the procedures he knew so well, and he imagined the village, dark and forbidding, the occasional dog barking as they passed the huts where families gathered, safe until morning from the unknown dangers of the night. And he saw also, in his mind's eye, the murderer doing the same.

'Could someone have seen you going there?' he suggested.

'I've been worrying about that for the past week,' Hurley conceded with a sigh, 'but I just can't see how. I've been over the drills and procedures and I've come up blank.'

'I think it's a long bow anyway at this stage,' Harry conceded. 'We'd have to then say that whoever saw you decided it was a good enough reason to then kill your man, or that the person reported to someone else who had a reason for doing it.'

'Both of those, particularly the latter, smell of Kopassus,' Hurley said carefully, 'but as I said before, there is no logical reason that I can see for them to risk everything associated with an assassination.'

'I agree,' Harry said finally. 'OK, I've got enough for now. If I could have a copy of your current database with all the reporting going back to the Ark, that would be smashing. I'll be looking first for something unique in your man's reporting, something that sets him apart from the crowd.'

'It's all here,' Hurley said tapping the CD container on the desktop to his left. 'How are you getting back to Maliana, by the way?' he inquired offhandedly.

But it was no casual inquiry. Hurley knew only too well the importance of the disk he was entrusting to Harry. In truth, they would both be happier when it was back where it belonged. The structure of Hurley's network, the identity of all the agents and contacts who risked their lives to work in secret, and all the information they had ever provided. As well as Hurley's investigation files on everything that had ever happened of security interest. It was the Holy Grail for those on the other side of the line, and it made Hurley very uneasy to part with it. Harry certainly sensed this.

'Don't worry,' he said smiling, 'I've got a vehicle waiting outside with one of my best guys — and she's armed.'

Hurley felt it would have to do.

'Now, before you go. My boss has restricted knowledge of your involvement to the CO, himself and me. You need to be aware that our knowledge of your activities is limited too. We don't know any of your people, or what they're doing or their cover jobs. You are the only point of contact for us.'

'Let's leave it at that, eh? It's nice and tight and if we need to open out a bit, we can look at that later. Listen, I've been thinking, how would you feel if I suggested to your boss that you work with me and my team on this for say, a month?' he enquired casually.

'What, seconded do you mean?' Hurley asked, surprised.

'Ezackly. My guys would benefit from having someone like you around and vice versa — you'd be the perfect conduit for what's going on here.'

Hurley worked through the options in his mind. On the one hand he had a clear responsibility to his own team. But working to resolve the murder was important too, and he was certainly curious about Harry's team and how it worked. He had some good people ready to take up the slack if he were absent for a short time, one or two who could really benefit from the experience.

'OK,' he said keenly. 'If the boss is good with it, I'm good too.'

'Alright, I'll see you in a few days if not before. It'll give me time to read myself in and go over all this stuff, run it through some special programs and the like. In an emergency you can call that cell phone number on my card.'

They walked together to the gate and stood under the old stone archway.

'Take it easy, Harry,' Hurley said as they shook hands. 'And it's great to see you.'

'Likewise, Mattie,' replied Harry, his eyes twinkling, 'and don't you worry, we'll get the bastard.'

As he watched Harry saunter down the ramp towards the

improvised car park near the town square, Hurley felt up-beat for the first time since the murder. Harry had never been one to associate himself with failure, and Hurley hoped his track record would run true.

10

BALIBO

UNITED NATIONS ADMINISTERED EAST TIMOR

....

January 2001

The baby Manuelito's cries were persistent and penetrating, such that eventually a small group of neighbours gathered at the house in response. In the burning heat of mid-morning they called out and offered to help those inside. But they were reluctant to interfere, and even more reluctant to enter the home of Senhor Jose da Cavarlho and his family without invitation.

Strangely, there was no answer to their calls. Concerned, they whispered furtively together and eventually agreed to enter the house and find out why no one was tending to such a troubled infant. Later they prayed and thanked God the child was too young to know what had happened in his own house.

In the front room, his father Jose laid with his throat cut from ear to ear, the ferocity of the attack causing blood to spray over the faded paintwork of the cement walls and floor. It also covered his arms and upper body. A swarm of flies lifted angrily from their blood feast as the frightened villagers recoiled from the sickly stench in the dank heat of the house.

Senhor Jose's head was almost severed, and the shiny white

vertebrae of his spine protruded from the little bare flesh that remained. His wife, Senhora Filomena, had fared little better. Her throat was also cut and she lay on her bed in the back room of the house, dressed only in the discoloured t-shirt that served as her night dress. Her long black hair cascaded across the bare mattress and was glued to the pool of sticky blood that had spilled as her life slowly drained away.

Her eyes remained open and fixed, staring in silent anguish towards the cradle where her newborn had lain sleeping. The child had slept on during the turmoil, knowing only his need for food and his mother's touch when he awoke. It would be some years before he would know he had been orphaned by a brutal killer who had come in the night.

The Giant told Hurley the story when he was called later in the afternoon to the house on the church road. The bodies had been removed by then and young Manuelito was taken away to be cared for by relatives. Hurley had sat in the heat on the porch step and listened as Stefan scrolled through the images he had taken on his digital camera, the violence evident for anyone to see.

The big man thought it was the same killer as the first murder, and this did not surprise Hurley. Though the method was somewhat different, it was the use of the blade that troubled them both. Again, the murderer was thought to have come about midnight, and again it appeared he had gained entry by permission, only to then turn on those who trusted him.

Later when Hurley had parted company with the amiable policeman, there was only one thing he had not shared with him. Instead, he shouldered alone the burden that another of his agents had been murdered.

The following day at the fort it was Hurley's turn to pass it all on to Harry who listened with growing concern. There was no doubt now that Hurley's network was under attack but much more doubt about why, and by whom. Between them they viewed the pictures the Giant had copied for Hurley and went through every detail, looking at the personalities, the opportunities of time and space and the potential motives, just as they had done after the first murder.

Again, they excluded this person or that, put a question mark over some but not others, and worked to separate the clear black and white from the amorphous grey.

'Well, that eliminates any residual doubt I had over your local interpreter I suppose,' Harry said resignedly, after hearing that Senhor Jose had spoken good English and had only had cause to fleetingly meet the young Eduardo. Importantly, he did not know Senhor Jose's secret status.

'Mate, I would have given the game away if Eduardo had been involved,' Hurley answered, staring away into space as the new information chunked away inside his head. 'One day I will tell you his story and what the militia and TNI bastards did to his family.'

Harry nodded as he pondered this, thinking that if it was definitive to Hurley, it probably was to him too.

'What's a clandestino, anyway?' he asked unexpectedly, silently reviewing the story Hurley had told him about this latest victim.

'We'd probably use the term resistance fighter,' Hurley began, 'but essentially they were also the people who were couriers, sustained the resistance fighters, provided clandestine support, moved weapons, hid those who were on the run, that type of thing.'

'And your man, Jose, he was one?' Harry inquired.

'Yeah, the real deal. A lot of people like to claim they were clandestinos now that the fight's over and the victory has been won, but he really was one, and a bit of a legend from what I've been able to establish.'

'Could his involvement have been a catalyst for this do you think?'

'Maybe, but then you'd be looking at payback or something like that if that's the case,' Hurley cautioned.

'Or perhaps him having secret knowledge of someone, or something that's now too dangerous to have?' Harry mused.

They chewed the fat, and Hurley watched as Harry put things forward, played with them and then excluded them within the parameters he had set in his own mind. It was a dynamic process and Hurley knew he was brilliant with the probabilities of this occurrence or that, and of accepting and rejecting possibilities until only the real answer remained. But all Hurley had worked to achieve was threatened and he harboured the great fear that even with Harry's help it might just take too long to resolve before another tragedy unfolded.

'Well, I've got nothing more to report from this end; did anything come from your work on the data base records, Harry?'

It was something they had not had an opportunity to discuss. Instead, Hurley's summons to Harry in response to the second killing had brought forward Harry's programmed visit.

'An analysis of the first victim's records has revealed nothing of note, unfortunately,' Harry began soberly. 'Nothing unique in his reporting or background that we can see. Now, with this *latest* development I can put the two histories together — we'll have a good chance of seeing some kind of pattern or connection if there's one. It's all we can do really, but one thing's for sure. If this is related to their background, their access or their reporting, we will spot it. Failing that, we will need to put some other aspects of the relationship, such as your operational procedures, under an even bigger microscope than we have already.'

Hurley knew that Harry was right but had been over this one in his mind a thousand times and was confident his methods were sound. He knew in his heart he had not given the other side a head start. What he did know was that probability alone negated that the two agents had been killed coincidently. The reality weighed heavily on him.

Harry understood Hurley's position as well as anyone might, and having reached a temporary impasse, he took the opportunity to change the subject. Flicking the clips on his briefcase with his thumbs while he balanced it on his knees, he opened the lid and pulled a large coloured photograph from it. He handed it to Hurley.

'Who's this then?' he asked casually.

Hurley looked at the photograph and could see that it had been taken in the small sterile departure lounge of Dili's Komoro Airport. He readily recognised the people featured in the picture, though wondered about Harry's interest in them.

The bear-like frame of his troublesome sergeant, Alan Campbell, was easily identifiable. Even though part of his face was obscured, without a hat his woolly fair hair and his powerful neck and shoulders made him immediately recognisable. It had probably been taken on his recent leave, Hurley thought, as he sought to second-guess Harry's spin on all this.

The lens had been looking straight into the face of the other subject and it certainly showed her in a good light. She was a young attractive woman on her first posting to the Australian Embassy. Unfortunately, she'd enjoyed too high a profile from the moment she arrived in country. She was known locally among the expatriate community as the Latte Girl. This was due mainly to her proclivity to patronise the restaurants and coffee shops that had begun to spring up in Dili.

It was perhaps the worst kept secret in East Timor, and probably Indonesia, that she also worked for the Australian Secret Intelligence Service.

'Yeah, that's my difficult sergeant, Alan Campbell. The one I told you about the other day,' Hurley began in a matter of fact way, pointing to each person in turn as he spoke. 'And her name is Gabrielle Tomms; she's a weasel.'

'Weasel?' Harry asked, his brow furrowed in confusion.

'She's a spook, Harry,' Hurley said in bland explanation, 'from the Aussie station in Dili.'

'Weasel.' Harry repeated slowly as he rubbed his chin between thumb and forefinger, obviously intrigued by the unfamiliar term.

'Yeah, I have a feeling *they* consider themselves to be slippery, cunning and sneaky,' Hurley explained, his eyes twinkling, 'but actually we call them that because they're usually out of control and all over the place like a mad woman's shit.'

Harry burst into a fit of laughter, immediately identifying the frustrations of working with the civilian intelligence services.

'So, what's the interest then Harry?' Hurley asked finally, very interested if it involved his own people.

'Nothing with this photo *specifically*,' Harry said deliberately, taking his lead from Hurley. 'I take it your man knows her in any case, and them talking at the airport is nothing out of left field?'

'Yep, he has a limited brief of the Dili station, but he certainly knows her through work-related issues.'

'What's the real interest?' Hurley pushed.

'I have another photo,' Harry admitted, appearing to choose his words even more carefully, 'but pretty poor quality. I've got the team working on it and I'll bring it over next time, but my thoughts are it's the same girl, that's all.'

Hurley sensed that Harry did not want to go further, so he left it alone. He was confident Harry would brief him on anything that was close to home.

'I'll be off then,' Harry announced as he placed the photograph

away in the briefcase and snapped the lid shut, the latches clicking in unison as he thumbed them closed.

'What sort of timeframe are we looking at, Harry?' Hurley
asked tentatively, trying not to signal his growing anxiety.

'My team will work on this all night,' Harry promised with a
smile, 'and I will be back tomorrow at… morning tea time, shall
we say? At which time you will make me a very big mug of tea
and having acquired me a bacon sandwich from your cookhouse,
we will talk about the way forward.'

Hurley smiled despite himself. There was a confidence in
Harry's words which was his way, but perhaps more than he felt.
But it was the only lifeline available in a worsening storm, and
Hurley grabbed at it for dear life.

11

BALIBO
UNITED NATIONS ADMINISTERED
EAST TIMOR

....

January 2001

Harry was early the next morning and intentionally so. Seeing his face, Hurley knew something had changed and he felt a quick kick in the pit of his stomach. He sensed it was good news.

'Marcelino Borges,' Harry opened cryptically as they sat down, eager to share the victory but also wanting to play it out for effect. It was his preferred tactic, Hurley knew, and it was hard not to get caught up in Harry's games.

'Yeah, he was a Firmi militia leader,' Hurley began, 'active in this area during the trouble and a very nasty piece of work. Unlike most of the leaders, he liked to be involved, get his hands dirty so to speak.'

'Where is he now?' Harry asked pointedly.

'Out of play, unfortunately,' Hurley remarked simply. 'Probably in some nameless, numbered refugee camp in West Timor where all the militia cowards are hiding. From memory, he was last seen about six months ago around Atambua, which is about fifteen clicks from here as the crow flies, and about five clicks on the other side of the border. Why?'

'The wonders of modern science,' Harry began excitedly, rubbing his hands together. 'As it transpires, the two murdered agents both reported having witnessed — not just heard stories but actually *witnessed* — Borges' involvement in atrocities prior to the arrival of INTERFET in September '99. And not only are they the only two sources from any agency who ever have, Borges' file at the UN Serious Crimes Unit in Dili is virtually an empty box. Plenty of hearsay and innuendo but anything of real value culled out. And I mean culled out; it is plain that there have previously been documents there that are now missing.'

Was this the breakthrough that Hurley had hoped for? He listened intently as Harry pushed on but struggled to find the connection.

'And it gets better,' Harry beamed, his enthusiasm infectious now. 'When your man Jose told the story of what he had seen way back when, it was also documented that his wife was hiding with him at the time, and that she could corroborate his story. Now importantly, *she* was never debriefed by your predecessors, but she was identified in *his* early reporting. It struck me as a little odd that the wife was killed in the second murder, particularly in a different room and in her bed. I'd like to entertain the possibility she could have been spared. But if she was a target in her own right, it explains it, don't you see? It's as good as it gets to confirmation we're on the right track.'

Hurley ran his hand back through his hair as he sought to process, and in some way find fault with Harry's revelation.

'Then it also means that whoever is behind the killings has access to our reports,' Hurley concluded, albeit reluctantly. He was filled with dread at what that might actually mean.

'Ezackly,' Harry chimed in triumphantly. 'Someone within your reporting chain is clearing the decks for Mr Nastypants. They either work for him, or he's getting this as a favour for something in the past — or more likely, something that is still to come.'

'Jesus, Harry,' Hurley muttered, the enormity of Harry's words washing over him like a tidal wave.

'So, tell me about this bloke Borges, everything you know,' Harry coaxed as he sat back in the chair with his eyes closed, hands folded behind his head. Hurley watched Harry and smiled inwardly. He knew that Harry could sense something, already felt they were close, and he could smell the quarry. And he knew what Harry wanted from him.

He wanted the soul of the bastard Borges, who he saw for now as the key to unravelling the puzzle. To know what made him tick, to see if he was the type of person they might target themselves. Or perhaps, whether he was made of the stuff to control others. For they had both long known there were only two types of people, those who controlled, and those who were controlled. Hurley stood and grabbed his hat from the table.

'You want to know Borges?' Hurley dared. 'Then let's go, and on the way back we'll pick up your bacon sanger.'

Harry quickly followed and caught up with him on the roadway outside the tent. They walked together in silence, through the fort gates and down the stone ramp. To Harry, it was obvious Hurley had something to show him, not just tell him, but to show him. Something that he felt might be devalued in the telling.

The short distance down the ramp brought them to the town square. It was dominated by its overbearing "freedom statue", the conquerors' legacy, bequeathed by the Indonesians to their enslaved people and standing guard over them still. They stopped briefly on the side of the main road that wound inland towards Maliana, the statue standing forbiddingly before them, and towering above.

It was overcast and the air was heavy with the threat of rain, the short walk had left both of them bathed in sweat. There were few people about; nearby some children played in the dirt at the side of the road and their happy, staccato shouts filled the air. Some called to Hurley when they saw him and waved. He smiled, answering them each by name. He turned to Harry.

'Of all the houses you see around this square, only these are currently occupied,' Hurley explained, pointing to two of the roughcast cement houses. Their paint was so faded as to be almost non-existent, and apart from rudimentary metal roofing they looked little different from the vacant ones. They were all dirty, faded and in poor repair. To varying degrees, the lush foliage had begun to reclaim them.

'The others are empty and belonged to Chinese merchants driven out by the Indonesians during the invasion of '75. Since then, there have been no Chinese living in Balibo, but local custom forbids the houses to be used by anyone other than the owners. That one over there is infamous as the place where the Balibo Five were murdered by the TNI,' Hurley related, pointing across the street to their right.

Harry nodded. He knew the story from his reading but noted the house in the photograph he had seen included an Australian flag painted by one of the journalists. No trace of it remained that he could see.

'And this one is known for a very different reason,' Hurley said as he inclined his head towards the nearest building. 'Locally it's referred to as the "Kissing House".'

Hurley walked towards the old house with its faded blue walls; it was pock-marked with bullet holes and had been defaced with graffiti. The building had once had a wide verandah, although no covering remained. An improvised memorial was positioned alongside the front door and contained offerings in varying states of decay. The ambience, and particularly the presence of the memorial, told everyone the Kissing House had not been a pleasant place.

Harry watched as Hurley bent his knee to the Roman Christ and then crossed himself before the memorial. He genuflected quite naturally and with grace, Harry thought. He expected nothing less of Hurley, though he knew all too well he was not a Catholic, and never had been. This was the public face of Hurley, and this was for his people who watched, and later talked.

It was just another of the almost subliminal ways in which Hurley showed himself to be one of them, which in the end could mean the difference between winning and losing. Harry had so often played the same game himself, in other places, at other times. Some of the children had stopped playing and watched in hushed silence as the two men entered the building.

Initially, there was nothing remarkable to attract the eye. The internal walls were superficially the same as those outside; faded blue, marked and grimy. Here and there, small pools of water left over from a recent downpour sat undisturbed on the smooth concrete floor. Their boots patted through them and the noise echoed around the empty house. They entered one of the main rooms.

It was the worst example Harry had ever seen, and he had seen quite a few. Two tours of Bosnia had cured him of any morbid fascination for such places. The volume of gunfire needed to reduce the cement wall to what remained was staggering. Huge chunks of masonry and mortar were missing and in a few places a finger could be poked right through to the next room. This was all the more amazing as the walls had originally been several inches thick. Harry did not need to be told that this room had once been a place of execution.

'And this,' said Hurley coldly, as he ran the blade of a small pocket-knife along the join of the wall and the floor, 'is blood and brain that will never be completely cleaned away.' He proffered the small blade to Harry who noted the sludgy dark residue on the tip of the blade. Still squatting, Hurley wiped the blade carefully on the sole of his boot and placed the knife away.

He stood and walked to the next room, connected to the execution room by a short hallway. Harry followed, the only sounds being the pitter-pat of their feet in the small puddles and the distant shrieks of the children outside.

Prior to that day, Harry would have said, though never boastfully, that he had pretty much seen it all. But he had never seen anything like the room into which Hurley took him now. There were no bullet holes or damage like in the execution room, in fact, the walls were in quite reasonable condition. They had only one discerning attribute, and it was certainly unique in Harry's experience — and it was how this place had gained its name.

Covering the four walls of the room, from about waist height to the average shoulder height of a man, Harry could see many hundreds of lipstick marks. The colour of each imprint was long gone; victim to time and weather, but the oil base left an indelible testimony of their presence. They were still easy to see, particularly if the wall was viewed slightly at an angle and the greasy remains were caught in the sunlight.

Close to each, and sometimes written between the lip marks themselves, were small inscriptions. Each included a name and a date. No one who saw them needed to be told what they were. They were the mute testimony of this barbarous place's connection with the human world. They were a macabre inventory of man's inhumanity — and what can be the inhumanity of men. Without doubt they were some kind of score card of evil, although what actually happened was hard to fathom.

'The owner of each set of lip prints was recorded,' Hurley began sombrely, reading Harry's mind. 'Thankfully in some ways, only Christian names were used. This at least provides some anonymity to the survivors, but they know each other and are eternally shamed regardless. In this room, Harry, hundreds of women, including girls as young as nine and women in their sixties, were raped over a period of a few months in late '99. Their lips were forcibly painted with lipstick and to the laughter and amusement of their tormentors, their faces were pushed into these walls. Not the walls in some far-away place Harry, or the walls in some black and white television documentary, but *these* walls. They were forced to kiss *these* walls while they were raped and terrified out of their minds so much they couldn't speak, and then they were raped again and again.'

'Borges,' Harry mumbled in understanding.

'Borges,' Hurley spat viciously in confirmation.

Hurley had spent endless hours with the survivors of this place and their families. Documenting their stories, establishing this piece of information or that, seeking the vital threads of evidence that could be passed on to UN investigators, and which might bring them or their loved one's tormentors to justice.

But in winning their trust Hurley also had to open his own heart, and in doing so, their pain and grief, their anger and shame, had wormed its way into him. He was tired and his voice was edged with their suffering, and his own frustration.

'There were others of course,' he continued on, 'but Borges was the ring-leader and a fully-fledged participant in all this — and all the other shit we've talked about before.'

Harry remembered Hurley's earlier briefing and was able to put an image to the name in his mind. He imagined the sight, the flames leaping and crackling in the night. And in the garish light, the villages littered with the handiwork of this bastard Borges and his militia thugs, drunken and drugged up, their eyes crazed and their machetes dripping with blood.

The old trucks, piled high with the corpses of those who dared to oppose him, or worse still who might identify him, speeding south on the road outside to sanctuary in West Timor. To sanctuary, and to destroy the evidence of their handiwork. And all the time the roads being cleared in advance by the TNI, the soldiers waving and cheering their militia proxies on. And, of course, other trucks bringing their human cargo to a dozen places like the Kissing House.

When Hurley was confident Harry had seen enough, they ambled back via the cookhouse towards the fort. It was a different story, a different Borges that Harry heard about on the way back as he tucked into his much-awaited bacon sandwich.

'He had a life before all that, of course, and quite a promising one it was, to be fair. During the Indonesian occupation, the young Borges enjoyed the political patronage of his very well-connected family. When he was growing up, he showed himself to be quite bright, and displayed useful political skills that would certainly be of benefit later on. Of course, during those times they didn't antagonise the Indonesian authorities too much. Instead, they played a waiting game, oftentimes distancing themselves from the more in-your-face "freedom at any cost" sentiment. He is actually a blood relative of both Xanana Gusmao, who will probably be East Timor's first president, and the Carrascalao family. They were once considered Timor royalty due to their dominance of political affairs, and they continue to exert significant influence among the power brokers. He couldn't have a better political pedigree really.'

By the time they arrived back at Hurley's tent, Harry had listened and investigated the heart of the man Borges. He sensed he was closer still to what he wanted. He sat down and wiped his brow with the sleeve of his shirt.

'So, he is a fucking bully and like all fucking bullies, he is as weak as piss,' Harry summarised as he passed judgement.

It was the way he had always done, Hurley reflected, free of any nicety and with assured finality.

'Which means he is being controlled, and it's for the future,' Harry went on, almost thinking out loud. 'They want his political nous and more importantly his connections, and they want him to do exactly what he's told. Someone is doing his dirty laundry to create a motivation, because there's nothing else. He needs a clean ticket to come home and they are trying to change the past. Which means also that whoever is in the driver's seat is naïve, because the past can never be changed. This in turn, of course, means that ultimately we will win, and they will lose.'

Hurley sometimes found Harry's perspective frightening, but always uplifting. He smiled at the simplicity.

'Surely the bottom line is if we're right, and that is the motive, it means that there's no reason for any more killings,' Hurley suggested, wanting to draw something more positive from it all.

'Mmm. That's true,' admitted Harry, seemingly lost in thought.

'Unless of course, we *create* a reason,' Hurley suggested, his eyes clear, his mind alert.

'What do you mean, Matt?' Harry asked suspiciously, though he had unconsciously moved forward on his chair, sensing excitement and eager to play.

'Well, I reckon that whoever this is, and whatever it's about, it is pretty high stakes. They've already killed three people that we know about to achieve their aim — to protect Borges' reputation. God knows what else they've done. I think people like that might be lured out one more time if they thought their plan was going to disappear down the shitter, don't you?'

Harry thought for a moment and then nodded, appearing to like the idea and processing the possibilities.

'It might prove to be the only chance we have of finding those responsible, it's true, but then I have a feeling you've already thought a bit about this and are way ahead of me,' he teased.

'What about this then…' Hurley started, pretending to ignore him. 'We engineer some nice, but not *too* juicy reporting that indicates there's *actually* another person who can put the finger on Borges. We guard the supposed source of this information and wait until they come to eliminate the new threat. And then nab them. Simple.'

'Jesus, Matt, do you know what you're proposing? We'd have to be very careful with the reporting. If this is someone up the chain, which is the way it looks, they'll surely smell a rat if it's too obvious. We will have lost our only chance if that happens,' Harry counselled, playing the role of devil's advocate.

'Absolutely,' Hurley agreed, nodding in confirmation. 'We have to write it like we're writing it for *ourselves*. Just enough, but not too much. I'll do that part and polish it off with a local flavour. Now, we need an idea for the source of the information.'

They each drifted into thought, but it was Harry who finally spoke.

'How about it comes from Senhor Jose?' Harry proposed with a smile. 'It could be written as the product from a meet you had with him *prior* to his murder. That way we don't endanger another agent and we can ascribe the information to anyone we choose as the potential source of this information.'

'I love it,' Hurley exclaimed slowly with a smile, 'And so would Senhor Jose.'

'What about bait?' Harry continued on, well into Hurley's plan now, 'whose head are we going to put on the block? Speaking figuratively of course.'

'Well, it's not just the person, but where they live,' Hurley cautioned. 'Ideally, we need someone who lives alone so that things don't get overly complicated, and we'll need someone who lives on suitable ground for laying a trap.' As Hurley spoke, he swivelled the laptop computer on the desk around so that he could view the screen and began manipulating the keyboard.

'We'll need a shooter too,' Harry piped in, 'for protection if nothing else, and a fucking good one as well. Do you have any special forces blokes with you?'

'Yeah, we have some Rileys with us,' Hurley answered absentmindedly, his voice and face deadpan as he attended to the computer.

'Rileys, what's that then?' Harry questioned predictably.

'Well, we can't refer to their real unit,' Hurley explained overseriously, 'it's so special and secret we would all disappear up our own arses, so we use a nickname. We figured that because they live the life of fuckin' Riley, then that was very apt.'

Harry threw his head back and roared with laughter. He immediately identified with the preferential treatment meted out to special forces soldiers the world over, treatment that left their conventional counterparts shaking their heads in disbelief. Like most soldiers, he had wondered over the years why these units employed stringent selection processes to find the army's hardest men, and thereafter treated them like spoiled Nancy boys.

For no logical reason that Hurley or anyone else could see, it had been decided at the highest level not to reveal that Australian Special Forces were operating with AUSBATT. In doing so, a great psychological weapon against the militia and a deterrent to Kopassus had unfortunately gone begging — but no amount of advocating this view had worked.

The official cover story was so unsustainable it just made everyone who dutifully trotted it out look foolish. At the same time AUSBATT were denying the presence of Special Forces, there were Australian soldiers who were different and apart from AUSBATT. The Rileys lived and ate in separate accommodation, drove different vehicles and carried varied and exotic weapons.

Much to the annoyance of AUSBATT's Regimental Sergeant Major, they only shaved when it suited them, and most wore their hair like rock stars. It was the worst application of operational security Hurley could ever remember — and he had known some shockers. The Rileys were so markedly different from others around them that even the children of Balibo knew they were Special Forces.

Nevertheless, for what Hurley had in mind they were the most suited and certainly the most highly trained and would need to be folded into the plan.

'Could we get someone attached for a few weeks do you think?' Harry pressed, regaining his composure.

'There's a bloke here that I joined the army with who'd be perfect for this job. He injured his ankle last week so he can't patrol at the moment, but he'd be pretty keen to do something useful I'm sure. Stevie is a good hand and if we speak to his boss, I'm pretty sure we can borrow him for a special job.'

'OK. Any ideas on the bait?' Harry prodded as Hurley continued to search through his computer files, an aerial map of Balibo now displayed on the screen.

'Yeah,' Hurley said finally with enthusiasm and sat back. 'I think we'll go with the village sorcerer.'

'Mate... mate,' Harry started warily, 'please tell me that we are not having a witch doctor involved in this plan. Besides, I thought they were all Papists anyway.'

Hurley chuckled. Harry often used pejorative terms for *Catholic*, but it was just another of his games. In fact, Harry was only very technically a Protestant himself. He was christened, against his will he would say, at a tender age into the Church of England. He had no formal links with organised religion of any kind, of which he was largely suspicious.

Nevertheless, he enjoyed adopting an almost Elizabethan perspective in which all Catholics were plotters of terror and a threat to the Sovereign. In truth, his own interest and his long years of secret work in Northern Ireland against the Catholic Republican target had given him an understanding of Catholicism which was probably unmatched outside academia. The funniest part was he counted Catholics among his closest friends, and it was these friends he teased most mercilessly.

'Yes, but you know how *popery* works,' Hurley chided him in return, 'they simply introduce their doctrines and accommodate those elements of the local beliefs they think are too entrenched to overcome without a fight. Instead they degrade them over time and eventually hope to eliminate them.

Most of the local people here were traditional animist and many of them still retain very strong links with those beliefs. The church turns a blind eye in exchange for a visible show of support for Rome. Add to the situation during the Indonesian occupation, where people had to align themselves with either the church or communism, with obvious ramifications for admitted communists. No wonder the church figures were so good.'

Harry nodded his understanding. It was an old story, unchanged in the telling.

'So, this geezer, he really is a witch doctor then?'

'Senhor Natalino is a very nice bloke who I know well,' Hurley explained patiently, 'and his English is OK, so we won't need an interpreter. He's more what we would term a herbalist or an alternative healer, but he does the magic thing too, believe me. And in the political power sharing with Rome, he is virtually the church number two here in Balibo. He fills the role of the warden and strangely, after Padre Alberto and the nuns have departed after mass on Sundays, Senhor Natalino addresses the flock and gives his spin on the party line — and they damn well listen too. It's very interesting. But in answer to your question, he is, and he will be perfect for this. Trust me.'

'OK,' Harry accepted, although still wary and clearly unconvinced.

'Alright then,' Hurley summed up. 'I will draft the report and tee up those other issues by tomorrow afternoon. We need to be ready to go from the time our bogus report is injected into the reporting chain, best case tomorrow night, I reckon. I will certainly know how we're travelling by tomorrow afternoon and if we need to adjust the plan we can do so. My first port of call has to be my boss and then the CO, to bring them up to date on your findings, and jack up the authority for what we are proposing, but the rest should be OK,' Hurley said with quiet assurance.

Harry nodded confidently. Hurley might just make this happen, he thought. He reached into his shirt pocket and pulled out a black and white photograph which he handed to Hurley.

'This is the photo I talked about yesterday. It was taken about a month ago,' he explained.

The image was slightly blurry and had obviously undergone significant enhancement to get it to its current stage. Nevertheless, the results were more than adequate. The female in centre-shot wore sunglasses and her black hair was tied back. She wore a *Save the Refugees* t-shirt and carried a clipboard under her arm. To the casual observer she looked every inch the humanitarian aid-worker, which she most certainly was not. Hurley nodded his head in answer to Harry's question of the previous day.

'That is the Latte Girl, no doubt about it,' he said confidently, tapping the photo. 'Where was this taken, Harry?'

'At a refugee camp between Atambua and Atapupu, about three miles on the other side of the border. Is she allowed to be on the other side of the line, do you reckon?'

'Jesus, not as far as I know, but I think it gets better,' Hurley speculated as he stood and went to the drawer of the desk. Ferreting around, he brought a magnifying glass back to where Harry sat.

'By pure chance I would imagine,' he continued as he focused the glass carefully on the photo, 'the photographer has captured the cab of the truck in the background with the door open.'

He handed the photo and glass to Harry whose brow had furrowed at Hurley's additional interest. He adjusted the glass as he focused on the truck in question.

'Sitting in that truck,' Hurley announced, 'looking nothing much like a driver I might add, is a man named Simon. He is also a weasel, and more senior. I have not met him, but I have seen him at the embassy and I'm pretty sure it's him.'

'Very interesting,' Harry murmured almost to himself as he tapped the photo against the palm of his hand and stood in readiness to go. He then handed the photo to Hurley. 'You keep this one, the Head of Station in Dili might be very interested. But we cannot disclose the source, you understand?' he warned, as he drained the last mouthful of tea from his mug.

'No problem, I'll brief him. As far as I'm aware West Timor is the domain of the Jakarta station and he will want to know if his people have been there in any case.'

They walked down the fort road together towards the gate, just another visitor being escorted out on another day. Harry turned to Hurley and held out his hand.

'I think this might just work,' he said, almost under his breath.

'I'd put money on it,' Hurley countered confidently, knowing Harry loved to tempt the fates. Somehow doing so dared them to a showdown and a result, one way or the other. It was an old game they played.

'How much?' Harry urged, his eyes challenging.

'Twenty quid says we get a result within the week,' Hurley said confidently.

'Done,' Harry said flatly, knowing that for the fates to be tempted there had to be a sceptic too.

And with that, Harry turned and walked away, whistling the jaunty refrain from the *British Grenadiers* as he strode down the ramp. Even though he had bet against it he didn't care, he felt there was a good chance Hurley's plan might work. In any case, there seemed little likelihood of the whole issue being resolved in the normal way. He reflected that if he did lose the bet, it would be the best twenty quid he would ever spend.

Hurley watched Harry go, and reflected he was glad to have him around. He marvelled at the circumstances that had reunited them and his confidence surged. Smiling, he walked back inside the fort walls. He had much to do.

12

Café Noi

Dili, United Nations administered East Timor,

....

January 2001

'We had some disturbing reporting last night, Gabby,' Simon Urquhart advised, quite deliberately but in a casual manner, as he slowly stirred his cup and replaced the spoon with a clink into its saucer. He sipped his tea and then looked up and smiled thinly, hiding his discomfort. 'Let's say we have a little *complication*.'

His emphasis served to forewarn Tomms and she was immediately suspicious — and alerted. She had enjoyed their lunch out and was decidedly upbeat, hoping, naively perhaps, that it would remain free of the tedium of work. Obviously not.

'What sort of complication?' she asked, perhaps a little pointedly, glancing around briefly to ensure no one was within earshot.

'Well, unfortunately reporting from within the military chain has thrown up a problem. An additional person who could testify against Borges actually,' he said almost apologetically, knowing the wider implication as well as she did. 'Someone who will also need to be... taken care of by *Hobbit*.'

The Café Noi was one of many new establishments which

had opened to serve the needs of an ever-increasing international community. The café was clean, the fare fresh and well-priced. Indeed, much of it was flown in from Darwin.

An Australian manager ensured that the meals were of the standard expected by his growing clientele. The colonial style tables and chairs, complete with their checked red and white tablecloths, gave it a homey country feel, which worked cunningly to attract the patronage of those who were far from home.

Urquhart had obtained a discreet table away from other patrons, which in any case numbered less than half a dozen and they were spread evenly around the table space.

'Simon, you've got to be joking,' she implored, irritated. 'I promised him there wouldn't be another.' There was an edge to her voice but there was little she could say or do in the environment he had so carefully orchestrated.

'Such a promise was evidently premature,' he said in a neutral, matter of fact way, as if distancing himself from both the decision, and the ramifications.

'I made that fucking promise on *your* advice, for God's sake, don't try and downplay it now. It's me who must front *Hobbit* and make it all happen again. I expect you to manage your part, just as I do mine,' she said coldly through gritted teeth.

Urquhart knew she was right — technically. He hated being put in this position, but he could also hardly be blamed for this latest reporting, which had only come to light after they had made a much more positive assessment. He previously had every reason to think they were well in the clear.

'We just have to view it as another operational obstacle that has presented itself,' he stated simply.

She glared coldly at him as she bought time by meticulously arranging her cutlery ready for the staff to take it, and her plate, away. The bastard, she could have scratched his eyes out. Indeed, one carefully manicured hand instinctively made a slight movement across the tablecloth towards him.

'It simply *has* to be done,' he urged, seeking momentum, 'otherwise the whole operation will collapse. Everything we've worked so hard for — me, you and *Hobbit* — will be for nothing.'

Urquhart watched as the anger rose in her face and neck.

'Do you know what he's been through up to now?' she asked rhetorically. 'Running around that fucking village at all hours of the night, planning and working at short notice — he could be compromised at any time.'

'We need it done Gabby, and we need it done as soon as possible. We can't have yet another source being afforded the opportunity to bugger everything up. Not now we've come this far. It's as simple as that.' She held his gaze but said nothing.

Urquhart stood and peeled off several small denomination US banknotes. He placed these on the table under his cup and saucer and retrieved his jacket from the back of his chair. She seethed as she watched him.

'Come and see me later and I'll brief you on the details,' he said before he turned and walked away, knowing she was quick to anger but would calm down. As he reached the heat and light of the street, he placed his sunglasses on and strode with purpose towards the embassy, his jacket hooked on one finger over his shoulder.

She was in whether she liked it or not, he thought, and she would realise sooner or later that his role in the whole thing was deniable if he chose it to be. Hers most certainly was not, and he had just enough to prove it, if he needed to.

She was *Hobbit's* case officer and the agent had killed already. He would kill again if he was told to and she would make it happen. He considered that his own plans were well on track and the risks were, well, acceptable for now.

Gabby Tomms remained alone at the table. He had planned the episode well, she thought. *Prick.* She sat facing the wall, her face unseen by the remaining patrons. It didn't matter though, they paid her no heed and the staff were busy; their playful banter and the clatter of pots and plates being washed carried to her from the kitchen beyond the counter.

Her lips were pursed, and her arms folded in frustration. Ignoring the *No Smoking* sign like everyone else in Dili, she lit a cigarette and drew heavily on it, exhaling both the smoke and with it, her frustration. Finally, she finished her cigarette and coffee and sighed audibly.

As her anger slowly dissipated, she felt something she liked far less. Rising coldly inside her, it felt like a slimy eel slowly wriggling in her lower belly. For a moment she badly needed the toilet, but she cut the thought off with an involuntary tensing of her pelvic muscles. It was fear, and she knew it. She didn't like it, but she knew it and would never admit it to anyone else, least of all Urquhart.

It was the fear she might fail, that she could not make *Hobbit* do what was needed and would look foolish as a result. She had been trapped by Urquhart, but ultimately, she had trapped herself; by agreeing to be involved in the planning of what had started out as a feasibility study and then become an unauthorised operation all on the promise of later unquestioned glory.

She knew she would forever measure herself by what she could make others do. Not what she could do herself, but by what she could make others do. The thought needled at her, poking at her confidence, annoying her, but she would never let him know that either.

By the time she left, the thoughts had not gone away but of one thing she was deadly certain. She would damn well push *Hobbit* down that dark road again, whether he liked it or not, and kicking and screaming if she had to. She was not going to fail, and he was not going to be the cause of it. There was too much at stake.

13

Balibo
United Nations administered East Timor,

....

February 2001

The sorcerer's hut was set well away from others in the village south of the town. It was separated from its neighbours by a small stream in full flood now that the wet season was reaching its peak. The building was otherwise surrounded by a thicket of dense tropical vegetation, which bordered the escarpment and the forest beyond. This grew knotted and tangled up to within a few feet of its walls and for all practical purposes it was impenetrable.

Hurley knew that any approach to the hut must therefore be over the small footbridge fashioned from palm fronds and wire. More importantly, Hurley knew the hut was rarely visited by villagers after dark. Strange things had been known to happen in this hut, or so it was whispered, and the superstitious folk were happy to give it a very wide berth, especially at night.

For a dozen nights since Hurley had first visited Senhor Natalino and told him their story, the trap had laid baited. While it was true, he had lost his bet with Harry, this was a technicality to Hurley and he remained confident. So, they waited still.

The sorcerer's daytime routine appeared relatively unchanged to anyone who may have observed him, although at Hurley's insistence he had found reason not to leave the confines of the town. Having gained the old man's cooperation in their conspiracy, Hurley did not want him falling prey to an attack in the bush or on the roads where he might be caught alone.

At last light each day he would return to his hut and at about the same time, Hurley would drive slowly through the earthen tracks of the banana grove nearby. Unseen in the rear of the covered Land Rover, Stevie would await Hurley's signal and then slip from the vehicle, moving silently to the old man's hut.

Here he would remain, guarding his precious charge until the next morning. Later each evening, Hurley would join the unlikely pair, bringing a hot meal and usually staying for a few hours to let Stevie get some rest if he wanted it.

As the three sat cross-legged on the hard, earthen floor, they greedily ate the hot spaghetti bolognaise Hurley had brought from the cookhouse. He was later than usual, and it had already passed midnight.

In the dim light of the flickering kerosene lamp, Senhor Natalino ran his long dark finger around the inside of his bowl and then lovingly popped it into his mouth and sucked the remaining sauce from it. His fingernails were chipped and broken, the longest parts protruding over the ends of his fingers, rough and stained from a lifetime of subsistence living.

Looking at Hurley, it was evident that the condition of his hands in no way lessened his enjoyment. He smiled broadly and nodded his thanks, his grin a mixture of irregular teeth, stained red-brown from betel nut, and black gaps where his long-lost teeth should have been.

The dark, weathered skin of his face was like a mask of dried parchment that had been pulled taught over the frame of his angular skull. By the dim light of the lamp it looked darker still.

In this setting Hurley knew why the sorcerer had such a fearsome reputation, particularly among the children.

Stevie sat easily against the large, rough-cut centre pole of the hut. He faced the only door in the round, traditional style hut and Hurley reflected that it was a real stroke of luck to have him along. He was wearing chest webbing over his camouflage uniform and the compact black form of a Heckler and Koch sub-machine gun hung loosely across his chest. It was secured to a harness around his neck and shoulders, the long silencer pointing down towards the ground.

As was his routine, the sorcerer drank a draught of herbs he had prepared and lay down on the ground to sleep, covered only by a rough striped blanket. The hut itself was filled with pots and tins and ceramic bowls of varying shapes and sizes. Some were fixed to the walls with wire or string and others lay in defined groups on the floor, although only Senhor Natalino knew what any of them contained.

Various herbs and special items he collected and hoarded, and which were needed for his medicine and his magic, concoctions mixed in ways known only to him from knowledge passed on by his long dead father. Potions to determine the sex of an unborn child, elixirs to cure the sick and poisons to hasten someone's journey to the next world. All this and more fell within his mystical domain.

Hurley extinguished the flame of the tiny lamp with a damp thumb and forefinger and the two soldiers sat in the muggy darkness. They savoured the thick, sweetened coffee that their host had brewed before he retired.

Occasionally they would talk quietly, mainly the odd comment answered in monosyllables, but for the most part they sat in silence, each with their own thoughts. Both of them had long ago learned the nights are always longest for those who lie in wait.

14

BALIBO
UNITED NATIONS ADMINISTERED EAST TIMOR

....

February 2001

It was the urgent little light on the panel Stevie had secured to the wall that first alerted them. Red for danger, blinking slowly at first and then pulsing rapidly before it slowed again and ultimately died. All they could say for sure was that something, an animal perhaps, had passed over the ground on the approach to the footbridge in which they had carefully buried the metal ground sensors.

But even before it had flickered and died, Stevie was on his feet, energised, with the sleek weapon comfortable in his hands. Together they peered through the small holes they had made in the wall and watched as a large black figure materialised from the gloom. It crossed the footbridge and approached the darkened hut, but the small sliver of moon overhead was no aid to its identity, even though Stevie donned his NVGs in readiness.

Behind them, the silent sleeping form of Senhor Natalino could be barely discerned. His breathing was slow and even and could just be heard. Together they watched as the dark form picked its way across the moist ground towards the sorcerer's hut, unaware a trap lay baited and waiting.

There was a soft footfall on the earthen step outside and then immediately, a light but urgent tapping on the metal door. It mirrored the beating inside Hurley's chest, which he felt sure the intruder could hear.

'Senhor Natalino, wake up. It's important,' the voice from outside urged.

Silence. The old man lay still, just as Hurley had requested of him, but his eyes were open now and he stared into the blackness.

At hearing the voice, Hurley's heart sank; just as his mind raced and he tried to fathom a reason why his sergeant, Alan Campbell, would be here. He could think of only one and as if in confirmation, the voice implored urgently again from outside.

'Senhor Natalino, open the door. Your life is in danger. Senhor Mateus has sent me to warn you.'

Hurley turned his face towards Stevie. He had given no such task to anyone and he felt numb as the realisation of what this meant hit home.

Hurley knew Stevie could see clearly and he raised his clenched fist in front of the other man's face, his thumb clearly pointing to the ground. He moved it up and down in a stabbing motion — the silent field signal was clear. The fact the man he knew on the other side of the door had been designated a threat was neither here nor there to Stevie. It was how he preferred it, simple and uncomplicated.

He acknowledged immediately with an exaggerated nod of his head, knowing Hurley would see him in the dark and know he was alert and ready. Hurley opened the door inwards with one smooth movement and stepped deftly into the doorway, facing the surprise visitor on the step as he did so.

In the faint moonlight it took a moment for the unsuspecting

Campbell to recognise Hurley and another for him to adjust to the unexpected turn of events. In that same time, Hurley noted Campbell's rifle was slung harmlessly across his back but that a large bladed weapon hung loosely in his right hand.

He paid no apparent attention to it but knew he had heard and seen enough. *It was that damned American K-Bar fighting knife he carried on his webbing,* Hurley recalled as he mentally kicked himself and then coldly pushed the thought aside. Campbell's posture stiffened and his foot scraped uneasily on the earthen step. Nervous and wanting to run perhaps, Hurley thought.

'Sir, what are you doing here?' Campbell blurted out incredulously, on the offensive and trying at the same time to sound casual and surprised. Also trying to imply with his tone that it was Hurley who was out of place and deflect questioning about his own presence.

And then, before an answer or challenge could be offered, he quickly filled the gap. It was nervous energy, and Hurley let him go. He hoped while he was talking, he might not have other things on his mind. Hurley too, desperately needed time to think.

'I... I... had an idea about the killings, you know, and thought Senhor Natalino might be a target too.'

Campbell was no match for Hurley, even under normal circumstances, but certainly not now the ante had reached such a level. Hurley's mind was reviewing every detail of the past few weeks, and every detail was now, sadly, falling into its proper place. Hurley now knew Campbell had killed before and had come tonight to kill again.

Twice he had come in the dark and gained entry as a trusted friend, and twice he had brutally murdered those who trusted him. The fact he had lied to Hurley during his enquiries seemed small meat now, but it rankled nevertheless. But Hurley wanted more, needed much more from Campbell now. He knew the *what*, but he wanted to know the *why* so much he could taste it.

'Exactly what are you doing here, Al?' he asked, his voice even and calculating and ignoring what Campbell had previously said. Not accusing, not unfriendly, but there was a strength and a menace to it and it was designed to weaken the big man's resolve.

'It's as I said,' Campbell reiterated, though carefully now and taking his time. 'I was thinking about the killings and worked out a theory there might be more, and that Senhor Natalino might be in danger.' It was bluff and bluster, Hurley assessed, but he played to the only tabled card.

'Explain to me how you worked that out, Al. *Exactly*. Tell me what information you used and how you drew that conclusion.'

'Well, it's obvious really,' Campbell began, but too quickly. 'I… I'll tell you what, let's go back to the fort and I'll show you on the computer how I worked it out.'

'Tell me now,' Hurley countered casually, his voice low and encouraging. But it was an order from his boss nevertheless and Campbell knew it and was pressured by it.

'I can't do that right now. To be honest, it wasn't me who worked it out, but that's about as much as I can say for now.'

His manner had changed to be strangely matter-of-fact, almost arrogant, Hurley noted. It was interesting, but they were lies nevertheless.

'Al, the number of people who could have known what you just said is very limited, so who told you?' Hurley pressed again.

'That's just typical of you,' Campbell suddenly spat back at him, animated and on the offensive now. 'Mr fucking I've-got-everything-under-control Hurley. You don't for a minute credit anyone else could think up something without you, do you? Well, there are people here actually achieving things that you don't know about, believe it or not. People with vision who are going to make a difference in this part of the world long after you've gone and been forgotten. And I'm going to be part of it instead of sitting around here, sidelined in your little tin-pot show, treated like a leper by every cunt and his dog.'

Hurley quickly analysed Campbell's response and knew this was the genesis, if not also the core of the problem.

'Regardless of how pissed off you are, with life or with me for that matter, I never figured you for one to work against us,' Hurley said simply.

'Work against you?' Campbell shot back, defensive now and throwing caution to the wind. 'You just don't see it, do you? I've been working for our side you stupid prick, *our fuckin' side*. It's just way over your head, that's all. The weasels said that you were trouble and should be kept in the dark, said that in the big show you didn't have it and never did, and they were right.'

Hurley had no desire to react, in fact, quite the opposite. He had learned something he needed to know, and more importantly, seen something he needed to see — it was the magic thread. The thread that when gently pulled would unravel the entire tapestry of deceit.

It already showed Campbell needed to hurt Hurley, wanted to ridicule him and rub his nose in it. It was payback for the treatment he had received at the hands of others, including Hurley. And he understood instinctively this was the means through which Campbell had been manipulated, but he needed more, much more.

'Which weasels?' Hurley asked, feigning indignation, playing the part Campbell needed and keeping the magic thread intact.

'Wouldn't you like to know?' Campbell toyed smarmily, but then he couldn't contain himself. Having one over Hurley was one thing, slapping him in the face with it was something altogether different, and so much more enjoyable. As Hurley knew it would be.

'Simon Urquhart,' Campbell began slowly and seemingly for

effect. 'Who else? Do you really think I'd get involved in anything like this without top cover from one of the big bosses?'

Hurley was incredulous but growing increasingly uneasy. He sensed from the telling of it that Campbell at least believed it was the truth.

'So, he briefed you up and authorised this…' Hurley searched for the right word, 'operation?'

'Yeah, but it's essentially my project,' Campbell boasted, believing beyond reason in what had been promised him by those who promise and never deliver. Hurley cringed inside and a sick feeling rose in him as the overall picture moved reluctantly into focus.

It was distorted by images of the Latte Girl with Campbell at the airport and of her with Urquhart at the refugee camp in Atapupu. Hurley knew Urquhart had no such authority within the Dili station, but he sensed this was not the time to tell Campbell the inadequacy of his story, and that he had obviously been deceived into believing a very different truth.

'Essentially?' Hurley pushed, but ever so gently.

'Well I can't do everything myself, can I? So, he gave me a nice piece of eye candy to help me out.'

'A *female* weasel,' Hurley acknowledged, taking his lead, his voice smooth, but cold. 'How very nice.'

'Gabby's good value,' Campbell spat back viciously. 'You're just jealous because she's out of your league. Besides, she's done a good job on this one.'

'And what would that be exactly, Al?' Hurley nudged again, albeit carefully, although there was little chance of Campbell drying up now his ego had taken over.

'Well, work it out bright boy,' he sneered, empowered now and the magic thread strong and unbreakable. 'If you were smart enough to work out your witchdoctor mate in there was next, you must have figured out anyone reporting against Marcelino Borges is for the chop.'

'But why, Al?' Hurley pleaded, knowing he was just directing the flow now.

'Because he is the chosen one. We'll engineer him into a position of political clout after independence to work for us, and we don't need anyone who can, shall we say, attest to his previous unsavoury activities.'

To describe Borges' past as *unsavoury* would have been laughable had it not been so shameful in Hurley's eyes. To be even considering him as an agent of influence was a slap in the face to them all and the work they had done. But it all clearly fitted with Harry's analysis and Hurley had heard enough.

'What about you, Al?' he asked, taking the subject where it needed to go.

'They'll facilitate my discharge from the army, and I'll reappear somewhere else as a newly-minted weasel,' Campbell said with smug finality.

It was fanciful and naïve, but the bastards had done their work. They had given him a dream to sustain him and make him do their dirty work. They would play, and he would pay. Hurley would have felt sorry for Campbell had the still form of Senhor Abrio, with the life drained from him, not entered his mind and chilled him.

'The question is, what am I going to do about you?' Campbell asked coldly, knowing he had already said more than he should. He knew now the operation could only be saved under certain circumstances, and Hurley was not part of the grand plan. Hurley knew it too.

'I think we should go and talk to the boss, try and sort some of this out,' Hurley suggested, trying to buy some extra time and finish it all without further violence, if he could.

'No fuckin' way...'

'Al, wait,' Hurley implored, his hands held out and open in genuine appeal, 'you don't know what you're getting into, I've got one of the Riley's with me...'

'Bullshit, you're just running scared.'

'Al, for fuck's sake. I'm being straight with you.'

As a skilled knife-fighter, Campbell did not seek to thrust out or stab at Hurley. Such a move was for rookies and too easily deflected or avoided. Instead, his left arm shot out, intending to grab Hurley and draw him close and onto the blade which would remain close to him and protected.

But in that same instant, when the unseen eyes from the blackness beyond saw the hand move and the blade come up, the fury that had waited patiently through the long nights was finally unleashed. In the short time between that moment and the end of his life, Alan Campbell felt only a dull thump inside his head.

The silenced bullets passed over Hurley's shoulder and impacted, the first into Campbell's forehead and the second through his right eye. Both continued their trajectory through the right hemisphere of his brain and exited somewhere out into the still night.

Though his head jerked backwards, for a millisecond it seemed to Hurley he might just maintain his balance, but then he staggered, the knife dropped from his hand and he collapsed onto the earth. The life was gone from him before he hit the ground.

Stevie was there almost before Hurley could react. Pushing roughly past Hurley, he pulled a torch from his chest webbing and turned the white light on. He bent down and quickly examined the lifeless form. The way he slowly stood up confirmed what Hurley already knew.

'Thanks Stevie, looks like I owe you one.'

'Jesus, Matt, we're going to have a hard time explaining this one,' Stevie said quietly, shaking his head as he turned back towards Hurley.

'Not at all, mate,' Hurley assured him, holding up the mini-cassette recorder he had taken from his shirt pocket and clicking it off as he did so. 'Not at all.'

'You cunning bastard!' Stevie said admiringly, grinning in the darkness.

'If only I really was mate,' Hurley countered sadly. 'There'd be four people alive now, including him. Such a fuckin' waste.'

'Anyway, look on the bright side, you've made me a celebrity.'

'Whaddya mean?'

'Mate, I've whacked one of your guys *legally*, I'm gonna get free piss for this for years.'

They both laughed awkwardly at the stupidity of it, but Stevie was right. The long-standing rivalry between their two groups would ensure Stevie's glass would never be empty, and the story would be retold many a time. In the end it would probably bear no resemblance to the truth, but no one would care. Hurley, on the other hand, would have to live with the regret of not being able to prevent the whole sorry saga from unfolding in the first place.

'Can you arc up your comms and talk to your ops?' Hurley asked finally. 'We need to get your boss, my boss and the CO out here right away, but just those three.'

'What do you want me to tell 'em?'

'Nothing yet. I'll brief them when they get here. Just tell them to come by vehicle and bring a body bag, that's all.'

15

International Compound
Maliana, United Nations administered East Timor

....

February 2001

The international compound in Maliana had grown to become a thriving complex. Situated within the grounds of the old Polri station, now the district CIVPOL headquarters, it was both home and work to dozens of UN and NGO workers. Initially it had been a tent city with few amenities and little sanitation. The ground was a quagmire during the wet season, and it had looked like a mining shanty-town.

It had blossomed from those humble beginnings and slowly but surely, canvas had given way to rows of largely white demountable huts, which glared under the cloudless sky. Each on its own concrete slab with its own humming air conditioner, the compound looked a trifle monotonous to Hurley, but it was neat and clean, and a far cry from what was originally there.

As he walked up the newly stoned path, he noted here and there that attempts had been made by some of the longer-term tenants to improve their little lot in life. Something of a green thumb himself, Hurley was momentarily distracted when he recognised the young shoots of a struggling frangipani and to his amazement, the striking red of a Scarlet O'Hara bougainvillea, delicate but winding itself skyward around a wire trellis, set for it by a loving hand. It could have been a cutting from his own garden in Brisbane.

He reflected that the towns of the border area tended to be rather drab and unfortunately this included Maliana, even though it was the largest town in zona Bobanaro. Each hut he passed bore the logo of their owners and words in scratched, permanent marker pen in a dozen different colours and languages.

Most had faded stickers affixed to the windows and doors and many of these had become scratched and partially removed over time. They were the leftover reminders of other missions far away, the battle honours of the temporary buildings and their tenants as they lurched from one third-world crisis to another.

Hurley had cause to visit the compound on a fairly regular basis, so his presence raised no eyebrows. He walked on, though anyone who knew him well would have seen he was preoccupied. He turned left off the main path and quickly found the hut he wanted, nestled up in the back corner against the security fence, the World Reach sign displayed in the window.

He mounted the single grated step and opened the door, immediately feeling the assault of the air conditioning after the relentless heat and humidity outside. He closed and locked the door behind him. Removing his cap, he wiped his face with his hands and ran them back through his hair, more in a gesture of exasperation than anything else. Inside, Harry was sitting at a computer, peering over the top of his half-spectacles. On Hurley's entry, he slowly removed them and looked towards the younger man, studying his face.

'I gather things didn't go well,' he said dryly, stating the obvious and knowing already in his heart what had happened and, in some respect, all that would follow from it.

'No, they fuckin' didn't, Harry,' Hurley exploded. 'We've been done over by our own side and I am fuckin' mightily pissed off.' With this he kicked the nearby wastepaper basket with all the anger and venom he could muster, sending it careering off across the cabin, its contents scattering through the air before they silently came to rest, littering the floor. Harry let it be.

'Tell me about the meeting,' he urged, as he moved to arrange two chairs around the small table near to where Hurley was standing.

Hurley remained standing for the moment and turned to fill a tiny paper cup from the nearby water cooler, little bubbles gurgling upwards inside the bottle as he did so. He threw his head back and drained the cold contents in one swallow, and then crushed the cup violently before throwing it towards the wastepaper basket lying sideways on the floor.

When he finally sat down, the strain in his face was evident, the anger and bitterness palpable in all his words.

'OK, so there wasn't any officially authorised operation — that's a certainty — but it's also cold comfort. Roger fucking Sanderson is also further taking the line that there wasn't any rogue operation between his people involving Campbell. His take is that it was all the invented ravings of Campbell, who they regard as unstable, and who is now very conveniently dead.'

Harry nodded, sensing where this might be going but allowing Hurley to finish his story. The very fact that a meeting had been convened at all had made Harry uneasy. In the first place, meetings of this ilk were about agenda, to create acceptable political solutions, and never to apportion blame or advise the dispensing of justice. The fact Hurley and his bosses had been summoned to Dili to discuss the "tragic circumstances" of Campbell's death with no less than the ambassador, the head of station and the senior Australian military commander, did not bode well with Harry from the start.

'So, they're saying there's no *prima facie* case for an official investigation,' Hurley lamented. 'And what's more, there's no proof that anything Campbell said on the tape is true, or that it's connected in any way with the weasels or the Australian government. The photography at the airport is a non-event, as they knew each other in an official capacity. The photo of the two weasels at the refugee camp in Atapupu, even if we can provide proof that it was taken there — which we can't without compromising your sensitive source — is regarded as an internal disciplinary matter and something for him to sort out with the Jakarta station.'

It was worse than Harry could have predicted.

'What's their explanation as to how Campbell knew to come to Senhor Natalino's hut then?' he asked, seeking to tie off the loose ends.

'They don't see they need to provide one,' Hurley explained, exasperated. 'There are a number of people who would have had access to it in the reporting chain, which is unfortunately true, and they are unconvinced he couldn't have accessed the information at our end. Now, even though we know this is categorically untrue, we cannot prove it. Sanderson even further muddied the waters by bringing up some fanciful notion Campbell may have been in league with some unknown third party who knew the same information, and that the story on the tape was an elaborate cover story they invented and gave to Campbell to protect themselves.' Hurley rubbed his eyes with the heels of his hands in frustration.

'Mmm,' Harry sighed. 'So the name of the service will be ever preserved, your government is relieved that there will be no controversial inquiry, particularly in an election year, and the military will solemnly bury one of its own in a sad case of post-traumatic stress disorder gone horribly wrong. I suppose everybody's happy then.'

'Well I'm fuckin' not,' Hurley said coldly, looking up at him. 'I want...'

'What do you want, Matt?' Harry cut in, his voice empathic but challenging. 'Revenge? Today you are red-hot angry because you have been betrayed. They have done what you would never do, and it is the anger of betrayal that burns the longest and with the most pain. But revenge is a luxury for lesser mortals, I'm afraid.'

'Why Harry?' Hurley shot back, his eyes blazing. 'Why in God's name am I not entitled to wring their fuckin' necks for what they've done?'

'Look, no one can deny you the moral perspective, but what would that achieve? The matter would end, and you would simply play into the hands of your government mandarins by cleaning up the mess for them. At the same time, you're then at risk of spending the rest of your life behind bars. Because when people die in these circumstances, other people come looking. Is that what you want?'

Hurley absorbed what Harry said, recognising the sense of it on one level, but wishing he could over-ride it, such was his anger. He sat in silence for a long moment before he spoke.

'Listen Harry, I haven't fully thought this through, but I ran it through my mind, over and over last night, I just couldn't sleep. I want you to listen, OK?'

'OK.'

'Do you remember what you told me when you first took me on board as an agent runner?'

Harry smiled. 'Of course I do. "They're each your personal responsibility. Every operational and personal detail. For now, they belong to you and you manage them for me, for us, and for what we stand for. You control their lives and you fight their corner, and argue for them, even with me. You speak for them and you do everything in your power to protect them, up to and including risking your own life, which will always be your decision. But when I tell you it's time to walk away, you do. And you don't ask any questions and you don't look back".'

Hurley smiled grimly, noting that Harry was word perfect, as always.

'That's right Harry, and it's the same mantra I've passed on to my people — because it's right. But you can't tell me to walk away this time. It's not your place. These vermin have killed two of my agents, not to mention the wife of one, and in doing so they have orphaned a young boy. By default, they have also killed one of my soldiers. I want a measure of payback here, and I think we can still get a modicum of success, but I need you to back me.'

'I can't write you a blank cheque Matt, you know that,' Harry counselled. 'What have you got in mind?'

He knew Hurley was right in principle. He would not, *could not* walk away from it completely.

'It will be complex, and I will need the help of you and your team, but I think we can still get a win out of this — and don't worry, it doesn't include killing them, as much as part of me would like to do that,' he spat viciously.

'Go on.'

'I think if we can get these two maggots to confess what they have done, we might at least get them off the street, if not more. In any case, I reckon it's worth a try.'

Harry pondered this. 'Matt, I'm listening, but the weasels and the Australian government have made it pretty clear that according to them, it just didn't happen. How exactly do you think we might get a confession? There's no way they'll allow us to question them, not under the circumstances.'

'I'm thinking more of tricking them into it,' he said simply, cold mischief in his voice now.

'I'm still listening,' Harry encouraged, wondering where this might go.

'Do you remember that story you told me years ago about the Special Branch man in Northern Ireland? The one who sold out one of your agents?' Hurley pressed.

'Yes,' Harry said, the memory rekindled, and his attention now front and centre. 'It was in the early days, I was green then, and thought at first it was my fault. Something I'd done or forgotten to do. They found my bloke, tortured to death and left naked in the Ardoyne, save for a black calico hood, and a single bullet in the back of his head. Left by PIRA as a message for other agents, you see. We checked everything to find the leak, and then we checked it all over again. Finally, we knew it was the Branch man, but these things are hard to prove, as recent events show. At the top level, the Branch would have none of it. There was no love lost between them and the army in those days, I can tell you.

'Anyway, my old boss had us dress as a PIRA security team, the most feared of terror units even by the terrorists themselves, and we lifted the unsuspecting copper from the lane behind his own house. We took him hooded and shaking to an abandoned farmhouse near Coleraine, though we tricked him into thinking he had gone south of the border and was a prisoner in the Republic. After we had given him a good kicking to soften him up and tied him to a chair, we removed his hood. We let him see what he thought was coming next, what we *wanted* him to think was coming next; the barbed wire, the axe-handles, the pliers, the batteries with the electrodes. All neatly laid out waiting for him. To save himself he told us of a secret deal he had previously struck with what he thought were *our* PIRA superiors. He claimed he had given up all his knowledge of British agents working in the Province in return for himself and his family never to be targeted by PIRA. Even though we knew it was true, we laughed at his story, and mocked him. Instead we readied the wires, and the electricity, even to the point of taping the electrodes to his balls with gaffer tape. From the shadows I watched him shit himself and can still see his bare foot tapping in a puddle of his own piss on the cement floor. He knew full well what would happen to a Branch man if he was not believed and to prove himself, he talked, and we couldn't stop him.

'In doing so he confirmed the information he had previously given up to PIRA. Of course, he had every cause then to think he had earned his freedom but at that point, a senior Branch man, a good pal of my old boss, walked from the shadows and showed himself. Only then did he realise what had happened. I had seen men cry before that day, but never like he did.'

'What happened as a result?' Hurley prompted, looking at the parallels and seeking the end of the story.

'He decided to retire after that, and topped himself the following year,' Harry said finally, his face deadpan and with no trace of regret. 'Some said he only got what was coming to him. I say he didn't get enough, but it was better than nothing. Sometimes we have to settle for better than nothing, which is something you're going to have to accept if we go down this path,' he counselled, his finger pointing a warning at Hurley.

Hurley nodded in return. 'OK, so I'm thinking if we had a scenario whereby we could work on one — or both of them — and trick them into confessing, we might have a chance,' he suggested.

'Do you think that's really achievable?' Harry asked sceptically.

'Think back to your own training,' Hurley began, animated

now. 'Beyond the question and answer stuff, what is at the heart of real interrogation?'

Harry worked to pull the words from the deep recesses of his memory. 'Theatre — it's a stage play for one, the creation of an environment in which the subject's reality is altered to create a motivation to cooperate. This is done through the management of their perception.'

'Because…' Hurley prompted.

'Because perception is truth,' Harry finished. They both smiled, but there was no pleasure. It was the smile of a growing conspiracy.

'OK, so we need a ploy,' Hurley summarised. 'A ploy strong enough to trick them into confessing — that's what we're saying.'

'Ezackly. At the moment neither of them has the motivation to provide the truth to anyone, in fact quite the opposite. We must engineer a situation in which they are motivated to do that. In order to achieve that, we need to create an environment in which they perceive it to be to their advantage to confess. Then they will do so. Their perception must be that something so terrible is going to happen to them they will risk confessing what they have done in the singular belief that they can be saved from that same fate. And only the fear of death can achieve that Matt, and because it can't be followed through it has a good chance of failure. Just like it would have fallen over in my story if the Branch man had decided not to play.'

'But the point is Harry, it *did* work. And while I admit there is some chance of failure, I can see plenty of scope for success too, and I think it's a chance worth taking. In the end, if it fails, it fails, but in my mind it's got to be worth a try,' he pleaded.

'I like the overall concept Matt, but is any confession we get worth anything in the big scheme of things?'

'Yeah, I suppose what we've said is all well and good, but at the moment I don't see any confession gained this way having any more weight than the recording I got from Campbell — they'd likely reject it as having been faked or gained through coercion, and we would be in deep shit for going down that path in the first place, just quietly.'

Harry nodded his agreement.

'The only way would be to get someone credible, ideally at a high enough level, to hear the confession and then verify it. Then we might be able to get them to influence someone to act on it,' Hurley suggested, his voice betraying the enormity of achieving that. They sat in silence while each processed what had been said, and where it might lead.

'Say that again,' Harry said suddenly, moving forward onto the front of his chair.

'Which part?' Hurley asked, confused.

'About getting someone senior to hear the confession and act on it,' he said, clearly running some idea around in his mind.

'I don't think we could get someone of suitable authority and credibility anyway,' Hurley said, almost dismissing it.

'I don't know so much,' Harry mused, clearly seeing some merit in what Hurley had said. 'You've actually given me an idea. I was due to meet with someone next week who might just fit the bill. If I can, I'll bring that meeting forward to tomorrow when I'm in Dili and explore the possibility. You leave that detail to me.'

They sat without speaking for some time, both thinking through the possibilities. It was Hurley who finally broke the silence.

'OK, what about this,' he began. 'If, and I say *if*, we could kidnap them together and isolate them for long enough to work on them, say two to three hours, *and* we could make one believe we were torturing with a view to killing the other, we could scare the living bejesus out of that one, maybe even enough to make them talk. You never know where that might go.'

'I like the idea,' Harry said, shifting in his chair. 'But doesn't that reduce our chances, just working on one?'

'Not really, in fact, it provides us with extra chances. Here's my thinking; if we torture A and B watches, then B has the moral problem of confessing to stop A from suffering. If that fails, then B is told that they will be next, so they'll then have to act to save themselves. If that sequence fails completely, then we simply reverse everything and start over. Remember that when we are working on one, it's a trick — the other is completely isolated. They don't know what's happened, so they are equally susceptible to the same trick. Understand?'

'Yeah, that makes good sense and I'm fucking glad you're not planning my demise,' he offered with a gleam in his eye Hurley recognised well.

'Still, it's only an idea,' Hurley cautioned, 'there's a lot of moving parts, not least of which is bagging them together.'

'Leave that for now too. As I said earlier, I have to sound out our potential prime witness which I'll do tomorrow, he might also be able to provide a little helpful information on more tactical matters like that.'

'Who is it you have in the frame, Harry?' Hurley asked curiously.

'You'll see soon enough if I can pull it off. In any case his presence is a pre-condition for the whole operation. Remember, no witness, no point, so no operation.'

'OK, agreed.' Hurley nodded. 'So, what do you see as the timeline for the op, supposing we get this witness?'

'Actually, it's very open ended, which is good. We could be ready to move and have everything prepped by Friday, tomorrow week that is, at the earliest. As to the window, it stays open.

You're here for another four months, I'm here for another six, the weasels and our witness remain in country — it's all open ended. After I've had my meeting tomorrow, I will let you know if it can go ahead. Following that, I will contact you with the actual date and we will RV in Dili for the planning and the op. Easy.'

'OK Harry, I'll plan it and do the questioning,' Hurley urged. 'But it will be complex, and I will need your team in support. Is that doable?'

Harry settled back in his chair and levelled his gaze at Hurley.

'Is that wise? For a start, they know you, even with your face covered, they know your voice. If this goes tits up, they will come for you and there will be hell to pay. Your career will be fucked.'

Hurley considered this for a moment, accepting that Harry's objection was born only of concern for him.

'Fact is Harry, I *don't* know Urquhart. I've seen him at the embassy once but never spoken to him. He does not know my voice. I know her though, I've met her a number of times.'

'Mmm. OK, so how's this for a compromise; we make a plan to interrogate them both if needed, and we work out the order later. We agree now that should this go ahead, you question Urquhart and I question the Latte Girl, and we plan the ploy around that, how's that?'

'Done,' agreed Hurley, nodding his head. 'But what about you?'

Harry shrugged his shoulders and had clearly thought it through. 'If it fails and I get sent home in disgrace, so what? That's all they can do. I reckon it's worth a try and I'd rather not die wondering if it would have worked, thanks very much.'

Hurley knew in his heart of hearts that Harry was right about the dangers of his own involvement. If it failed, the weasels would scream blue murder and there wouldn't be any excuses to fall back on. If he was identified, he would be an easy target and would bear the brunt of their anger.

The weight of officialdom would certainly come down heavily on him. Although Harry made light of his own fate if they failed, it was still a big call but one he was obviously prepared to make. Hurley understood why, and that he was doing it not just for him, but for those who had died, and because it was right.

He smiled and nodded. 'Thanks Harry, I appreciate it very much, and so would they.'

'It's as it should be,' Harry acknowledged with a slight nod.

Hurley stood, placing on his webbing and retrieving his rifle. 'I'd best be off and get out of your hair, you've a long drive ahead.'

They walked together to the door and Hurley opened it, stepping down to the ground and placing his cap onto his head in one motion. The heat was all-consuming again as the cool of the hut was left reluctantly behind. Harry stayed in the doorway propping the door open and looking down at the younger man.

'We'll know tomorrow if the gods favour us,' he said.

Hurley smiled. His mood had lightened since the opportunity for action, and retribution, had presented itself.

'Send word as soon as you can after your meeting tomorrow, and if it's a go then we'll really get to work.'

Harry nodded but Hurley did not see him. Instead, he turned and walked purposefully away. He was resolute; the script was being written and those involved would play their parts. It was a debt that must be paid.

Harry went inside and sat again at the table. He made a cup of tea and gazed out of the window for a short while, and then began packing some items into his much-travelled leather overnight bag. He would need to get to Dili tonight in order to arrange the meeting for tomorrow.

As he prepared his departure, he hummed softly to himself. Operationally, he was stepping it up a notch and it gave him comfort to think that in far off Dili, two murderous traitors were waiting. Unbeknown to them, the birds of prey had already begun to circle.

16

DILI
UNITED NATIONS ADMINISTERED EAST TIMOR

February 2001

Harry watched the house, or more correctly the large green security gates that dominated the residence, from the passenger seat of an old black Pajero. He had adjusted the side mirror to allow a perfectly framed view back along the roughcast footpath. The house stood in a pleasant enough street in the west of Dili, an area that was a step away from the more ordinary parts of the town and a quantum leap from the slums and poorer areas that proliferated throughout the country.

It was an area which had become fashionable with those governments and NGOs needing to house their staff in circumstances more in keeping with their first world sensitivities. As one of the preferred homes, the house behind the green gates had been repaired, renovated and painted; security specialists and tradesmen from Australia had fitted it with all the required bells and whistles to ensure the occupants lived as comfortable a lifestyle as possible considering the environment.

But security was poor, Harry's team had noted during their reconnaissance of the area. To them, it beggared belief that a counterinsurgency campaign was being waged only forty miles to the south-west, but here there were no UN or contracted security patrols. The individual houses, although gated and fenced, were not guarded around the clock. Any security for the individual officials involved also seemed non-existent. If pro-Indonesian militia groups really wanted to make a statement, the team reported, it was here they could do it best and with little risk.

There were a few other vehicles around at this time of the morning and the Pajero merged comfortably with its surroundings. Harry was not alone. His driver had parked the Pajero discretely along the road, facing the direction they anticipated the person they were waiting for to walk in. Harry's team had learned enough of the person's habits to predict he would appear in the next ten minutes and walk in their direction, and then on towards the main road.

As they watched, the heavy gates, topped with a row of razor wire, began to slowly open under their hydraulic assist. A man in a grey suit appeared, and with him, a woman of about the same age. Like him, she was tall and thin. It had been twenty years since Harry had seen either of them, but he recognised them both instantly.

Her name was Marjorie, and she was dressed in a sleeveless blue print dress and wore simple leather sandals. Her hair was that attractive shade of grey that former blondes carry with such grace, slightly less than shoulder length and tied back in a neat ponytail. A young Timorese woman, barefoot and wearing a bright pink t-shirt, also appeared from inside the gate. She was carrying a yard broom too big for her and began awkwardly sweeping leaves from across the front of the gates.

Marjorie had no hat with her, and Harry reckoned she would return inside the complex once she had bid the man goodbye.

As if on cue, she held her face towards the man and he kissed her gently on the cheek. He placed his wide-brimmed hat on his bald head and strode off in the direction of the main road, and unwittingly towards the Pajero.

'Bingo,' muttered Harry's companion. 'I love it when a plan comes together.'

'This is only the start,' Harry warned, 'there's a lot of work to do yet.'

They watched the man's image grow larger in their mirrors as he walked purposefully towards them. In the background, the two women disappeared back inside, and the big gates slowly closed.

The tall man was oblivious to everything around him, and only the footfall of his leather-soled shoes filled the air as he closed the distance between them. Harry timed his move to perfection; judging the man's pace and approach, he deftly opened his door and stepped out in one fluid motion.

In an instant he was standing on the footpath and the two men were face to face.

'Hello Roger. Long time, no see,' Harry smiled genially.

The man was startled at first, being pulled from his own thoughts with a jolt, but he quickly recovered and realised who it was standing in front of him.

'For God's sake! Is that you Harry? You gave me such a start. What the hell are you doing here?'

'Actually, I have a story to tell,' Harry said cryptically as they shook hands. At the same time, he pulled the rear door open and beckoned Roger Sanderson inside with a slight movement of his head.

'We'll give you a ride. We can stop off for coffee on the way and talk.' It wasn't an offer or a question, it was an instruction, and Sanderson didn't sense he could refuse, indeed he had no reason to do so. He climbed into the back of the Pajero and they were away.

Harry's driver dropped them at a small, rather dingy café a short distance away which had been pre-selected for several reasons. Firstly, it wasn't normally patronised by Westerners, and Harry wanted to avoid the possibility of any unexpected guests. Secondly, it had a small, pretty, cobbled courtyard to the rear with only one table — and Harry had pre-booked it. Lastly, the team had reported the coffee was excellent and Harry always said that if you had a tough job ahead, you may as well enjoy whatever you could about it. Coffee was one of those things, and it would be a tough job, Harry knew.

'So, what's this all about then? A little bit cloak and dagger, eh?' Sanderson asked searchingly. His unguarded words warned Harry that his antenna was up, and he was now highly alert, although nothing showed outwardly. Sanderson took his hat off and placed it on the corner of the table, happy that the roofed trellis overflowing with multi-variant bougainvillea would shade them and protect his shiny head from the hot sun. They sat in silence for a moment and around them a rooster heralded the morning. Harry was happy to take it as his cue.

'I'm actually working Roger, and it seems that circumstances have caused our paths to cross,' he opened cryptically, with a dashing smile.

Sanderson nodded and busied himself pouring coffee into both their glasses from the elegant metal pot the waiter had set down.

'How intriguing. Do go on,' he said finally as he looked up with a bland expression.

'Alright, I'll be as succinct as possible. A few days ago, you met with your ambassador, the senior Australian military commander, and two intelligence officers from AUSBATT — Major

Tony Fletcher and Sergeant Major Matt Hurley. The topic of discussion was the murder of two agents run by AUSBATT, and the wife of one, and the tragic death of an Australian soldier. OK so far?' Harry offered enticingly, cocking one of his thick dark eyebrows towards Sanderson in challenge. Sanderson said nothing, but his face visibly paled.

'The reason I know this, Roger, is that I am in East Timor managing a covert counter-intelligence capability in support of the deployed force. I was called upon to investigate the suspicious deaths of those agents. Together, myself and Hurley established that two of *your* people, Urquhart and Tomms, have been running some type of operation, the purpose of which is to cultivate a wanted war criminal named Marcelino Borges as an Australian agent of influence. The vision was that with his family and political connections he might be engineered into a position of political power in the new East Timor, and thus be a great insider, perhaps even a decision maker, when issues like the Timor Gap oil and gas treaty are negotiated by your two countries. So, *your* people talent-spotted a surly and disaffected Australian soldier and then recruited him to do their dirty work. Subsequently, he eliminated those who could provide eyewitness testimony of Borges' crimes against humanity on their behalf. Moreover, I have very good reason to believe they pruned Borges' file at the UN Serious Crimes Unit here in Dili, such that there is no longer a record of the crimes he has committed. How am I doing so far?'

'Harry, I–'

'I'm not nearly finished,' Harry interrupted smoothly, lifting his hand slightly from the table and facing his palm towards his prey. Sanderson squirmed on his chair, but Harry was relentless, and the look in his eye said that he wasn't going to entertain any argument.

'So, at this meeting the other day, it was *agreed* that none of the aforementioned ever happened. Conveniently, the murderer himself has been killed in self-defence. And even though there is a recording of an admission by him which reveals the entire story — which I might add is supported by all the known facts — the official version is it never happened. To add insult to injury, you, not them Roger, but *you*, muddied the waters by suggesting that the recording was some sophisticated cover story provided by some unseen third party who may miraculously have had the same operational aims. Please correct me Roger, if I'm getting any of this wrong,' Harry paused, his words dripping with sarcasm.

Sanderson sat uneasily in his chair and did not want to meet Harry's gaze. He was clearly annoyed he had been placed in this position. He could have elected to walk away at any time though, and Harry had considered the possibility of him doing just that.

For this very reason, Harry's driver now sat easily at what was the only exit to the courtyard. In any case, Sanderson was like a deer in the headlights now and Harry reckoned he would stay to the end. As if in capitulation, he poured another cup from the coffee pot and sighed. Harry did not miss a beat.

'So, the outcome is, there will be no inquiry, no punishment or sanction for your people, and the death of the soldier will be attributed to mental health issues. A good outcome for many I suppose, but not for me.'

'What do you want, Harry?' Sanderson implored suddenly, looking at him sharply. 'Politically, there can be no inquiry, there's an election at home in a few months and the ambassador will not countenance it — full stop. If this got out it would be catastrophic for our relationship with the new East Timor, it's that grave. And if there's no inquiry, I technically have nothing to hang on those two, who have plausibly denied everything and put me in the invidious position where I have been forced to support their denial to hold up the government's end. It stinks, I don't like it, but there you are.'

'You asked me before what I wanted, Roger. I want you to do me a favour, that's all. You owe me a favour, Roger. In fact, you once said those very words to me. *Harry, I owe you everything, if there's anything I can ever do to repay you, I will, I promise.* And now I'm calling in the mark, Roger.'

Sanderson rested his elbows on the table and held his head in his hands. He did not look up. It was true, he did owe Harry, and he had said those words. In fact, as the years went by, the debt became ever greater. Now it was finally being called in and it all came back to him in a rush.

It was more than twenty years ago when he and Harry were on attachment to MI6 headquarters in London. It was before the great monolith that now stands in Vauxhall Cross had ever been built and filmed incessantly on the big screen.

Headquarters was the very ordinary Century House in those days, with its quaint old humming and bumping elevators, the polished linoleum floors and the uniformed, moustachioed commissionaire standing sentinel on the door.

They were both outsiders then; Harry from the army and he from the Australian service, and they had warmed to each other. It was also the time before computers when the registry girls brought the files around on a squeaky trolley twice a day; once in the morning and once in the afternoon.

On the top tray, working files were collected and passed out in an endless cycle of filing and distribution. And on the bottom tray were the tea and coffee urns, the white crockery cups and saucers, and the obligatory government biscuit, waiting patiently for distribution in each saucer.

Peggy was one of those registry girls. Leggy Peggy the boys called her, but not to her face, although she well knew she deserved her moniker. He had warmed to Peggy too, and she to him; and so she became Peggy Weggy to him, just for a laugh, their little joke.

Marjorie's suspicions had first been raised at the office Christmas party — how cliché it was, he had often reflected — a quick kiss and a fumble with Peggy Weggy in the cloak room, all harmless enough he had thought. Until Marjorie had confronted him, and like most wives she had that uncanny ability to know just who was missing from a party at the same time a husband is.

He had largely gotten away with it after much strenuous denial and claims of being sick in the toilet. But it wasn't that simple the following week when Marjorie found the note in his overcoat pocket with the name of a small boutique hotel and *Room 14* underscored. Having read the note, he had stuffed it back in his pocket, and then, and only because the weather had turned, he had taken his raincoat instead.

Marjorie had come across the note while hanging his coat in the closet and it was all downhill from there. She had rung Harry's wife Jean, all in a tizzy by then, having worked herself up, and had proclaimed she was going to the hotel to confront him.

Harry had done the obvious and called him at the hotel to warn him. Sod's Law held that in their earlier lovemaking the telephone receiver in Room 14 had been dislodged from the cradle by an errant foot, and Harry could not get through. Sod's Law further held that the night clerk would be some type of foreigner and not able to understand the message Harry was trying to convey. In fact, the more Harry talked the more it sounded like it would be worse if he let the clerk loose in Room 14.

In desperation, Harry had jumped into his old Ford Escort and belted across town to the hotel to warn him. He beat Marjorie by minutes only, and when the door was opened to her knocking it was Harry, looking shamefaced with his hair tousled and only in his underpants, with Peggy Weggy in Room 14.

For his part he had listened from his hiding place in the bathroom as the scene unfolded. Marjorie, aghast at Harry's betrayal of Jean, and feeling guilty herself for doubting her own husband, learned he was working that night and Harry had given the note to Roger so he would know where to contact him if anything came up.

Peggy Weggy thought it all rather amusing and held the sheet up over her mouth, her eyes wide, and then giggled uncontrollably once Marjorie was gone. Sanderson was never sure it didn't become one of those great enduing stories told among the registry girls down the generations.

Unknown to him, it *was* still talked about from time to time, but Harry was the celebrity that night and his name had entered service folklore — courtesy of Peggy Weggy in Room 14. Any action considered vaguely funny and gallant was now still referred to in registry as *doing a Harry*.

Sanderson, for his part, had been forgotten, but he had vowed that night to change. There would be no more playing away, and he had truly held to his vow. It was something that could have cost him his marriage and his career, and he knew it.

In a sense, his career, and certainly finally being appointed Head of Station, and all the happy years he had enjoyed with Marjorie and the children since that night, would never have happened if it wasn't for Harry, and his quick thinking. There really was only one way to go. He sat back, beaten.

'I'm listening,' he croaked emotionally.

'I want you to hear their confession. I want to kidnap them, interrogate them and trick them into confessing what they did — and I want you there to hear it, and then I want you to act on it.'

'You're out of your mind Harry, you can't do that,' Sanderson blurted out, wide eyed and incredulous.

'I can, and I will. But I need you there to hear it because when I say act on it, I mean get them dismissed from the service. That's the end state if we're successful; they get sacked. The recording we already have can be misattributed and ridiculed, and you can say it is worthless if you wish, but you can use their confession if you've witnessed it. In the process, I won't physically harm them; you have my word on it.'

'It's too much Harry, and anyway, it would never work,' Sanderson said dismissively.

'I think it might, and I know a lot more about this type of thing than you do. I want you to repay the favour you bloody well owe me,' Harry pressured him.

There was a lot running around in Sanderson's mind. On a point of honour, he should repay Harry and let the gods decide his fate. One part of him wanted to do just that. If those two did confess, he could go to the director general and have them removed from post, he probably could get them sacked. Once they confessed, they would have nothing to use in complaint, and no case to mount against their dismissal.

Even if it went to a tribunal, they would never win a case with the meddling inspector general. A few strategically timed rumours to the right people and even the most well placed of their backers would abandon them, that's for sure.

There was a good chance the DG would support him and you never know, if it all went *really* well, he could pass it off as his own initiative, his way of tidying up and ensuring the good name of the service, following what he could then portray as a clearly unacceptable outcome the first time around.

He worked these thoughts over in his mind and made his decision.

'OK Harry, I'll do it for you, but on one condition.'

'Depends.'

'If it doesn't work, they don't see me or know that I was ever there.'

'Agreed. But if it does work, you must show your face so they know they've confessed in front of you and the cat's out of the bag.'

'Agreed,' said Sanderson.

Harry had seen himself at this juncture when he planned the encounter, but he knew self-congratulations were premature. He also knew he needed something more — something that would work away inside Sanderson's mind and hold him to his commitment — something that would provide a deterrent should he get cold feet or find it all just a bit hard to follow through.

Sanderson was essentially weak, and Harry knew it. A debt incurred long ago could easily evaporate or be rationalised away if things got too difficult. And he and Sanderson both knew that Harry wouldn't be running off to tell Marjorie what really happened all those years ago. So, just as he knew he would eventually have to, he played his trump card.

'I'm relieved we've been able to agree on this, and that you've been kind enough to repay the favour you've owed me all these years. I'm very glad for you… and Marjorie.'

'That's an odd thing to say, Harry. What do you mean?' Sanderson asked suspiciously.

Harry looked Sanderson straight in the face, and leaned imperceptibly closer, his eyes measured and resolute. There was a hardness there that the Sandersons of the world could never match.

'Because if I had failed to secure this agreement, Matt Hurley would have killed both your people in pretty short order. And be under no illusions he hasn't the resources, the capacity and the motivation to do so. You must understand his position, call it revenge if you want, but he is loyal and determined and he feels responsible to resolve it. Three people have died down there, and a child has been orphaned, all by the cavalier actions of your people.'

Sanderson gave a short laugh, but it was brittle, and he was clearly uneasy.

'That may have actually solved a problem for me,' he admitted, trying to be a bit too blasé now that he felt most of the pressure had lifted from him. 'It would've got those two out of my hair, for sure.'

'Not for long Roger,' Harry countered blandly.

'What do you mean?'

'Because then Matt Hurley would have killed you, and you need to understand something. He *will* kill you if he doesn't get the outcome we've talked about. It may not be next week, or next month, or next year, but he will come for you, and he will kill you.'

'Jesus Christ, Harry, this whole affair wasn't my doing! You'll have to talk to him, he must be raving mad!'

'I have, and I won't cheapen it by trying to change his mind. I played a part in training him, and he's not rogue or raving mad, in fact, he is quite sane and very good at his job. They were his agents, Roger, and the soldier was his sergeant. It's his call. There was a time when you knew what that meant.'

'But it wasn't my doing,' he pleaded weakly.

'Be that as it may, I'm sure there's an apt metaphor about ships and their captains but I won't bore you with it now,' Harry remarked, twisting the knife that was well embedded now.

They looked at each other in silence as the past hour or so of words and thoughts worked its way around inside their minds. The small, happy chirping of the birds playing in the nearby bushes was the only sound to accompany their thoughts. It was Harry who broke the silence, knowing he needed to maintain the control and moral authority he had established.

'Anyway,' he smiled, 'let's not worry about that for now, let's get on with the details of how this will work, shall we? Because there's some things I need from you in the first instance.'

With that he stood up and pulled a crisp US twenty-dollar bill from his shirt pocket. Folding it once across the middle, he placed it on the table. He walked back to the Pajero with Sanderson, knowing full well he had played all the right cards.

17

BALIBO

UNITED NATIONS ADMINISTERED EAST TIMOR

February 2001

Hurley moved slowly along the dusty road leading from the largest of Balibo's villages back towards the fort. Intermittently, he waved or spoke briefly to the locals as he passed. Small groups of children, barefoot and dressed in threadbare clothes, moved around him like flocks of seagulls before their attention was diverted elsewhere and they drifted away, their squawking slowly fading as they moved on.

He spotted the white Toyota as he entered the town square and made a beeline towards it, his pace quickening in anticipation that Harry might have news, and particularly the news he wanted. He could hear the engine running as he approached the vehicle and saw Harry inside, content to sit in the air-conditioned cab rather than walk up to the fort in the heat of the day.

Harry was sitting comfortably in the driver's seat, gazing out the windscreen as Hurley climbed into the cab and pulled the door closed behind him with a thud. He said nothing and settled himself into the seat. Harry turned his head slowly towards him.

'It's a go,' he said without fanfare, but there was an underlying excitement in his voice.

'Jesus,' Hurley whispered. It was more than he could have hoped for. 'So, who is this mysterious benefactor Harry, or is that a surprise for later?'

'Actually, it's someone you know quite well,' Harry teased.

'Really?' Hurley said, his face betraying his scepticism. 'I can't think of anyone who fits the bill and who would do this for us.'

'It's Roger Sanderson,' Harry said evenly, watching Hurley closely.

Hurley was gobsmacked. He turned to face Harry, his eyes wide and mouth half open in disbelief.

'You're joking, right? The same Roger Sanderson who supported *their* story, and tied this all up with a bow for them?'

'Ezackly,' Harry confirmed. 'However, it might be that dear old Roger was caught between a rock and a hard place. It seems he couldn't really do much else at the time and was looking more at, shall we say, *reputational* issues, which I'm sure included his own self-interest. That's no excuse at all by the way, but the bottom line is he owes me a very big favour and he's decided to pay up.'

'Is there anyone you don't know, Harry?' Hurley finally asked.

Harry chuckled. 'I suppose it's always good for people to think one is infallible, and better still if one can occasionally pull it off, just to keep the myth alive,' he said primly. They both laughed.

'It's a very *old* favour actually,' he went on, earnestly now, 'but not nearly strong enough to hold his nose to the grindstone under pressure. For that very reason, I made some other shit up that will help him stay focused and on task.'

Hurley began to laugh again, but seeing the beginnings of a mischievous smile playing at the corners of Harry's mouth, he stopped.

'What other shit would that be exactly, Harry?' he asked slowly, and very deliberately.

'Well, I do like to link these things to the emotion of the situation, and send a good moral message as well. I think emotion makes people believe things they normally might not. You gave me the idea the other day when you were so pissed off, after the meeting went badly.'

'Go on,' Hurley prodded, clearly suspicious now.

'Well, I simply told Roger that if you don't get the outcome you want — the sacking of those two fucking dirt bags — then you will kill them.'

'You said what?' Hurley burst out, incredulous.

'Yeah, and here's the clincher…'

'There's more?'

'You bet. I also told him that in the future, at a time and place of your choosing, you would come for him, and kill him too.'

Hurley smiled slowly at first, and then began to laugh. Harry joined him and the sound grew to fill the cabin.

'Seriously, it's important you know that Matt,' Harry implored, breaking into their laughter. 'While it is most unlikely to come up as a topic of conversation between the two of you, you must act as if it is true, and your words, actions and demeanour must support it, without ever stating it explicitly. He must believe it, you understand?'

'Sure, I get it. In fact, I might just enjoy it.'

'OK. So, as it turns out, Roger has already been able to provide us with some useful information to get started. Apparently it's common for some certain embassy staff to go out and paint the town red on Friday and Saturday nights, with Saturday night being the more common. Do you know Club ET?'

'Yeah, Club Echo Tango, on the beach front north of the city.'

'Good, I'm thinking at this early stage to build something

around that. Roger says these two often go together for conve-
nience, to share a vehicle, so we can get straight into some serious
recce this coming week and we'll see what that turns up in the
way of options. Can you get up to Dili mid-week do you reckon?'

Hurley ran his hand through his hair before he answered.

'Wednesday would work best. The boss has been happy to cut
me some slack to work with you and things are fine here.'

'That sounds good, actually. It will give the guys a couple of
days to work on things before you come up. That way, you can
provide your input and we have a couple more days to tweak
things with your input. Best case, we might just be ready to go
on the Saturday night. If not, no problem, we work on the plan
and hold it over for the following week.'

'And we keep doing that until the time's right.'

'Ezackly. On Wednesday, I can pick you up from Australian
HQ and take you back to Casa Dili. Can you be there at midday?'

Hurley nodded. 'Mmm. Casa Dili — The Dili House. I take
it that is your covert base up there. How does it work with me
going there?'

'It is. It's actually owned by the British foreign office and has
been for years. Brian Ashby came across it when he was setting
up the initial deployment and was able to secure it, ostensibly for
World Reach but without their knowledge of course, and turn it
into our main operational premises. As to your concern, it's no
problem. I have decided you have a need to know, and besides,
the guys are looking forward to meeting you,' he said with a wink.

Hurley gave him a quizzical look.

'Matt, they've been with you throughout this. They've been
working in the shadows with me, not just on this problem but
other problems that affect this mission too. When those treach-
erous pricks did what they did to you, they did it to all of us. It's
personal now. The team know your background and they know

your reputation. Most importantly, they know that you and I go back, and we're mates, and that's good enough for them. I've worked with some of these guys before in a dozen other places just like this. Some I trained, just like you.'

It was a big deal, and Hurley knew it. While they may all be working towards the same end state, it wasn't common practice to drop the curtain of secrecy and potentially risk compromising the big moving parts of any covert operation.

'I appreciate it Harry, you know that.'

'I do, but there's no special treatment. You need to be there if we are to get the result we're looking for, it's as simple as that.'

'I appreciate it anyway, and I know how complex these issues can be. In the meantime, I better go and let you get back to Maliana.'

'OK, before you do though, what's your first thoughts on how to approach these two. What's your take on them?'

Hurley moved his gaze to the windscreen and stared into the distance, weighing the targets up against each other as subjects for interrogation. When he spoke, he chose his words carefully because he knew what Harry needed.

'The Latte Girl I know. She is selfish and totally up herself; she's a looker and she knows it, and she's used to getting her own way. Intellectually she's a lightweight and hides behind her private school education and her language skills. She doesn't care a tinker's for anyone except number one, and I reckon she'd be hard pressed to lift a finger to save anyone else but herself. Intrinsically, she's tough though, not so driven by emotion and so probably less likely to be captured by the theatrics of inter-rogation. Urquhart, I don't know, as I said, but I've asked around here among my own team and made some discreet enquiries back home with people I trust. He prides himself on being a schemer, he's a good strategic thinker and a good talker too, but not so tough. He is more emotional and so more likely to act rashly and be tricked and controlled by the ploy, so long as he falls for it. But the same imagination that is the strength in his vision is his weakness here. He told one of my guys he actually made a play for the Latte Girl when she first arrived although realised shortly after that he'd made a big mistake, handing all the control cards to her. Nevertheless, I think he'd see it as the right thing to try and be gallant, although he would probably fail in the follow through if his own well-being was on the line. I wouldn't piss on either of them if they were on fire.'

'OK, this is good. I'll take that last comment as unprofessional and an emotional product of recent events. Not that I disagree, mind you.'

Hurley looked straight at Harry and nodded his head in silence, clearly having been distracted and missed Harry's joke entirely. By his distant look there were many things running through his mind.

'Which means,' Harry summed up for them both, 'that Urquhart is first in the frame to watch *her* suffer, because he is the one most easily controlled, and the most likely to break.'

'Yeah, I reckon that's the way to go. You and I can talk at length in Dili on the approach and the questioning for both of them. Have you had a think about the physical components of the ploy? The theatre will need to be top notch, Harry, if we're going to carry this off. You know that, right?'

'I do, Mattie, I do. For that reason, I've briefed a couple of the team who are working on just that problem while I'm away from Dili. They know the degree of difficulty and we'll maintain the initiative by keeping strict control of the timing and events, and most importantly, exploiting the dark. It will be done outside at night with only enough artificial light to serve our purposes, which is for them to see what we want them to see.'

It was a sound concept. Without split-second control of events, things wouldn't happen as they must for the desired effect, and the darkness can be used to hide all the unwanted detail. What's more, the dark makes people see what they want to see, or more correctly what they fear most and *don't* want to see, and Hurley knew it.

'Sounds good, Harry. I'll see you Wednesday at midday, and I'm guessing that by the evening we'll know pretty much where we're headed. I'm looking forward to it.'

'Luvvly jubbly,' Harry said, rubbing his hands together. 'And don't worry, my team will be all over this by the time you get there. See you then.'

For a short while, Harry watched Hurley in the rear-view mirror as he disappeared up the ramp towards the fort gates. Then he slowly drove out onto the main road and pointed the vehicle east towards Maliana. He had much to think about, and it would be a very busy week.

18

DILI

UNITED NATIONS ADMINISTERED EAST TIMOR

....

February 2001

Australia's military headquarters in Dili was a two-storey concrete structure originally painted white, but the colouring had long faded. The building fronted towards the road and featured a large covered portico. The grounds were protected by a tall metal fence topped with razor wire.

At the rear was a newer, single story block used for accommodation. Overall, the HQ had housed a large number of people in relative comfort since the initial INTERFET deployment in '99. The Dili Dwellers, as they were known derisively by soldiers serving on the border, had improved their lot over time.

The buildings were air-conditioned throughout, and demountable shower and toilet blocks had been installed. A large covered area between the two main structures housed the Dili Surf Life Saving Club. In truth, it was simply a bar from which the residents could obtain ice-cold drinks at bargain basement prices, but its creation continued a long-standing military tradition to establish similar such clubs whether there was a beach within cooee or not.

The club was also the focal point for Friday night happy hours, and functions organised to lessen the boredom of the Dili Dwellers. Hurley remembered well the time he had driven up to brief the Australian commander on some burning issue and had stood cooling his heels in the bar talking to a staff officer dressed for the night as Paddington Bear.

He had stood there in his sweaty camouflage fatigues, with mud caked up to his knees — courtesy of a flat tyre on the trip up — as he listened to the music blaring. A pink fairy with a wand had suddenly appeared and placed a drink in his hand. He had found it most disconcerting.

Hurley whistled as he showered and allowed himself a few moments of cheeky extra time before he reluctantly turned the water off. He ran his hand back through his hair and headed back to the accommodation, a towel wrapped around his waist and his toothbrush between his teeth.

His kit lay strewn across the bunk as he sorted through it and repacked his overnight bag. He quickly dressed in casual civilian clothes and surreptitiously placed his Browning pistol into the Velcro flapped bottom of his backpack for easy access.

It was totally against Australian and UN regulations for someone dressed in civilian clothing to carry a weapon. Like many others, however, Hurley was happy to risk the flack if he were caught rather than be unarmed in the event of a militia attack or a mugging.

The former was not likely in Dili, but the latter was very possible. He grinned to himself as he remembered just how dangerous Dili could be. *Red Week* — the week prior to Christmas — had seen more people wounded at HQ than in the border regions for the first time, though these were not the work of pro-Indonesian militiamen.

Instead, these resulted from "unauthorised discharges" brought about through nothing but poor weapon handling. Still, not all UDs resulted in injuries and in one celebrated incident a shot was fired clear through the wall of one office into the next, missing those on the other side by millimetres. The story was a much-needed pre-Christmas tonic for troops serving on the border.

Hurley sat on the step of the portico in the shade, awaiting Harry's arrival. There was no one about in the heat of the day and the carpark in front of the HQ was quiet except for the incessant buzzing of the bees attending the nearby bushes. A dozen or so white UN vehicles were neatly lined up, gleaming in the sun like parading soldiers awaiting inspection.

When Harry arrived, he propped outside the gate and jauntily sounded the horn; it was certainly easier to wait outside than go through the bureaucratic tedium of gaining entry to the HQ. Hurley waved to the guard on duty as he passed through the gateway and after throwing his gear in the back of Harry's vehicle, jumped into the cab.

Harry appeared relaxed and in good spirits, and Hurley took this as a good sign of what lay ahead.

'We'll be there in about five minutes,' he offered as they moved off. 'We'll have lunch first and then I'll get the team to brief you on where we're at. I think you'll be pleased. They've worked really hard and loved it.'

'Sounds good, especially lunch,' Hurley beamed. It was what he had been hoping. It was certainly new territory for him to be doing such an important and complex operation with people he didn't know, but he had faith in Harry and his team and had leaned on them heavily. He just hoped he could live up to their expectations.

Harry turned off the main road and began winding his way through the minor roads of an old residential area unknown to Hurley. The area was tired, not overly so by Dili standards, but the houses here were larger and had previously been more up-market. They pulled up at a double storey residence that was painted a Tuscan sand colour, the window shutters and the eaves neatly trimmed in black.

Harry activated the remote control on his key fob and the heavy metal security gates began to withdraw from their centre point. They drove through onto a cobblestone area beyond and stopped in the shade of a large Jacaranda tree. Harry then waited until the gates were fully closed. This was the drill, Hurley thought watching him, for which each team member would be responsible when they came and went.

Looking around, Hurley could now see the house in its true setting; the manicured lawns, the garden beds colourful and well kept. There was a wide variety of palms and succulents, and hibiscus and frangipani within his immediate eye line. Trees had been strategically planted and had matured to shade the property to perfection.

The centrepiece was a magnificent dragon tree, but Hurley also noticed the orange spray of a Royal Poinciana and a tropical Magnolia among those on display. It was like an oasis amid the tired and hot world that seemed to perpetually surround them, Hurley thought. It gave him a good feeling.

His professional eye noted the two-meter high cement wall surrounding the entire property. It was painted the same colour as the house and inset into the top were dangerous jagged pieces of broken glass. Security lights discreetly overlooked the wall.

'Casa Dili,' Hurley remarked, professional admiration evident in his voice.

'Casa Dili,' Harry acknowledged, 'and you're right, this is a cracker. It's an absolute gem, and one of the nicest places it has ever been my good fortune to work at. But you haven't seen any-thing yet.'

Harry led along the neat cobbled path that took them around to the back of the property. It was only then that the lawn tennis court came into view and Hurley chuckled out loud.

'It comes with the turf, I'm afraid,' Harry conceded with a smirk as they walked on. Hurley sniffed the unmistakable aroma of meat and onions sizzling on a barbeque, though he was hard pressed to see where it was coming from and could not hear it.

Instead, the tropical garden sounds of the insects and birds at midday were all that were on offer. Hurley realised that the house was, in fact, square and not 'L' shaped as he had first thought. This meant the house was probably twice the size he had reckoned from his first impression.

The barbequing was occurring inside the square and as they approached the house, Hurley could see a cobbled arched walkway to about the height of the ground floor. It led through to an inner courtyard and Hurley thought it may have just been possible to drive a small car through it.

At the entrance they passed two formidable black ironwork gates which, while ornamental, were functional too and could secure the inner courtyard. But Hurley's growing appreciation did not prepare him for the reality to come. As they walked the short length of the walkway, they passed two large doorways that in turn led off to the right and left into the interior of the house.

The courtyard was spectacular. Designed in the style of a Mediterranean villa, perhaps a testament to its Portuguese roots, the courtyard was tiled with sandstone and decorated with large potted plants. Centrally, a tiered fountain was prominent but at the same time not imposing; it gurgled softly amid beautifully chosen plants and was trimmed with a low box hedge.

The house design meant that in the hottest part of the day the courtyard was comfortable and in natural semi-shade. The sizzling of the barbeque could now certainly be heard; it was situated in the far corner and partially obscured by the fountain. Hurley could see it was surrounded by cookers and watchers, like most barbeques.

A long trestle table surrounded by chairs and laid with a simple white cloth stood close by the barbeque crowd. The cookers and watchers numbered just over a dozen, and they chatted happily among themselves. They did not seek to interrupt the arrival of Harry and their guest.

'This is fantastic, Harry,' Hurley said finally.

'Ezackly,' agreed Harry with a wink, 'and one of the reasons I'm glad this is a closely guarded secret.'

'Who does the maintenance? It must be pretty labour intensive keeping up these appearances.'

'Yeah, interesting story there too. You'll remember this place has been on the foreign office books for years. Well, when Brian looked into it, it seems that back during the Portuguese years, pre-'75, the UK Government maintained some sort of quasi trade commissioner who contracted a local family through their business here in Dili. When the last incumbent left for Blighty during the Indonesian occupation, around the early 90s, the family continued to maintain the property and look after the security as they always had. Essentially the patriarch of the family became the caretaker and his family the willing workers. Seems that they simply put in an invoice to the company here in Dili and it gets passed on to the FO and paid through some bizarre bureaucratic process that should have ceased years ago. It continues to this day and the family have grown rich on the proceeds. But you can see the results.

'So we see Senhor Da Costa and his family almost every day and they do all the work and cooking for us. They think that we work for World Reach and other assorted NGOs and the like of course, and they are instructed not to come into the lower east wing,' he said indicating over Hurley's shoulder. 'We've told them that we have volunteers and interns that work for their supper and are required to clean and maintain that part of the house. It means we can secure items and do operational stuff in that wing if we want, but it leaves the big kitchen, dining and sitting areas in the west wing, and the grounds for them to look after.'

Hurley looked around and his eye was drawn upwards to the balconies overhead. They were trimmed by ornate black iron-work in a style similar to the walkway gates.

'So, is it the living quarters upstairs then?'

Harry followed his gaze and nodded. 'Basically yes, upstairs are bedrooms and bathrooms. Perfect for our crew plus the odd blow-in like me and you. Not everyone is here all the time, so we're never overcrowded. Anyway, we'll do a tour later. Let's go and meet the troops and get some scoff, eh?'

Harry led Hurley over to the gaggle surrounding the barbeque and introduced them all to him. He quickly learned their names, listening to their voices and accents which were varied in such a big group. Few people would recall the names of a dozen people at first blush, but Hurley had no such problem and had trained himself to remember many more. It was one of his little party tricks.

Hurley was surprised to learn that among Harry's team there was a face from his past. She wasn't with the group initially but instead he noticed her approach from the kitchen. Carrying trays of bread and salad, she eased her way gracefully to place them on the table.

Her hair was different, cut shorter no doubt for the heat, and now a dark lustrous red. She would now be in her early thirties, Hurley reckoned, but it was definitely her. The things you recall about people were never constant, he mused; sometimes it was their voice, sometimes a certain mannerism, sometimes their laugh or just the way they held their head.

With this woman it was her walk; she moved with a confidence and athleticism about her that he remembered finding attractive the first time he had ever seen her. He was reminded of that now, although he pushed the thought away by habit.

It had been six busy years, and he remembered her as a young Royal Military Police investigator from the dark days of the mission in Rwanda. There were very few Brits in that particular mission and she and her colonel, the UN Provost-Marshal, had naturally gravitated towards their antipodean cousins for sanity — away from all things Africa and away from the UN.

Having settled the trays, she turned to look at Hurley and smiled. It was friendly and impish, and for a fleeting moment Hurley thought it a smile that crossed a lot of miles and had meanings he did not quite understand.

'Stone the bloody crows, Maggie Redcap what are you doing here?' he burst out with a wry smile. The team laughed good-naturedly, and with appreciation of the nickname Hurley used for her — a British Army term denoting the distinctive head dress worn by the RMP.

In fact, Hurley's team had called her that in Rwanda, in order to distinguish her from another British corporal with the same name who was tall and thin and had been less kindly nicknamed Maggie Broomstick.

Unfortunately, the appearance of *this* Maggie also caused a nagging guilt to quickly surface in Hurley. Some three years before, after the car accident in which his wife had sustained her terrible injuries, Maggie had written to Hurley.

It was a heartfelt letter and it spoke to her friendship and compassion for his situation. Hurley had not returned her letter, and he made a mental note to address this with her later. For her part she showed no hint of any of this and was clearly in the moment.

'I'm here because of you, Matthew Hurley,' she accused him tartly, her voice proud but playful, and mocking him in reproach nevertheless. The group's laughter pealed again at her riposte, and Hurley played his part as the chastened schoolboy. He already felt very much at home with this group and was confident it boded well.

'Let's eat!' Harry called out above the hubbub as the last of the cooked meat was delivered to the platters on the table.

Hurley was guided to a seat next to Harry, who was seated at the head of the long table. They placed Maggie next to him, likely because they knew each other, he thought. The others spread out and were quickly engaged in silly banter and witty, but harmless insults towards each other. A ritual that no doubt rolled on day after day and was part of the glue that held the team together.

They were easy going and tight knit, a very pleasant bunch. The setting reminded Hurley of an extended Italian family lunching on a summer day, with the patriarch *Don Aroldo* at the head of the table surrounded by his much loved and loving family. Hurley couldn't supress his amusement.

'What's so funny?' Maggie asked, her head askew, smiling and curious.

'Maggie, if you can't see what's funny about this scene, you need to get out in the real army more,' he suggested playfully.

She nodded. 'You're right, we're very lucky.' And then lowering her voice, as she leaned over and poured him a glass of water. 'I meant what I said, you know.'

'What, about being here because of me?'

'Yes.'

There had always been a precision to her language, and he was immediately reminded of it. She wasn't one to say 'yeah', or 'yep' and such like. She spoke crisply and with clarity, and her English Home Counties accent was easy on the ear. Some would say just a little bit posh. Hurley liked it, in fact, the thought came to him that he liked it a lot.

'You couldn't have known but it was you who wooed me to the world of intelligence. I watched you and your team in Rwanda and saw how much you enjoyed your work. I left knowing I wanted something more. As soon as I got back to the UK after that mission I applied for Special Duties. I certainly haven't been disappointed. And so, here I am. In a sense it really is all thanks to you.'

'Well, I would correct one small detail,' he said, his voice taking on an apparent serious tone. 'We never *enjoy* ourselves, its only ever *professional satisfaction*. But apart from that, I love a success story as much as the next bloke,' he conceded with a broad grin. In truth he felt just a little chuffed he had played some part in her change of heart, and career.

'So, what's happened to you in the meantime?'

'First up, I was fortunate to get a tour of Northern Ireland in before the big wind down.'

'Ah, so you joined the club, eh?' Britain's longest war had been the crucible for many a stellar career, particularly in special duties intelligence. It was still viewed, rightly or not, as the yardstick against which all other operations were measured.

Hurley sensed this would remain the case until either the last Northern Ireland veteran had retired, or some major conflict eclipsed the memories of the past. In the British Army you were a member of that club, or you weren't, it was as simple as that.

Hurley was not measured by the same yardstick. As an Australian, he was not expected to have served there and instead he had made his name in other places, although he acknowledged what he called the *genetic link*, all his British trainers and mentors had served with distinction in Northern Ireland, and they had learned everything they knew the hard way.

'I suppose you're right,' she reflected, pursing her lips and nodding in acceptance. 'Mine was all recon and surveillance though, the joys of being a female operator really. It's where I was needed at the time. I don't regret it though; it was a great experience.'

Hurley reckoned she was hiding her light under a bushel. He pictured her for an instant, armed and driving alone, one-up, or even on foot, in that cold, dangerous and God-forsaken place under the noses of the PIRA heavies and learning their secrets to bring them down, and doing it in style. She wouldn't have been there otherwise.

She didn't miss a beat, and Hurley sensed that some of this was nervous chatter. He was slightly confused. She wasn't the type to be nervous; perhaps his presence in Casa Dili had upset the status quo. He hoped not, but he understood that visitors here would be very unusual indeed.

'And then I had a break and followed on pretty quickly into Bosnia and then Kosovo,' she continued. She was keen to talk, and she appeared to enjoy Hurley's attention. For his part, he was happy to listen. There were things he didn't want to talk about with her yet, and it made it easier for her to talk. He noted she did not raise those issues, and he was very thankful.

'How did that go?' he prompted.

'Oh, you know, caught a few war criminals, wrapped up a Serbian agent network, worked undercover for a time supporting counter-human trafficking. This and that,' she said casually, even playfully, and smiled radiantly.

'So not very busy then,' he agreed, playing it down as she had.

'I met Harry in Bosnia,' she said simply.

'Ah, so *very* busy then.' They both laughed, knowing full well there was never any navel gazing or thumb-twiddling when Harry ran the show.

They chatted and laughed easily together. Hurley reflected he had always thought highly of her, and if he was brutally honest with himself, had always found her attractive. In what seemed a strange warping of time, it appeared as they talked that no time had passed since he last saw her.

She was razor sharp and had been a crack criminal investigator when he first knew her; but she was uncomplicated and, well, nice to know and to have around. He suspected she had transitioned easily into intelligence work. Indeed, if she hadn't, she probably wouldn't be part of this team.

When he learned she was a trained interrogator and it was she Harry had tasked with the management of the ploy that was so important, he felt a piece had fallen into place. Something made him feel very comforted to have her on board, and he also liked the idea of working with her again.

Hurley chatted to her and the others in his vicinity while they all plied themselves with the barbequed meat and a variety of salads that had been made. He learned that Rommel, whom he had met earlier, had gained that nickname because his real name was Montgomery, and that Freon was so named because he was "cool". It was true; he dressed smartly, and his suntan and hair were just so. Hurley did not judge him though and knew his abilities would not be in doubt.

Merlin had earned his moniker through his technical expertise and his magical fingers. Maggie was but one of a formidable group of young women on the team, all confident and easy in their own skin. Lucy, Janey and Michelle were all outgoing and friendly; Hurley didn't know anything of what they could do, but he was buoyed by their quiet self-assured manner, and their measured demeanour.

Hurley noted there was no alcohol on the table. That would be Harry's orders. Harry loved a drink, and too much sometimes, but there was always a time and a place. Harry would want the briefing to go well. It would be complicated and very detailed, and alcohol didn't fit with that in Harry's mind. After lunch as they all walked to the east wing, Hurley noticed the iron work gates were closed and locked. Work time.

19

Casa Dili

Dili, United Nations administered East Timor

....

February 2001

After passing through a short hallway with a walking rug running down the centre, the group entered a large and airy room through an internal archway. It was high-ceilinged and had probably once been a sitting room, but it was now devoid of normal furniture.

Instead, Hurley was surrounded by the paraphernalia of operations; whiteboards on easels, tables, computers and screens, wooden map-drawers, photographic gear and tall metal cupboards packed with technical gear. One of these was more robust than the others and locked; it most certainly contained weapons.

In the corner, banks of radios and walkie-talkies were on charge, their little lights steady and green, or blinking red, looking for help. On the walls, there were maps and photographs, and more maps. Hurley noted they ranged from complete coverage of East *and* West Timor, down to various villages and towns, some of which were not known to him.

It was a room Hurley would have recognised anywhere in the world. Ten or so chairs were placed in a rough semi-circle and a tall, athletic man, introduced earlier as Toby, nodded towards the group to sit.

'OK,' Harry started, calling for quiet. 'The first issue is the take-down. Toby, as group leader I'll get you to brief us all on that activity. Take it away, mate.'

Toby's group moved to the front and it included Derek, Max and Freon. Hurley was sure that at least Toby and Derek could have played rugby for England, and with the other two it was evident they had chosen the four largest and most powerful men in the team for the capture. Why would you not, Hurley thought ruefully.

They produced a detailed map of the area around Club Echo Tango and Hurley recognised it easily. It was laid flat on one of the small tables and had some 3D aspects; a white model van and a green cotton-wool hedge between the carpark and the club entrance.

On another table was a larger scale map of the section of the hedge closest to the carpark. Hurley couldn't help but note Harry's team had been very busy over the preceding days, and their work was very exacting.

Toby briefed them on the mechanics of the take-down. He used a ruler to point to various locations as he spoke, and Max moved the little van and figurines depicting the various actors to show how events were unfolding. The two traitors were given the code-names Hansel and Gretel for the operation. At the completion of the brief, Derek and Freon rolled the big TV screen forward to centre stage.

'OK, what you're going to see now is the take-down itself. I can tell you we have practiced this quite a few times and have perfected what we were hoping to achieve. Of course, we'd welcome suggestions if you have them.'

This was no humble platitude. Hurley instinctively knew this team sought nothing less than perfection and would consider anything that might help them achieve it.

'We would like to say a very big shout out to Lucy and Stan for their beyond the call on this one. They were pounded into the ground untold times and are bearing the scars I'm afraid.'

There were murmurs of praise all around and then a quick round of spontaneous applause in acknowledgment of Toby's comments. Hurley had noted the purple welts on Lucy's arms when they were first introduced, and Stan was sporting a sticking plaster over his left eye which Hurley suspected covered several stitches. He certainly couldn't fault their dedication.

Freon pushed the start button and the screen came to life. Toby's team had evidently practiced in a large open building somewhere, it looked as if it might be a hangar or a dockside shed. There were heavy chalk markings and some coloured crosses drawn on the concrete floor denoting critical locations.

As they watched, Hansel and Gretel dressed in smart casual clothes strolled into view, but of course it was Lucy and Stan playing the traitors. When they reached a certain point, four figures in blue overalls and black balaclavas burst forward and all but consumed them.

A pair allocated for each, they quickly and easily overpowered them and held them to the ground as the action of them being tranquilised was played out. Within seconds they adroitly manhandled the comatose forms and relocated them, processing them for the move to the van.

As quick again, they moved them to the van. The whole thing was lightning fast and brutal to the senses; the aggression was controlled and targeted, but not harmful. Most importantly it was slick and evidently well-practiced.

The screen went black while Toby explained they had also practiced a number of likely scenarios; these included a variance in the walking distance between the two, the order in which they were walking and if aggression was displayed by one or both of the targets.

When the screen came on again, and then for a third and fourth time, the same take-down occurred but accommodating the explained changes. Each was smooth and professional. Hurley already knew they wouldn't commit to the take-down unless the situation favoured their rehearsed actions.

If circumstances were unfavourable, they would simply abort and wait for another opportunity. Time was on their side. Toby switched the TV off. There was silence while the group analysed what they had seen.

'Right. Any questions?' Toby offered.

There would be none from the team. This request was for Hurley's sake, as he had been out of the loop during all their hard work and preparation.

'Thanks Toby, that was very slick,' Hurley said, nodding slowly and knowing credit should always go where it was due. Standing up and walking a few paces, he picked up one of the syringes from the box on the table. 'I'm wondering though, what exactly is this stuff?' He winced inwardly at the thought of the hypodermic being thrust into his own neck as he had seen role-played on the video.

'Ketamine,' Toby answered. 'The doc says it will do the trick one hundred per cent. I have a table to work out the doses for each of them by weight. The injections will be intra-muscular by necessity, we don't have the flexibility or time to go IV and it will be getting dark. Still, they will be sedated in one to three minutes and general anaesthesia will take effect within three to eight minutes. It can last from twelve to twenty-five minutes depending on the individual. No major reactions or after-effects are anticipated and there is normally no interference with breathing. I don't envisage any major problems,' he finished confidently.

Hurley nodded. It was impressive. They had done their homework to the letter. From what little he knew, the drug was a good choice.

'Is there a doctor or medic on stand-by?' he asked.

'Yes,' Harry put in quickly from the back. 'He will be mobile with Howie and less than two minutes away at all times. I have promised they won't be hurt, as you all know, so it behoves us all to keep that in mind. I shall also cover that when I give final orders on Saturday morning.'

They all nodded their understanding.

'Right,' said Harry. 'Maggie will lead the ploy and myself and Matt will conduct the questioning as part of that, so Maggie will start the brief for the next activity. Please, all to the next room, and take your chairs.'

They all moved noisily through another archway for the next briefing, the metal chair legs clinking as they hit each other and scraping on the floor as they did so. This room had been meticulously prepared, and Hurley sensed this was Maggie's work. There were two tables. The first one, in full view, contained a detailed model of a house.

It was green and had no roof, so anyone standing around could look down into the rooms. Around it there were thick bushes and trees with walking tracks marked in white on a black background. While Hurley had taken this in, Freon had wheeled the big screen TV from the other room, and it was now oriented for them to watch.

They all quickly adjusted their chairs, the metal legs scraping into position on the ceramic tiles and sending a shudder up Hurley's spine. Maggie cleared her throat.

'Right. At first it might seem this brief is in reverse order but bear with me and you'll see the reasoning. I'd like you to watch the rehearsed ploy which has been recorded; please do try and find fault, just as we have, and continue to do so. After that, I'll talk through the mechanics and add detail to the model to demonstrate how it was done. Now before it starts, I want you to focus and remember you are looking through the eyes of Matt and Hansel; what you see on the screen has been filmed from *their* position. Gretel will be out of action and blindfolded while this is happening. Lights please.'

When the video started, the environment was dark. It was spotlighted to highlight only those aspects they wanted to be seen. Hurley was mesmerised as the action unfolded in front of him. As they watched, the squirming body of Gretel, played by Janey, was manhandled across their view and raised up, to be suspended by her wrists from a large wooden beam.

She was dressed in oversize grey overalls that had been tightly knotted at the ends of the hands and feet. A black hood covered her head. A female figure in blue overalls and a black balaclava, it was Maggie, mounted a step ladder and tied the ropes that fixed Gretel to the beam. There was about a metre and a half of rope that allowed the body to swing.

Maggie could then be seen securing Gretel's legs to large concrete blocks on the floor which stretched her body taught. Gretel's body vibrated with anxiety and fear as she struggled, and the muffled sounds of pretend terror carried to them. Maggie carefully selected an item from a nearby table and walked over to Gretel.

As she did, the spotlight's beam played on the metal bar in her hand. She raised the bar and struck Gretel with all her might in the lower leg. The sound of metal on bone was unmistakable and sickening; a quick intake of breath was heard from more than one person in the room. Gretel shook and screamed, but it was only a muffled cry that carried to them. What followed was brutal and was intended to be so.

Maggie belted Gretel so hard and so much that the bones were evidently broken, indeed, at times could be heard breaking. She worked in set areas, the lower and upper legs, and the lower and upper arms. Bloodstains were eventually seen to seep through the fabric of the overalls. As she was struck, muffled cries of anguish carried to them and occasionally, the body went limp as it apparently retreated into unconsciousness.

When this happened, Maggie picked up a water bottle and squirted Gretel's head, bringing her to wakefulness again, only for the pain to continue. When the torture was complete, Maggie walked slowly back to the table and set the now blood-ied iron bar down. She exchanged it for a 9mm semi-automatic Beretta pistol. Moving close to Gretel she cocked the weapon and pointed it at the hooded head. She fired once and the sound alone told Hurley the shot was real; and caught in the spotlight for all to see was the bone and brain matter explode from the back of the head.

The room was deathly quiet, and Hurley was speechless. It was what they called in the interrogation game "scene per-fect". He slowly stood up, still watching the screen. His face was engrossed, intent.

'Could you play that back, please Maggie?' he asked quietly. 'But only from the start to where you first strike her.' Hurley and the group watched again as the images replayed. All around him were silent. Once the beating started again, he said in a low voice, 'Again please, to the same point.'

Hurley knew it had to be there. Somewhere, Maggie had switched the bodies from the live squirming body of Janey to a dummy. He carefully watched the sequence over again. He saw as before, Gretel carried, moving and evidently alive, to the beam. He saw as before, Maggie secure her to the beam and then her suspended form hanging there with her legs free, and still moving, still alive. It was at this point he found what he was looking for.

At this very second someone walked in front of the spotlight that was trained on Gretel and for a fleeting instant nothing more, there was complete blackness before the light returned and the scene was resumed. He saw as before the body of Gretel still hanging, suspended as it had been a microsecond before, while Maggie busily secured her feet.

Reality told Hurley that Janey was not having her legs and arms broken in the following scenes, and nor had she been shot in the head at the end. The switch must have happened there.

'Again please.' Hurley's voice was almost a whisper and his eyes never left the screen. After watching it for the third time, Hurley confirmed the point in his own mind at which the switch happened and smiled broadly. But he still couldn't *see* it, even though he *knew* it and was looking for it. He also knew that on the night, it would happen once, and the human mind and eye would fill that microsecond for Hansel just as it had for them. He would have no idea it wasn't a complete sequence.

'I know in my gut what you've done, Maggie Redcap,' he admonished her playfully, amid subdued laughter from the others. 'But I can't see it. It's brilliant, and more importantly, it will work. Now, show me how.'

The admiration in Hurley's voice was evident. It was shared by the amazed onlookers, most of whom were seeing the video for the first time. Harry, who had seen it many times, chuckled quietly to himself. Maggie felt herself blush, and she was thankful the room was still in half darkness.

'Lights please,' she said. 'Spread yourselves around this model so you can see, if you will. I will populate this model to represent what you have seen and how it works.' She was focussed and in total control. Hurley watched her and was in awe of what she had done in the time she had available, and what he sensed was still to come.

From a shoebox, Maggie produced a handful of small figurines of different colours; signifying the team members, Hansel and Gretel, and Sanderson.

'These are all the people involved in the ploy,' she began, as she positioned the figurines around the green house. She then went through and named them all, pointing as she went so that everyone listening knew where everybody would be. 'It is imperative that when people are sited, they do not move from those places unless told to do so. Those who need to move as part of the ploy will be advised and know their parts. We have a scene to present to Hansel, but neither he nor Gretel can see Sanderson. Sanderson, however, must hear the confession. We have set it up accordingly.'

Maggie had them all hooked, and looking around surreptitiously, Hurley could see it. She reached into the box and pulled out a piece of dowelling. She carefully put this in place across one of the rooms, from wall to wall and parallel to a wide doorway on one of the main outside walls. She fixed it in place with modelling clay.

'This is the beam from which both Janey and the dummy will be suspended, as you saw in the video.' As she spoke, she carefully wrapped string around the beam and connected two figurines. 'Matt will be with Hansel. This location has been chosen because of the angle of vision to the beam and is designed to maximise what Hansel sees, and at the same time to facilitate Sanderson watching and hearing Hansel but being unseen by him. Now, the switch. You will note that the beam is positioned close to, and parallel with, the large open doorway leading to the outside of the house. This allows us to have *two* bodies hanging from the beam at the same time, one being Janey and one the dummy, but with one pulled and held at the outside through the doorway and importantly, not visible from Hansel's position as you all saw in the video. Simply by swinging the bodies on the ropes, we can have whichever one we want on display.' With this she manipulated the figurines slowly and demonstrated how this was achieved. 'We have a system of ropes that enable us to do this deftly, and with confidence. At the moment required, Merlin walks in front of the spotlight and stays until the switch is complete. That's it really. Are there any questions?'

The team waited for Hurley's response. In truth it was masterful; as good as anything Hurley had ever seen, and the briefings and the aids had brought it all to life.

'Do you already control this house?' Hurley asked.

'Yes, and we have done since we started our rehearsals. The nearest habitation is about three miles away. Maggie picked up several air photos and a number of ground level shots and handed them to Hurley.

'Becora,' he stated as he examined the photos, and Maggie nodded in agreement. He knew the area and was also aware it was a good choice for this job. 'Did you consider a technical break of the light for the critical moment?' he asked.

'No,' she replied, shaking her head. 'It seemed to work so well we never developed it further.'

'It may prove helpful to use both,' Hurley suggested. 'If you were to put in a kill switch and Merlin was to activate it as he moves across the light, it then acts as a fail-safe. Without it there could be light leakage dependent on his exact positioning, and which could ruin the overall effect. I understand you actually want Merlin walking across, because Hansel will see this in his peripheral vision and that information will help trick his mind,

I certainly get that, but this would make the most critical aspect safer.'

Maggie considered this and Hurley could see her mind turning over as she did so. She was going through the actions with the new idea and seemed comfortable. She turned to Merlin and raised her eyebrows slightly in question. Merlin nodded confidently.

'Aye, that's no problem,' he added. 'And to tell the truth, in the early practices I had a wee bit of trouble positioning my legs exactly right to block out the light, this will eliminate that problem once and for all.'

'Thanks Merlin, we'll do that. And thanks Matt.'

Hurley nodded in acknowledgment and continued. 'Do you have a pistol with a silencer? The reason I ask is we don't want the real Gretel to hear a gun shot, which she would even with earmuffs on. If the ploy fails with Hansel, the plan is to reset and do the same with Gretel. If she is watching later and it goes to the point of the execution, she might put two and two together, and it could be enough for her to twig and bring it all down. If we are at that stage, we will have come very close to failure, and I wouldn't want to jeopardise what would be our last chance. In any case, the visual impact effect of a silencer is the same — I would suggest even better.'

Maggie nodded. It was a good point, and not one they had thought about.

'You're right,' she decided. 'We can make that happen and I will practice with it tomorrow.'

'I suppose the elephant in the room is what's under the sheet on that table,' Hurley suggested, turning to point to the second table which was in the corner. 'I take it that is the dummy, yeah?'

'It is. If I could get you all to move around there, I'll show you.' As she spoke Maggie moved between the wall and the table and waited while they repositioned themselves in front of her. She grasped the sheet by one corner and pulled it off in one smooth motion, laying it on the floor to the side.

All eyes focussed on the dummy lying motionless on its back. It was dressed in grey overalls knotted at the feet and wrists, just as Hansel and Gretel would be, and just as they had seen in the video. It had a black hood that was knotted at the nape pulling the material taut over the face.

'This is a demonstration model only for today's brief. The real Hansel and Gretel dummies are in the big cool room ready for Saturday night. Each of them has been constructed using the traitors' vital statistics — height, chest, waist and hip measurements. You will see why we must keep them refrigerated.'

With this she pulled a knife from her belt and flicked the blade open. Inserting the blade at the bottom of one leg, she slit it upwards to the underarm of the overalls and pulled the material back. Hurley saw it was a clothing mannequin made from a resilient hard spongy material.

Large parts of the lower and upper leg had been cut away and packed with thick slabs of meat and shards of large animal bones. These were tightly bound in place with strong black cable ties. She slit the arm sleeve from the wrist to the shoulder. The arm was similarly constructed; with the packing area concentrated around the forearms and the upper arms.

Maggie then cut the hood from the head revealing a cutaway section filled with offal. She held up a pneumatic device with a tube that went down inside the overalls and could be covertly operated by her from along the leg of the dummy. She squeezed the device and a stream of yellow, vomit-like material ejaculated from the mouth of the dummy into a geyser. As it made its way through the air towards them the group jumped to avoid it. They all laughed in mock horror as it splashed on the floor.

'This gives us an option if we need to stall for effect, and I get that signal from Matt,' she explained. 'Are there any questions about the dummy or use thereof?'

'Why did you go for grey overalls, rather than white, for example?' Hurley quizzed.

'We started with white, we thought it would look better in the spotlight and the blood would look more authentic. In fact, both of those things proved not to be correct. White is too stark, and it showed some imperfections we want to keep to ourselves. As to the blood, it's too raw. With the grey, it seeps nicely and stains darker — and works better with the imagination.'

Hurley nodded, enlightened. 'We noticed in the video that the dummy moved and groaned although it was subdued because, ostensibly, Gretel was gagged. But these sounds were synchronised with the blows. How did you make that happen?' he asked.

'Janey remains trussed up and gagged while she is out of sight, but as comfortable as possible.' She looked over and smiled at Janey who winked in acknowledgement. For not the first time, Hurley was warmed by their mateship, and their keenness to do whatever the team required to make it work. 'Toby watches my arm and when I strike, which is always very orchestrated and predictable, a millisecond before contact he puts a sharp pressure on Janey's neck. She then makes the appropriate sound. We can move the dummy like it's vibrating, or move its head using fishing line which can't be seen at a distance. If we want a period of unconsciousness, Toby doesn't touch her neck, so Janey is silent until Gretel is revived, and on we go again.' Maggie looked around, her eyebrows raised expectantly, seeking more questions.

'I have just one more Maggie,' Hurley offered, his brows knitted in curiosity. 'How are you and I communicating during the ploy? I mean, there will be times when I want you to stop, or pause, to give Hansel time to think about what he's seeing and measure his response. Particularly, we wouldn't want the execution scene happening without it being synchronised with what I'm saying to him, right?'

'Excellent point and well made,' she said with a slightly embarrassed laugh. Reaching under the table she produced a small black box with two lenses on the front — one green and one red. There was a button on the top. 'Matt will have this with him,' she explained to everyone as she pointed the box towards them. She turned it on, and the green light shone out and when she pressed the button on the top it turned to red. She pressed it again and it returned to green. 'Matt will show this to Hansel, and it will become an integral aspect of the interrogation. He will know it is the mechanism through which Matt controls events and he will seek to control the box. It will be pointed towards the area of the beam where I will be working, and I will take my cue from the lights.'

Hurley grinned and nodded. Simple is always best, he thought.

'Thanks everyone,' Maggie finished up. 'Over to Matt now for a rundown on the speaking part he will run with Hansel, and Harry will run with Gretel if we get to that stage.'

Hurley moved out to the front and stood before the group. He looked around at each of them as he gathered his thoughts. 'It's impossible to stand here and tell you exactly what we will say to Hansel, or to Gretel if it does come to that,' Hurley began. 'What I say must be relevant to what *he* says and does, and I'll be looking to use that, and how I think he's reacting, to feed off him. As you all know, this isn't a game where we can write down the thousand questions we want to ask or the things we think we might want to say. Anything he says could make any of that redundant or it could provide an opportunity we want to exploit. What I can talk to however, is our information requirement and a number of themes I will be presenting to him right from the start. Firstly, our information requirement is to extract enough information via confession regarding the events of the previous few months; the murder of my two agents, the murder of one of their wives, and the unfortunate death of one of my soldiers who became involved. I will know when this requirement is met when I get the nod from Harry, who will be with Roger Sanderson.

'Now for the themes; firstly, he will damn well know he is in a world of hurt, and that I am in complete control. It goes on until I make it stop. Secondly, in order to stop what is happening, he needs to cooperate, and that means only a full disclosure of the events will suffice. Thirdly, if he does not cooperate and be truthful with me, I will have Gretel brutalised beyond his comprehension and eventually killed, and he will be next. He will know it will not stop until he is dead, but before that there will be a great deal of pain and suffering. Remember he will have watched Gretel getting her treatment so he will be aware of what's coming. Harry and I have looked at their personalities. Our assessment is that this is the best way to achieve our desired outcome. I have every confidence that we can win, with this team and with this plan,' he said emphatically, pointing towards them and catching Maggie's eye. He waited to let his words sink in. 'Finally, let me congratulate everyone on the amount and quality of your work over the past few days, and the effort you've all put in. It's absolutely outstanding — well done. I can't thank you enough for your creativity and hard work, for myself, and… for those who didn't make it. I reckon the only thing that could bring us down now would be the gods pissing on us from a great height. So, let's do it. That's all Maggie, unless there're any questions for me.'

'Alright, thanks Matt. Final rehearsal is scheduled for tomorrow night, so we'll need everyone there for a walk through-talk through and we'll make those minor adjustments we discussed.

Transport will leave here at 2000 hours sharp. Be there, be seen there, impress your friends,' she finished up, smiling. They all laughed in appreciation, and probably with some relief. They were on track and opening night was only a few days away.

'Huzzah!' Harry bawled, fist high in jubilation. 'That's the bar open then.'

They chatted and laughed together easily as the gaggle streamed out towards the west wing. By the time they got there, bottles and glasses had appeared, evident by the clinking sound of glass. The music was already on; the Rolling Stones. The Brits loved their music and Hurley loved them for it. It wouldn't be long before the singing started.

'The pizzas will be ready in about twenty minutes,' Max boomed out above the racket, and they all hooted and cheered. They had briefed the afternoon away and the mention of pizza made Hurley feel very hungry.

'After seeing Maggie's dummy, I'll never eat steak again,' he whispered to Harry, and they both chuckled.

20

Casa Dili

Dili, United Nations administered East Timor

February 2001

It was some time later when Hurley spied Maggie on the other side of the room. Having looked after him at lunch, she had kept her distance during drinks and allowed him to spend time with the others, getting to know them, and they him. But Hurley was a kindred spirit to them all and this had proved easy for everyone.

She caught his eye and smiled mischievously, slowly bringing a bottle and two small glasses into view. Hurley could see it was a bottle of red wine and he gave her a look of mock horror. She laughed and inside he did likewise thinking, *she has a mind like a steel trap.* He was immediately transported back to another place and time as she hoped he would be.

He nodded conspiratorially as he recalled the last time they had shared such a bottle. Towards the end of her tour in Rwanda she was promoted to sergeant, and as the Provost Marshal was away on leave, he felt it only right they celebrate such an important milestone. So they locked themselves in her office at UNHQ and drank the only bottle of alcohol they could get their hands on.

It had a label neither of them could read and it was the cheapest, nastiest bottle of wash-down red wine either of them had ever tasted. They had talked and laughed the afternoon away, cackling like schoolchildren and trying unsuccessfully to keep quiet as the bottle emptied. Luckily, his team had come back to collect him, and she had somehow managed to get to her lines and sleep till the next day.

She weaved her way through the throng of arms and legs and stood above him as he leaned back in the comfort of an armchair.

'Allow me to take you on a tour of Casa Dili, Mr Hurley,' she said demurely. 'Come on,' she urged, tilting her head in the direction of the door.

The music and happy hubbub of the sitting rooms died away as they moved further away into the coolness of the house. She guided him through the remainder he had not seen, and they returned through the rooms where she had briefed earlier.

It was all quiet now and the dummy had thankfully been returned to the fridge. She had been outstanding, and he must find a way to tell her, at the right time, he thought. The house was amazing, and the library was a hidden treasure. The shelves were almost empty, but the atmosphere was intimate.

It was one of the few rooms carpeted wall-to-wall, and the smooth leather Chesterfield furniture looked original. It had the feel of a reading room in a London club, and Hurley guessed the original occupant had tried to replicate exactly that.

'Sometimes my parents send me the UK papers and I bring a cup of tea here and read them in the peace and quiet,' she said wistfully. Hurley smiled and envied her the luxury; he had not had time to read a newspaper for months.

As they walked up the marble staircase only their soft footfall and the murmur of their voices could be heard. Even the sounds of the tropical night did not penetrate here. The first-floor balconies were wide and decorated with urns and plants similar to the courtyard. They stopped at one point and leaned on the balcony rail, chatting easily, their arms almost touching.

'All our rooms are up here. The two big corner rooms are bathrooms, ladies at the east end, gentlemen at the west end,' she explained, mimicking a British Airways flight attendant as she extended her arms in either direction and put on an obviously fake smile. They both laughed.

'And this is my room,' she said casually, opening a nearby door and standing aside to allow Hurley to enter.

It was a pleasant, comfortable room. It could have been a mid-range hotel room in Bali or Thailand, complete with teak wardrobe and cabinets, and polished parquet floors with colourful mats. The double bed had a multi-coloured coverlet and a white mosquito net cascading around it; fixed from four hooks in the ceiling it gave the impression the bed was a four-poster.

A rattan fan rotated slowly overhead making a tick-tick-tick sound, but it was enough to ensure the air was moving and cool. The windows were slightly open, but the slatted external shutters had been pulled closed. There was a dressing table with her personal items and a marble hand basin sporting a single brass tap.

'I like it. I like it a lot,' Hurley remarked with conviction as he walked around nodding admiringly. 'If you saw where I usually sleep, you would know why.'

'I've seen where you sleep,' she said mischievously.

He turned to her, surprised. 'Really, when?'

'I had to visit Balibo on a job just before Christmas. I asked around the fort, but you were away on patrol. It was wrong really,' she confessed. 'We're not supposed to seek out people we know because of the complications of the job but I felt, well, for old time's sake...'

Their eyes met and Hurley briefly felt uneasy. He was

beginning to see Maggie in a completely different light. For an instant he felt like he was a on a very fast train hurtling along a single track with no scheduled stops. It wasn't a bad feeling, just unknown. She looked away quickly and he wondered if his thoughts had been too transparent.

'Anyway, I walked through the Sergeants' Mess accommodation with the Regimental Police — what's the sign outside say? *The Balibo Backpackers.* I liked that, and quite by chance I saw a bunk with a green trunk underneath it, stencilled with your name. I left a packet of sweets on your bunk.'

'Bloody hell,' Hurley remarked, incredulous. 'I remember that! Damned if I could work out where they had come from. I thought I had a secret admirer.'

She laughed easily. 'You did. Come, sit with me,' she said, as she placed the bottle and the two glasses on the small wicker table and sat in one of the matching chairs, each of which had a red cushion. She patted the other.

Hurley poured and offered her a glass. They talked for what seemed like a very long time. He reflected he had not allowed himself to enjoy a woman's company as much for as long as he could remember. He learned about her older brother, the lawyer, and his family and her two nieces, whom she evidently adored.

She talked about her parents and her horse, Atlas. She told him of her schooldays and her friends, and how she had joined the army so she wouldn't have an ordinary, boring life like so many of them now did. In turn, Hurley gave of himself much that he did not offer to many.

She learned about his parents, now long gone, his love of sports, the outdoors and travel, and that he always had a book on the go. She remembered little things they had talked of in Rwanda all those years ago, and she was able to weave them cleverly into the conversation. At one stage he had to convince himself it wasn't the wine talking, but in truth, they talked a lot but drank very little.

'I owe you an apology Maggie,' he said finally, adopting a serious tone.

'Oh?'

'I very much appreciated — I *still* very much appreciate — that you wrote to me after… the accident. I'm sorry I didn't answer your letter. I should have and it was wrong of me not to. It's no excuse, and I don't expect you to understand or forgive me, but… I simply didn't know what to say.'

'I understand–'

'No, let me finish,' he cut in, needing to end what he had started. 'It's no excuse but it's even harder to talk when you have feelings for people. I felt if I wrote back I would have poured my heart and soul out to you, and I don't know what scared me more — that I might do that and show too much of myself, or that you might be burdened by it.'

She reached over and placed her hand over his, her eyes were moist and held his, but this time it was he who looked away, afraid at what she might see. In one slow but deliberate movement she went to him and sat easily on his knee. She said nothing. In its own way it was assertive but in another it was almost prim. It was certainly not wanton.

She re-filled his glass and handed it to him, before picking up her own from the small table. Hurley did not move to accommodate her, but neither did he reject her. In truth, he was in that nether world between comfort and discomfort. Just as he was comforted by the warmth of her friendship and her closeness, he was discomfited not only by his own desire but by hers, which he sensed.

The last thing Hurley wanted to do was hurt Maggie. She had done nothing to deserve that, and everything to deserve much,

much better. In truth, Hurley had been dealing with what was happening now for a long time. For years after the accident he had known he would eventually be brought into the new reality of his life, and that the old one had changed forever. Not his fault, not anyone's fault, it just was.

He had been in denial and put any thoughts of someone new aside, sometimes even aggressively, and instead throwing himself into his work. But Maggie was different, and always had been. He knew that now. The decision came to him that if she was to be the agent of that change, then so be it.

She offered up her own glass for him to drink from, and he reciprocated, interlinking arms as they drank. It was symbolic, and he knew it just as she did. He placed the glasses deliberately on the table and reached his hand to the nape of her neck, as she relaxed and closed her eyes at his touch. He moved his hand along the line of her jaw wondering at the softness of her skin and held his hand against her cheek.

She returned the pressure and opened her eyes. There was no going back now, for either of them. Their lips found each other easily but they both held back, terrified for their own secret reasons. He was fearful she might see him as overly eager and seeking only physical pleasure; she was afraid he might be scared away. In truth, neither of them had anything to fear.

Hurley's slate grey eyes held hers. They were orbs of the most brilliant blue, the pupils now dark pools, dilated with her arousal. He could see no judgement there, just laughter and light — as much as he had ever seen. When he finally spoke, the words were redundant, for she had read his eyes too.

'I haven't… for a long time,' he croaked, his voice thick with emotion and rising desire.

'I know,' she whispered, not trusting herself to speak at all.

If anybody had later asked them what happened after that,

neither could have said with any real certainty. As if in a trance they took the clothes from each other and drank deeply of each other's bodies; each saw only what they had always wanted, as if in the fulfilment of a prophecy. Frenzied, they touched and kissed, and lavished pleasure upon the other. When they finally joined as one Maggie felt at some point she might faint and may even have done so. Hurley was in some far-away place where there was only her and he held her tight, lest he lose something precious he had just found.

She lay on her back, nestled safely in the crook of his arm.

'I can't stay, you know,' he offered softly, apologetically, but knowing the subject needed to be broached.

'Actually, you can,' she answered playfully. 'You've been allocated the room next door, but no one is going to be concerned, I assure you.'

'What about the team, Maggie? I don't want to make things difficult for you, or them.'

'That is simply not an issue, Matt.' Her tone told Hurley the subject was well and truly closed, and he was glad he was spared that complication.

'Awesome,' he said light heartedly, as he visibly relaxed. 'Where have you been all my life?'

Maggie bit her lip, but to no avail.

'I rather fancied you in Rwanda, you know,' she confessed. She hadn't wanted to say it, but she was thinking it and it slipped out anyway.

'Did you?' he asked curiously. 'That's very flattering.'

'I remember the first time I saw you,' she continued, as she watched the fan circling overhead. 'I was standing on the HQ balcony with your MP Sergeant, do you remember him?'

'Yeah, Adam. He was killed in a car accident you know, about a year later.'

'Really? That's awful. How sad.'

'Yeah, he was good bloke, helped us out a lot.'

'Anyway, we were standing there, and you were dressing down a soldier who had a loaded weapon inside the compound. I thought you were so strong and authoritative, but not abusing your power or showy like some do. You definitely caught my eye.'

'I don't remember that at all,' Hurley said, amazed for not the first time at the things people remembered.

'So, I turned to Adam and asked who you were. He told me *that's CSM Hurley, he's one of the few people round here with their shit in one sock*,' she said, deepening her voice to mimic Adam.

They both giggled. 'I loved it, *shit in one sock*. Whenever I hear that expression, I think of you.'

'I'll take that as a compliment, I think.'

'You piqued my interest and then a week or so later I was in Cyangugu on a job, and I'd gone up onto the heights overlooking the town. I saw an Aussie Land Rover in the distance, parked at the crossing point into Zaire.'

'Go on,' Hurley said slowly, his own interest now piqued for an altogether different reason.

'I watched through the binoculars and saw a white NGO vehicle come across and you met it on our side of the border. And then out of this vehicle steps a stunning blonde who hugs you and you kiss her on the cheek. You then get into her vehicle and drive away towards the NGO compound with your team following. I remember thinking, you couldn't write this into a movie script.'

'Bloody hell,' Hurley murmured, amazed.

'I have to say, I had a little pang of jealousy,' Maggie said primly. 'But on the other hand, I'd learned you were…' she was about to say *married*, but changed her mind, because he still was and she didn't want that conversation with him right now, so she said '… not available. And that made me think, oh, he's just like all the rest; what happens on deployment, stays on deployment.'

'Oh, thanks very much for the vote of confidence,' Hurley said, pretending to be hurt but playing it up.

'No, no wait,' she said quickly. 'So, I mentioned it to Adam at my next meeting and he winks and tells me not to worry, *she's a worker bee, not a queen bee, and the only honey Hurley is interested in is information.* That's when I learned your real intelligence role and that your company sergeant major position was a cover. I have to say that made you all the more mysterious and interesting Matt Hurley.'

'Is this story actually going somewhere?' he asked playfully.

'Stop being such a lad,' she teased. 'Anyway, later when I learned she was your courier who went back and forth across the border to your agents in Zaire, and the plan for her emergency extraction, well that sealed the deal for me.'

Hurley suddenly went very still. His eyes had cleared, and his breathing had almost stopped. He too watched the rattan fan circling overhead. Tick-tick-tick.

'How did you learn about that?' he asked warily, his voice thinly edged. 'Adam didn't know that.'

'Don't be angry Matt,' she soothed. 'Your team told me because they cared for you, and they wanted to watch your back. They knew that if you enacted that plan, the world would surely go mad and you would need me and the Provost Marshal to be on side and help clear up the mess.'

'I wouldn't have asked you to lie,' he said suddenly, defensively.

'I didn't say you would, and I don't need to be asked if it's the right thing to do either,' she admonished him in return.

They lay in silence and she knew Hurley's thoughts had returned to those times. She nuzzled into him and her eyes twinkled.

'I have to say Matt Hurley, I thought you so gallant, and I was a young, impressionable girl then,' she said playfully and with faux confidence, flushing slightly with the embarrassment of her own candidness.

'It's not that really,' he explained, playing it down. 'I was taught to care about my agents, by Harry actually. It makes them work better, and easier to manage. In any case, it's no big deal. I made her a promise and after that there was no going back on it.'

Maggie raised herself up on one elbow and faced him, her brow creased.

'Would you really have done it? Would you *really* have walked across that tatty little bridge at Cyangugu and into that guard-house, and then brought her out at gun point?' she challenged him.

'No Maggie,' he answered evenly, holding her gaze. 'I would have run across that tatty little bridge and killed them all to get her out. That was the deal. And I wouldn't have thought twice about it from that day to this, regardless of the consequences.'

The enormity of his response hung between them. She remembered too, watching through the binoculars seeing him kit up, put his webbing on and check his rifle when the white vehicle had first come into view, though she had not mentioned this, and it had meant nothing to her at the time. She saw in his eyes it was all true, and it confirmed everything she had ever thought of Matt Hurley and heard about him from others. And she had made it her business to hear plenty.

'So why *did* you promise her? She knew the risks, surely.' It was Hurley's turn to smile.

'You never found that part out, did you? I never told the guys either. Has that been burning a little hole in your pocket ever since?' he chided, poking her in the ribs.

'Maybe,' she conceded playfully and squirmed against him. 'Maybe it was just because she was young and beautiful.'

'She certainly was Maggie, it's true. But that wasn't the reason.

She'd been raped in a previous mission, a lot of the NGO girls had been, and are still. Sadly, it almost comes with the turf in Africa. You know that, and you've seen similar in Bosnia and dozens of other shit holes. She was gutsy, but she was absolutely terrified that if they stopped her vehicle and took her into the guard-house they would gang rape her, and then throw her away, or worse, destroy the evidence.'

'Oh, my God. I'm sorry Matt, I didn't mean…'

He stroked her hair. 'It's OK,' he soothed. 'Anyway, I promised her it wouldn't happen while she was working for me, and that we'd always be there to watch her come over. That's all there was to it. That's why we took the vehicle down every time to meet her at the crossing point. Over time, we worked a relationship with the border guards, and they came to think I was her boyfriend. That was the cover. I figured they would be less likely to take her if they knew we were waiting and had skin in the game. But I won't ever say I didn't shit myself every time she came over.' His eyes hardened and he pursed his lips at the memory.

'Well, I thought it very brave of you then, and it makes my pants very wet now to think about it,' she teased him.

'You're not wearing any pants, now go to sleep, it's late.'

'I don't think so.'

Hurley turned fully to face her and smiled down at her. She brought her hand up from under the covers and touched his upper lip ever so lightly, running her finger against the grain of his growth.

'You had a very sexy moustache then.'

'I did, even if I do say so myself. Alas, they are no longer in fashion. Anyway, you used to be blonde.'

'I coloured my hair, but I was never a blonde,' she corrected, 'as you would bloody well know, Matt Hurley, if you'd been paying any attention in the last hour.'

He chuckled at her clever joke and smiled inwardly; she had a private side that was funny, naughty and extremely attractive. It complemented all the positives he already knew in her and had been reminded of in the past few hours. He looked at her face. She too was thinking back; he could tell from the look in her eyes. Then she leaned forward and began to run the tip of her tongue across his lip.

This time it was not at all like the first. This time they emptied each other of everything; it was raw, and the pleasure was acute to the point of pain, but it was as if in a dream. At some stage during that dream she felt herself going, no, she let herself go, to a place she had never been.

It was then she pleaded with him, *say my name*, and he did, though he didn't need to be told. It told her he wanted her as much as she wanted him, and it pushed her over into an abyss of joy she had only ever dared to dream of.

The sound that came from him was primeval, a visceral sound as old as time. It was everything — love and pain, heartbreak and guilt, but most of all, hope — and she held him tight throughout. It told her the chains that still shackled him to the past had been loosened, and everything would be alright in the end. She knew that not only did she love him, but that in time he would love her too, and in the way she needed to be loved.

Hurley half woke during the night from the deepest of sleep, confused. They had fallen asleep exhausted, with the small night-light still on, and although he could see the room around him, his eyes were not of this world and it made no sense to him at all. At one stage he murmured, incoherently, and listening she heard it was about the orphaned baby, Manuelito.

In another instant he was looking for his weapon, as tired soldiers sometimes do. She turned off the light and soothed him as only a lover could, and she held him as he drifted back to a place where there was no pain. Unknown to him, her eyes moistened the pillow behind him, but she held him and slept the sleep of the saved.

It was daylight when Hurley woke fully, the birds near the house were already busy and he could hear roosters across the neighbourhood competing to declare the day open for business. He heard a dog bark and a few cars drove by; he wondered why Maggie was not there beside him.

He pulled on his trousers and walked around the room bare-chested, looking at the little things he had not seen the night before. Her room was ordered and neat, just like she was. On her desk-like dressing table were photos of her parents and her brother, the nieces, and Atlas the horse.

Astride another nameless horse long ago sat a teenage Maggie, wearing the uniform of dressage; her dark red hair cascading down her back as she posed, innocent, smiling and hatless in her riding boots, jodhpurs and sleek black coat.

Hurley reflected that he had made love to this woman but had never seen her in a dress or a skirt; not even in a photograph. There was nothing in sight to indicate there was anyone special in her life. He had not asked her and wondered why. Was he afraid of her response, or did the question not need asking? Surely, she would have said so if it were true?

In a cup on the small marble basin were two toothbrushes. Each had a white handle, but one was new and still in its cellophane wrapper. Next to the cup was a bottle of water. He smiled to himself, *she thinks of everything.* He ripped the cover off and brushed his teeth, washing away the previous night's wine with a carefree laugh as he watched himself in the mirror above the basin.

He had known this time would eventually come and was relieved; there was no guilt looking back accusingly from the mirror. Instead, he liked what he saw. No sooner had he done so than Maggie returned carrying two steaming mugs of tea which she placed on the small table. She was dressed in khaki tactical trousers and a sky-blue polo shirt. Her face was fresh, without make-up and her hair had been towelled and was still damp from showering.

'You look fantastic,' he commented, his pleasure evident.

'Why thank you, sir,' she said, her cheeks colouring slightly. He reached and cupped her face softly in his hand. She moved her head and kissed his fingers. Hurley knew her eyes were closed to keep the memory and make time stand still. They sat on the bed, drinking their tea in happy silence. He laid his arm around her shoulder and she leaned in easily. With his other hand he held hers in her lap. There was already comfort in their closeness and they both sensed it.

'Maggie, I want you to know you're special to me,' he confessed, somehow wanting her to know that while he didn't know where it would go, or how it would end, it wasn't a passing fancy either. She bit her tongue. She wanted to throw herself at him and hold him, tell him she loved him — had loved him for a long time — but she didn't.

Like all the women who have ever lived, Maggie sensed the danger. She knew his situation, and that he had to travel at his own pace along a path that few men did, and while there were things she desperately wanted to say, they would only make the journey more painful for him.

'As you are to me,' she said softly, but the meaning in her eyes was clear nevertheless and Hurley drank it in, as she hoped he would. He hugged her and then kissed her fleetingly on the lips. It did not have the urgency or the passion of the previous night, but his touch comforted her.

'It will be a big show Saturday night,' she said, trying to sound brazen and confident, but falling somewhat short. Clearly, she was working through what was to come and Hurley sensed her unease. She wanted success and was worried it might elude them, although she had said nothing of this to him. For his part, he had no such qualms; about success, or about her. Now was the time he had waited for. He held her shoulders and locked eyes with her.

'Maggie, what you've set up is truly brilliant. It's the best I've ever seen. You've worked so hard and done so much, it's fantastic. And the team we have can make it work. People will talk about this one forever, believe me. You'll be terrific, so don't worry. And the final rehearsal tonight will confirm it all.'

It was exactly what she needed to hear, and he was the person she needed to hear it from. She hugged him tightly and beamed.

'Let's go and get some breakfast,' she said eagerly.

21

Club Echo Tango
Dili, United Nations administered East Timor

....

February 2001

Club Echo Tango was a popular nightspot for the expatriate community of Dili. Located close to the beach in the north-west of the city, it was *the* place to be on Friday and Saturday nights. It had quickly become an off-duty haven for the swelling international community of Dili, all of whom flocked to the club each weekend.

The few locals who frequented the venue were either business moguls, the riders of some particularly lucrative gravy train, or they were involved in organised crime. These groups, as always, were not mutually exclusive.

The music provided by local bands would play from early evening until closing time about two am. Many of these entertainers were highly talented and could easily have cut a decent living in Australia but at Club ET, as it was known locally, they sang only for their supper.

Alcohol was dirt cheap and shipped into Dili by the container load from both Darwin and Kupang in West Timor. It flowed like water and was consumed at an astonishing rate by those who had little else to occupy their time. And when they tired of the alcohol and the gossip, and the bumping and grinding of sweaty bodies on the parquetry dancefloor, there was always drugs.

Marijuana, cocaine, amphetamines. Heroin, and any of the chic designer drugs. All found their way into East Timor and all were available at Club ET — for a price, of course. There was very little scrutiny of the endless stream of soldiers, internationals and NGOs constantly arriving and departing East Timor.

There was less scrutiny still of consignments believed to contain important medical, humanitarian or building supplies. The club was periodically placed out of bounds to Australian military personnel for a variety of reasons, but drugs were always high on the list.

The silver Nissan Pathfinder driven by Gabby Tomms passed the front entrance of the club. It turned off onto adjacent land opposite the beach that had been converted into a car park. Simon Urquhart sat comfortably in the passenger seat, enjoying the air-conditioned comfort and the latest Faith Hill compact disk he had earlier loaded into the sound system.

The level of the carpark was lower than the club property by about a metre, and an arched walkway of sorts had been beaten through a dense thicket of palms and vines that grew messily between the two. It was like a hedge that was out of control.

A few rough concrete steps had been placed to facilitate access up to the path and it was the only access to the club entrance, meaning everybody who came from the carpark was forced to take the path or walk the long way around. As she always did, Tomms selected a position on the far side of the carpark.

While it was a longer walk from the pathway, she knew it would make for a more convenient departure later. *It always turns into a shit fight*, she had complained to Helen, her older and usually disapproving support officer, earlier that day.

Helen had nodded understandably but *shit fight* really was an understatement.

The combination of alcohol and testosterone, and a general lack of driving ability, had produced some memorable moments at Club ET. The carpark was regularly turned into a rally circuit of hoot-roaring drunks and the presence of CIVPOL did nothing to reduce the chaos.

There had been numerous minor injuries, many of which had gone unnoticed by their intoxicated owners or worn as a badge of honour the following day. On one occasion, a Kenyan army officer had somehow become wedged under the wheels of a car as its owner displayed his skills doing doughnuts on the slippery ground.

The ensuing scene as two hundred drunk revellers of varying ethnicity, language and medical ability tried to render the unfortunate African first aid would have been funny, had it not been so tragic. The victim was quickly forgotten in a collective mood of apathy and returned home as a paraplegic. The carpark culture then continued like nothing had ever occurred.

As they left the vehicle Tomms activated the auto-lock from her key ring, waving the key fob in the general direction of the vehicle. The blinking indicators confirmed to her, and those who watched her, that the locking mechanism had engaged, and she turned to walk towards the club. Urquhart loitered near the rear of the vehicle with his hands in his pockets and fell into step beside her as they crossed the carpark and entered the walkway.

She briefly noted the light-coloured van parked near the walkway entrance, but her thought was fleeting. It had been a pressure week for sure. Exciting in many ways, but oh, so stressful too. She wanted to dance, and she might even get a skin full. Why not? After all, *he* could drive them home. And so *he* should, after the shit *he* had caused.

After all, it was his fault the week had gone the way it had.

Thankfully he had proved cunning enough for them not to have been exposed, but she had made a mental note to be much more careful of him in the future.

Later, she would remember nothing of the light-coloured van, the carpark or the walkway. It was dusk, so the last of the day was fading, and the cloudy sky added to the growing gloom. Neither of them noticed the hooded shapes that appeared as the darkness of the foliage engulfed them. And they would only vaguely remember their legs being taken quickly from under them and strong arms pinning them.

They smelled too, but only fleetingly, the moist ground as they were pressed onto it, and felt the strong, gloved hands that tightened across their mouths. Behind them, a single figure moved quickly to place a large sign reading *Danger: Walkway Closed* across the entrance, preventing others from entering as they had done.

As they lay face down, their attackers heavy over them, there was only the quick jab of the needle in the side of their neck, heads swirling and then blackness. Then they were quickly dragged off the main path onto a smaller track that led deeper into the thicket to a small semi-cleared area previously prepared for just this task.

Firstly, strong woven adhesive tape was wrapped across their mouths and around their heads, ensuring that only their nasal passages were free. The attackers then dressed them in large oversize grey overalls, knotted at the feet and hands. Their arms were quickly bound behind them and their feet trussed. Yellow, spongy earplugs were carefully stuffed into their ears and the tape wound around their heads, covering their ears and eyes completely.

Lastly, the attackers pulled black cotton hoods over their heads and secured them with a knot at the back, tightening them across their faces. The attackers used another smaller track they had made to carry the pair and place them into the side-loading compartment of the light-coloured van. Over them they fitted a wooden structure that then looked like a packing crate sitting on the floor of the van.

Three of the attackers then quickly pulled of their masks and climbed into the van, Max took the wheel and Toby and Derek sat on the floor in the back with the crate. The door was pulled closed by the figure who had erected the sign — it was Lucy — and the van quickly moved off. The headlights only came on after it had moved away a safe distance from Lucy and Freon, both now hidden from view in the tree line.

The capture had been better than at the rehearsals, they would say later on. As she watched the van turn onto the main road and head away towards the east, Lucy pulled a mobile phone from her rain jacket. She keyed the pad and then listened briefly to ensure connection before shutting it off. She gave the thumbs up to Freon and they melted back into the vegetation. There was still work to do.

They donned night vision goggles and then quickly and expertly cleansed the area, placing anything that belonged to them or the traitors into a black plastic bag. After they finished with the site, they swept back along the track towards the car-park, clearing as they went. They had their orders and worked quickly; not a word was needed between them.

The growing humidity and the threatening sky reassured the pair there would be rain by the early morning and the entire area would then be a quagmire; any tell-tale marks would be obliterated within minutes of the first drops splashing on the earth. Once they had disposed of the warning sign, the pair unlocked the Nissan Pathfinder and Lucy drove them away towards the east.

22

DILI
UNITED NATIONS ADMINISTERED EAST TIMOR

....

February 2001

The security gates closed with a faint hydraulic hum and the Land Cruiser pulled quietly out into the city night. The safety of Casa Dili was now behind them. It was sultry and still; rain would come in the early morning Hurley reckoned as he shivered. Harry had the air-conditioner switched to blizzard mode and the cab was icy-cold.

They turned onto the market road and entered the traffic flow, heavier in this more populated part of town. The market lay about two kilometres ahead of them in the darkness, but would be nothing now but sad, empty wooden frames waiting for the light and colour of dawn to become shops and stalls again.

Harry pointed the vehicle towards the north-east of the city, just as Hurley expected. The footpath lining the road was rough and uneven. Here and there pieces of concrete and stone were missing, broken up and taken away, the need greater somewhere else in the city.

The branches of the huge trees growing at the roadside threw sinister shadows on the dark ground. There was little light coming from the buildings they passed, these were all set well back from the road and inhabited only during the day by various UN and NGO agencies.

Before long they crossed the *Mota* Santana, originally a small river but now reduced to a wide stormwater drain. It was filled almost to capacity from the recent rains, bearing its sludgy, debris-ridden morass down to the sea. Clouds of mosquitoes and other insects of all shapes and sizes were momentarily frenzied in the headlights as the vehicle moved on into the night and negotiated the now dark, unpopulated streets.

'This area's out of bounds to UN troops, y'know?' Hurley said flatly as the small stone bridge over the Mota Santana disappeared behind them. The area did indeed feature on the prohibited list promulgated by UNHQ. This was largely to prevent naïve UN soldiers, staffers and aid workers from getting themselves mugged, or worse.

There had been one murder and more muggings and rapes than UN officials would care to admit in these wild areas on the outskirts of the city. The prohibition also meant that the UN had no responsibility to patrol there, which suited the non-swimmers, and was certainly a relief to the Portuguese military, who were responsible for Dili and its environs.

They had quickly earned themselves the nickname of the Armoured Cappuccino Brigade due mainly to their proclivity to look smart and park their white pristine patrol vehicles outside the Dili coffee shops for the greater part of the day. They had largely come to the mission for a good time, not a hard time, and to ensure they were ideally placed for a spot of neo-colonialist influence and intelligence gathering at the expense of their former abandoned colony.

'Yes, but not to us,' Harry answered as he looked straight ahead.

His voice was calm but determined, almost menacing really

but only in the way that true strength of purpose can be to those who never know it. The time was close, and it would not be easy, indeed there were significant risks.

Harry was steeling himself for another show, going through his own internal preparation, using processes that had seen him through before. Processes he had been taught by a master unseen and unknown to Hurley in the generation before.

Hurley was doing the same. Unexpectedly, Harry threw back his head and effected a high-pitched aristocratic British voice and made an effeminate flourish with his left hand.

'Begone ye scoundrels and ne'er do wells, for we are about the Queen's business, and that truly be most secret business in protection of the Realm!'

They both laughed, just as they had done so many times in the past. It eased the tension, as Harry knew it would. Another turn and they entered the *desa* of Becora. The suburb of Shitsville.

Harry drove as if he had lived on the ground all his life. Hurley figured he had probably been there twice, maybe three times, including their trip for the rehearsal. But he knew also that Harry had memorised all the team's planning, including the street patterns, the landmarks, every bump and ditch.

Christ, it had been notebooks and butcher's paper in the old days. Yards of it, all taped together across the ops room walls with the streets drawn in permanent markers. To Harry it was just another piece of ground to be learned, to be dominated.

Berlin, Belfast, Zagreb, Dili. It made no difference to Harry. As they drove, the headlights picked out mounds of bricks and concrete. Earth had been somehow scraped or bulldozed into heaps beside the shells of the burned-out buildings.

Craters large and small were scattered about. Refilled daily by the rains, they were black holes in a grey moonscape, gazing up like so many lifeless eyes as the vehicle rushed by. Corrugated iron, timber, car bodies, debris and rubbish of every kind was littered all around.

By day, the area was scavenged by urchins and the elderly from the surrounding villages. Only the rats scurried about now, happiest in the dark and startled briefly by the noise and light from the vehicle. The derelict houses stood as dark, silent sentinels as Harry skilfully negotiated the back streets.

Up ahead a red light blinked twice, and Harry slowed the vehicle to a halt and turned the headlights off. They waited while their eyes adjusted to the night. The owner of the torch came into focus beyond the bonnet of the vehicle, it was Michelle.

'Here we go then,' Harry advised, as he eased the Land Cruiser forward, following their guide at walking pace along the rough overgrown track.

Michelle's long legs were already encased in blue overalls and she wore a pistol at her belt. She was not yet hooded, and her blonde hair acted as a point of light as she walked ahead of them. Hurley was silent as he watched her walk.

Harry's pager suddenly beeped into life. The piercing alarm startled Hurley who was pensive and lost in thought. Harry calmly reached to his waist and turned it off.

'Pick up complete,' he said with finality. 'They'll be here in sixteen minutes.' The wheels were well and truly in motion. 'Let's go,' he announced.

Michelle had chosen a hideout for them between two buildings shrouded in foliage. They positioned sheets of black calico across the windscreen and bonnet and in front of the grill, before standing back to survey their handiwork. There was no reflective surface to be seen and they nodded their satisfaction in unison in the darkness.

Hurley led off and negotiated the track which, following the rehearsal, was familiar to him and he knew would bring them to the green house. Harry followed in silence and before long they stepped up onto the slab of the old house. Hurley could see the beam with the aluminium stepladder standing next to it.

Maggie came over to them. She was wearing a head torch attached to elastic straps although the light was switched off. She handed Harry a portable UHF radio and Hurley watched as he fitted the earpiece into his ear. He turned to Hurley; his voice lowered.

'Right then, as you know the emergency RV is the small house ruins fifty yards away at the end of the track that leads from that doorway,' he explained, indicating the doorway they had entered. 'If anything happens to me, or when I say, you get there. I might mention that if this eventuality occurs, bloody quick smart would be very fucking handy.'

Understatement; one of Harry's many specialties, thought Hurley as he smiled at Maggie.

'It will be manned throughout. You'll then be taken away. Any questions?'

He looked at Harry and shook his head.

'Right, as you know we have this entire area under control. We are the sole occupants of the cordon. I am in radio contact with the watchers and will know well in advance if anything is about to turn to a box of frogs. Hansel and Gretel will arrive in the next few minutes and we will start when Sanderson gets here. Afterwards, you and I will disappear as previously discussed. The team will fix this place and that will be it. OK?'

Hurley nodded. It was crunch time and his throat felt dry. In contrast, his shirt was drenched. Harry, on the other hand, appeared to be in his element and in control, as always. As if on cue, Maggie brought over a white plastic squeeze bottle from among a stack of items she had been sorting through, most of which remained concealed by a folded tarpaulin.

She offered it first to Harry, but he declined. She turned to

Hurley. He nodded and took the bottle, drinking deeply as he squirted the tepid water into his open mouth, his head held back. He thanked her with a nod and handed the bottle back. She smiled and took the opportunity to briefly squeeze his hand before she returned to the beam. *Good luck.*

Harry walked over to the entry they had used and moved outside while Hurley followed. They each donned the blue overalls Maggie had left at the doorway and placed the balaclavas in their pockets. Propping himself against the wall, Harry pulled out his tobacco pouch and from it, a cigarette that he had rolled and placed there for this very occasion.

His match flared briefly as it was struck, and their night vision was temporarily ruined. He opened an old, much-travelled tobacco tin and held it at his waist. Into this he carefully placed the used match and the spent ash from the cigarette.

The end of the cigarette burned brightly, albeit briefly, as he drew strength from it. The aroma passed to Hurley who, although never a smoker, found the smell of real tobacco sweeter and more pleasant than that from manufactured cigarettes.

And so, we wait, together again, Hurley thought. Just like the time we waited together long ago, in the hills of southern China. So cold that night, the winds howling and bitter from the snows beyond, Hurley remembered, as he stared into the night. Not like tonight. The sweat flowed down into the small of his back and he shivered at the memory.

Running his hand through his hair, he felt the perspiration from his forehead as he did so. There was treachery then too, but that was the evil that came with their business. Back then they learned from the technical wizards that the last guide to bring their man, Hurley's man, back inside Hong Kong had betrayed them to the Chinese. Tricked, he had been turned to betray the special life placed into his care.

So together they hatched a plan. To steal their man before he met the traitor, and let the trap wait, baited and open, the traitor empty handed. It was a given Hurley must go over, his face known and trusted, but Harry had gone too.

So together in the darkness they had breached the wire and crossed the rugged hills, skirting the frontier villages to wait on the lonely road to Nan Shan Mountain. The young agent runner and the old master. Together, in the freezing hills of southern China.

Hurley recalled with fondness the childlike smiling faces of the small, nut-brown men from Nepal. Gurkha warriors, guardians of the frontier, gazing in open adoration at the two *sahibs* who would cross the wire and go into the hostile land beyond. Beyond, and into the hills of southern China.

They were all Recce Platoon men, hardened and born to war in a mountainous land far away. All soldiers and the sons of soldiers, living for war and ready for war now. Hurley knew that if he had called for volunteers, they would have drawn their fabled *kukris* in a heartbeat, and then crushed him in their rush to be first.

But this was not their battle, this was his battle and a secret one. His and Harry's. The Gurkhas had led them out and waited to cover their return. They knew the frontier ground, knew the Chinese guard posts and the patrol patterns. Nobody knew them better.

Gurkha battalions had spent generations watching the other side and trapping those who sought to breach the wire. Watching, and waiting. And they did that now through the long cold night. Hours later in the false dawn they stood to, hearing before seeing. Sensing running feet on the earth.

And then it was Harry leading with the compass, his old para smock billowing out behind him in the bitter wind, his chin up and determined. And Hurley pulling his charge by the hand, willing him on, knowing that the old man's strength was almost gone. Knowing also that if the old man faltered, he would never leave him. And Harry knew it too.

Exhausted, all of them, and running; running for the wire and running for their lives. And then when Harry fell on the rocky ground and smashed his face, two of the wiry warriors broke from cover and dashed forward. Against orders of course, two hundred metres, three hundred maybe — into China. Just to help him up and spur him on.

Two others had broken from their listening post in the dangerous growing light and appeared from nowhere at Hurley's side. Sensing the condition of Hurley's man, they quickly hoisted the frail body onto their shoulders and together they had all sprinted for the line.

In the blur that followed there were the sirens and the flares. And there was the shouting and the fear. There was always the fear. But there was sanctuary beyond the wire and they brought Hurley's man home into Hong Kong.

England one — China nil! Harry had cried with obvious pleasure, blood streaming down his face, as they all lay panting and exhausted, but exhilarated, in the safety of the RV inside the wire. Things were always simple to Harry.

But that was then, and this was now. Hurley smiled at the memory and willed his mind back to the present, and his focus to the task ahead. Behind him he could hear Maggie moving unseen items around in preparation.

Some were obviously heavy as the tell-tale noise of them being dragged across the concrete slab grated on their ears as they waited. Also, the tinny sound of the aluminium stepladder being positioned, then re-positioned.

He let her be, knowing she would ask if she needed help. The rehearsal had told him without doubt that everything was ready. He now had to rise to the occasion and play his part. In his periphery he could see the illumination of the small beam from her head torch now as it played around the room while she worked. Enjoy the wait, Harry always said, because you never know what the waiting will bring.

The sound of the van was faint at first and then grew louder, the noise making everyone uneasy, as it always does to those who wait in the silence and safety of the night. Then the engine died as the van was halted at the end of the track. In the new silence Harry butted his cigarette stub in the little tin and screwed the top closed, placing it in his pocket. Finality.

The sliding door of the van was clearly heard in the still night and then they carried them in, each as a single package. Gretel was brought in first. She was still unconscious, and they handled her easily, like a ragdoll. They placed her gently in the room furthest from the beam and her watcher, Michelle, took up residence sitting protectively on the floor next to her.

Hansel was conscious but did not struggle. Instead, his head moved from side to side in an attempt to make sense of his situation. It was as if he was looking, as if he were listening. And he was reaching back into his training to find a point of reference, but there was none.

Nothing Hansel had ever learned would prepare him for what was to come. Hurley also knew he would be thinking there would come a time for talking, for negotiation, for regaining control. He was right, and they had wagered everything on this. They carried him through to where he would sit with Hurley and secured him to the chair.

Word came over the radio that Sanderson was inbound, expected in about two minutes. It was the signal for them all to cover their faces. Harry and Hurley looked at each other in the half dark and both nodded, their faces set and determined. They shook hands and donned their balaclavas. Hurley turned and walked away — towards the stage. It was another show for another night.

It was also time for Harry to take his seat and as he did so, the spotlight came on. Merlin too was weaving his magic. The area under the beam was now set and brought into stark relief.

Only those things that needed to be there were visible; Maggie, the ladder, the ropes, the concrete blocks. On a field table Maggie had neatly laid out the items she needed; a water bottle, towel, the iron bar and the pistol with its silencer.

Beyond the beam and invisible to Hansel, were Toby and Derek. They held the dummy back ready for its delivery to Maggie, and there was another field table ready to rest Janey on once the switch was made.

Harry sat behind Hurley and out of Hansel's sight, Sanderson's chair next to him. Everything was as Maggie had briefed and the model of the little green house had magically come to life — soon the last of the figurines would be in place and the curtain would go up.

23

BECORA

DILI, UNITED NATIONS ADMINISTERED EAST TIMOR

....

February 2001

Hurley sat on his chair close to Hansel, quiet and unmoving. Hansel was secured to his chair around the ankles and thighs, and with his wrists and forearms to the arms of the chair. The chair itself was secured to the ground with large stakes, immovable.

He was still hooded, and he breathed heavily and unevenly, his head moving periodically, like the antenna of a trapped insect seeking information from its environment. He did not try and resist his bonds after an initial struggle, realising it was useless.

Sanderson sat behind them and shifted uncomfortably in his canvas chair. He always found camping style furniture unable to accommodate his long frame and he wriggled to find some degree of comfort. Harry sat next to him, and between them they occupied the best seats in the house.

Sanderson could see that Harry had gone to quite some trouble to achieve what he wanted; good. The last thing he wanted was one of these bloody army types out of control and seeking revenge against him. After all, it wasn't his fault those people had been killed, he had nothing to do with it.

But he wanted an outcome too. He was ambivalent as to whether the theatrical extravaganza laid out before him would work, of course, but he was trying to keep an open mind. He would be careful to be graceful when it all fell apart and came to nothing, which it probably would. Importantly, he will have paid his long-standing debt to Harry. It would be a win-win from his point of view.

Suddenly, Hurley held his right hand straight up in the air. It was the signal to all those on the main stage that he would start, and that Hansel's hood was about to be removed. It was also the stand-by signal to bring Janey as the struggling Gretel across Hansel's field of view, and literally string her up.

Hurley reached over and removed Hansel's hood in one fluid movement. He then, without ceremony, ripped off the woven duct tape from around his eyes and ears. Hansel yelped into his gag and said something indistinguishable as the tape pulled clumps of hair and skin away.

His eyes blinked rapidly as he tried to focus. Hurley then pulled the earplugs from his ears and put them down next to his own chair.

'Listen to me,' Hurley began. His voice low, measured and authoritative. He made no attempt to disguise it; Hansel did not know him and the fact he had an Australian accent was incidental. If the ploy was successful and he found out Hurley's identity later on, it wouldn't matter. 'In a moment I will remove your gag,' Hurley continued on. 'You are not to cry out, you are not to speak. You will speak only when I tell you to. Nod if you understand.'

Hansel watched Hurley through eyes that were calculating, but fearful, nevertheless. There was a lot going on in there,

Hurley thought as he looked into them. Hansel nodded slowly in acknowledgement and Hurley ripped the tape from his face in three distinct movements, each time a new raw pain as skin and hair were roughly ripped away.

'Who the fuck are you?' Hansel blurted out as soon as his mouth was free. Within a millisecond, Hurley slapped him, very hard, with his open hand, right across the face. The sound of the smacking blow carried to everyone on the night air. Hansel recoiled in shock and cowered away from Hurley as much as he could, but he shut his mouth nevertheless.

'I said not to speak until I tell you, do you understand?'

Hansel nodded solemnly, and Hurley knew the rules were established.

'Let me set the scene for you, Urquhart,' Hurley began, noting Hansel's unease when his real name was used. 'In a moment, a colleague of yours, Ms Tomms, will join us. However, she is not to be as lucky as you. If you watch your front and orient yourself towards the light, you will see her emerge and be carried to the beam you can see there. Do you see it?'

'Yes,' Hansel mumbled, unsure where this was going but obviously very uneasy about the possibilities.

'Once she is there, I will ask you a series of questions. If you answer those questions truthfully, and give me a full account, no harm will come to Ms Tomms or to you. If you attempt to deceive me, or refuse to answer my questions, that person you can see there at the beam in blue overalls, do you see them?'

'Yes.'

'That person will hurt Ms Tomms a great deal, and I won't be responsible for how much. As you will see if you are foolish enough to resist me. Do you understand?'

'Yes.'

'You need to understand something more. I control everything here. I control the beginning of the pain, and the end of the pain.' Hurley reached down and retrieved the black box. 'If you look at this box you will see that it has a green light and a red light. If the green light shines towards that person there, they will continue to inflict great pain on Ms Tomms, if the red light shines towards them, they will stop immediately and wait. Do you understand?'

'Yes.' Hansel's eyes were fixed on the box with dread.

'What colour light do you need to shine for your colleague?'

'Red,' Hansel spat out, petulantly.

'And how do you do that?'

'By answering fully and truthfully.'

'Good.'

The simple question-easy response pattern was a conditioning technique that would help erode Hansel's will to resist and assist him on the road to cooperation. Hurley placed the box down and turned it on. Maggie saw the green light and motioned for them to bring Gretel forward.

Hansel watched the squirming, protesting Gretel brought forward by two burley figures, also in blue overalls. Her screams were well muffled by her gag, but they were still audible. She was hoisted up and held in the air under the beam by strong arms while Maggie secured her wrists into the prepared ropes.

Hurley watched Hansel closely.

At first his eyes darted around the scene, which was normal. He was afraid and doing what animals do when they sense danger — looking for a way out. When Gretel first came into view, he was visibly distressed. He watched her squirming and groaning, and his jawline tightened. He sweated heavily, particularly on his forehead, but his eyes did not leave her.

It was the first time he had shown how the lack of control affected him and he pushed hard against his bonds, almost rocking his chair in place. It showed Hurley he had bought into the theatre of it and believed what he saw was true. It also told Hurley that he would play his role as the tormented prisoner.

Together they watched Gretel being tied by her hands and then without realising it, Hurley held his breath. It was in anticipation of the critical moment, and as Merlin walked in front of the spotlight and killed the light. Before he knew it, it was over.

When the light went out, none of them had any night vision and it worked better than it had on the video or at rehearsal. The light simply reappeared a microsecond later and there was Gretel, having her feet tied to the concrete blocks. Seamless. It had worked, just as they had planned and hoped for.

Hurley knew that in the background, Janey was safely held by the strong hands of Toby and Derek and that they would lay her carefully on the field table to rest. Hansel had no such knowledge and could draw no such comfort. Gretel was now suspended, squirming like a marionette, with Toby pulling the strings.

'Now, shall we turn the light to red for Ms Tomms' benefit?' Hurley began, almost politely.

'Yes.' Angry and reluctant to play but forced to do so.

Hurley switched the light to red.

'OK,' Hurley said. 'Over the past month or so, two Australian agents run by AUSBATT were murdered in their homes in Balibo.' Hurley watched Hansel's face as he delivered the introduction and noted the immediate look of guilt and fear. While normally the master of his own body language, this was made almost impossible with his arms and legs tethered, and his body desperately sought expression. Hurley thought Hansel already understood what was required, and that he also sensed what Hurley knew, but he was under no illusions it would be easy getting it from him. They were in for the long haul and their planning had prepared them for it. 'In addition, the wife of one of those agents was also brutally murdered and their child orphaned, and an Australian soldier who had some involvement in these events was also killed.'

'I don't know anything about that,' Hansel spat out. But in an attempt to distance himself from the events, it was too quick and too forceful.

Hurley's voice remained even, there was no change at all in the delivery.

'For the only time tonight, I am going to pretend I didn't hear that. Because if you said that, what colour would the light need to be?'

'Jesus Christ. Green, fucking green,' he almost yelled, angry and not realising he had just admitted his lie.

'That's right, because what you said was a lie,' Hurley confirmed for him. 'And what happens if the light turns green?'

'She… will be hurt.'

'That's right. So what colour does Ms Tomms need from *you*, what colour are *you* personally responsible for?'

'Red… red,' he gasped urgently.

'Good. Now, I want you to tell me, in great detail, what you know of those events, including your involvement and that of Ms Tomms.' Hurley leaned over, his finger poised menacingly over the light switch.

'I… can't. I don't know anything about it really,' he stated desperately, but without conviction.

Hurley knew Hansel's choice of words pointed to his guilt anyway, and his attempt at distancing himself would be short-lived. He turned the light to green and Hansel watched transfixed, powerless and now part of a tragedy from which he could not escape.

Maggie walked deliberately over to the table and selected the iron bar. There was no haste, in fact, quite the opposite. It was designed to allow the opportunity for his imagination to work and they had catered for this specifically.

In a brilliant moment of theatre, when she returned to Gretel, Maggie dropped the bar on the concrete floor while she seemingly adjusted her belt. The heavy clang of the bar hitting the floor ensured that everyone watching, but especially Hansel, knew it was hard, and iron.

Sanderson watched, aloof and mildly amused. Well, Urquhart had called their bluff on that one, hadn't he? What were Harry and his merry men going to do now, he thought. Had they really thought Urquhart was going to fold that easily? He wondered what the back-up plan was. After all, it wasn't as if they could bludgeon whomever it was strung up down there with that iron bar, was it?

When Maggie picked up the bar and turned to face the beam, the light was still green. She positioned herself and raised the bar, which was caught nicely in the beam of the spotlight. Metallic and sinister, just as they had planned. With the deliberation and predictability they had rehearsed, she brought it thumping down onto Gretel's shinbone.

Gretel screamed and the muffled pain carried easily to Hansel. He cringed and lowered his head. He was desperately trying to find a way out. He was a person who always had an answer, always a scheme, always in control, just as they had learned about him. This time, there was nothing.

He looked up just in time to see the bar come crashing down again, and the sound of breaking bone was unmistakable. A small colouring, dark in the spotlight, was forming on Gretel's lower leg. Hansel knew it was blood and that it was red. His head fell and he vomited into his lap. He clenched his jaw tightly.

Sanderson nearly sprang out of his chair when he saw and heard the first strike. For a start he was not expecting for her to be hit at all, let alone the way it happened, and his stomach almost turned. He had been duped, he knew that now, but didn't know how.

His agitation was almost palpable and Harry, sensing this,

reached across to him and waved a cautionary hand towards him, complemented by a steely eye. It said, *control yourself, everything is alright and I have kept my promise.* Sanderson didn't like it, but he did as he was bid and as he had agreed.

Hurley turned the light to red and Maggie paused, wiping the bar slowly and deliberately with the towel as she waited. Gretel vibrated on the rope and moaned in pain. The anguished cries carried to Hurley and Hansel.

'Now,' Hurley continued, unabated and unaffected, his voice still even and unemotional. 'You can see how unpleasant this is for Ms Tomms. However, I will continue this until I have all the information I need. Look at me,' he directed Hansel.

Hansel looked into Hurley's face and Hurley saw that he was already beaten. He just didn't know it yet. He was in that world where something, somewhere was telling him he could make it right, the way he wanted it to be. He was wrong, and Hurley knew it. Only Hurley's eyes could be seen shining out from the balaclava and there was no mercy for Hansel or Gretel to be found there. Hansel's face dropped and he wept with frustration, as men often do.

Hurley felt the plan was unfolding well. His deep understanding of the rhythm of interrogation told him they were on track. To practitioners, these things had a musical quality of their own, and Hurley had a good ear.

'Now the light is red, we will have had a little break,' Hurley said condescendingly, as if to a child. He was taking Hansel, by the hand, in small steps. 'What involvement did you and Ms Tomms have in those events about which we spoke?' He reached for the switch and Hansel rallied and took a deep breath.

Hurley watched him and exhaled audibly, sending the message to Hansel he knew he was preparing to lie. This alone, he knew, would further weaken him.

'I don't know, I just don't know,' Hansel pleaded, apparently exasperated, but again it was unconvincing.

Hurley turned the light to green and Hansel dropped his head.

'Fuck!' he screamed loudly through gritted teeth.

'Look up now!' Hurley ordered sharply. 'If you are going to condemn one of your own, have the guts and the decency to watch it happen.' When Hansel tried to look away again, Hurley reached over and held him firmly at the back of his neck by the hair, his head faced directly towards the beam.

Maggie put the towel down and moved in. Again, she belted the lower leg and the blood pool seeped and widened. The sound of crepitus that carried to them across the night was stomach churning. Gretel cried out like a lost soul in the night and began to choke. There were some panicked movements of her head as she seemed to fight for breath, Toby working the strings.

As Hansel watched, spellbound, Maggie dragged over the stepladder and positioned it next to Gretel. She mounted the ladder and when she was high enough, she drew a knife from her belt and flicked open the blade. With the point she surgically cut a small hole in the hood and into the tape covering Gretel's mouth.

As she did so, she activated the pneumatic device at the side of Gretel's leg and vomit spewed forth in a stream under pressure, arching towards the ground and then as it died, dribbling down her front. Maggie dismounted the stepladder and methodically placed it against the wall. She grabbed the water bottle from the table and squirted Gretel in the face so that her hood and head were drenched but free of muck.

It was too much for Hansel. He was highly agitated, and his legs began to shake uncontrollably, his feet drumming a tattoo on the ground. He was cursing incoherently, and his face was flushed. The perspiration dripped from his face and head.

Hurley watched him closely and knew the anger and the moral dilemma that was raging unresolved inside him, and also that he must keep the pressure on.

Maggie had regained the iron bar and was moving in to resume her violent assault. She positioned herself and started on Gretel's thigh. She rained blow after blow and each time the smacking sound might just as well have been on Hansel's head. He could not look away as Hurley held his head tightly, and when he tried to close his eyes, Hurley turned the light to red.

'If you close your eyes again, I will bring someone to hold them open,' Hurley warned him coldly. 'If I have to, I will borrow that switchblade and cut your eyelids off so you will never close your eyes again, do you understand?'

'Yes,' Hansel said, subdued, terrorised and compliant. It was a further step along the path. Hurley marched on.

'What part did you play in the events surrounding the deaths of these people we have talked about, and what part did Ms Tomms play?' It was determined and relentless. It would not go away, and Hansel knew it.

'I... I... I don't know, I don't remember,' he begged, as unconvincing as he had previously been.

Hurley turned the light to green and Maggie moved in again. Hansel's head dropped and he sobbed heavily, the mucous and tears dripping into his lap, mixing with the slime of vomit already gathered between his legs.

Hurley grabbed his hair violently and held his face towards the beam. Maggie brought down another crashing blow, the blood pool grew, and Gretel screamed. She was now shaking like a wounded rabbit caught in a trap. Maggie raised her arm again.

'I... I...' Hansel blubbed through his tears. Hurley turned the light to red and waited.

'I'll tell you if you let her go,' he muttered weakly, playing the only card he thought he had. Hurley mused with some satisfaction they had predicted his chivalry to perfection. In truth, he had no card to play at all.

Hurley quickly turned the light to green and Maggie's arm came down. The result was the same as before and Gretel's scream carried to them. Hurley turned the light to red.

'Don't ever think you can dictate a bargain to me,' Hurley warned him menacingly. 'I am in control and I make the rules, not you, do you understand?'

'Yes,' he whispered, broken.

'It will help you to further understand that once Ms Tomms is broken and bloodied, she will be of no further use to me. At that point I will kill her, and you will have caused that. It will be *your* responsibility and *yours* alone. If you look down carefully on that table near the beam you will see a pistol. Do you see that?'

'Yes, yes.' He nodded vigorously, agitated and fearful now.

'Only you can stop that happening, do you understand? And when she is disposed of, you will get the same treatment. And if you do not cooperate, you will be killed too.'

'You fucking prick. You can't fucking do that...' Hansel spat venomously, wide-eyed now and terrified. Hurley reached for the switch.

'Wait... I...' Hansel blurted out urgently. Hurley's hand hovered, waiting to hear the words he wanted to hear.

'I can only tell you what I know,' Hansel conceded, seeking compromise. But his voice was soft, and it was the sound of compliance and defeat.

Hurley let the silence hang between them for effect before he continued.

'Tell me everything you know and keep talking until I tell you to stop or there is no more,' Hurley instructed, his hand now withdrawn from the switch.

'Alright,' Hansel murmured reluctantly. 'There was an operation, run from our station. It was a private operation, something we were working on to later present as a successful fait accompli to the bigwigs, if you like.'

Hurley listened and smiled inwardly. Behind him, Harry did the same. While it wasn't over yet, this trickle would become a torrent and Hurley would channel it all in the right direction, just as they had planned. Hurley had thought they would either have worked on half the dummy before Hansel capitulated, or it would come at the execution. It was some relief that it came early.

Sanderson couldn't believe his ears. This charade was actually going to work. He listened intently as Urquhart tripped over his words in an effort to give his interrogator what he wanted — and talk himself and Gabby into the ranks of the unemployed as he did so.

As often happens with the perspective of bystanders, he egotistically thought himself immune to such trickery, and considered himself unlikely to have fallen for the ploy. He was immediately forgetful that was exactly what had happened to him at the beginning.

'It involved a former militia leader,' Hansel looked for the right words. 'A politically well-connected Timorese who we felt might prove a good agent of influence after independence.'

He took breath and gathered his thoughts. Hurley knew he was editing and would get more selective as he went on. The use of the pronoun *we* was always to deflect blame, but that would be sorted out in the later questioning. He would be forced to face his own responsibility, and Hurley could smell blood now.

'Who is that militia leader?' he asked pointedly.

'Marcelino Borges.'

'Go on,' Hurley urged.

'I couldn't do it all alone so I brought Gabby in on it. We

went over into West Timor and met Borges. His pre-condition was that we destroy all the evidence that pointed to his part in criminal activity and that we…' he pursed his lips and sought to find suitable wording, '…that we remove any evidence of people who might be able to testify against him. Can I have a drink of water?'

'No. Go on,' Hurley directed. The social rule of reciprocity did not apply here. Hansel had no choice now. He swallowed, licked his lips and carried on, the taste of vomit acrid in his throat.

'We visited UNHQ and were able to cull Borges' file at the Serious Crimes Unit; from the AUSBATT agent reporting we identified initially three, and then a fourth person who could testify against Borges. We had the first three people… eliminated. That's all I can tell you, honestly,' he finished, believing his narrative complete.

He had taken a final big breath and let it out, thinking that because it was cathartic to him it was all he needed to do to save himself and Gretel. But everyone edits when they talk, and Hansel was no different. All the teeth would eventually be pulled.

'You have begun to tell the story, but there is much more you can provide. You need to understand that I will ask you a series of questions concerning your narrative. If you fail to answer, or lie to me, it is back to square one, do you understand?'

'Yes.' He was compliant now his decision was made, and he had begun to unburden himself. In the background Gretel moaned unnervingly, helpful in keeping him focused.

'When you say a private operation, what do you mean?'

'One not technically sanctioned by our Head of Station.'

'When you say "technically" what do you mean?'

'Unauthorised.'

'At any time was the Head of Station aware of what you were

doing, perhaps putting himself in a position of plausible deni-ability?' *Sanderson will love that*, Hurley thought, *fuck him too.*

'No, not at any time.'

'Why did you see the need to present such an operation as a fait accompli anyway?'

'I had a number of plans vetoed, including this same idea. I thought rather than keep plugging away, if I could put a big success on the table, no one would be able to ignore it and its genesis would be forgotten.'

'And of course you would get the credit for it, the credit you deserve?' Hurley asked, reading the weakness of him.

'Yes, I suppose so.'

'You suppose so, or that is the truth?'

'It is the truth.'

'When did you bring Tomms into the operation and what was her role?'

'After I had the initial idea, I brought her on to do most of the leg work. Primarily to be the other half of the operation and to recruit an agent that could assist us in the border area. That was about mid-year last year.'

'Why did you need an agent in the border area?'

'We needed someone with access to the agents run by AUSBATT.'

'Why?'

'So that those identified as posing a risk to exposing Borges could be eliminated.'

'What do you mean by eliminated?'

'Killed.'

'Be specific. Do you mean murdered?'

'Yes.' Softly, almost inaudible.

'Speak up.' Hurley ordered, his voice still even.

'Yes.' Clear, but guilt-ridden.

'Who were those people, the ones who were murdered?'

'The two AUSBATT agents and the wife of the second one.'

'What were their names?' Hurley asked simply.

Hansel swallowed hard. 'I don't know,' he muttered again, almost inaudibly.

Hurley too, swallowed as he braced himself.

'For the record their names were Senhor Abrio da Silva, Senhor Jose da Cavarlho and his wife Senhora Filomena. Their orphaned son is named Manuelito.' It was the only time Hurley gave him any information and he did it to twist the knife he was now holding, and he did it for them all, and out of respect for the dead.

Hansel looked up at Hurley, ashamed. For the first time he appeared to truly appreciate this wasn't going to end well for him regardless of what the outcome might be. He was broken. If his arms had been free, he would have held his head in his hands. He lowered his head and began to sob softly.

'How were they murdered and who did it?' Hurley marched on relentlessly.

Hansel sniffed. 'They were stabbed by the Australian soldier that Tomms recruited, Sergeant Campbell, the one that was shot and killed by AUSBATT.'

'Why did Sergeant Campbell do that?'

'He was a tasked agent; he did as he was told.'

'Who told him to do that?'

'Tomms.'

'At whose direction?'

Silence.

'At whose direction?'

'Mine.'

'What was his motivation to work for Tomms?'

'A mixture; friendship, appeal to self-esteem, disgruntlement with the army and his treatment. He felt marginalised and unappreciated. He was made to think he might get a job with the service later. He was a good Indonesian linguist; we probably could have found something for him.'

'Did he have an agent number, or a code name?'

'Yes, *Hobbit*.'

'Did you ever meet him?'

'No.'

'So Tomms was his only case officer and she directed him.'

'Yes.'

'Did you hear any recordings of the meetings between Tomms and the agent *Hobbit?*'

'Yes.'

'Where are these recordings now?'

'In my safe at the office.'

'How was *Hobbit* contacted for tasking?'

'He travelled weekly to Dili for work, so it was easy to arrange meetings and to cover them, so it was not suspicious. We also gave him a mobile phone for exclusive use with us.'

'How did this arrangement work?'

'It was a point to point mobile, used as a single unidentifiable channel. It wasn't used for any other purpose.'

'Where is this mobile phone now?'

'I don't know.'

'Where is the one you used to contact it?'

'In Tomms' safe at work.'

'Did you or Tomms target any other person as a potential agent in this operation?'

'No.'

'Where did you meet Borges and how many times?'

'I've met him twice, once at a refugee camp in Atapupu, and once at a house in West Timor where he lives.'

'Where is that house?'

'It sits on the three-way road junction immediately north of a place called Tullamalae, on the road to Atambua.'

'Describe it.'

'It's a double story white house trimmed in blue and gold. It has a security wall around it. It is the only major cement dwelling in that area.'

'What is the means of contacting Borges now?'

Hansel bit his lip, and his tone changed slightly.

'We cannot contact him; he sends a courier with written instructions when he wants to talk to me. They place a note under my door at home.' Hurley considered this and thought it a lie, but he continued on.

'How many times has this happened?'

'Three.'

'When were these occasions?'

'I don't know the dates off hand; the first time was when he approached me early last year. It was this approach that gave me the idea of the operation and we met in the house I mentioned a week later. The second time was some weeks ago to organise the meeting in the refugee camp at Atapupu. The third time was last week.'

'What was the substance of the latest communication?'

'He wants to meet at the house I talked about before.'

'When does he want to meet?'

'At midday two weeks from tomorrow.'

Hurley silently drew breath. *This was gold.*

'Midday on Sunday two weeks from now?' he repeated casually.

'Yes.'

'Do you know why?'

'No.'

'Do you have this note or any of the others?'

'No. I destroyed them after reading them.'

'What are the security procedures for meeting Borges at this house?'

'I am to stop about five hundred metres north of the house and stand next to the car for about five minutes. I will then walk slowly towards the house and he will open the gate when I get there.'

'Is he expecting a particular vehicle?'

'I don't think so. When I last went, I used a four-wheel drive I hired in Dili.'

'Is there a danger signal, to alert him?'

'Yes, the headlights will be left on.'

'Who culled Borges' file and how was that done?'

'Tomms. She had access through a contact at UNHQ with the SCU.

'What is the name of that contact?'

'Captain Chip Granger, he is an American army officer.'

'Was he involved in the culling of that file, or knew about it?'

'No. He simply facilitated access.'

'Do the culled documents from that file still exist?'

'Yes, they are in my safe at the office.'

'Is everything you have told me the truth?'

'Yes,' he spat. Compliance. And then anger. 'Fuck you to hell, you bastard.'

Hurley ignored him. It was just the bravado that bubbles up at the end, which helps the Hansels of the world believe they have been stronger than they really are. Instead, he looked over Hansel's shoulder and straight at Harry and Roger Sanderson. Sanderson's face was ashen. He nodded angrily that he had heard enough and held up his own recording device on which he had taped the interrogation. Harry slowly nodded his agreement.

'Is there anything more you would like to tell me, or ask me?' Hurley enquired.

'Why? Why the fuck have you done this to us? Why the fuck do you care?' he pleaded. He was washed out, exhausted. He was also angry and frustrated beyond expression, but still selfish and content in the thought he might escape with his life.

'If you have to ask me that, it proves you are unworthy. In any case, I'm sure you will have that discussion with your boss in due course.' Hansel looked up uncomprehendingly into Hurley's face but saw only cold hate in the grey eyes beyond the balaclava.

24

BECORA

DILI, UNITED NATIONS ADMINISTERED EAST TIMOR

February 2001

Sanderson sat for a moment gathering his thoughts. Finally, reluctantly, he uncurled his long frame and stood up. He was certainly free of his debt to Harry, but he had also made his own bed here, and he was forced to lie it. He moved around in front of Urquhart and looked down.

'Yes, your boss — that would be *me*,' he said with emphasis, his own emotion and frustration evident. He looked and sounded like a school principal dealing with a recalcitrant pupil. Urquhart looked up into Sanderson's face, his jaw dropped, and his red-rimmed eyes were wide with disbelief.

'Roger, thank God you're here! For God's sake, help me out, they've kidnapped us and they've hurt–'

'Oh, shut up Simon,' Sanderson cut him off tiredly. 'I've heard quite enough from you tonight.'

'You don't understand…' Urquhart blurted out urgently, searching for sense in what was happening, not comprehending how Sanderson had come to be there in the first place.

'Oh, I very much do understand. I've been sitting in that chair there,' he stated flatly, pointing behind Urquhart. 'And for the past hour I have listened to you and watched it all unfold. I heard everything you said, and importantly, everything you *confessed*.'

Urquhart was speechless with confusion.

Harry beckoned Merlin forward and he began cutting the cable ties, first the arms, then the legs. When he was free, Urquhart stood up very slowly and groaned slightly as his cramped body, and his brain, came back to life.

'Who are these fucking people and what are you doing here?' he spat at Sanderson. 'By God, if you are part of this you will pay dearly.'

Sanderson had heard enough; it had been an emotional journey for him too and he was now angry. He had listened to Urquhart's ego and had heard how he had sought to usurp his authority. Suddenly, he grabbed Urquhart roughly by the front of his overalls and pulled him roughly towards the beam. Urquhart protested as he struggled to keep up, the knots on the bottom of the overalls hindering him.

It wasn't what Harry or Hurley really wanted, but they looked at each other and let them go. Hurley certainly had confidence there was nothing they could do that Harry's team couldn't cope with. Besides, it might prove interesting. He followed them closely and at the same time he waved his hand in the air to let the team know it was OK.

At the beam, Sanderson leaned over and screamed into Urquhart's face. 'She's not hurt, no one's hurt! You stupid bloody idiot! You have been done over by a cheap vaudeville tent trick.' With this, he reached for the dummy on the beam and tore open the front zip, exposing the mannequin and the beaten meat and bone beneath.

Urquhart gawped in disbelief and struggled to process what he was looking at. The confusion was etched into his face. In the background he could now also see Toby and Derek, guarding what looked like another dummy. He turned around in confusion, his face manic, and his mouth searching for words.

'But, but… but I saw them bring her here, I saw them bash her with…' he spun around and spied the iron bar on the table and reached for it. Somehow, even though his hands were still knotted off with the overalls, there was enough slack for him to grasp the bar through the material. The look on his frenzied face told them all just what he wanted to do with that bar. As he lunged for Sanderson, they all heard the cocking of the pistol and froze.

'Put that down, *now*,' Maggie ordered, the weapon levelled at Urquhart. His eyes were wild with rage and something more now, humiliation. Maggie was cool and unflinching, the sinister form of the Walther P99 with its silencer was unmoving in her hand.

'Well if everything else here is a fucking lie, why would I even think that gun is real?' he challenged her, screaming, his eyes blazing.

With that, Maggie turned slightly to her left and with a single-handed stance shot the dummy in the face. Everyone witnessed the brain matter spray from the back of the head as the heavy nine-millimetre round did its work. In a pure chance event, the bullet severed the fishing line that held the head upright and it slowly, almost comically, slumped forward onto the chest of the dummy. Maggie quickly re-levelled at Urquhart. There was no doubt about her intent, or her ability to carry it through.

'Put the bar down, *now*,' she commanded, her voice cold and menacing.

Urquhart slowly lowered his arm and the bar dropped to the ground, the sound echoing on the concrete. He slumped and followed it. He was truly broken now as the full realisation of what had happened washed over him. He sobbed quietly and Hurley kicked the bar away with his foot.

Harry motioned for Tomms to be brought forward and Michelle appeared, guiding her; her arms were still bound behind her back and she remained hooded. She was frog-marched forward to the beam. Harry wanted no further drama. He turned to Sanderson.

'Their car is parked at the end of that track,' he explained, pointing. He reached into his pocket and pulled out the keys to the Nissan Pathfinder and threw them to Sanderson. 'All their possessions are in the car. Get them out of here and then do what you need to do. Only then is it over. Leave her bound and hooded until you get to the car and then give the overalls and hoods to my people. The car is facing towards Dili — just drive and stay on the same road. A vehicle will shadow you until you are safely back. We'll talk next week but remember what I said.'

Sanderson nodded curtly and skulked away. He half-pushed, half-carried Urquhart as he guided him down the track. Michelle guided Tomms who walked gingerly; inside the overalls she was barefoot. As she walked, she remained oblivious to all that had happened.

Hurley sat down on the field table and removed his balaclava, wiping his face back through his hair. Merlin did the same and patted Hurley affectionately on the back. Hurley grinned and nodded in recognition of the magician's efforts. Harry smiled and pulled his old tobacco tin from his pocket.

Inside there was a cigarette, it was called Victory. It was one of those black and white things that Harry really liked. The match flared, and after it, a small cloud of blue smoke billowed triumphantly skyward.

The others likewise removed their balaclavas. Toby and Derek freed Janey from her bonds; they cut the overalls off her quickly rather than undoing the knots. She was exhausted and dripping wet with perspiration, but she smiled broadly knowing it had all been worth it. They helped her off the table and each of the big men threw their arms around her.

Maggie went to Hurley and perched next to him, holding his arm. Hurley stroked her hair; it was sopping wet. *They had done it.*

'You were magnificent Maggie,' Hurley said, in awe of her performance. 'But remind me never to have a pistol close at hand in our bedroom,' he teased. She exhaled and leaned against him in silent thanks. She liked the sound of the term *our bedroom.*

'I was scared,' she confessed readily. 'I didn't know if Harry really wanted me to shoot him if he kept going or not, I thought I'd just do what came naturally.'

'No matter how bad things get, you do what you can, with what you've got, where you are,' he muttered, passing on wisdom he had learned himself, long ago. In truth, Hurley had watched her stare Urquhart down and had stood transfixed as she had done something most people couldn't.

And all that after the performance of a lifetime. She was indeed formidable. A life with her could prove very interesting, Hurley thought, and not for the first time since their night together.

At the car, Michelle supervised the freeing of Tomms. She let her remove the duct tape which she did carefully but not painlessly. Urquhart did as he was told. He could see the pistol on Michelle's belt and feared another confrontation if he rebelled. It was a good decision. They each removed their overalls and left them in a pile on the road with the hoods.

Sanderson moved in behind the wheel. Michelle retrieved Urquhart's watch from the plastic bag and handed it to him. She gave Tomms the bag with her handbag and shoes as she slid into the back seat. For what seemed like a long moment she looked Michelle in the eyes, two pools shining out from her balaclava. She thought those eyes were smiling and that a victory had been won. She was right.

She was smart enough to ask no questions though, preferring to keep her powder dry. She was at a loss as to what had happened, but something had. Something big. She had never seen Simon look as he did now; dishevelled, distraught and beaten. He was obviously traumatised and did not want to speak to her, or anyone.

She felt she would know the answers soon enough and her sixth sense told her it wasn't going to be good. She watched as Simon went around the front of the vehicle and got into the passenger seat. His shoulders slumped immediately and he too, remained silent.

25

AUSTRALIAN EMBASSY
DILI, UNITED NATIONS ADMINISTERED EAST TIMOR

....

February 2001

Sanderson drove fast and straight to the embassy. His long frame hunched over the wheel, he was malevolently silent and his face intent. For their part, his passengers did not speak either. When they arrived, that spell was broken.

'Look Roger, what the hell's going on?' Tomms demanded.

He rounded on her, angry and frustrated. 'Shut up Gabby. Just shut up. Everything will become clear.'

She baulked. It was like being slapped in the face. He had never spoken to her like that before, indeed she didn't think he had ever spoken to *anyone* like that before. She and Urquhart cooled their heels while Sanderson roused the security staff and the outer doors were opened. Sanderson was prepared, she noted grimly, he already had the master key for the inner door and used this and his card to gain entry.

Once he had gained access to the station, Sanderson motioned angrily for them to enter. It was eerily silent, the usual sound of machines and the background bustle of the staff going about their normal duties was missing. Strangely ominous. Sanderson switched the lights on, and the fluorescence brought stark reality to life. They all looked terrible, and each sensed it was only going to get worse.

'Into Gabby's office,' Sanderson growled, pointing the way. 'Open your safe Gabby, and no bullshit, get it open now.' She complied; indeed she was left with little option. 'Now hand me the mobile phone you used to contact *Hobbit*,' he ordered sharply.

Her face betrayed her growing understanding, and fear.

'Roger, I'm sure–'

'I said shut up Gabby, there'll be time for talk later. Hand me the phone.' She ferreted in the drawer and did as she was bid, giving Urquhart a venomous look as she did so. His eyes were downcast and would not meet hers. Sanderson snatched up the phone and checked he could access it before he placed it in his blazer pocket. 'Leave that safe open. Now, to Simon's office,' he snapped.

When they arrived there the procedure was the same, as they had both predicted.

'Hand me the documents from Marcelino Borges' culled file, and the recordings of Gabby's meetings with *Hobbit*,' he directed Urquhart.

'You fucking prick!' Tomms exploded, rounding on Urquhart. She was caught unaware as to how implicated she might be, and how much she had been betrayed. 'You kept copies of those tapes, you bastard! Was that your insurance policy if you couldn't control me, or needed someone else to blame?' She sneered vehemently, her eyes needle-points of hate.

Urquhart said nothing, and the blood drained from his face.

'Shut up both of you,' Sanderson barked, as Urquhart pushed the items reluctantly across the desk.

'Leave your safe open and get into my office, both of you, *now.*'

Sanderson sat them both at the small conference table.

'Now, this is how this is going to work,' he started angrily. 'You will both keep your mouths shut — throughout. I will play the recording of tonight's little adventure. I am doing this not to continue Simon's pain, even though I'm sure it will, but to ensure you both have equal access to what has been said, and at the same time know each other has also.'

With that, he reached forward and placed his micro-cassette recorder on the table and pushed the start button. Urquhart flinched, and in his mind he saw the light change to green. They sat for over an hour, captives in their own station. Once a safe haven, it had now become a prison.

Neither would look at the other, or at Sanderson, but all were perversely mesmerised by the tape. At times they squirmed, or bit their lips, or gasped. Hurley's voice, neutral and cold, carried to them and controlled them still.

Urquhart was re-traumatised as he listened to his own voice, but he now suffered the indignity of group humiliation as he was forced to endure it all a second time. To him it sounded like someone else's voice; weak, disembodied and far away, but his words were clear and incriminating. Sanderson was amazed at the power of the theatre just listening to the soundtrack, and found himself reliving each scene.

Tomms quickly realised what had happened while she was hooded. She brought none of the trauma and emotion the others two did to the table and, because of this, her mind was working better than theirs. But she also knew as she listened that the secret house she and Urquhart were building had been demolished before it was even finished.

Just this week they had been able to fight off the first assault, the first accusation, and with Sanderson's unwitting help too, which had been pivotal. But there was no evidence then and that wasn't going to happen again. Urquhart had said far too much and given them too much evidence to support it. He had also said things he couldn't have known if it really had been a fiction.

Tomms found the more she listened to the tape the less she could blame Urquhart for being tricked; she was clever enough to listen and hear how it had been done. She could not only hear the cold delivery of Hurley as interrogator; masterful, relentless and ruthless, but also the anguished cries of the tortured dummy in the background, and the responses of the harassed, humiliated and ultimately vanquished Urquhart.

But apart from Hurley, *who were they?* She heard a British voice while she was still hooded, not clearly, but a British man nevertheless. The only other voice she heard was at the car, the woman's voice had also been British. *Was that relevant? If so, how?* She had not seen any faces. *Had Urquhart?* She couldn't know, and she couldn't ask.

When the tape stopped, they were all silent, emotionally and physically spent. Sanderson stood up and retrieved the recording from the table.

'You are both fortunate I am not empowered to lock you up! Go home, both of you,' he said, his voice tired and embattled. 'Be back here at nine o'clock on Monday morning, *sharp*. Talk to no one here or at home about these events. I will have more information for you then. Do not return to my station in the meantime. In any case, you will find you have no access,' he warned as he threw the keys to the Pathfinder on the table and they skidded towards Tomms. 'Now, get out!'

The two of them trudged from the embassy as if in a dream, exhausted and beaten. Neither spoke to the other. Downstairs, Tomms got into the car and waited, but Urquhart ambled by with his hands in his pockets, like a sleepwalker, beginning the long journey home by himself. She watched him walk down the street before gunning the engine and speeding off towards the town.

26

....

February 2001

Harry sat at the centre of the long table in the courtyard. The team gathered around him, each with a steaming mug in front of them. Stay-at-home Bill had made hot soup and a platter of chunky sandwiches which they all devoured greedily.

Their herculean efforts were evident; they were all weary-eyed, their hair matted and their clothes grimy with sweat. But the buzz around the table was all jubilation.

'OK. First things first, and I'll keep it to a minimum. I know it's five o'clock in the morning,' Harry began glancing at his watch. 'And I know you're all tired. We achieved ezackly what we set out to achieve tonight. Fantastic effort, and well done to everyone. I am very pleased, as is Matt,' he said as he motioned towards Hurley. Hurley acknowledged with a nod and a tired smile.'

'So, good job. Let's get an update to tie things off. Lucy.'

'The take-down was without incident, Harry. The site is clean.'

'Michelle.'

'The interrogation site is clean Harry — we were never there,' she said with finality, shaking her head.

'Stan.'

'The Pathfinder was driven back to the Aussie Embassy. It was outside for an hour or so and then Hansel and Gretel came out. They didn't speak to each other that I know of. Sanderson stayed inside and the lights remained on. Gretel drove back towards the centre of town — very fast. I shadowed Hansel, who walked home, much the worse for wear.'

'Thanks. Howie.'

'The Doctor was no problem. He is now tucked up in bed. He said you owe him a bottle of very good whiskey.' Harry nodded knowingly, and smiled.

'Freon.'

'The van has been sanitised and returned to the unsuspecting owner. No problems.'

'OK, thanks for that everyone.' Harry summed up. 'As I said, a good job — no, a *great* job. But it isn't over yet.' The timbre of his voice surprised the group and they all looked up from their mugs expectantly.

'Merlin.'

'Thanks Boss. When they were captured earlier this evening, Harry had Toby remove Hansel's watch as part of the takedown. It was returned to him along with their possessions when they left the site. That watch is now an active audio transmitter and will remain so for about two weeks. It has a range of a few hundred yards, give or take, and the battery life is not very predictable either.' He allowed a moment for the information to sink in, and then pushed a small black recorder across into the middle of the table.

'This is a recording taken from the time they left the site. We shall be monitoring and recording twenty-four/seven to see what comes up.' Harry revealed, a tight smile on his lips and his eyes twinkling.

Despite their weariness, the team was immediately rejuvenated. They all knew what this might mean. Hurley was speechless and Harry caught his eye. There was an evil glint there and Hurley couldn't help but laugh inside. There was always another surprise with Harry, but where would this one lead?

'Thanks Merlin, first class,' said Harry. 'I don't have to tell anyone here that this will mean twenty-four/seven surveillance shifts as well. We must keep the receiver within just a few hundred yards of Hansel to exploit it, and we'll do that primarily from a vehicle. One saving grace is that Merlin has installed a receiver, from which we can download, in the lane at the back of Hansel's house. That means when he is home, it goes to the receiver, when he leaves home, we stay within the prescribed distance and the receiver in the vehicle will pick it up. I'm hoping that in his current state of mind he actually stays home, but you never know. Any questions?' Harry offered. There were none.

'You all need to be crystal clear as to why we are doing this. This isn't something clever I thought might be interesting and fun to do. It could serve us in two ways. Firstly, it will allow us to monitor to some extent how Sanderson is dealing with the problem he now has. By being privy to all the discussions he has with Hansel we will know if he is keeping his promise to us, or not. We might get lucky and have Gretel in on those discussions too. It might also provide us with information about the extent of Hansel's involvement and actions. We shouldn't be naïve enough for a moment to think he has told us the truth, the whole truth and nothing but the truth tonight. The fact is, we didn't have the environment or the situation where Matt could exploit some of the lines of enquiry. We have to be satisfied that he coughed as much as was needed, plus a little bit more, and that we have what we have. But if he is further involved with a third party, or with Marcelino Borges beyond what he would have us believe, we might have a chance to find out. And I will bet a lot of money that after what he has been through, if he can, he will contact someone. Any takers?' he challenged, daring the gods again.

There were none, just a table of tired smiling faces.

'OK. Merlin tells me the discussions inside the embassy tonight confirm Roger is behaving as he said he would, and the other two are, shall we say, estranged and suitably downcast. Critically, we know the evidence that Hansel alluded to in his interrogation has been acquired by Sanderson. There will be a meeting of all three at nine am on Monday, which means we have half a day to sort ourselves out because I want you guys back here at noon today. Except, of course, the first surveillance shift — which started five minutes ago. Any problems?' There were none.

Harry looked around with great admiration at them all. There was no one in that room that did not feel the warmth of pride Harry felt in them, including Hurley.

'Off you go then, and get some shut-eye… Maggie, could you stay for just a minute please?'

There was a general burst of noise as their chairs scraped on the stonework and the group made its way eagerly towards the stairs, and their beds. As the noise faded away Harry took his cue.

'You did a fantastic job tonight, Maggie. Much of our success pivoted on it, well done. As they say in the movies, it's a classic,' he smiled, watching her face.

She was beyond tired now; the past few weeks had been tumultuous for her in more ways than one, and Harry knew it. But he also knew he needed more from her. He knew already that if events developed in a certain direction, Maggie could have a big role to play. And it would be dangerous. She needed to be at the top of her game.

'Thanks Harry, it was a great team effort and I was glad to be part of it. As you say, there are no big parts and no small parts, there are only working parts.'

Harry chuckled at having his own mantra fed back to him.

'I know all that Maggie,' he said dismissively, 'but I also know ops, and I know rugby. A team might play well and win, but there's always a place for individual excellence. That was you this week. Thank you.'

'Thanks Harry, I loved it all,' she said, valuing his praise.

'Now, this new operation,' he said, 'and I stress as we move on it is a *new* operation. Accordingly, it means that Matt will not be briefed in.'

Maggie stiffened, 'I wouldn't say anything to Matt unless you said to Harry,' she said defensively, feeling her loyalty had been questioned.

Harry reached over and placed his hand over hers. 'Maggie, I know that. I just wanted you to be clear, that's all. You and Matt both mean a lot to me, you know that. And I know what you mean to each other, even if one of you hasn't quite worked that out yet,' he said mischievously, holding her gaze. Despite herself, she smiled, and the colour rose slightly in her cheeks.

'I don't yet know how this might work out,' he admitted, 'that's why I need options, and Matt doesn't need to know. He has to go back to the border tomorrow, and he has the FSG to run, and with it a million problems of his own. I don't want to add to his woes by having him think about things he doesn't need to, or to worry about you unnecessarily, OK?' He nodded solemnly, as did she in return. 'Now go and get some sleep, I have a feeling it will be a busy week for all of us.'

By the time Maggie mounted the marble stairs and crossed the landing to her room, there were little cracks of yellow light show-ing under some of the doors and in the background she could hear the soft sound of the showers running in the bathrooms and the dulcet tones of Merlin singing quietly.

She smiled to herself and opened her door, expecting to see the night-light on and Hurley there, waiting for her. But the room was dark and empty. After a flash of concern, she realised Hurley had probably gone to his allocated room next door to let her sleep.

While she was appreciative of such consideration, it wasn't what she had in mind at all. Instead she wanted the warmth and the strength of him, and to share what they had achieved together. She certainly didn't want to risk not seeing him before he returned to Balibo the next morning.

Quickly she went to the bathroom and showered; the warm water washing away the grime and the perspiration, but not the memory of the night. She towelled her hair quickly and shook it out. Donning her silk robe, she tip-toed silently along the landing to Hurley's room and opened the door.

It was dark within and as she crossed the floor to the bed, she could just make out Hurley's sleeping form. Standing, she undressed, leaving her robe on the chair with Hurley's clothes before she peeled back the cover and slid in next to him.

Hurley said nothing. Instead, he pretended to be asleep. She climbed in gently next to him and moved close, her arms embrac-ing him. She kissed his back lovingly as she snuggled into him, her damp hair cold and tickling the back of his neck.

'Go to sleep,' he mumbled, pretending to be more asleep than he really was.

'No,' she said, and laughed. It was a happy girlish sound like music, Hurley thought, and then he couldn't help but laugh too.

27

Australian Embassy
Dili, United Nations administered East Timor

February 2001

When Urquhart and Tomms arrived at the embassy on Monday morning, things had already changed. Their passes would not allow them entry, and they suffered the additional indignity of having to sign the visitor's book and wait for an escort.

When the station was advised of their arrival, Sanderson dispatched his most junior functionary to shepherd them upstairs. It was a sign of things to come, and they both sensed it. They were ushered upstairs into Sanderson's office and sat at the same table they had early the previous Sunday morning.

Their attempts at conversation with their erstwhile colleague were met with an awkward but frosty silence. They could smell coffee brewing in the machine down the hallway but were not offered the opportunity to partake. It was the beginning of the end, and they both knew it.

When Sanderson arrived, he dismissed their escort with a curt nod and closed the door. He sat opposite them, his coffee in front of him, further tormenting them.

'Good morning,' he opened formally. 'This is how this is going to work. Firstly, I will give you the party line. And when I say *party*, I mean the Head of Mission, Australia's Ambassador to East Timor, the Director General of the Australian Secret Intelligence Service, and me, Head of Station, Dili.'

He let his introduction hang, just for effect.

'All of what I say has been discussed and agreed by those parties,' he continued pompously. 'At the end, you may make any comments you wish, and they will be recorded.' He opened a notepad on the table in front of him and placed his silver pen diagonally across the page.

'Last Saturday night,' he began, 'I authorised a training activity in counter-interrogation for select members of my staff, namely you two. I had previously obtained approval from Canberra to do so.'

They watched Sanderson carefully, and both realised this was going to be a very clever stich-up. Not that either saw themselves as blameless, or that they might not deserve what was coming to them, but Sanderson had obviously been very busy.

It was true he had been a survivor over many years, and they had clearly underestimated him. A day and night of soul-searching had also brought each of them closer to the reality of their situation. Sanderson cleared his throat and continued.

'Quite unexpectedly during the training activity, as part of a complex interrogation strategy, certain compromising information was divulged. That information supported a previous, and very serious, accusation that an unauthorised operation had been run from this station. Moreover, it provided additional checkable information and material evidence to support the assertion. This evidence is in the form of the culled UNCIVPOL Serious Crimes Unit file of Marcelino Borges, and a mobile phone purchased with station funds — since exploited to confirm multiple contact with an unauthorised agent. Also, the recordings of meetings with that unauthorised agent, at which he was clearly directed to take illegal action; specifically, to kill certain AUSBATT agents. To this end, I have reluctantly presented these circumstances to the DG who has supported the termination of your employment from the service — with immediate effect. The HOM has also been informed. The weekly flight to Darwin leaves on Monday mornings. You will both be on next Monday's flight. You will continue on to Canberra where you will be met by a HR advisor from the service. This person will finalise all your administrative arrangements. In the meantime, for the remainder of today, and under supervision, you are both to hand over your case files to others in the station whom I will nominate. After that you can consider yourselves on gardening leave and without access to the embassy work areas. I already have your passports and I will have your travel arrangements sorted, and the details brought to your homes. You are to make yourselves available to me to cover off on any issues that come up as part of your handover, and the materials I am personally going through from your respective safes. Firstly, do you understand everything I have said?'

They both nodded in unison.

'Do you have any comments to make?' he asked.

'I think it unfair those discussions were taken without us present and able to represent our own interests,' Tomms said haughtily, with confected indignation as she sat ramrod straight in her chair. Her eyes were now blazed, and she held Sanderson's gaze, but it was brittle, and Sanderson had expected it.

'I will, of course, note that for the record,' he said perfunctorily as he picked up his pen and scratched it across the page. He looked up.

'Off the record, I would have thought a murder victim, or

an orphaned child perhaps, could claim some element of gross unfairness towards them, but not you two,' he spat, glaring at her. She averted her eyes guiltily.

'In any case,' he continued casually, 'should you wish to present yourselves as victims, or having been unfairly treated once you are back in Australia, the DG advises you to — and these are his words — *fill your boots*. You have no leg to stand on for a complaint via any avenue. Our legal advice is that if we were to examine the issue closely, there would be a *prima facie* case of conspiracy to murder that could be raised against each of you. If you want to go down that road, please feel free to do so. My reading of the situation is the Australian Government would prefer a quiet end to this, and so should you. You have potentially done enough damage to Australia-East Timor relations without exacerbating the issue. In any case, the DG may terminate the employment of anyone, without recourse, with whom he has lost confidence. You may be assured he has lost confidence in you both.'

'Who were those people the other night?' Urquhart queried lazily, clearly nothing to add to what had already been decreed, Sanderson noted.

'Trainers who specialise in that type of activity for our benefit. Let's just say there were… unintended consequences,' Sanderson said artfully.

'Why was Matt Hurley involved?' Tomms interjected, showing that she had evidently recognised his voice on the recording.

'Sergeant Major Hurley has a certain expertise in this area, as I'm sure you both now realise. I asked him to assist,' Sanderson lied smoothly. 'But in respect of Hurley, there is one aspect you should both keep at the forefront of your minds. Something you might like to mull over before you go off trumpeting that your human rights have been infringed. I have it on very good authority that it was Hurley's preference when this whole business first came to light that you both be eliminated — yes, killed for what you had done.'

They quickly looked at each other and then at Sanderson in horror, their eyes wide and their mouths agape. Tomms nervously pulled her long black hair back into a loose ponytail and then let it fall free. Urquhart shifted uncomfortably and was obviously affronted.

'That's totally ridiculous,' he blurted out, and then he realised what they had done, what *he* had done. He reflected it wasn't really ridiculous at all, and Hurley wouldn't be the first person in the history of the world to apply the old adage *an eye for an eye.*

'Is it?' Sanderson cut into his thoughts. 'The Matt Hurleys of this world take these things quite personally you know, and that sergeant was one of his. It's a relationship the likes of us will never quite understand. Moreover, they still teach a connection with their agents that we once did too, but that is now long gone — and with it some of our effectiveness I might add. They can be quite traditional in their approach but quite innovative and flexible too, that's why they can sometimes achieve things we can't,' he said cryptically, and let it hang between the three of them.

'And don't for a minute think Hurley doesn't have the means or the motivation, I assure you he most certainly does,' Sanderson warned, feeling the need to sell the product now it was off the shelf and on the counter. 'Fortunately for you both, I feel comfortable from information I have since obtained that your sacking will assuage his anger to the point where you will both escape with your lives. My advice would be to see this as a big win, because his kind can always be relied upon for one thing, to follow through on their obligations — as misdirected as we might think them to be.'

As he counselled them, Sanderson gave no hint that he believed his own life had also been in the frame, and that he needed to sell a win to his two wayward officers in order to ensure his own skin remained intact too.

28

CASA DILI

DILI, UNITED NATIONS ADMINISTERED EAST TIMOR

....

February 2001

Harry sat with Merlin and Toby in the ops room reading a newspaper; they were gathered to hear the recording of the nine am meeting at the embassy. There had been nothing of note from Urquhart's watch from early the previous morning as he had stayed at home alone. They heard dishes being washed and music playing; from the other noises they heard he probably got drunk and slept most of the day away. Nevertheless, the watchers maintained their vigil and the receiver in the lane did the job.

When the little speaker crackled into life, Merlin adjusted a small dial and Harry closed the paper. He folded it in half and laid it down for later. He took a long sip from his tea and listened, as did the others.

The quality was good; the voices sounded disembodied and there were other unidentified noises that came and went, but it was clearly audible. They listened intently as Sanderson laid down the law, and as the outcome Harry and Sanderson had discussed was unceremoniously dished out. Merlin turned the switch off with a click.

'Well,' Harry summed up, nodding slowly to himself, 'old Roger has certainly held up his end of the bargain by the sounds of it. We must have scared the living daylights out of him,' he said with a wry smile. The others chuckled.

'They're for the high jump alright,' agreed Merlin.

'Matt will be well chuffed with this outcome for sure,' Harry mused. 'It's ezackly what the doctor ordered. But the timing might be very helpful to us too. If Urquart is further involved, now that he knows he is to be sacked he might be more likely to contact others he is involved with. Thanks to the gods he also has a full week to do something before he's packed off back to Oz. Are we all hooked up to cover him, Merlin?'

'Aye, we have him covered at the embassy and if he goes home there's no problem. If he goes off with her or down into the town, the watchers will be on him.'

'OK, put someone on that and let me know as soon as anything interesting pops up,' he said, indicating towards the speaker.

Harry hummed to himself as he returned to the newspaper; there was a lot going on in his mind and some part of his brain was processing while he read. When he had finished, he picked up his mug and walked it through to the kitchen, running water into it and leaving it to dry on the wooden stand. For a moment he stood looking out the window at the quiet beauty of the grounds.

'Harry! Harry!' Merlin yelled, moving erratically through the house looking for him.

'In here!' he called from the kitchen. 'Keep your shirt on, me old son.'

Merlin's face appeared around the corner of the kitchen door, his face flushed and animated.

'Harry, you need to hear this. Urquhart went home and made a call from a cell phone.'

They hurried back to the ops room and Merlin connected

the speaker, while Toby was called and hurried in from outside. A little voice squeaked from the box; it was Urquhart. *'Bon dia, Senhor.'*

'Yes, I'm well, thank you. But there is a matter of some urgency. The meeting for Sunday week, we need to cancel that for security reasons — can we move it forward to this coming Sunday?'

'Yes, same place and same time, but this Sunday. I will be driving down from Dili.'

'Yes, OK. Same arrangements, same security.'

'Can you get… the sponsor there for the meeting?'

'Well, say it's important, there have been some changes outside our control, and we may have to revise our plan.'

'That's all I can say for now.'

'Yes, one thing. I've misplaced my passport. I would appreciate if the sponsor could facilitate my passage across the border. Please advise me if that isn't possible, but the matter is urgent.'

'OK. See you then.'

Merlin turned the switch and the speaker clicked off. They were all silent and looked at each other as the enormity of what they had heard washed over them. Even though they heard only Urquhart's side of the conversation, it was earth shattering from an operational perspective, and they all knew it.

'Yeees!' cried Harry finally in triumph. His hunch had paid off, and it wasn't going to be a wild goose chase for the team after all. Toby and Merlin nodded and grinned.

'Toby, get everyone together please and we'll have an update brief in an hour,' Harry directed, checking his watch.

He sat back in his chair, his eyes fixed like a hunter. He was certain he could smell blood now.

29

Casa Dili

Dili, United Nations administered East Timor

....

February 2001

As the team assembled there was an underlying feeling of expectation and excitement in the ops room. Harry couldn't help but feel it too.

'OK. Have a seat everyone,' he said, rubbing his hands together. 'I have an update on what's happened, and then I'll talk about where to from here.'

Harry was careful to measure his delivery. He knew from looking at the group that some of them had been raised from their beds, and others had been relaxing or doing other work. Stan and Rommel still had their tennis racquets with them. With this in mind, he went through the information and brought them all up to date on everything that was known, and particularly the implications of the latest mobile phone call.

'With what we have,' he explained, 'we assess the person at the other end of this call is likely to be Marcelino Borges. In the call, Urquhart also referred to a person he called "the sponsor". We don't know who this is either, but he has been asked to attend the meeting. We assess from the context this person is more powerful than Borges and could have higher militia, or even intelligence or government connections.'

He paused to allow the details to sink in. A ripple went through the group; eyes widened, and eyebrows were raised in appreciation, the excitement level going up another notch.

'We have been learning more about Borges since he first came onto our radar, and Maggie's agent *Stiletto* has done some great work tracking him, and even photographing him in the refugee camp at Atapupu, ironically, the same bloody day that Urquhart and Tomms were there. This presents a possible opportunity to predict where he will be, and at what time, and get ahead of the game. I say possibly because we simply don't know if Urquhart lied about that part. But we are going to take the chance and act on it, as if it is true. If it isn't and we come up blank, then we simply withdraw and await our next opportunity. Borges is fair game for us as a senior militia figure wanted for crimes against humanity, and if you need any extra incentive, you should ask Matt Hurley to take you on a tour of the Kissing House in Balibo,' he finished sombrely.

Maggie knew the story too, and she saw that Harry's eyes were saddened, but it was fleeting, and they quickly steeled to the task ahead.

'So, boys and girls, we are going to lift Marcelino Borges from the west and bring him here into UN detention.' He let his words hang for effect, to let them absorb, but it wasn't needed. Each of them just wanted to be part of it — *no big parts, no small parts, just working parts.*

'This is my intent,' Harry continued. 'Borges is the main game, and we go for him providing it is safe to do so. Whoever this sponsor is, we want him, or her, photographed. We want the conversation from those who attend that meeting. If the sponsor is a major government or intelligence player, then that is hugely significant from a counter-intelligence perspective. Also, under interrogation, Urquhart admitted it was Borges who first approached him, although he maintained the operation was his idea. I am beginning to doubt that. I consider it is at least possible someone more powerful is pulling the strings and they have let Urquhart think he is in control. In any case, what we get will be valuable to a variety of authorities. The complicating issue is that in order to achieve that, we need to be within a few hundred yards of that house. Any questions for now?'

'Harry, do you have any idea about the size of the team yet?' queried Lucy, as keen as anyone for a plum role.

Harry shook his head slowly. 'No Lucy, not yet.'

Harry felt their pain. Indeed, he had been them once upon a time. But there would always be other operations for those who might miss out. 'Toby will be the operational lead,' he announced. 'We will speak separately and then he will do some preliminary planning. We'll get back to you as soon as we can. We will continue to monitor Urquhart's watch to see if new information comes to light. We need to be responsive to any changes that might arise, so we need to maintain the watchers on station too. From that point of view, everyone will remain involved in one way or another, I can assure you,' he finished up, and smiled wickedly.

They all laughed. The lights of the fairground were in sight, and they all secretly hoped they would get a ticket on the main ride.

30

CASA DILI

DILI, UNITED NATIONS ADMINISTERED EAST TIMOR

....

February 2001

Harry had a brief word with Toby and then let him be. Toby quickly made a space for himself in the ops room and, with blank paper in front of him, began his task. It was routine at Casa Dili for the person chosen as the lead to be assisted by the others, as much or as little as they wished.

If Toby wanted coffee, it would be brought to him. If he wanted maps, or photos, or other information, these would also be brought to him. But he was not to be interrupted. It was Toby's style though, to do much of his own legwork. It gave him time to think, and time to put all the pieces of the puzzle together.

Harry certainly hadn't chosen Toby on a whim. He had watched the young man take the lead on the takedown of Hansel and Gretel and was well pleased. While Toby was a big man, he was trim and athletic. His amiable personality and pleasant looks belied his true mettle, and the grey that appeared prematurely in his dark hair gave him the air of someone older.

Toby was a Royal Marines commando, indeed he was the only team member not from the army, which was why the others ribbed him so relentlessly, as did Harry. But Toby was a deep well-spring of experience too, particularly for someone not yet thirty.

And there was something else. Harry knew in his heart that ten years from now, it was someone like Toby who would stand in his place. To be that person, there were certain rites of passage and what was to come might be one of those.

It was true that promotion to sergeant had come quickly for Toby, with all the gravitas that brings. But Harry also knew that upstairs in his room, a memento of a very different time had pride of place for Toby. Something not displayed boastfully but kept quietly as a reminder of his journey in the world, and the things he valued. It was a talisman from his past, and a standard he set for himself, and his future.

For sitting neatly on Toby's bookcase upstairs was the *kepi blanc* of a foreign legionnaire; the coveted white kepi earned by a teenage Toby in another life, and then many times over in his five years with the *2e Régiment* Étranger *de Parachutistes*, the Foreign Legion paratroopers, with whom he had trained in Morocco, Corsica and South America, and served in half a dozen African countries.

Toby was adept in the art of rural surveillance and Harry's discrete enquiries had uncovered something else; he had once been forced to survive alone for ten days longer than planned on a bleak rocky hillside in Libya, overlooking a terrorist training camp. Yes, Harry knew all their secrets and yes, Toby was a good choice.

Toby started with the maps and the photos, and when he did want coffee, he went to the kitchen and made his own. He was seen gazing out the window watching Stan and Rommel playing very bad tennis and smiling to himself.

In truth, he had quickly put the bones of a plan together, and then had gone about methodically putting flesh on those bones; accepting and testing this idea, rejecting another, and then considering some modification or alternative before he moved on to the next part of the problem.

By that evening Toby had enough for Harry. He had taken his dinner in the ops room and picked at it as he finalised his plan. Shortly after, he sought Harry out in the library.

For over half an hour, Toby talked, and Harry listened attentively. He did not take notes or ask questions along the way. Instead, he sat back on the Chesterfield sofa with his feet up and his hands behind his head and listened. Occasionally he closed his eyes.

As he did, he absorbed the plan; gave it structure and watched it work in his mind's eye. When Toby was finished Harry sat in thought for a few moments, slowly winding the longest hairs of his eyebrow around his finger as he looked out the window.

His own operational life had taught him there was rarely just one right way to do something; often there were many ways that could work, but there were always a few that probably couldn't, and these had to be avoided. Toby had found a way.

'That will work Toby,' he said finally. 'Good job. Let's develop that concept.'

Toby nodded in acknowledgement but knew the process was not over by a long shot.

'How did you choose the team?' Harry asked unexpectedly.

'Well, it has to be Maggie; *Stiletto* is her agent and they've worked together before. Maggie has also been to West Timor numerous times before and she is a trusted face. If we want to get the best out of *Stiletto*, then it's a no-brainer.'

Harry knew it to be true, but wanted to know the young man's reasoning, and wanted to know Maggie was the right choice for the right reasons.

'And Rommel?'

That position could have gone to a number of people, and no

doubt there will be disappointment,' he conceded. 'We have several who are rural OP trained but Rommel has another special skill I want in my back pocket.'

'Oh, what's that?' Harry quizzed, curious.

'He's a combat medic,' Toby said simply.

Toby's eyes met Harry's and held his gaze. They both hoped Rommel's extra talent would not be needed, but Toby was prudent to include it nevertheless. Harry couldn't fault his thought process on that score. The moment reminded them both of the uncertainty and danger that might lay ahead, but neither looked away.

'What about yourself?' Harry said, motioning towards him.

'I took a long look at the options Harry, and I think with my background it's best if I go. I'd also like to be there to manage anything out of left field. I will know the plan better than anyone, so I'm best placed to put it together, and to make good decisions if things go wrong.'

Harry smiled inwardly. It was what he had expected. Toby could have appointed someone else to lead the operation on the ground and coordinated it all from Dili, but that wasn't quite Toby's style, or Harry's for that matter and they both knew it.

'Now, the insertion; you've got Maggie going in with *Stiletto* in the NGO truck, the same one Borges will come out on. You and Rommel are inserting in a hire vehicle and then handing that on to Maggie for the Saturday night, is that right?'

'That's right. We'll go in at last light Saturday but there's nowhere to hide our vehicle for the time we're there,' he explained, as he selected a large photo of the house and its surrounds from among the material he had brought and passed it to Harry. 'The area is pretty bald. There are a couple of good options for our OP but nothing for hiding a vehicle. If it's in the area it will be found, and questions will be asked. Borges is a fugitive; he will be sensitive to any changes in his environment and we could lose our advantage if he's spooked. So, the vehicle will have to be taken away and brought back the following day to pick us up,' he summarised.

Harry looked at the photo and nodded appreciatively. It made complete sense.

'The only other way is to insert through the AUSBATT AO and go in on foot from the border. We're talking about six miles,' Toby suggested.

'No, that isn't an option,' Harry said firmly, shaking his head. 'This isn't a UN operation and they can't be complicit. It would compromise them, and it would be a diplomatic nightmare. We are not UN troops; we provide support to AUSBATT as an ally but we are not force assigned. In any case, it would be dangerous, and we couldn't do it covertly. We'd be picked up on the ground surveillance radar or even seen by the locals, who would report it to the FSG. There might also be SF ambush sites set to catch militia infiltrators coming the other way. Having said all that, if things do go to a box of frogs and you need to extract back *through* there, that's fine because the deed will already have been done. In that case we could RV on the border and I could get Matt to clear the way. If you're under the pump though, that will be the longest six miles of your lives,' Harry warned evenly.

Toby nodded solemnly and Harry watched his young sergeant.

'Let's be straight Toby, there'll be no possibility of an extraction by chopper. Its Indonesian sovereign territory and even my influence has its limits,' Harry said with a thin smile.

'I understand, Harry.' Toby smiled in return, but the message was understood.

'Now, about the options for lifting him,' Harry continued, 'I like the idea of talking him out of the house under the guise of needing help and I think you're right; *Stiletto* can manage that. I'm also happy with you and Rommel going over the wall, provided he isn't pre-warned, otherwise it's too dangerous. He holds all the cards in a situation like that. But I'll have to veto your third option of driving through the security gates,' he chuckled. 'As much as I'd like to be there to see that — or be at the wheel for that matter.' They both laughed.

'Seriously though, it gives him too much warning and it's too dangerous. He's in there, and he's on his own turf, and we know he's armed. He's also a killer. Remember, if you have to come home without him, that's the way it is. Your plan gives us a good chance of lifting him on our own terms without unnecessary risk we can't mitigate.'

'OK Harry, I'll go and put the finishing touches. Do you want me to let the team know?'

'No. Unfortunately, it falls to me to deliver the bad news.'

31

BATUGADE
UNITED NATIONS ADMINISTERED EAST TIMOR

....

February 2001

Maggie sat in the shade of a tall palm at the roadside and watched the truck come through the checkpoint. In a previous life the old truck had transported TNI soldiers, but it had long since been retired from military service. It had been sold as part of a job lot to one of the many NGOs operating in and out of West Timor, and it regularly ferried people and goods on the main route between Atambua and Dili.

Today it was empty, and the tarpaulin that usually covered the cargo section was folded neatly in the back, tied down with a large blue strap. It moved forward in the queue as another vehicle was processed, and then stopped. Moved forward, and then stopped.

With each move it crept closer to the checkpoint manned by the TNI on the western side and the UN on the eastern side. As the truck came abreast of the first checkpoint a soldier in the dark camouflage uniform of the TNI with his rifle slung behind him stepped forward. He went to the driver's window and spoke with the driver. After being handed the required papers and perusing them, he handed them back and waved the truck forward.

The boom gate opened and allowed it to pass. Empty trucks like this were of little interest to the TNI, they plied their trade regularly and were well-known, as were many of their drivers. The process was cursory at the UN checkpoint too, and after sighting the driver's papers it was again waved through.

Maggie watched all this from her vantage point and walked to the side of the road as the truck approached. It slowed to a halt next to her and the door opened; she climbed up into the cab and the truck moved off slowly into the town.

Batugade was like small third-world border towns the world over; dusty streets, buildings in poor repair and embryonic businesses on the main road that came and went as the locals tried to eke out an existence. The bottom line was people didn't go *to* Batugade, they went *through* Batugade.

The truck eased into the shade near a small cafe that had defied the odds and become somewhat of a semi-permanent fixture. Across the road a small and ever-changing line of vehicles came and went as people bought supplies for their trips east to Atambua, or west to Dili.

Others simply stopped for a quick break, or a coffee or Coke before they continued on. Toby and Rommel sat in the front of a mud-splattered grey Toyota Hilux and watched as the old truck stopped and Maggie climbed down from the cab.

When the driver emerged, Rommel spluttered and almost spilt his coffee. He recovered to the laughter of his companion.

'Bloody hell! Did you know *Stiletto* looked like that?' he blurted out incredulously.

'Not exactly,' Toby said softly, laughing. 'And just as well probably.'

'Did you even know *Stiletto* was a skirt?' Rommel asked, almost accusingly, as if he should have been told earlier.

Toby ignored the implication. 'She comes highly recommended, and she's important for this operation,' he summed up, but still smiling.

They both watched *Stiletto* as she walked alongside Maggie to the café. She was what is sometimes referred to as classically beautiful, and she moved with a graceful feline quality. Her almond shaped eyes were covered by her sunglasses, but it was easy for any observer to fill in the gaps; she had long, shiny black hair, skin the colour of honey and cheekbones you couldn't buy in the best New York clinic.

She was not overly tall but her long legs were encased in taut canvas trousers, shaping her femininity. She wore a loose denim shirt with three-quarter sleeves that was modest, but it did nothing to hide the perfection beneath.

Neither of her observers knew she was a *mestico*, a person of mixed race; in her case a Timorese mother and a Portuguese father but this would have been obvious to local onlookers. She had certainly skimmed the cream from both ends of her genetic pool. She wore two large sized golden earrings which gave her a slightly gypsy air as she walked.

The café was a run-down, ramshackle affair, and the cement walls needed a new coat of paint. But it had a reputation for serving good coffee and for being clean. The hard, wooden tables outside were regularly scrubbed with boiling water to keep the flies away. It was *Stiletto* who motioned to the owner for their order.

'So,' she said seriously, dropping her voice slightly. 'I am told that everything is prepared, just as you asked. But tell me *menina*, who is it we are snatching from the west?'

'I'll fill you in on all the details on the way down,' Maggie replied, pretending to be officious.

'It must be someone *very* dangerous, I think,' *Stiletto* pushed playfully.

'Now, why would you think that?' Maggie asked coyly.

'Apart from all the other arrangements and the short notice, I think Starsky and Hutch will be there to provide the muscle, to help us,' she summarised, smiling mischievously.

'Starsky and Hutch?' Maggie quizzed as her eyes wrinkled in confusion.

'The two *amigos* in the grey twin cab behind me, *menina*, they are yours, are they not?' *Stiletto* suggested. Just as she was now doing, injecting Portuguese words into her speech gave her a cosmopolitan air. 'The taller, dark-haired one at the wheel, very handsome. I think he would like to take me dancing, or maybe just… take me,' she said playfully, leaning sensually on the last two words. 'He is honourable and kind, but a killer nevertheless,' she continued without judgement. 'And his younger, fair-haired, and left-handed friend, who is funny and clever, but not a killer.'

Her eyes held Maggie's gaze. For not the first time Maggie was gobsmacked with her tradecraft. The insight it provided her was beyond anything Maggie had ever known, and it was what had kept her alive. As her handler, Maggie knew a great deal about *Stiletto*, but there was much she did not know.

She was a British agent from MI6 and enjoyed a fearsome reputation. She had received bespoke training and had worked in Portugal and Brazil before being sent back to her country of birth. It was from here she had been loaned to Harry's team and allocated to Maggie.

'Bitch,' Maggie said in faux judgement, chuckling. *Stiletto* smiled and reached down, tapping the frame of her sunglasses with a neatly manicured nail. She had placed these on the table with the lenses angled *just so* in the afternoon light to provide a mirror-like surface, affording her a clear view behind.

They both laughed. When *Stiletto* did so, it was throaty and raw, natural and uncaring. Men found it very attractive, indeed they found everything about *Stiletto* attractive. It was a valuable asset, but in no way was it the limit of her talents.

Maggie smiled despite herself. 'I'll fill you in on all the details on the way down, including our friends,' she said playfully.

They were silent while the owner brought two steaming espressos in glass cups to the table. He swept the US dollar bill *Stiletto* had left for him from the table and pocketed it.

'*Obrigado*, Senhorita.'

'*Nada*, Senhor Alfredo.'

'It's Borges,' *Stiletto* persisted softly when Alfredo had drifted away to another table, out of earshot.

All handlers know there are times to lie to their agents, sometimes for their own good, and sometimes for the greater good, but Maggie knew this was not one of them.

'Yes, but no more questions for now.'

Stiletto seemed happy enough with this, vindicated, and energised. They finished their espressos and walked back to the truck. The hottest part of the day was behind them now but without air conditioning it would still be a hot, uncomfortable couple of hours in the old truck, Maggie thought. At least she could rely on *Stiletto* for company; they were a good team.

'Tell me one thing, Josefina,' Maggie asked as they approached the truck. 'How did you know the fair one is lefthanded?'

'I didn't until you confirmed it, by not contradicting me. But if you watch people drink in the front seat of a car, if they sense they are not in danger they always use their gun hand to hold the cup, yes?' She flashed Maggie a winning smile. 'And you must tell me one thing also *menina*,' she countered. 'You must tell me all about this man who has put such a spring in your step.'

Maggie's eyes widened and she shook her head in wonder as she climbed up into the truck, knowing she had said nothing about the events of the previous week to anyone.

32

Indonesian Province of West Timor

....

February 2001

'Here we go then,' advised Toby, as he watched the old truck pull away and turn back towards the border. He would fall in behind them soon enough but not too close, and not so it looked as if they were travelling together. Both vehicles passed easily through the checkpoints; their papers were good and the girls smiled, and like girls everywhere, they easily passed muster and were waved through.

The grey Hilux, four cars back, got more scrutiny because it was a hire vehicle. Nevertheless, the papers describing the occupants as malarial research workers were in order, and there was no delay. No one in either vehicle thought it would be that simple on the way back.

They followed the coastal road as far as Atapupu, enjoying the smell of the sea, the cooling effect of the water sparkling off to their right, and the accompanying sea breeze. As *Stiletto* drove, Maggie stretched her legs up over the dashboard, her feet resting against the windscreen.

The old gearbox was putty in *Stiletto's* hands. She drove with practiced skill, the changes smooth and the sound of the engine

« 270 »

mesmerising. She kept a watchful eye on the road behind; at times she could see the grey Hilux, and at other times it virtually disappeared from view, only to re-appear like a cork that had bobbed back to the surface. There was no urgency, no panic, no change of speed from its driver.

'I see the dark haired one is confident also, not afraid to make a mistake. I like that,' she stated simply, largely keeping her thoughts to herself.

'His name is Toby if you must know,' Maggie explained with a smile, judging that Toby had certainly caught her eye.

'*Bonito* — that is his new code-name,' *Stiletto* announced.

'*Bonito?*' Maggie queried.

'Handsome,' she replied with a whimsical smile as she looked over, her arms astride the big steering wheel. And they both broke into laughter, the cabin filling with the happy noise of their shared conspiracy.

'And the fair one?' *Stiletto* enquired, once the noise had subsided.

'Rommel,' Maggie replied.

Stiletto nodded thoughtfully. 'Like the general?' she asked, her face curious.

'Just like the general. But don't ask, it's just English humour,' Maggie explained.

They stayed on the main road as it wound its way through Atapupu, and then headed inland towards Atambua. The truck was quickly surrounded by hills of a hundred shades of green, and with thick vegetation which had given life to small villages, built out to the side of the road.

As they passed each one, the mixed smells of livestock and decay, hearth cooking and kerosene found their way into the cabin through the open windows. Maggie found it strangely comforting. They chatted easily, always comfortable in each other's company as the miles quickly passed beneath the wheels.

Before long they were driving through the large sprawling town of Atambua. At first, they kept to the main road, the dirty dusty streets of the town leading off to the right and left, a hotch-potch of houses, factories and large government buildings lining the route, all of which looked to have been built without rhyme or reason. The colourful bustling crowd went about their business, noisy cars choked the air with fumes and motorbikes zipped in and out of traffic, their horns tooting and blaring.

Maggie watched them all, but none paid the truck or its occupants any heed. At the point nominated by Toby, they left the main road and headed west towards Tullamalae. They wound their way through narrow streets and lanes where the vegetation was up to the roadside and tracks led to houses or small villages now set further back from the road.

There were few other cars travelling in either direction but when one did pass by, they raised their hands in greeting and blared the horn as was the custom. On a chosen, isolated stretch of road the truck down shifted and slowed to a stop, the engine still running. Maggie walked back along the roadside knowing the Hilux would soon appear.

When Toby and Rommel arrived, they quickly donned their rucksacks, spoke briefly with Maggie and then melted into the vegetation. *Stiletto* thought they were dressed like hikers, but were soldiers again before they passed from view, watching them in the rear-view mirror. Maggie climbed into the driver's seat and flicked the lights.

The vehicles moved off as a pair now and a minute down the road they passed the white cement house trimmed in blue and gold, the house where Borges was hiding; the house where everything would happen tomorrow. Each glanced briefly as they passed by but there was nothing to see, nothing to tell them what was happening inside, or even who might be there.

As the darkness engulfed the forest, Toby and Rommel made their way stealthily towards the location Toby had chosen as their hide. They moved slowly and deliberately, skirting the house from a safe distance and keeping it on their left-hand side. At one stage they saw a light in the house through the trees and squatted on the forest floor, listening.

But they heard nothing and moved on. Around them, the sounds of the early night carried to them. Here and there a bird squawked and far away a dog barked, but otherwise it was only the reassuring buzz of the insects.

They walked on silently, and alone. Within the hour the forest thinned, and they were out on open ground and moving up the escarpment at the rear of the house. They found the thicket of bushes Toby had chosen that overlooked the house, the one that would allow them to look down into the compound surrounding it. The one close enough for them to hear the voices inside through Urquhart's watch.

Maggie and *Stiletto* drove on into the night, the beams of their headlights playing around erratically in the darkness of the forest. Finally, Maggie saw the red stop lights of the truck flicker up ahead and the orange indicator burst into life.

Stiletto turned off and led them up a bumpy winding track, the headlights struggling to make sense of the world around them as the path ahead and the surrounding forest was intermittently illuminated, and then plunged back into darkness.

At the end, unseen hands opened the gates in readiness and when both vehicles moved into the safety of the floodlit yard, the gates closed behind them, the hum of a diesel generator in the distance the only sound once the engines were stopped.

Toby and Rommel settled silently into the undergrowth, deep

within the thicket they had chosen. They set to work; making ready their kit, checking another time that the radio and walkie-talkie were switched off. The last thing they needed was an unexpected transmission booming out on the night air.

They checked as best they could that when the light came, they could not be seen and then they ate hard rations washed down with a flask of lukewarm tea.

Then they slept, back to back and head to toe against each other with their weapons close at hand, knowing they were in the enemy's land. They would wake in the dawn, and then the test they had set for themselves would begin.

Maggie watched as the old couple gathered *Stiletto* into their arms. On the trip down Maggie had listened in wonder to the story of where they were going and who she would meet. The man was *Stiletto's* uncle, her father's brother, and Portuguese. He was tall and wiry with a pleasant and proud face. His hair was wavy and grey, as was his well-kept moustache.

He wore a soft linen shirt and trousers, with canvas shoes. The woman was Indonesian. She was small and graceful, and her skin was dark and smooth. She wore a striking floral skirt that touched the ground and her long black hair was bound in matching material.

Maggie knew they were both clandestinos; veterans of the secret war that had worked to free East Timor, and that they had given their son in the long campaign.

'I am Migel Pires and this is my wife Susanti, welcome to our home. Any friend to our dearest Josefina is a friend to us,' Migel said as he approached Maggie, his hands outstretched to take hers. When he did so, his hands were warm and strong. Just like him, Maggie thought. He kissed her formally, alternating to each side of her face as he did so, before he stood back. 'All is in readiness, Senhorita Margarida.'

Few people — except some in her own family — called her *Margaret* anymore. She smiled, liking the new, Portuguese version. He spoke in English for her sake and she was grateful. While it was subtle, in reporting to her he also acknowledged her status and that what he had done, he had done for her. Maggie knew that *Stiletto* had arranged this.

'We will pack the truck in the morning, and I will show you the special rug,' he said, with a twinkle in his eyes that Maggie knew the years had not dimmed.

'*Obrigada*, Senhor Migel. Whatever we achieve tomorrow, will only be because of you and your family.'

He beamed and gave what Maggie now realised was the family trademark smile. 'Come, let's eat, you must both be starving.'

33

....

February 2001

Toby woke with a start in the pre-dawn chill and listened. He heard nothing of concern. The crowing of an early rooster carried to him across the hills and the urgent movements of the smaller birds around him were growing with excitement as the dawn beckoned.

The faint, pleasant smell of wood smoke wafted in the air. He poked Rommel in the back and then pulled on the green coveralls from his rucksack. He eased himself out of the hide at the rear, contouring the ground and taking care not to break the line of the thicket.

When he was free, he crawled down the escarpment into dead ground and waited for the sun to rise and fall across the hide. The day dawned cloudless and the sun's new rays danced across the escarpment, eventually striking the thicket.

Toby viewed the hide from various angles and was pleased; he returned using the same route and wormed his way back inside. They had chosen well, he reflected, even though the work was done largely from maps and aerial photographs. In the past this had caused some of Toby's biggest headaches but today, they were blessed.

By mid-morning the humidity within the hide had intensified; the greenery surrounding them sucked the heat in. Thankfully, it shielded them from the direct blast of the sun but they both sweated profusely. They knew they were secure; the small birds within the thicket chirped and had now come to accept their new visitors. They popped around them, occasionally sitting on them or their kit.

They rested between spells, watching the house and the surrounds, taking turns with the binoculars. It was the car horn that first alerted them. They heard a vehicle pass on the road to their right but thought little of it.

When it stopped at the house the driver sounded the horn, loudly, and just once. A small, rat-faced man wearing a grimy t-shirt walked from the house and opened the gates. He wiped his nose on his forearm as he waited sullenly for the black Mercedes C180 sedan to drive inside before closing the gates behind it.

Toby watched through the binoculars, with the faint clicking of the shutter in the background as Rommel worked the camera with its long lens. He captured everything — Rat-face, the car, the registration plate, and finally, the man they presumed was probably the sponsor.

He was an older man in his mid-fifties, Toby reckoned, almost certainly Indonesian. He carried himself with confidence; like that of a successful businessman. He was small and neat, and he wore a navy-blue blazer with gold buttons that caught the sun, and beige trousers, both of which were tailored for him.

The collar of his crisp white shirt was open and beneath it, the hint of a gold chain loose across his chest as he walked. He did not speak to Rat-face who stood off to one side and made no attempt to engage him in conversation. Instead, he walked directly to the house and was lost from view.

'Wow, did you get all that?' Toby whispered.

'Yeah, no problems. He looks impressive — like me in another life, rich and powerful,' Rommel summed up for both of them. 'And that car is last year's model,' he added approvingly, being the car enthusiast that he was.

They could do nothing more, so they waited and sweated, and drank; Toby used skills he had learned in the Foreign Legion and sipped small amounts of water, which he held in his mouth for protracted periods before swallowing slowly, Rommel guzzled incessantly when he felt the need.

As each plastic bottle was emptied, they used it to urinate in, and then scooped out a hole in the earth and buried it, rather than carry them all away with them. Carrying them in had been hard enough.

They actually heard Urquhart before they saw him. Faint intermittent sounds of music drifted into Rommel's ear and he reached over and tapped Toby's arm.

'He's punctual if nothing else. Glad he's got the car radio on,' he whispered.

Toby took the offered earpiece and listened. Nodding, he checked his watch. The code-word that Urquhart had crossed the border at Batugade had come through to them on the radio over an hour before, so he was not unexpected.

Toby noted the quality of the signal from the watch was much better than he had expected; he had high hopes the decreasing proximity and the quiet house would make it even better. He handed the wire with the attached earpiece back to Rommel and trained the binoculars on the approach road. Merlin would be overjoyed at the performance of his toys.

As they watched, a silver 4WD came into view. It caught

the sun momentarily and glared, temporarily blinding them. It slowed and stopped in the area they had anticipated, and the driver stepped out and stood by the car. It was Urquhart, in soft trousers and a casual cream shirt and they both recognised him at once. He wore sunglasses and a dark baseball cap, and he waited by the side of the car, pretending to read a map.

Inside the yard, a slim figure with an angular head and unkempt hair appeared. At once their hearts leaped. It was Borges. Now they knew he was there, and the next part of the operation could go ahead, provided a few pieces of the puzzle fell into place.

Rommel worked the camera again, missing nothing. Toby watched as Borges rolled an oil drum over to the far corner and climbed on to it with some difficulty. He peered over the wall. Borges watched Urquhart and the car, and he watched the road, looking for something out of place, someone who didn't fit.

He was especially attentive when the figure began walking up the road towards the house, knowing this was the time he was most likely to see something move in response. But the area was desolate and when he was satisfied, he ambled over and unlocked the gate, and waited.

As soon as Urquhart arrived at the gate, Toby and Rommel had a running commentary, listening as they watched.

'*Botarde*, Senhor Marcelino, I see that the sponsor has made it,' Urquhart said, gesturing towards the Mercedes.

'*Botarde*, Senhor Simon.' Borges nodded and they shook hands. Borges secured the gates and they walked up the path to the house together.

Inside, but now unseen to Toby and Rommel, the three sat around a low table with a fan circling overhead. Urquhart helped himself to a glass of water from the ice-water jug on the table and wiped his brow.

They spoke English for Urquhart's benefit, but the listeners were just as pleased. *Thanks be to God*, Rommel thought as he lifted his eyes skyward.

'I'm glad you could come, Rio,' Urquhart opened in his smooth manner, seeking to take control.

The sponsor ignored him. 'What is so urgent and what are these security reasons you speak of, Simon?'

'Well, that's the thing, you see,' Urquhart continued, wrong-footed slightly, 'I have been moved back to Canberra at very short notice, due to fly out next Monday in fact, so I think we need to re-think how the project might work.'

The sponsor contemplated this, but his dark eyes revealed nothing.

'Why are they moving you at such notice, is there anything I need to worry about?'

'No, not at all,' Urquhart soothed. 'But if we continue as we are, I shall have to identify someone who can take the project over, without anyone becoming aware. It will take time.'

'What about the woman?'

'Ah, some bad luck there. She is being returned also, part of a bigger, service-wide reorganisation I'm afraid.'

'I don't like such coincidences, Simon,' the sponsor said evenly, his eyes narrowing. 'How do you propose continuing this from Australia? How do you hope to re-establish Marcelino's credentials and make him attractive enough for the Australians to accept him from there?'

Urquhart had not planned for such defensiveness; he knew there would be a considerable amount of money to be made over the future Timor Gap negotiations and treaty, and he wanted to be part of it. He had thought they did too, and that their greed would trump any intelligence victory. He was beginning to think he may have read them incorrectly.

'Have you destroyed the dossier of Marcelino's involvement in pro-Indonesian activity?' the sponsor asked unexpectedly.

'Yes,' Urquhart lied, swallowing hard and sweating, but not from the heat.

The sponsor locked eyes with him.

'I understand from my people that you and your assistant have been terminated from your service and are returning to Australia, so what assistance can you now be? Not only will you be in Australia, you will not have access to the people we need.'

Urquhart was shocked at this revelation but tried to retain his composure. *How the hell did he know that? He must have people on the security staff at the embassy, for Christ's sake.*

Urquhart recovered quickly. 'I can control people inside the service from the outside,' he boasted, unwittingly confirming the truth of what the sponsor had just said. 'Let's just say there are things I know that would encourage people to cooperate and work towards our goal. You can be assured I would be loyal to our joint interests, even considering these changed circumstances,' he finished smoothly.

The sponsor smirked, his white teeth forming a perfect line across his dark face. His eyes remained expressionless.

'Like you have been loyal to your own country?' he laughed mockingly before he went on. 'I think we may have run out of options for you and you now have little to contribute.'

With this he drew a handgun from inside his blazer and levelled it at Urquhart. It was a Colt snub-nosed revolver; a small neat handgun now held in the small neat hand of a very ruthless man. 'Indeed, I might be worried that you would pass on information against me or my interests in order to help yourself.'

'Wait–' Urquhart implored, his hands held out, palms forward. He had not seen this coming, and in the end his naivety had been his undoing. The sponsor said nothing more and simply fired once, hitting Urquhart in the chest. The blood stain spread almost instantaneously, and Urquhart fell back in the chair and lay still, his eyes staring blankly towards the ceiling.

It could have been two gunshots; the first arrived via the wire into their ears, the second an instant later, the report of the real shot carrying to them from the house. They were both stunned and turned to look at each other.

'I think they've just shot Urquhart,' Rommel said disbelievingly.

Inside the house, the small man walked over and shot Urquhart again, this time in the centre of the forehead. It was a kill shot, but it wasn't needed.

This shot was also heard in the thicket, and it echoed like the first.

'You better believe it,' said Toby. 'Keep watch and keep listening.'

There were three voices in the ensuing conversation; it was in Indonesian and from the tone, the sponsor was calling the shots.

'Damn!' cursed Toby, 'We'll have all this later on record, but it isn't much use to us now.'

As they watched, Rat-face rushed out and opened the gates, running up the road to retrieve Urquhart's vehicle. As quickly as they could manage, he and Borges loaded Urquhart's body into the luggage compartment of the vehicle which they backed up to the house.

A large bloodstain was clear on the front of Urquhart's pale clothing and his face was chalky white, except for the blood stain on his forehead, which had trickled down his face.

Rommel captured it all, the camera clicking incessantly. Finally, they placed an old blanket over Urquhart's body and shut the rear door. Toby and Rommel heard nothing more, the watch was now locked in the car. When the sponsor reappeared, he calmly got into the Mercedes and drove away in the direction he had come from.

Rommel got this on film too, and their attention was only drawn back to the house by the sound of Urquhart's car starting. It burst from the compound and out onto the road towards Tullamale.

'Just a driver visible inside, must be Rat-face,' Rommel said, as they watched Borges close the gates and walk back inside.

They stared at the house in stunned silence for a brief moment before Toby reacted.

'That's us then, we're on. Borges is alone now, we've got him.' He began putting the kit away in his rucksack, motioning for Rommel to do the same. 'Get Maggie on the walkie-talkie,' he said urgently. 'Tell her to stand by, we're moving to our final positions. We should be there in ten minutes and we'll call her in.'

34

Indonesian Province of West Timor

....

February 2001

It was the unmistakable aroma of bacon and eggs cooking that pulled Maggie reluctantly from her slumber. At first, she thought it was a dream but quickly realised where she was and it was real. There were other morning smells too, and equally enticing; freshly baked bread, and coffee. *Stiletto* was already up and dressed, and she knelt next to Maggie's bedroll to rouse her.

'An English breakfast for an English guest,' she said brightly, showing no nervousness about the day ahead. But Maggie saw she was already dressed for it; she was wearing brown riding boots, the leather soft and nourished, under her canvas trousers and the gold earrings of yesterday were gone, replaced with more practical studs.

She had already donned a wide leather belt at her waist which was partially obscured by her loose white blouse. Her long dark hair was held back tightly in a ponytail.

'Mmm. That smells delicious,' Maggie murmured. 'Migel and Susanti have gone to so much trouble to make me welcome. I'm very grateful, you know.'

She was too, for everything. *Stiletto* beamed. In Portuguese culture, it was important not just to be a good host, but to be recognised as one too.

'You have five minutes, *menina*,' she commanded playfully as she tapped her watch and then disappeared out the door.

It had been a night Maggie would always remember fondly. Hurley had told her there were times on operations that stayed with you forever and made your life rich. They tended to be a crazy blend of the most amazing times, times you would split your sides laughing about later, and sometimes there were the dangerous times.

But it was mostly about the people you shared those times with. She knew now he was right and why he treasured his own memories so much. Susanti had prepared a sumptuous chicken stew the previous evening, thick with flavoursome gravy and root vegetables; and they had washed it down with a tasty wine Migel had made himself from wild fruits of the forest.

It was a Portuguese specialty, he said, his eyes twinkling. Afterwards they had relaxed on the old leather sofas, comfortable with the thick colourful blankets wrapped around them against the chill of the mountain air. They talked and listened to Migel play his guitar by the fire, his long artistic fingers caressing the strings and stirring the soul of the instrument, and the hearts of his listeners.

And, after much coaxing and laughing, *Stiletto* agreed to sing, which she did with the voice of an angel making the eyes of her uncle Migel moist with tears.

After a sumptuous breakfast, Migel shepherded them outside into the compound. Maggie stared at the truck and was immediately overwhelmed, and somewhat embarrassed. While she had slept, unseen but trusted hands had loaded the truck with all the props they needed to get back across the border.

There were tables and chairs of all kinds, bed frames,

mattresses and packing boxes, and other bric-a-brac, all piled high and tied in place. Indeed, it looked exactly like the dozens of NGO trucks that passed through the check points every week, all carrying the household goods that were needed by the thousands of returning refugees. So, the truck looked exactly like it should.

But Maggie had no need to feel embarrassed. Migel and his helpers had wanted to do this, needed to do this. And it was their task, given to them by *Stiletto*. As members of the old clandestino network, their secret tasks now came much less often, and in truth, not at all.

This was their day back in the saddle, even though they would never know the reason behind the task — and none would ever ask — they had gone about it with relish. *Stiletto* had also acted as a cut-out. The secret helpers knew her and her uncle but had never seen Maggie before; there was no knowledge of her or her role in the task and *Stiletto* had engineered it so. For Maggie, and for herself.

Migel smiled sheepishly. 'You like, Senhorita Margarida?'

'Migel, it looks fantastic,' she beamed. 'Thank you so much, and please thank your people. But you should have called us to help,' she scolded him playfully, as she went to him and embraced him warmly.

'Come, look at this,' he said excitedly. 'It has been made by a dozen loving hands.'

With this, Migel led them both to the front of the truck and dropped the side frame. Reaching up, he pulled on a large roll of carpet and wiggled it out onto the ground. It was evidently not as heavy as it looked. They all gathered around.

When he unrolled the carpet, a wicker capsule, like a long birdcage, was revealed. At each end, plugs of carpet representing the rolled edges had been meticulously sewn in place to hide the capsule and make the carpet roll look solid, and normal. It was into this capsule they would bundle Borges and smuggle him across the border, and the dimensions had been given to the secret workers to ensure the correct fit.

Into the capsule, Migel had already placed the compressed air bottle and the attached face mask, duct tape and cable ties they would need. Maggie was speechless. She had been assured by *Stiletto* that the product would be *perfeito* — perfect. In truth it was a work of art and it exceeded her wildest expectations.

She smiled broadly in appreciation and they all clapped to celebrate the success. While she trusted *Stiletto* and had tried to put her worries aside, it was in her nature to think detail and it had weighed on her mind. She had a newly found confidence everything would go well.

Stiletto clearly wanted to linger after they had restored the truck, and Maggie knew why. In their plan, Borges would see *Stiletto* and would live to potentially pass that information on to others. They both knew it would be too dangerous for her to return to West Timor, and this could easily be the last time she would see her family.

Maggie let it be, and they drank coffee and laughed while they talked in the shade of the verandah, savouring every moment. But by late morning, they needed to be on the road. It was *Stiletto* that finally prompted the move, and after gathering her Tio Migel and Tia Susanti in her arms she turned away, her cheeks wet with tears.

Maggie embraced them too and shared their pain. She thanked them again for all they had done. These two had played such an important part, and any success would be theirs too. *No big parts, no small parts, just working parts.* The vehicles set off down the same track that had brought them the night before with the truck leading.

Stiletto did not look back; it was not her way. Maggie waved from the Hilux and sounded the horn merrily, for both of them. Once they were back on the main road the travelling was easy again. There were few cars on the road, and they wound their way back through the hills towards their target.

The previous night they had spotted a derelict *Pertamina* service station and assessed it as a good place to lie up and wait for the call from Rommel. They pulled off the road there and hid the vehicles from view, sitting in the cab of the truck together, waiting.

'You will see them again, I'm sure,' Maggie consoled her, but she was unsure how this might happen. Their work was not always predictable, which they both knew.

'If I can, I will,' *Stiletto* said philosophically. There were no tears now, just the sadness of parting in her eyes.

When the walkie-talkie crackled into life, Rommel's voice told them he and Toby were moving to their final positions. They looked at each other and nodded.

'Are we good?' Maggie asked, the coach now with her head cocked and challenging her premier athlete.

'We're not just good, we're brilliant,' *Stiletto* replied in her very best posh English accent, mimicking Maggie. They both laughed. It was their little ritual each time before they went into the belly of the beast.

Maggie looked into her eyes and could see she was focused and determined. She was ready. Maggie returned to the Hilux and the two vehicles were again on the move, this time Maggie leading but travelling more slowly.

This tactic was used to minimise any time they needed to be stationary at their next planned stop, which would be about a mile short of the house. Here they would drop the Hilux and await Rommel's final call that would set everything in motion.

Maggie timed it almost to perfection, and they were stopped only a few minutes after she had climbed into the truck when the walkie-talkie crackled again. She slapped the dashboard in triumph. Toby and Rommel were in position and it was show time.

Maggie watched as *Stiletto* loosened her hair and shook it out gently. Straightening her blouse, she carefully pulled it taut across her breasts. She left the top button enticingly undone and the collar rakishly unfurled, creating a splash of cleavage to die for.

From her backpack she pulled a red lipstick and made a small mark on her fingertip. This she rubbed gently into her lips, leaving just a tease of colour and bringing them to life. *My God, she is in the wrong job*, thought Maggie. She turned and grinned at Maggie. The truck burst into life and they were away, the clock was now ticking.

35

February 2001

Stiletto brought the truck to a halt near the house; parallel with the front wall of the compound but close to the corner where they knew Toby would be in hiding. She and Maggie walked the short distance to the gates together. Their intention had been to call out from the gates and lure Borges there, but to their surprise and delight they found the gates were closed, but not locked.

Maggie looked at *Stiletto* and they read each other's thoughts. They opened the gates and walked up the stone-lined path to the house. Rather than mount the few steps to the house they called out to lessen any perceived threat.

'Hello!' *Stiletto* called out melodically and in a friendly manner. There was no response. Maggie had a sensation they were being watched; *good, he will certainly like what he sees.* They knew Borges spoke English and planned to use that so Maggie could follow what was being said.

'Hello!' *Stiletto* called out again in a playful sing-song fashion. This time, they heard footsteps inside and the door opened. It was Borges. He was of medium height and slightly built. His hair was black and greasy, although it looked freshly combed. His clothes seemed too large for his frame, both his trousers and his shirt, which was worn lose, tended to hang on him.

His shoes were brown and scuffed and did not match his clothes. *Stiletto* noticed the unnatural fit in his waistband, and she knew there was a gun or a knife hidden there.

'Hello, what can I do for you two… ladies,' he said smoothly in his thickly accented English.

Meanwhile, his eyes scanned them both, taking everything in, assessing. They knew he was checking them and the context; they thought he had probably heard the truck and seen it come to a halt from the upper floor and was making a judgement he was safe.

But his decision was dictated by opportunity, and lust as they knew it would be. Finally, his eyes settled on *Stiletto*, but not in appreciation. Instead, his eyes were predatory, and he undressed her in his mind, as they knew he would.

Like all women, *Stiletto* knew but she was practiced and pretended not to notice. He didn't know, but the hunter had already become the hunted.

'Our truck has some problem,' she said with her winning smile and a hint of vulnerability. 'We hoped you might be able to help us.' She delivered this with just the right tone of playfulness, knowing his lizard brain would process it as her desire for him.

'Of course, let me see what can be done,' he offered expansively and smiled, but it was not a kind smile. It was cruel and exposed his discoloured teeth. *Stiletto* knew he was brutal and greedy, that he was a killer, and that he did it for fun.

He moved down the stairs and stood between them looking from one to the other, before his eyes returned to *Stiletto*. She did not miss a beat and flicked her hair slightly, accentuating the line of her neck and cleavage as she began walking away, knowing he would surely follow.

She could sense he wanted to touch her. He was already close, and she could smell sweat and the cheap *Kretek* cigarettes on him. She turned to engage him as they walked, and his eyes told of everything he wanted; her eyes held his and told him she might let him do anything he liked.

As Maggie turned around to fall in behind them, she felt a light shudder of fear and stopped, uneasy. It was something she could not describe, and nor had she experienced it before. Borges and *Stiletto* continued to walk ahead and disappeared around the corner of the gate.

They were still close; she could hear *Stiletto's* hypnotic voice caressing her prey as she closed in, leading him towards the trap that waited. Maggie felt compelled and she slowly turned back and looked towards the house. But there was nothing.

Dismissing it, she shook her head and moved to make pace and catch them up. As she turned away, a rat-like face edged around the door frame, and a beady emotionless eye watched her walk away. His attention was drawn to the outline of the pistol under her shirt, safe in the small of her back, or so she thought.

Rat-face knew then his boss had been tricked. Time was critical. In a simple movement, he quickly stepped into the doorway, took aim with his own handgun and fired. Maggie heard and felt it as one. She was propelled forward by the force of the round as it struck her in the back and she fell, face first onto the rocky ground.

Dazed, and with blood already seeping around her, she battled to stay conscious. In her head she heard Hurley's voice from far away, gentle but persistent — *do what you can, with what you've got, where you are.* She struggled to grasp her pistol and rolled onto her back.

Her hand was already warm and slick with blood, but she held it, just, before she heard another shot from the doorway, and tensed. He would kill her now.

But she was not hit again. She raised her own weapon from

the lying position and her vision danced on the small target framed in the doorway. *Centre of seen mass, centre of seen mass,* she remembered from her training. With the last strength she could muster she steadied and took the shot, and then fell into blackness, the pistol falling gently from her hand and the life draining out of her.

Stiletto and Borges had walked only a dozen steps beyond the gate when the first shot rang out. Borges was quick — *Stiletto* had to credit him — and he reached instinctively for his own gun, but it was a mistake. With his arm across the front of his body and his elbow up, *Stiletto* easily smashed his larynx with the side of her hand and unbalanced him, pushing him heavily to the ground and smacking the back of his head as he fell.

The gun clattered free and in a flash she was on him, her knee driving into his sternum and taking the last of his breath away. The long sinister blade had been drawn like metal lightening from its hiding place at the back of her waist-belt and was now poised to take his life away.

'If you make one small move, *serpenta*, I will gut you with pleasure,' she hissed through gritted teeth as she locked the cold, merciless eyes.

Borges was used to getting his own way, particularly with women. He was not used to being insulted and called a snake, but he was a pragmatist — he didn't want to end up dead like one either. He was dazed and he swallowed hard and repeatedly, his large Adam's apple moving up and down as he gasped and attempted to recover use of his throat.

All the while the razor point of the long blade pushed in on the skin over his jugular. He could feel his own heartbeat against the tip of the blade.

'Put your arms behind you, one at a time,' she commanded. His eyes held hers but he could see no weakness there, and a lot of hate; a wrong move would be the end, and he knew it. He complied reluctantly and was helpless with her weight pressing down on him.

What happened? Has Maggie been hit? Her mind raced, and then the realisation hit her — there must surely have been someone else in the house.

'Maggie! Maggie!' she called desperately towards the gate, but there was no response. She looked back towards the gates. At the sound of the first shot Rommel had sprinted from his hiding place around the corner and dashed through the gateway with his pistol drawn.

Immediately, a second shot rang out. Transfixed, she watched Rommel stagger back through the gates, his face drained, his head and fair hair awash with blood. He fell backwards on the ground and his foot twitched, and then he lay still.

She turned to the sound of running feet. Toby was moving quickly towards her from the other corner but not sprinting. His movements were measured and efficient, his resolve evident. He jumped over her and Borges to retain the close cover of the wall, and then held at the gates, his pistol drawn — just as she knew Rommel should have done.

There was another shot from inside and then Toby committed to the cauldron. *Stiletto* held her ground. She knew if they were to achieve anything today, Borges was the key. If all was lost, she would slit his throat and melt away. She pushed her knee harder into his chest and held the tension on the long blade. Borges knew looking into her eyes she would run him through for sport if she had the chance, so he did not move.

When Toby reached the gates, he could see Maggie lying on the ground, her chest covered in blood, her pistol raised towards the house. He saw her fire once and the figure in the doorway collapsed. He jumped forward into the yard.

His mind raced. Maggie and Rommel would have to wait, the initiative had to be regained, and he knew it. The house was the threat and he had no choice now but to clear it. He went forward and bounded up the stairs, seeking cover at the doorway. He shot Rat-face in the head before he moved through the doorway.

When he reappeared, he went quickly to *Stiletto* and together they manhandled Borges back inside the gates, throwing him roughly to the ground.

'You'll never get away with this, you scum,' he snarled at them, aggressive now he had regained his composure. 'My people will hunt you down and kill you, just like your friends there,' he smirked, jerking his head towards Maggie's body.

Stiletto kicked him very hard between the legs and he writhed on the ground, groaning and swearing. Without ceremony, Toby uncapped the Ketamine injection he had taken from his thigh pocket and stabbed the needle into Borges' neck.

He grunted but was unconscious in a few seconds and Toby held his head up by the hair and let it fall back on the ground to make sure. They dragged Rommel back inside the yard and shut the gates. They both knew what needed to be done and they quickly got to work.

It was bad, thought Toby, but it looked worse than it was. Rommel had been shot in the head, but he was the luckiest of men; the bullet had creased his skull and opened the flesh up like a tin can from front to back, taking most of his left ear in the process. But it had not penetrated his skull.

There was a lot of blood, and Toby reckoned he would have a headache for a month, but he would live. Maggie lay still and was deathly white; from what they could make out, the bullet had gone into her back and exited her chest, but thankfully high up and well above the heart.

In truth, she too had lost a lot of blood and needed attention, but she was alive, and they had to keep her that way. Together, Toby and *Stiletto* applied the field dressings from Rommel's trauma kit, and they injected her with morphine.

'Tell them she has had morphine,' he said pointedly and *Stiletto* nodded.

As they finished up, they looked at each other and began to nod in joint understanding. *We can still do this.*

'Do you think you can get Maggie and Borges back across the border?' Toby asked, sceptical, yet hopeful.

'Yes, I have a plan. What about you? You can't go through the border with his head bandaged like that, they will arrest you both.'

'I have a plan too, but we have to move. We have no idea if anyone has heard the shots, or if they might come looking, but if someone does come, you have to go,' he said earnestly, his eyes bright and determined.

Stiletto glanced at Maggie and then gave him a look that said that wasn't going to happen. Toby decided there was no time to argue.

They worked quickly. *Stiletto* backed the truck into the yard, and they closed the gates. It was an isolated road and there had fortunately been no traffic but working inside the gates was safer still. They slid the carpet from the truck and unrolled it.

Together, they bundled the now comatose Borges into the capsule. It was a snug fit. *Stiletto* fixed the cable ties around his wrists and ankles and Toby fitted the face mask, ensuring the flow of air from the attached bottle. They secured the mask with duct tape and covered his eyes too, placing the air bottle behind him.

Together they rolled him tightly in the rug, ensuring the end plugs were secure and looked the part. They did. Finally, it took their combined effort to slide the carpet onto the flatbed of the truck; parallel to the cab and hard up against it.

Over this they placed the other carpet rolls, so it was simply one of many, and then repositioned other furniture and bric-a-brac above and around it. They stood back briefly to admire their handiwork and smiled nervously to each other. *That will work.* Toby secured the side frame and then checked the cargo from every angle. *It had to work.*

Maggie was like a ragdoll. Toby carried her easily and laid her gently across the seat in the cab of the truck. She flopped and moaned in pain, but she was not fully conscious. They propped her up in a sitting position.

'Wait here,' *Stiletto* said and rushed away towards the house. When she returned, she had three dark shirts, a hat, and two bottles of Indonesian *arak*, the locally produced rum. Toby had inserted a saline drip into Maggie's arm, and he anchored the bag to the frame at the back of the seat.

'Leave this in as long as possible. Just pull this out slowly and apply pressure here so it doesn't bleed,' he explained, pointing to the place where the needle was inserted.

Stiletto watched and nodded. She leaned Maggie forward and, giving Toby the weight, she cut Maggie's blood-stained shirt from her, using it to mop up blood smears from around her. Toby watched her work with the long knife, understanding now how she had earned her name, and her fearsome reputation.

He noted Maggie's dressings were largely clean, meaning the flow of blood had been staunched. A good sign. But her bra and upper torso were soaked, showing just how much blood she had lost. A bad sign. They managed to clean her down and dress her in a dark blue shirt. *Stiletto* fixed the buttons in place and tucked it in neatly, leaving the drip arm free.

'I will lay her across the seat and nurse her head for the trip up, and then sit her up while we go through the checkpoint,' she explained to Toby.

With the *arak* she doused one of the shirts and wiped the surfaces of the cab, removing the last of the blood smears but also leaving the heavy fumes of the rum in the cabin. She emptied the bottle on the ground and jammed it between the seat and the passenger door. With the other bottle, she emptied half the contents and replaced the lid, laying the bottle next to Maggie. Toby nodded; her strategy clear. *Smart girl.*

'That's good. I have to get the other vehicle,' he said quickly. 'If anyone comes, please go,' he implored.

Stiletto knew he was right this time and nodded. It was Maggie's only chance and the only way they would get Borges away, even if it meant Toby and Rommel were sacrificed. She felt sick at the thought, but she understood.

When Toby returned, he noticed *Stiletto* had changed into a black shirt; it was a men's shirt and on anyone else it would have looked like a rag. On her the rolled-up sleeves and jaunty collar looked like it had come from a fancy boutique.

He backed the Hilux into the yard as she secured the gates. They laid Rommel on the back seat. The dressings were holding; there was no new bleeding although he was falling in and out of consciousness. Toby put a drip into him also and hung the bag on the suit hook before he rolled up *Stiletto's* old bloodstained shirt and placed it under Rommel's head.

'OK, go,' he said. 'I will radio ahead for a chopper to meet you at Batugade. I will tell them we are coming up through the AUSBATT AO from the border.' He pulled out a map and laid it on the bonnet. 'Near here at… Maudeko.' His finger came to rest on the map. 'I will wait for them to call me forward so it is safe.'

She nodded. 'Yes, if you follow this road after Atambua,' she indicated as she ran a blood-stained nail across the map, 'it will bring you to within about one kilometre of the border, but when you can go no further you must leave the car because it will be too rocky and steep.'

She looked at him and he could see her concern, knowing what this would mean with the wounded Rommel.

'Yes, I know,' Toby said determinedly, acknowledging her thoughts and steeling himself for what he knew lay ahead. 'Now go.'

She climbed into the cab while Toby opened the gates.

'Good luck,' he called above the noise of the engine.

'I will see you on the other side, *Bonito,*' she called back.

But before he could ask her what she meant, the old truck lurched forward and was on its way, out the gates and turning onto the road. She did not look back, and the truck quickly passed out of view, the sound of the engine fading away as she worked expertly through the gears.

Toby scanned around to ensure nothing compromising was left behind. He kicked dirt over the blood stains and dragged Rat-face inside the house, pulling the door locked behind him as he returned. He picked up the weapon that had shot Maggie and Rommel, unloaded it and placed it into his rucksack.

Glancing around, he left the yard for the last time and pulled the gates shut. They might just be lucky, he thought, as the Hilux sped off towards Atambua.

36

AUSBATT HEADQUARTERS, FORT BALIBO
UNITED NATIONS ADMINISTERED EAST TIMOR

February 2001

Hurley's weekly conference was always held on Sundays. Sunday wasn't officially a holiday but by unspoken agreement it was usually a slower day for all UN forces in East Timor. AUSBATT was no different.

Hurley took advantage of this and each Sunday his teams would converge on his headquarters from their outstations; an opportunity for him to have face time with his people. After the work was done, it allowed them all some time to relax, shoot the breeze and have a few laughs. All before his busy bees packed up and returned to their own hives.

Hurley leaned on the post securing one end of the privacy screen of his tent. Before entering, the troops placed their weapons, webbing and equipment in semi-ordered piles near the entrance and then filed inside. Hurley was proud of them for sure, and there were few who understood the difficult work they undertook.

He took the opportunity to share a quick joke or comment in passing while they settled themselves. The day was cloudless and already steaming hot; thankfully a light breeze flowed through the tent and the smell of freshly brewed coffee made it almost pleasant.

Most of the group removed their camouflage shirts and sat down in their khaki t-shirts. A few were busy making mugs of tea and coffee and then handing them around to the others seated on the collection of assembled chairs or on the ground.

In the middle was a flat tree stump which served as a table. A collection of coloured brew mugs with steam rising from them was already beginning to accumulate there. Before they had settled and Hurley had a chance to begin, they all heard boots crunching on the gravel outside.

'Knock! Knock!' The visitor called out, awaiting a response. Hurley smiled and it was mirrored by the group. They all recognised the voice of Private Murphy, one of the combat intelligence analysts.

'Come in, Spud!' Hurley called.

A shy young face poked reluctantly around the corner of the privacy screen. The young soldier was very much in awe of the FSG, and hoped his career in military intelligence would someday lead in that direction. For his part he certainly didn't want to draw the ire of the more seasoned members by overstepping the mark. In truth, he was universally liked and had no cause for concern.

'Sir, sorry to interrupt your meeting. There's a call for you, on the sat-phone in the Ops Room.' Hurley's face probably said it all. This was odd; all his people were gathered in front of him, essentially there was no one to call him. His brow furrowed in curiosity. The messenger was slightly unnerved and referred to a piece of paper in his hand.

'It's someone from World Reach, sir, a… bloke called Harry. He said you'd know who that was. He says it's urgent.'

Hurley tensed inside. This couldn't be good news. Harry

would always arrange to meet him or visit AUSBATT under the arrangements they had used previously. He had a strong sense this was serious.

'I'm on my way, thanks Spud,' he said, his face betraying none of his concerns.

He turned to his operations sergeant. 'Jodie, you start please, I'll be back directly,' Hurley advised as he disappeared out of the tent with Spud, leaving the chatter of the group behind him.

'OK, settle down,' he heard Jodie say in the background as she got proceedings back on track.

As he made his way to the Ops Room, Hurley chatted with the young soldier, but he was turning a number of things over in his mind at the same time. *What could this be?* It surfaced in his mind that Harry had been hard to contact in the last two weeks, in fact since the interrogation of the weasels.

So too had Maggie, he reflected. They had not even arranged their little celebration. *Had this distance been deliberate? Did it have something to do with today's summons?* He told himself that Harry's team were busy too. He knew they had other operations that were ongoing, and that he had no need to know about them. It was the way their world worked, and it had to be respected.

Hurley walked into the Ops Room and the sat-phone receiver was sitting unattended on the table. Around him, the current shift buzzed as soldiers attended map boards and computer screens, too busy to care about his visit. Hurley steeled himself and picked up the receiver.

'Harry, Matt. What's the problem?' he asked directly.

Hurley listened for a good thirty seconds. To anyone paying attention, it was obvious the voice on the other end was telling a story. As Hurley listened, in his mind it seemed like a developing ops problem and he attuned his thoughts to that. Until, at one point, his jawline tightened visibly.

'Is it Maggie?' he asked pointedly. 'Harry, is it Maggie?' Hurley forced urgently, obviously unhappy with the previous response.

After a short interval Hurley spoke. 'I will see you there in thirty minutes,' he said tersely as he rang off and then walked quickly from the Ops Room.

As much as he felt like it, he did not run. Hurley subscribed to the old army superstition that if seniors run it can scare the soldiers. It was an oft used joke but one his habit did tend to reflect. Besides, his own calculation told him he would make it to Batugade in time — just. He needed to think through a couple of things first though.

Hurley was aware that his own people were very perceptive. You simply couldn't put that amount of natural talent and specialist training in one tent and expect otherwise, he thought ruefully. In fact, that's exactly why they were there. He didn't want to deliberately mislead them, but it wasn't time for them to be fully briefed either. He didn't yet know what that brief would look like anyway.

He gathered his thoughts as he re-entered the tent. The group stopped and looked to him. 'OK guys, sorry for the interruption. I've been called away as part of a bigger job. There isn't time to brief you all now, but I'll close the loop when we next get the chance. Jodie will complete today's conference and I'll be here to follow up next week on any points. Please ensure you keep Jodie informed on any issues. That's all.'

They watched as Hurley gathered his webbing and rifle from under the table and when he looked around the group, his attention fell on one of his young sergeants; a burly soldier with dark hair and an open face, with friendly, but strong and determined eyes.

'Jack, can I see you please?' he asked as he headed outside. The look Hurley gave Jodie said *don't wait for Jack* and she nodded intuitively. Jack followed immediately and they stood by the Land Rover.

'Jack, get your gear and a trauma kit, and tell no one please. I'll see you back here in five and I'll brief you on the way.'

Jack was one of Hurley's protégés, and commanded the busy detachment at Batugade. Hurley never showed him favouritism, but their relationship was well known. There were always the ones who would carry the light in the next generation, and Jack was one, just as Hurley had been. For his part, Jack knew he would be told exactly what he needed to know, plus a little bit more.

More importantly, he knew he could trust Hurley and the reverse was also true, no matter what. It was Hurley's way and it was more successful than most. It not only taught them more, it prepared them better for the unexpected. Jack had a feeling this was the unexpected.

For Hurley's part he would have chosen Jack on most accounts anyway, but he was also a patrol medic, just as Hurley was and at this point, Hurley figured he could use all the help he could get. Within minutes, the two were fully booted and spurred, and the camouflaged Land Rover rolled out of the fort gates with Jack at the wheel.

'Where are we going?' asked Jack, not unreasonably, before they got to the main road junction.

Hurley looked at his watch. 'I need you to get us to Batugade in twenty minutes, Jack.'

'OK,' he said as he turned right and pointed the vehicle towards the coast. It would be tight, but he reckoned it was doable.

Hurley seemed lost in thought until they passed the outer limits of Balibo, and Jack opened the vehicle up on the main road. He knew the road between headquarters and Batugade well, and he drove quickly, but safely and efficiently. Hurley settled back in the seat, cradling his rifle.

'OK, Jack. I will tell you a story, it won't be all the story, but you can ask any questions you want, and I will answer them if I can, or tell you I can't. OK?'

'Yep,' answered the young sergeant, already intrigued and now secretly excited. The unexpected had now materialised, and he was part of it.

'At Batugade, head for the UN helipad at the airfield near the checkpoint. When we get there, you will meet a man named Harry...'

Hurley gave the shorter version of his complex personal and operational life with Harry, but he left nothing out. In fact, Jack had heard snippets of deeds done and close shaves Hurley had shared with the legendary Harry.

He knew that Harry was the spymaster who had trained Hurley in the generation before, and that much of what Hurley had passed to him, not just in knowledge but in attitude, had come from Harry. He was now passing the same on to his own soldiers.

'Harry is in East Timor running a covert counter-intelligence team in support of our operations here,' Hurley continued, 'it is sourced from the British Army and is not on the UN books.'

'Jesus, does the CO know?'

'Yep, but now you are one of the very few others who do. They have a wide-ranging remit that includes all CI aspects and extends to high value militia targets that may be connected into the Indonesian government or intelligence system.'

Jack nodded, processing the information, but he couldn't help wondering where this was going. 'It was them who investigated the murder of our two agents,' Hurley added sombrely.

Jack stopped nodding and turned to Hurley. 'Did they kill Al Campbell for his involvement?' he asked pointedly.

'No, most definitely not,' Hurley assured him. 'I was there

that night. He was taken out by one of the Rileys when he tried to kill me. But it was my work with Harry that lured Campbell there in the first place, I admit.'

Jack was happy with this. He knew if Hurley had been there, there was no conspiracy he needed to worry about.

'Anyway,' Hurley went on, 'we are going to the helipad to RV with a medevac chopper. Sometime in the next hour, a truck will come across from the other side, and in that truck is a wounded person who has been shot. That's why the trauma kit, in case we beat the chopper and we're needed.' Jack's eyebrows rose appreciably, but he said nothing. This was getting more interesting by the minute.

'And there's something else you need to know, Jack,' Hurley offered quietly, almost reluctantly.

'What's that?' Jack asked, curious to see where this might go.

'The wounded person is a woman, and I am involved with her.'

Jack looked askew at Hurley, his face uncomprehending. Hurley looked forward, his face hardened and his eyes looking far away. Jack had a thousand questions and knew Hurley would answer them, but he also knew this wasn't the time to ask them all. For now, there was one issue he wanted to resolve.

'Involved? Is she an agent?' Jack pushed, confused and seeking clarity on their role.

Hurley gave a small smile despite the circumstances. 'No Jack, I mean personally involved, *romantically* involved. She is a British Army agent runner, a member of Harry's team; it is her agent who is risking both their lives to bring her over.'

'Fuck,' exclaimed Jack, gobsmacked. It never ceased to amaze him the things that could be going on in the background. He couldn't begin to process the full situation but knew it would all become clear as events unfolded. He was less sure how allied — but non-UN — cross-border operations were going to go down if it all went to shit though.

'Quite,' said Hurley reading his thoughts, his eyes fixed on
the road ahead.

37

Batugade

United Nations administered East Timor

....

February 2001

As they sped into Batugade and passed the CIVPOL station, Hurley noticed the Giant standing outside talking to two officers from the station. He leaned over and pressed the horn, waving out the window as the group looked up. The waving figure of Stefan disappeared in the rear vision mirror as they raced on.

The chopper was already there when they arrived. The blades were still rotating slowly, cooling down, so it had not been there long. Hurley directed Jack towards the small concrete building at the side of the airfield. As they drew closer, Hurley could see Harry, standing next to a black Land Cruiser in a serious huddle with Merlin and Lucy.

The chopper, a white Puma with UN markings, had the sliding door open and inside they could see it was rigged for medevac. Michelle was there with a man Hurley didn't know. It was probably the doctor. *God, he hoped it was the doctor.*

Hurley felt his demeanour change as they drove into the airfield. He was pensive and agonising over a situation he could not control but was swept up in nevertheless, and he knew it. The unexpected involvement of Maggie and the uncertainty of her condition had skewed his thinking, knocked him off kilter.

'Jesus,' he spat in frustration through gritted teeth, all his worlds colliding.

Jack could read his boss. He knew things could go very wrong if Hurley unloaded on his old friend over this. As Hurley had always encouraged him, he did what he thought was right and jumped in.

'Matt,' Jack said calmly, locking eyes with Hurley, 'if you think I'm out of line just tell me to shut the fuck up. But from what you've taught me, a plan like this would never have been hatched if it wasn't likely to work. Whatever it is that has gone tits up, I'm guessing it's a major freak circumstance. No amount of planning can accommodate everything, you know that. We work on what's likely, and what's not. That's what operations are all about — risks and rewards. It's why we have back-up plans, and why we have back-up plans for back-up plans. I'm guessing since we're all still talking that we're still in the game, and like you always say, if you're still in the game, you can still win. And that guy out there is a legend,' he stressed, cocking his head in Harry's direction. 'Jesus, I owe him, and I've never even met him. You know in your heart he is not to blame. Here endeth the lesson,' he finished up, using the very words that Hurley himself often did in the same way.

Hurley exhaled and visibly settled. Sometimes you just had to hear it from someone you trusted rather than the little voice in your head, he thought.

'You're right, Jack,' he admitted. 'I knew I brought you along for a reason. Thanks mate.'

Hurley was back, Jack mused, *and if we can win, we will.*

Harry watched Hurley open the Land Rover door and moved

to meet him halfway. He tried to read him and see where he was at; he knew that this would not be easy for him, just as it was not going to be easy for any of them. He had seen the two of them talking in the front of the Land Rover and knew it was connected.

Hurley couldn't help but notice Harry was limping heavily as he approached him, and it temporarily caught his attention.

'What have you done, Harry?' he said, motioning towards his leg.

'Ah, I knew that bloody tennis court was trouble,' he answered, clearly irritated by the unexpected injury. It was probably giving him more trouble than he would admit, and Hurley smiled despite himself.

'Is there any update, Harry?' he asked, working to keep himself in check.

Jack had reframed Hurley; there was nothing he could do for Maggie yet, but he certainly wasn't enjoying the feeling of helplessness that accompanied other peoples' operations — particularly those that had gone wrong.

'Nothing yet unfortunately,' Harry answered, clearly concerned also. 'We got a transmission from Toby telling us about Maggie, which I told you about on the phone. But they obviously have a problem with their radio because the last part of their transmission wasn't readable and there's been nothing since. Merlin is monitoring as we speak. They had intended to drive through here with the truck, so we have to wait for now to see what unfolds.'

'They?'

'Toby and Rommel are the other half of the team.'

'What's Plan B for them?'

'To walk out through AUSBATT.'

'Where from?' Hurley asked, concern etched on his face.

'Atambua plus a bit more.'

'Jesus Harry, that's over ten clicks,' he implored.

'I know, but that's only if they can't drive out remember, and they'll drive as far as they can.'

'Right. Do you have comms with the truck?'

'Technically yes, the short-range walkie-talkie they've used for coordinating on the ground is with Maggie's gear, so if *Stiletto* remembers she will let us know the truck is in the queue.'

'She? Is the agent a woman?'

Harry nodded.

'Is she any good?'

It was a reasonable question, but under the circumstances Harry couldn't contain himself, the tension had clearly got to him too.

'No,' he said, his words dripping with sarcasm, and his eyes aflame. 'I picked the worst fucking agent in the southern hemisphere to do a really important job and watch over the life of one of my best operators.'

They looked at each other stony-faced, and then both broke into something of an embarrassed grin; a smile of shared pain and understanding.

'Actually, she is bloody fantastic. If it can be done, she will do it,' he confided with absolute conviction.

Merlin walked over from sitting in the Land Cruiser and nodded to Hurley. He was awkward and didn't seem to know what to say. Hurley could see they were all under the pump. Merlin turned to Harry.

'Harry, they're in the queue. They just came up on the walkie-talkie.'

'Whose voice was it?' Harry asked eagerly.

'*Stiletto's*. She said they were eleven cars back and then she giggled and said that Maggie was drunk, and she couldn't wake her, but that it was OK because they hadn't spilt a drop.'

They all absorbed this before Harry spoke.

'OK, it's all veiled speech. I'm thinking she's worried about the walkie-talkie being intercepted by the TNI. I reckon the giggle is a deliberate positive signal; it tells us Maggie is alive. She's not awake, means she's unconscious. I think she has a plan to bring her across pretending she is pissed and has passed out. And *they have not spilled a drop* — the package is intact,' he summed up.

It was a high-risk strategy, Hurley thought, but it was the only game in town. It was certainly Maggie's only chance.

'*Stiletto* seems pretty capable, Harry,' Hurley conceded. 'What package would that be exactly?'

'I will tell you her story sometime,' Harry said cryptically, 'and we'll worry about the package when they're safe. Come on, we'll go down and watch them come over.'

Hurley went via the Land Rover and updated Jack who nodded, taking it all in.

'Here, take my rifle, I'll just take my pistol,' Hurley said as he handed the weapon to Jack.

Jack gave Hurley a long hard look.

'Don't you be doing anything stupid now, boss,' he warned with a smile, knowing Hurley well and how high the stakes might be.

Hurley gave him one of those *I'll do whatever I have to do* looks and Jack pursed his lips, knowing there was nothing more he could say, but that he would back him regardless.

Hurley easily caught Harry up as he was struggling into the front of the Land Cruiser. Harry had the walkie-talkie and Merlin and Lucy were remaining at the airfield, Hurley noted. They drove the short distance in silence and unwittingly parked in the shade of the very palm where Maggie had watched the truck come over the day before.

They watched the line of vehicles and willed them forward. Their truck inched its way painfully forward as the vehicles in front were gradually cleared. It served no purpose being impatient, the TNI guards were routinely checking most cargo, and their truck was always going to get the same treatment.

Hurley held his breath as he watched it move into the search bay, it was now the object of attention. *Stiletto* had cleverly placed the truck behind another truck with a similar profile. The guards had given it a cursory search and when the driver climbed back into the cabin, *Stiletto* called out to him and waved, yelling out she would see him in Batugade.

The guard saw this, as *Stiletto* knew he would, and he naturally thought the two vehicles were travelling together. Subliminally, she knew that since there were no problems with the first truck, he would link the two in his mind and be less likely to scrutinise hers.

The guard came around to her window and motioned for her to get out. She complied immediately, handing over their papers and flashing him a winning smile. He responded with a reserved nod. They watched as he perused the papers, holding them as he walked to the back of the truck, looking into and among the cargo.

He asked *Stiletto* to pull down a packing box and open it. She complied and when he was satisfied, she had him assist her to replace it. They watched as she laughed with the guard while they manhandled the crate back on board. *She is a cool customer,* Hurley thought as he watched her.

She then followed the guard as he walked down the passenger side of the truck. He looked in, under the mountain of furniture and prodded the rolls of carpet. *Stiletto* said something and they both laughed, him shaking his head. *No, he did not want to buy any carpet for his house.*

When they reached the cabin, a discussion ensured and finally the guard opened the door. A bottle fell to the ground with a clink, and *Stiletto* picked it up. Seemingly embarrassed, she quickly placed it back in the cabin.

Hurley could see the guard was now clearly displeased; he could smell the cabin and saw the half empty bottle in Maggie's hand. He shook her on the arm, but she just moaned. He lifted her hat and checked her face against her passport.

She was pale, but only as much as someone drunk might be, and *Stiletto* had carefully applied makeup to her cheeks and lips. She looked more like she was asleep. *Stiletto*'s body language was of contrition and apology. *I'm sorry, she is just a young girl, too much drink, she will be sick tomorrow. I can assure you this will never happen again*, it said.

In the Land Cruiser they held their collective breath and waited for it to end. There was a moment, as there always is, that stood still for Hurley. A moment when it could have gone one way or the other.

In that instant Hurley drew his pistol and cocked it, and at the same time realised Harry had already started the engine. Their eyes met briefly. *Whatever it takes*. He knew then why they were the only ones in the vehicle.

Stiletto sensed the moment too and her hand went casually to the back of her waist. Only Harry knew the significance of that, and that the guard was seconds from death if he made the wrong decision. Harry covered Hurley's pistol with his hand.

'Wait,' he urged, knowing it was in *Stiletto*'s hands now. The guard looked back along the long queue and made his decision. Handing back the papers angrily he dismissed her, and the boom-gate began to rise. *Stiletto* ran to the cabin thanking him, and the truck was quickly on the move.

There was no halt at the UN checkpoint; Harry had weaved his magic and arranged for it to go straight through, and the boom-gate was already up. *Stiletto* powered through and towards them. Hurley jumped from the Land Cruiser and stood by the road until the truck slowed near him.

Meanwhile Harry turned the Land Cruiser around and headed for the airfield with a screech of tires. Hurley jumped up into the cab, squeezing himself in, his back to the windscreen.

'Follow him,' he ordered without ceremony, pointing to the Land Cruiser.

Hurley pulled Maggie's cap off and cupped her face gently with both hands. She was deathly white, and her face was cold.

'My name is Matt,' he said finally, turning to face *Stiletto* as she drove.

'I know who you are, Senhor Mateus,' she said mischievously, 'I am Josefina.'

'Thank you for what you have done, Josefina.'

'I think it was a very close call,' she admitted seriously, the enormity finally hitting her as she manoeuvred the truck into the airfield and brought it to stop behind the Land Cruiser.

Hurley lifted Maggie down from the cabin and together they all laid her on the stretcher from the chopper. Michelle began securing the straps across her while the doctor checked the dressings and her pulse, his stethoscope moving from place to place. They folded a beige blanket over her.

'She had morphine one hour ago, and a drip,' *Stiletto* reported to the doctor. He nodded and continued.

'OK, we're out of here,' the doctor finally announced, and Hurley and *Stiletto* hurriedly carried the stretcher to the chopper.

Maggie rallied slightly as they fixed the stretcher in place and her eyes fluttered open, but she seemed far away. *Stiletto* reached for her free hand and squeezed it as Michelle readied the drip and the doctor administered it.

'Are we good?' Maggie croaked weakly, knowing it was her.

'We're not just good, we're brilliant,' *Stiletto* said tenderly.

Hurley leaned forward and kissed her cheek.

'I love you Maggie Redcap,' he said softly, for her ears only.

'I know,' she murmured, and fell back into blackness, the faint trace of a smile on her pale face.

CHAPTER 38

BORDER REGION
INDONESIAN PROVINCE OF WEST TIMOR /
UNITED NATIONS ADMINISTERED EAST TIMOR

....

February 2001

As soon as the chopper lifted off, *Stiletto* grabbed Harry urgently by the arm.

'What word from the other two?' she urged.

Her concern was obvious and he shook his head, confused.

'We've heard nothing, Josefina. We're expecting them to RV here at the airfield. They told us by radio you were coming through and Maggie was wounded, but then they were unreadable. We've heard nothing since.'

She steeled herself and Harry could see the wheels turning inside her head. There was bad news, he could feel it.

'They are coming out on foot Harry, and Rommel is wounded too, he was shot in the head,' she exclaimed, her face drawn.

Harry was stunned, but it was fleeting. His brain was already processing the implications of this revelation as *Stiletto* pulled a map out of Maggie's backpack. She spread it on the bonnet of the Land Cruiser and Harry looked over her shoulder.

'Here,' she explained, moving her finger from place to place across the map as she spoke. 'This is where they will come out. They will wait, just on the other side to be called forward. They will drive to here and be forced to go from there on foot.'

'Timing?'

She glanced at her watch. 'The earliest they will arrive in that area is about half an hour from now, if Toby can make it carrying Rommel.'

Harry quickly gathered them all at the side of the truck.

'OK people, today is not nearly over,' he told them. 'A quick update. Toby and Rommel are coming over through the AUSBATT AO, although thankfully, only the last few miles will be on foot. I say thankfully because Toby is carrying Rommel, who has a head wound.'

He let this sink in and for them all to process the implications. They were all soldiers, except for *Stiletto*, but even she knew what this meant, and she had seen it in Toby's eyes before they parted.

'Because of that wound they could not drive out, they would never have gotten through the checkpoint. Josefina estimates that they will arrive in this location here, near the village of Maudeko in half an hour at the earliest,' he explained, as he pointed to the map.

'OK, so how long to get there, and then go forward to the border?' Harry asked, naturally turning to Hurley, but he deflected to Jack with a curt nod. It was his turf and he knew the area well.

'Fifteen minutes, no more,' Jack said confidently.

'Good,' Harry summed up, 'then time is on our side.'

'Josefina, please,' he said, motioning her forward.

Together, she and Harry dropped the side frame of the truck and with Lucy's help they wiggled out a large roll of carpet, letting it drop to the ground. Jack and Hurley looked at each other, wondering where this was going.

When they unrolled the carpet, to Hurley's astonishment, a

figure was encased inside what looked like a thin bamboo cage. Harry pulled the frame away and ripped the face mask from the figure. The captive gasped as the duct tape was torn from his skin. Harry stood back.

This was the package, Hurley realised. Whoever this person was, he was deemed important enough to have risked lives, including Maggie's, to snatch him. Hurley looked down at what was a pathetic figure, but he meant nothing to him.

He was a weedy man with an angular face, his hair was unkempt, his clothes were grubby and ill-fitting, and he was exhausted from his journey inside the capsule. His skin was pale, and Hurley surmised he had been drugged before being connected to the air bottle Harry had ripped from his face.

Hurley turned to Jack who also shook his head.

'Matt, on behalf of the team, allow us to present Marcelino Borges,' Harry announced.

They looked at each other. *We wouldn't have taken the chance we did for nothing,* his eyes said, and Hurley knew it was the truth.

Could it really be Borges? Hurley thought, looking at the figure on the ground. He turned to Jack, who had retrieved a black plastic folder from the Land Rover; it was a mug shot collection of the twenty most wanted militia figures, complete with their descriptions.

The photo of Borges was indistinct; it was old and grainy, and he had previously sported a wispy black beard. He had also carried more weight, and this had filled his face out in the old photo. Jack read aloud from the folder.

'He has a large scar on his left calf and is missing the top of his right index finger.'

Hurley moved forward and grabbed the captive who recoiled from him in confusion and fear. Jack drew the bayonet from his webbing and slit the left leg of the captive's trousers, before tearing it up along the seam and exposing the scar, exactly where it should be.

They then grabbed his right hand and held the fingers out, extended. The top of the index finger was clearly missing.

'Bloody hell, it is Borges,' Jack exclaimed.

'It is,' Harry said with quiet confidence. He was happy that it was confirmed, although the team had been certain when they mounted the operation, thanks to *Stiletto's* information.

'Well, I am not a member of UN forces,' Harry said in apparent disappointment, 'so I can't arrest him, and neither can my people.'

He turned to Hurley and gave him a thin smile, with one eyebrow raised. Hurley nodded and approached Borges as he removed his handcuffs from his webbing. Borges knew it was over for him and he lay still on the ground, clearly not recovered from the journey. But he knew he was now in East Timor, where there was a warrant for his arrest, and that he could no longer count on the protection he enjoyed in Indonesia.

As Hurley placed the handcuffs on his wrists and closed them up, they all heard the ratchet slide and the finality as they clicked shut. It was the end they had worked for. Hurley stood up, looking down at the wretched figure on the ground who glared back at him through gritted teeth.

It came to *Stiletto* as she watched Hurley that he thought briefly about the Kissing House, and the many victims he knew and had interviewed; the images saddened his grey eyes momentarily and then they cleared. His jaw hardened. He spoke clearly for them all to hear.

'Marcelino Borges, by the authority vested in me in accordance with the United Nations mandate for East Timor, I am arresting you for murder, rape and crimes against humanity.'

There was a moment of silence before the small group broke

into spontaneous but subdued applause. They had earned this, Hurley thought, and sacrifices had certainly already been made. It was a day that could get bleaker still, but they deserved their high point. He looked around the group, holding their collective gaze.

'Thank you to everyone involved,' he said solemnly, his voice thick with emotion. 'This means a great deal, to a great many people.'

They all nodded in unison.

'Right,' said Jack, 'we can drop this scum bag off at CIVPOL on the way through to Maudeko. How do you want to do that, Harry?'

'Let's go in your vehicle, Matt. Merlin, I need you and the radios with me, the remainder hold here until we get back. I'll radio an update.'

'I'm coming too,' announced *Stiletto*, no room for discussion in her voice. 'I promised Maggie,' she lied, before Harry could refuse her.

Harry pursed his lips, seemed to consider this and then acquiesced.

'OK, let's refurbish the truck first. Lucy, I'll get you to get it out of here and back to Dili. The rest of us will go in the other two vehicles.'

Within minutes they were parked outside the CIVPOL station. Hurley and Jack escorted Borges, Jack holding him by the scruff of the neck as he guided him forward, his legs hardly touching the ground.

'Stefan, I'm glad you're still here,' Hurley announced as they entered the station. 'For the record, I have arrested Marcelino Borges and I need to transfer him into your custody. Can you do that for me? I'm in a hurry.'

'Marcelino Borges?' The Giant considered this for a moment while he ran the name through the database in his head.

'Ah, he's very naughty,' he said finally, his face breaking into a wide grin and his finger gesticulating as he might towards a child. But he was clearly impressed.

'And where did you find him?' he prodded softly, his head cocked, his eyes assessing Hurley.

'I saw him at the airfield in Batugade, confirmed his identity and arrested him,' Hurley said truthfully, even if a bit thinly. 'If you need anything else, I'll come to the station tomorrow in Balibo.'

'Very good, Mr Hurley. I will take care of him and be arranging his trip to Dili, no problems.'

He took possession of Borges who was dwarfed even more by the big policeman than he had been by Jack. He wrapped his huge hand around Borges' upper arm to take formal control of him.

'Thanks Stefan. We must go, duty calls,' Hurley called as he threw him the keys to his handcuffs and disappeared out the door.

They raced back along the sealed road towards Balibo, knowing once they left the bitumen and turned off for Maudeko it would be slower going. Jack checked his watch at the turn and was comfortable they would still make their window.

Knowing what he knew now, it was unlikely the pair would be early, he reasoned. More likely late, if they made it at all. His heart was with them, but he knew the odds were not. As a soldier, carrying a wounded mate out under those conditions did not bear thinking about, particularly in this fearsome heat.

In the rear-view mirror, Jack could see Harry and *Stiletto* deep in conversation.

'Big debrief going on there,' he said to Hurley, nodding towards the mirror.

'Yeah, they will take this one apart to see what went wrong,' said Hurley glumly, 'but as you rightly said, it's not necessarily anyone's fault.'

'She's bloody impressive,' remarked Jack. 'And not a little bit hot as well.'

They both chuckled.

'Too true,' agreed Hurley as some huts came into view, 'I owe her for sure.'

The village of Maudeko comprised only a dozen dwellings, a couple of old cement houses and others made of wood, corrugated iron and palm fronds. They slowed down to drive through the village for fear of hitting a stray dog or a child, and the smell of the cooking fires and general decay invaded the vehicle.

Jack waved to all the brown faces that turned to watch them. They all knew him from his regular patrols, and they waved in return and smiled as he passed. Maudeko was in Jack's area and if a car came with people they did not know, or people came through the village at night from the border, it was Jack the villagers reported it to.

They paid no heed to the white Land Cruiser or the people who travelled with him; if they came with Senhor Jack, they were welcome. They pushed on slowly for a few kilometres past the village; the road turned into a rough bumpy track which was often impassable during the wet season.

Luckily for them there had been no rain for over a week and the surface was bone dry, and hard, the rough-dried mud cooked by the sun into ruts like concrete across the track. They stopped at the natural end, after which only foot trails snaked off into West Timor; little tracks used by traders, smugglers and militia insurgents.

They all gathered around the back of the Land Rover. Hurley and Jack had slung their rifles across their backs.

'I've radioed our ops to report we are following up a possible militia sighting in this area,' Hurley began. He turned and faced directly west and held both his arms extended. 'The border is about two kilometres in this direction. Another two clicks beyond that is where the guys have said they will hold, if they can. My suggestion is we wait for their call. They could come up on either the radio or the short-range walkie-talkie, so we listen, and we wait.'

'Yes,' Harry agreed. 'That's ezackly what we'll do, for about an hour. And then we will re-assess. Merlin, are both those channels good?'

'Aye, Harry. No problem.'

Jack pulled *Stiletto* aside. 'Josefina, can you show me exactly on the map where they have travelled from, and how?' he asked. 'I might be able to do a more accurate prediction from that.'

She nodded and returned with a map from the Land Cruiser. They perched on the tailgate of the Land Rover and Jack questioned her subtly to find the detail he needed.

She could see his process and liked the big man and his exacting, no-nonsense style. He was friendly and dependable, and she sensed his strength of purpose. Jack went meticulously over the details. The start point. The start time. The type of vehicle. The route she had recommended. The likely obstacles. Traffic density. Road surfaces. Where they would likely leave the vehicle.

After that he looked at the ground and measured the gradient and the distance, not as the crow flies but across the steep ground. He used his own experience to factor in everything, as if he was doing the trek himself. Finally, he looked up.

'How big is Rommel?' he asked.

Stiletto looked around the group. 'Similar to your boss.'

'How fit is Toby?'

'Very fit I would say,' she said confidently.

'Field fit?' asked Jack, his eyes narrowed, looking for something more. She looked confused.

'He's a Royal Marines commando and prior to that he was a

Foreign Legionnaire,' Harry interrupted them both with a tired smile, 'and he is field fit.'

Stiletto raised her eyebrows. Jack smiled and nodded.

'OK, good,' he said as he put his head down and did a few more calculations.

Finally, he looked up. 'I reckon it will be fifty minutes from now before they get to the nominated point, plus or minus five minutes,' he announced with a wry grin. It buoyed them all. Regardless of how accurate it might be, they at least had something to hang their hats on while they waited.

Hurley helped Jack lay out the trauma kit with the gear they would probably need and they readied two drips for insertion. They then packed it all away in the order it would be needed, stripping out the things they judged were not required in order to lessen the load.

Then Jack made tea. He brewed a big pot from the gear in the Land Rover and used the metal canteen cups from his and Hurley's webbing to distribute it among the group.

'Will this do any good?' *Stiletto* challenged him when he offered her the cup.

Her spirits were low, Jack thought, which was probably not her usual style, although it had been some day and she had come out a winner. She was impressive, and no doubting it. And like few women, she had that special something, he thought, holding her gaze.

'Can't say,' he answered casually, 'but there's an old army saying — tea never made any situation worse.'

She smiled tiredly and accepted the cup, realising she had not eaten since breakfast at her uncle's compound. That seemed so long ago, she thought, as she greedily drank the hot sweet brew.

Jack read her thoughts and returned with a packet of ration biscuits. Her eyes lit up. She thanked him with the trademark

Stiletto smile as she ripped the plastic with her teeth. It was infectious and Jack laughed with her.

39

Border region
Indonesian Province of West Timor /
United Nations administered East Timor

....

February 2001

It would be talked about for years to come and would also be roundly denied as an urban myth. Jack himself would always humbly say it was more arse than class, but it was nevertheless true.

Within the window he predicted, the walkie-talkie crackled into life and they heard Toby's voice, weak and exhausted, and on his last legs for sure. But it was Toby.

Against all the odds, he had made it to the RV with Rommel on his back. And all on a day so hot you could cook an egg on a rock. Hurley listened to Toby's transmission with the others and his heart sank.

'He sounds absolutely fucked,' he said finally, his concerns mirrored in the faces around him. 'We will just have to go forward and bring them in.'

Jack quickly retrieved the rolled-up stretcher and the trauma kit from the Land Rover and appeared, as if by magic, at Hurley's side.

'I reckon three should go,' he said, 'with Toby that makes one

« 327 »

on each handle of the stretcher on the way back. We'll never do it any other way.'

Jack was right. Hurley looked around and quickly did the numbers. Harry was most definitely out of play, there was no way he'd be doing anything on that leg. He looked at Harry and saw the bitter acceptance of his fate in his old friend's eyes. *We won't be doing this one together.*

'I agree with Jack,' said Harry, 'so it will be–'

'I'm going,' *Stiletto* interjected, no compromise in her voice at all.

'I'm in too,' said Merlin quickly, sounding a little chirpier than he actually looked. While this type of activity was evidently not his forte, he had obviously taken the course to volunteer rather than be volunteered. He too, had done the numbers and knew he was needed.

That left one more position they needed to fill. Hurley pulled Jack aside and they walked away a short distance, out of earshot of the others.

'I know you want to do this Jack; I can see it in your face, but I can't let that happen,' Hurley explained, almost in a whisper. 'If you're compromised over there, it will be an almighty shit fight, you know that. And I will wear it for being so cavalier as to let you go. If it all goes to custard, I'm in the frame whether I go or not, so it may as well be me.'

'I'm happy to take the risk,' the younger man said earnestly.

'I know you are mate, and I appreciate it. What's more I'm quite sure you'd make a good fist of it. You're a bloody good soldier and an equally good medic. But that's not the issue now. It's also potentially dangerous; if we run into the TNI it only takes a mistake or a miscalculation and it could get really grim. If anything happened to you, I have to face your wife and kids and explain exactly why I sent you into West Timor, in contravention of UN and Indonesian law, to recover someone you didn't know, over whom you had no obligation. Try and imagine what that conversation with Lisa would look like, because it's looking pretty fuckin' painful to me,' he pressed the younger man.

Jack grinned despite himself. 'Yeah, I get ya,' he conceded reluctantly, and his face said the decision was made, and accepted. 'So, what do you want from me?'

'I need you here as my rear link on the radio. If I call for you, I need you to come; can you do that for me?' Hurley implored.

'No problem,' Jack said, nodding his head.

'Jack, let's be clear. I will only call you if I need to save a life, do you understand?'

'Yep,' he agreed solemnly.

'And I need you to monitor our ops radio net. If you hear a fighting patrol or the ground surveillance radars have picked us up as intruders you need to manage that, OK?'

The big man nodded, understanding how dangerous that could be.

'And another thing,' Hurley urged, dropping his voice further and turning his back to the group. 'I want you to promise me something. If anything happens to me, I want you to tell them I ordered you to be here and be involved, OK? There's no point taking extra flak you don't need.'

'Don't worry, I'll fix that,' Jack said, and then in response to Hurley's challenging look he capitulated. 'OK, I promise,' he said, and they both grinned.

Harry watched the two soldiers talking, close together. He knew well the conversation that was taking place. They could all see that Jack was up for the task and eager to go. He was also younger and probably more physically suited to the task than Hurley, so would have been a good choice.

But Harry also knew that would not be the outcome, and for

all the right reasons. He watched as Hurley fed the younger man his shit sandwich and watched as the two discussed the reasons and noted the body language between them.

But when it was over and the message was passed, the two were closer, not further apart and it was a testament to Hurley's leadership that in the space of seconds, Jack was ready and accepting of the new task Hurley was asking of him.

When Hurley and Jack returned to the group, they all knew Hurley was coming. Harry pulled him aside.

'I'm sorry it's come to this mate,' he began.

'You know there's no need for that Harry, it is as it is,' Hurley acknowledged, grasping the arm of his old friend and mentor. 'The only focus now is getting those two home, so let's get on with it.'

Hurley led them out, not just because he was more familiar with the ground, but that role now naturally fell to him. The going was mainly downhill, which meant of course, it would be uphill on the way back. They put that out of their minds as they walked down the steep earthen track and occasionally clambered over the sharp rocks. Periodically Hurley looked at the map and then put it away and pressed on.

When they got to the border it was marked by a rocky stream-bed through which trickled shallow rivulets of water, washing lightly over the rocks. The only sounds in the quiet of the forest were the birds and the tinkling of the water as it meandered through the glade.

Here and there deeper pools were stagnant, their contents black and dirty. In the shade it was oppressive and musty with the smell of bird droppings and general decay. The area would only be cleansed after the next storm when the stream would come violently crashing through and fill the riverbed temporarily before the whole process began over again.

They propped on the East Timor side and waited. It was the

last safe ground and Hurley pulled the binoculars from his webbing and scanned the terrain on the other side for some time. He knew it well but from an opposing perspective; he knew the militia infiltration routes and he knew why they used the ground as they did.

Now he needed it too; concealment from the air and from any potential observers on the ground.

'I don't anticipate any problems, but we do get TNI patrols in this area from time to time, so we need to be careful,' he whispered to the others.

He pointed into the distance. 'We'll head for that rise in the ground on the other side about a click away.' They both nodded. Merlin's expression said it looked a long way off. 'I reckon if we're lucky we may even be able to see Toby and Rommel from there,' Hurley encouraged him.

As they crossed the border Hurley felt like a naughty boy; he knew he shouldn't be there and his only excuse if they were caught would be a navigation error. How he would ever explain the presence of his eclectic group of friends in civilian clothes, including a woman and one with a bullet wound in his head, was anyone's guess.

He put the thought out of his mind. As he had said to Harry, it is what it is and very occasionally, the cover story locker is empty. Today, even the shelves had been removed. They pressed on, moving easily now. It was still downhill, but the surface was grassed and softer on their feet, and the gradient too had eased. But they still had to get back, and they all knew it.

They wound their way slowly towards the knoll that Hurley had identified earlier. He picked his way carefully using the low ground and moving between the pockets of foliage, clumps of the thorny bushes that dotted the landscape, keeping their profile below the line of sight should anyone be around.

Each time they reached the bushy cover they rested, and Hurley again scanned the landscape. He took no risks and used an old foot track he found to lead them to the top of the knoll.

Once there, he looked for a safe place close to the area Toby had nominated, a good tactical location to protect a wounded man. A place he might choose himself.

'What colour shirts are they wearing?' he finally asked *Stiletto*.

'Light blue, and green.'

'Bingo,' he announced after a further traverse of the binoculars, 'have a look there.'

Stiletto eagerly took the binoculars and pointed them in the same direction. She could see Toby in his light blue shirt sitting in the shade of the bushes and her heart lifted. It wasn't over yet but this was surely a sign they might just do it.

'Merlin, can you give Toby a burst on the walkie-talkie and tell him we're inbound from the north, mate?'

'Aye Matt, happy to do that,' he said cheerfully as he keyed the handset and sent the message.

Two words on a radio can't usually convey very much, but Hurley thought it was the happiest *Roger, Out* he had ever heard. They continued on and were with them within fifteen minutes.

Seeing *Stiletto*, the relief on Toby's face was manifest.

'You got through. I knew you would, well done. How's Maggie?'

'She's fine Toby, she'll be OK,' *Stiletto* reassured him, praying there was truth in her words. She rubbed his arm instinctively as he sat resting against the bushes.

'What about you?' she asked, concern etched in her expression as she watched his face. It was drawn and grey. The effort had been even greater than she could have imagined. The heat of the day still scorched down on them and the weight of Rommel had taken an enormous toll.

His clothing was soaked, his face was grimy with sweat and dirt. His eyes were filled with muck at the corners and they had lost their clarity.

'Good to go,' he said with spirit and a tired smile. She knew then she had picked him right when she first saw him. He would walk until he dropped to save his friend and he would never give up. She bit her lip, fearing he was close to exhaustion but knowing there was still so far to go.

Hurley asked Merlin to keep watch and he handed Toby a water bottle.

'G'day mate, I heard you were in a bind. Thought I'd just pop over the border and see how things were going.'

Toby smiled despite himself. 'Thanks Matt, I'm all out,' he admitted as he undid the screw-top and drank deeply.

Hurley set about replacing Rommel's drip. 'And drink all that, ya gunna need it,' he warned Toby over his shoulder.

Hurley thought better of removing any of Rommel's dressings. There was no fresh blood and he reasoned it might only make things worse. Surprisingly, he had a strong pulse. It was a good sign. They laid him on the stretcher ready to go.

'I gave him a morphine shot when we left the vehicle,' Toby said, 'unfortunately, he's been pretty much head down across my back since then. God, he needs that stretcher, and so do I,' he joked to himself.

But it was no joke. Toby was knackered. Not only was he on the back end of a high-octane day in which two of his team had been shot, he had just carried one of them in relentless heat for over an hour uphill and over rocky ground.

But he was strong and determined, Hurley could see it in his face and he knew his training had prepared him for this. He looked at his watch. It would be another hour and more to get them back to the vehicles, and all uphill.

'OK, let's go. Take it nice and easy, for Rommel's sake. Slow and steady wins the race,' he chirped as they each took a handle and moved off, Rommel's drip bag hanging from Hurley's webbing. *However it ends, this will be a day to remember,* he thought.

When they first set off, Hurley's plan was to stop every fifteen minutes and break for five. That idea simply did not fly. After less than ten minutes, they needed a break and he rested them for ten. That became the pattern as the little group struggled up the rocky escarpment towards the border, hiding periodically under the cover of the thorny trees, like lost ants trying to get a sugar cube back to the nest.

After one stop they were about to set off and Toby pushed them back to ground well into the shade of the canopy, gesticulating wildly and his face anxious.

'Chopper!' He yelled through gritted teeth.

At first Hurley was confused and thought Toby might be delirious, but quickly the noise grew. Soon the TNI helicopter was roaring overhead at low altitude, so low that the foliage overhead shook from the down thrust of the rotors.

When Hurley looked up, he saw the ominous green belly of the chopper and the brown face of the crewman riding at the door, leaning on his machine gun. But he was looking out and away, towards the border. It buzzed over them like an angry wasp and then was gone as quickly as it had appeared.

'Jesus Toby, you've got fuckin' good ears, thank Christ,' Hurley said wryly as they moved off, not knowing if the sortie was routine, or hunting for them. Hurley knew they were all thinking the same. He gritted his teeth and pushed them on; in the end it didn't matter, the solution was the same — get moving and get home.

There were no complaints and all Hurley heard from the others was their panting from the relentless heat and the groans of their physical exertion. For not the first time, he was proud to be with them. Their clothing quickly became bathed in sweat and pasted to their bodies.

Hurley gave his bush gloves to Merlin and *Stiletto* to ease their burden but still their hands blistered from the weight and friction of the old wooden handles. They were soon bloody, the skin ripped from them.

They all alternated handles to spare their hands and aching limbs and the group grimly struggled on, earning each rest period and needing it sooner every time, not any cooler in the shade but at least protected from the burning rays of the sun. At each break, Hurley scanned the area through his binoculars, ensuring it was clear before they set off.

They were almost in sight of the rocky streambed marking the border when a movement in the shadows attracted Hurley's attention. It was a figure in dark camouflage fatigues. He motioned the group to lie down quietly in the grass and he crawled forward to check the area.

At first he thought it might be a militia insurgent. He cursed, *Jesus, the first militia I see and I'm on the wrong bloody side of the border.* As he watched though, his concern grew. There were several figures walking around and they were all dressed the same.

It was much worse than he had first thought. It wasn't a militia group, it was a TNI patrol resting in the shade, right in front of them and blocking their path to safety.

Hurley slowly crawled back to the others and briefed them on what he had seen.

'Listen,' he whispered, 'we're not in any shape to go the long way around. We'll have to backtrack too far and it will take the last of our reserves. We will have to wait them out. The danger is if they move in our direction.' He let them absorb this and continued, 'If that happens, and it looks like they'll walk over the top of us, I'll crawl away from here across the low ground and then show myself at a distance, and by doing so draw their attention away from the group. They will arrest me and I will be able to play lost. Don't worry, that will all be sorted out at a higher level, but it will leave the way open for you guys to push over the border to safety. One last guts effort, can you do that without me, for Rommel?'

They all nodded, grim faced and exhausted, but realising Hurley's plan was the only option. Toby caught his eye. *Thank you for doing this for my team.* He knew as well as Hurley did that it was equally possible the TNI would fire at Hurley first, with results neither of them could predict. Hurley nodded his acknowledgement, but his eyes were resolute. *It ain't over till it's over.*

He crawled forward again to better monitor the patrol. The team lay in the grass and waited, knowing that if Hurley was to sacrifice himself, he would move from where he now lay and they would then have to judge when to go, and do it quickly.

As Hurley watched, the soldiers began to pick up their weapons and those that had taken their shirts off were getting dressed again. It was the moment of truth. Hurley tensed as a soldier walked towards him out of the streambed, but then he suddenly changed direction.

He was an outrider for the patrol, the main effort was along the streambed and he paralleled them as the patrol moved off across Hurley's front; they were obviously using the border as the patrol focus. He let his head fall face first in the grass in gratitude. *We might just make it.*

He waited for some minutes after seeing the last soldier disappear from view, and then by experience he waited some more before crawling back to the group.

'Let's go,' he said, sounding as happy as he really was.

They had a second wind now after a longer rest and they moved as quickly as they had all day, up the gradient and across the streambed, and into East Timor. They stopped a safe distance inside and their relief and excitement was palpable.

For all intents and purposes, they had made it. They carried the stretcher with renewed vigour now and didn't baulk on the steep ground that had been so easy on the way out but tested them now, the sharp rocks biting into the soles of their boots.

Before long they were on the brown earthen track Hurley knew would bring them to the road, and back to the vehicles.

When they broke into the clearing, Hurley could smell coffee. Harry and Jack were brewing up for their return and they both looked up to see the team stagger the final yards and lay the stretcher on the ground.

They all collapsed around it, breathless. But their faces said it all — *we did it*. Harry and Jack came up and congratulated them, patting each of them on the back. But Harry's eyes shone with admiration and the debt owed to Hurley for the part he had played, without which he knew they may not have carried the day.

Hurley nodded and grinned, his eyes and teeth showing out from his grimy face. They all laughed together; relief now they could say it was done. Jack helped Hurley check Rommel while they loaded the stretcher into the back of the Land Rover.

A hot drink syrupy with sugar brought a contented smile to Toby's lips, but they applied another drip to him anyway. Jack said Toby was as dry as a dead dingo's donger, and although only Hurley understood exactly what that was, none of them needed to be told he was dangerously dehydrated.

With *Stiletto*'s help they sat him in the back of the Land Cruiser with the biggest mug of tea that could be had. She sat with him, talking with her hand close to his arm. Hurley caught his eye and winked in admiration; soldier to soldier. No one had given more than Toby. Hurley knew it was a guts effort to remember, to talk about, and to inspire others with.

There was a call over the radio, and they watched, hushed and waiting as Harry listened intently, one ear to the radio and a finger pushed into the other to help him hear. Hurley watched on too, helpless.

'Good news everyone,' Harry announced finally, as he limped back to the group. 'Maggie has just come out of surgery and all is well. The chopper is inbound at Batugade in thirty minutes, and we need to be there.'

A weary cheer went up and *Stiletto* caught Hurley's eye with an impish grin. *Our girl is OK.* She had brought Maggie home against the odds and they would both live to tell the tale. *Thank you,* his eyes said in return, and they both smiled in secret conspiracy.

Before long the vehicles were working their way back through Maudeko, a small village of no real importance, but a place Hurley would remember for the rest of his life.

40

Casa Dili

Dili, United Nations administered East Timor

....

February 2001

Hurley found Harry in the library at Casa Dili, surrounded by reports and papers of various kinds.

'Jesus Harry, I have to say it was a bit disconcerting having Michelle turn up unexpectedly at sparrow fart this morning at HQ looking for me.'

'Sorry mate, sit down. I need to speak to you before you head up to see Maggie, that's all,' he said, apologetically. 'She's alright, you know.'

'Yeah, I know, Michelle told me. So, what's all the ballyhoo?'

Harry collected his thoughts. 'In short, I need you to speak with Marcelino Borges,' he answered without fanfare.

Hurley was completely taken aback. 'I don't actually want to be in the same room with that bastard, Harry.'

Harry nodded. 'I understand that. And I would do this if I could, but the fact is I can't. You're the only person I trust to pull this off, and one of the few who can actually get in there to do it.'

'What's the problem?'

'It seems Borges is something of an international celebrity

since he's magically turned up,' he said with a wry grin. 'He's the highest profile militia insurgent in detention — ever. The press is having a field day, trying all sorts of tricks to get to him for an exclusive interview. So, the UN has shut the gate, only UN officials can talk to him. As a badged UN member, and his arresting officer, you can apply and get time with him, I can't,' he explained simply.

Hurley understood, but also that it was more complicated still. 'Even so Harry, the conditions aren't appropriate. The visiting room is almost a public forum, you have to pay dirty top dollar to get what I think you're talking about, time in a private cell, no guards hanging around — and more importantly — me not getting strip searched on the way in,' he finished with a distasteful look on his face.

Harry chuckled. 'Yeah, I know. It cost me three hundred US and your meeting is at ten tomorrow morning. You'll have an hour, hour and half tops.'

Hurley closed his eyes and exhaled, exasperated. It was typical Harry but he could also sense the urgency. He knew Harry never put people out over a trifle.

'It's that important, mate?'

'Yeah. Let me fill you in on the full story of the recent operation, believe me, you'll need it all to talk to Borges. And then I'll give you something very interesting to read.'

For a good hour Harry told Hurley the complex story of the operation to capture Borges. Hurley couldn't help but be impressed, and a little embarrassed. He knew he had been too critical when things had gone wrong, and it came back to haunt him as these things often did.

He had seen things at the time through the lens of Maggie's wounding, and it had skewed his thinking. That said, he knew it was not held against him, least of all by Harry. All the team loved Maggie and Hurley knew their relationship was universally accepted. He also knew there wasn't one of them who took exception to his attitude that day and saw it only as protective of Maggie.

He became engrossed in Harry's telling of the tale, as he always did at these times. Harry was ever the master storyteller, his keen mind missing nothing and every detail at his fingertips. In the telling Hurley learned what they had heard from the listening device in Urquhart's watch, and all that had come about from it. *You couldn't make this stuff up*, he thought as he listened, spellbound by Harry's narrative, and then by the tape which culminated in Urquhart's murder. It blew his mind.

Harry turned the tape off and Hurley picked up one of the photos.

'Who is this bloke Rio?' Hurley asked finally, pulling it all together in his head and pointing to the dapper Indonesian in the photo.

'He is the sponsor and his name is Rio Hermanto. He's a senior BAKIN counter-intelligence officer.'

Hurley's eyebrows rose. It was all grim but breathtaking stuff, he had to admit. But seemingly to him, the story had a natural end and he was curious as to what else Harry wanted to wring from it.

'Well, that sure takes the cake, Harry. So, what is it you want me to read that takes this to a new level?' he asked, his brow wrinkled in curiosity. 'It seems to me that Borges is in custody, and Urquhart got pretty much what he deserved.'

'To a certain degree, yes,' Harry agreed tentatively, and then handed Hurley a single pink sheet of paper. 'This is the translated transcript of the audio taken immediately *after* the shooting of Urquhart; the original was in Indonesian.'

Hurley nodded and sat back on the Chesterfield sofa. He read through the document and as he did his face paled. The tide of anger and hate rose in his throat. He looked up to see Harry staring knowingly back at him.

'That fuckin' bastard!' Hurley spat, 'This *does* take it to a whole new level.'

'Yes, it does. So, you see, it is that important,' he said quietly to Hurley.

'And what exactly do you want from Borges?' Hurley asked, his eyes narrowed and ready for a fight, his anger fuelling the hatred he now felt towards the real cause of all their pain, the one on whose shoulders it had rested all along.

'Everything, my old mate. Everything about the personalities, the connection, the relationship, the operation. Everything,' he said resolutely, the anger in him too, and barely subdued. 'I want every-fucking-thing, and I want to finish it.'

Hurley's jaw tightened and he nodded his understanding, he needed no more persuasion.

'Have you thought about how we might get Borges to talk?' he asked finally.

Harry selected a thick fawn-coloured file from the nearby pile and passed it to Hurley. It was well thumbed and dog-eared.

'Yes, but let me know what you think. You can have a good look when you come back this afternoon. This is part one of three by the way.'

'Actually, I was intending to stay overnight with Maggie at this… secret rest home you have her hidden away in,' he said with a cheeky grin.

'Were you now? Well young fella, you better get to work then,' Harry ordered, his eyes twinkling, 'because I'm not telling you how to get there until you've done your homework.'

'Jesus Christ, Harry!' Hurley implored, knowing already it was a lost cause.

'He will not help you, and in any case, I told Lucy you wouldn't be there before ten thirty anyway.'

'Thank you so much for organising my social life,' Hurley said, his voice dripping with sarcasm.

Harry smiled broadly. 'Well, look at it this way, that's three hours away, aren't you glad now you were up so early?'

41

The Jesuit Refuge
United Nations administered East Timor

....

February 2001

The old house stood alone above the city, high on the escarpment and with a commanding view back across Dili. It could only be reached by a single twisted road that was sealed in places, but it was badly pot-holed and in disrepair. As Hurley drove the Land Rover carefully around the bends, the sea breeze blew fresh through the open windows of the cabin and the canvas covering flapped uncontrollably.

The morning was bright and the sky a startling blue; it complimented the seascape laid out before him perfectly, even though the vista disappeared periodically through the trees as the vehicle wound its way up the heights. It also mirrored Hurley's mood. It had been ten days since he had seen Maggie at the airfield in Batugade, and he had waited for nothing else.

The house had once been the headquarters of the Society of Jesus in East Timor, and home to the most senior Jesuit, the Father-General. Hurley gleaned the story from Harry when he had finally relented and given Hurley the directions to Maggie's refuge, but not before Hurley had prepared for his confrontation with Borges.

The team had acquired temporary use of the house, through a friend of a friend, or so Harry said, for use in Maggie and Rommel's convalescence. Although Rommel had since returned to Casa Dili, both he and Maggie had spent the absolute minimum time in the national hospital in Dili before being quietly relocated to the Jesuit house.

Behind them, no record remained that anyone with their names had entered the hospital, and certainly no one with a gunshot wound was ever admitted on the fateful day Marcelino Borges was snatched from West Timor.

As he approached the house, Hurley thought the setting looked vaguely Mexican. The small semi-circular gravel drive was centred around a large cactus bed and the house, low set with wide verandas amidst an arid landscape, was populated by cacti and potted succulents, some hanging from baskets on the front veranda.

As he brought the vehicle to a halt, he could see Lucy leaning on the porch railing. She smiled and held a finger to her lips, so he did not sound the horn as he had planned. She came down the stairs to greet him.

'G'day Lucy, how's tricks? Apart from pulling hospital picket, that is,' he teased.

Hurley knew from his discussions with Harry that each of the team was being rostered at the Jesuit house to watch over Maggie while she recovered. Looking around, he could think of more arduous duties.

She seemed to read his thoughts. 'I'm grand thanks Matt, and yourself?'

'Good thanks. How's the patient?'

'Well. Very well in fact. The doctor was here earlier and says she will be well ready for her leave in a few weeks. He comes each day and changes the dressings and it's looking better each time.

She still has a bit of pain with big upper body movements, and her nights are restless, but they say that will pass.'

He nodded and turned to walk with her back up the stairs. She touched his arm lightly to stop him, her face close to his.

'There's just one thing,' she warned, her voice a whisper.

'Oh?' he said, attentive and his brow wrinkled with concern.

'She's talked a little about the wound, fair enough, but I think she's thinking about the scars. I think the beach holiday you two have planned in Australia might a bit confronting so soon after the incident. I know I wouldn't want to be the only woman on the beach with an in/out bullet wound scar in her back and chest,' she said conspiratorially, holding his arm and watching to see his reaction.

Hurley nodded understandingly. 'Thanks Lucy, leave it with me.'

'She's on the veranda at the back. And you didn't hear that from me,' she said, smiling kindly and making way for him to enter the house.

It was a cool and airy house with high ceilings, exposed beams and large rattan fans circulating slowly, keeping the air in constant motion. It contained a tasteful mixture of European and local furniture and had a comfy, homey feel. Hurley noted the large ornate crucifix on the main wall guarding the entrance, the carved body of Christ in eternal agony as it stared forbiddingly down on all non-believers. Like himself, Hurley thought.

He passed through the impressive public rooms and poked his head slowly around the large doorway that led onto the rear veranda. It gave him a secret side-on view of Maggie as she relaxed in a wide swinging chair, the Savu Sea pristine and glistening in the background.

He caught his breath and waited, content to watch as she painted her fingernails, a bright cherry red that matched her lipstick. The colour had returned to her cheeks and he closed his eyes momentarily, pushing from his mind the last vision he had of her at the airfield in Batugade, her face so deathly pale then.

She wore a loose-fitting white t-shirt through which he could just discern the outline of her bandaged chest, and navy-blue shorts. Her legs were smooth and sun-kissed, and her leather sandals showcased her toenails, painted in the same colour she was applying to her fingernails.

Her movements were fluid and careful as she applied the polish deftly with the little brush, first one hand and then the other. Her foot moved slowly against the tiled floor, just enough to keep the chair in slow motion as she did so.

She hummed as she worked, and it was a bright, happy sound. It came to him that he wanted her badly, and as she applied the final coat to the last nail he stepped around the corner.

'Hello pretty lady,' he announced, with more emotion than he had planned. She looked towards him and her eyes lit up. He knew they mirrored his own.

'Matt,' she mouthed, almost soundlessly, her hand reaching towards him automatically and then returning to pat the striped canvas seat next to her, beckoning for him to sit.

Hurley noted she did not try to stand, and he bent over, eager to kiss the lips that were offered to him, and holding her face gently, letting her decide when to end it.

She held his face too, her hands soft and warm. He noted her eyes were closed, holding the moment and the memory. It was her way.

'Jesus, don't be doing that,' he said finally, breathless. 'You never know where that might end.'

'That's against doctor's orders actually,' she said primly, goading him.

Hurley laughed and nestled next to her. He put his arm

gingerly around her shoulder, but his touch was very light, and pensive.

'I'm not going to break,' she said, happy for him being there and to have his care all the same.

'I'm staying tonight, even if I have to sleep on the couch,' he said, pretending to be put out.

'I'm sure we can do better than that,' she said playfully.

'Harry said the doctor has signed off on your leave,' he said enthusiastically. 'That's great news.'

'Yes, I can't wait for us to go away. Is yours confirmed?'

'Yep, Jodie, my ops sergeant was very happy to swap.'

'That's brilliant! I shall have to send her a big thank you,' she said warmly.

'Listen Maggie, I've been thinking. I know you were keen when we first talked about having leave together, saying you wanted the classic *sun, surf and sex* holiday in Oz...'

'I did not!' she said in mock horror, smacking his arm playfully.

'Well, I heard the *sun and surf* and filled the gaps in for myself,' he said, grinning and interlocking her fingers with his.

'But you know what? I'm fed up with the heat, it's giving me the pip to be honest. Also, Jack was saying that brand new skin is very tender and vulnerable to sun damage, so we'll need to be careful not to get sunburnt. That all-over tan you promised me will have to wait till next summer I'm afraid,' he explained, feigning disappointment.

She glared at him in jest and then her face was serious. 'I had some worries about the sun too,' she conceded, half truthfully.

'So, it's settled then,' he said, without allowing her to elaborate. 'I'll have a look at some other options that might keep us out of the sun, maybe a train trip, cool and air-conditioned. We could even nip over to New Zealand, it's always cooler there at this time of year. You'd love it.'

'Could we do that do you think, Matt?'

Hurley could see the thought relaxed her.

'Sure. I don't care where we go Maggie, I just want to go with you. So, don't you worry about it anymore. Doctor Hurley's orders.'

She smiled and hugged his arm, pressing her head against his shoulder.

'I had a good chat with Harry this morning about the operation,' he said, changing the subject.

'I know, he was up here a couple of days ago and gave me the third degree for the post-operation report.'

'I'm sure he didn't,' Hurley corrected her, 'but I'm also sure he got what he needed, for everyone's sake.'

'Yes, but I kept something from him,' she confessed softly, her eyes downcast.

Hurley turned to face her, put his hand under her chin and locked eyes with her, looking for the answer that would make this right. He waited, watching. She bit her lip.

'I knew he was there Matt, the man who shot me, and Rommel. I felt him there, I even turned around to check. And then I turned my back on him,' she started all in a rush, it was all tumbling out now.

'Hang on a minute,' Hurley interrupted. 'Just back up. You *felt* him there. Did you actually *see* him?'

'No. But I could feel him there, so strongly I was afraid, and so much so I just had to turn around and check. But there was no one there. So, I paid it off, and turned away. And look what happened.'

Her eyes were moist and alert, and suddenly regretful. Hurley could see in her eyes she had gone back to the house where she was shot.

'OK. Listen to me,' he counselled earnestly, but softly. 'You did right not to mention it to Harry. It doesn't add any value to the post-op report or the lessons learned, but it is something *you* can learn from. What you describe is instinct Maggie, some people have it in spades and others not at all. The boffins think it might be the highest form of analysis, the sub-conscious mind processing information and sensory cues from the environment. We just don't know, you may have heard his footfall, or heard him draw his weapon, smelled him, or anything, we just can't know.'

There was a long silence while she processed this.

'I suppose you're right,' she conceded.

'I am right,' he urged, 'and don't doubt yourself. You were magnificent that day. Toby told me how he got to the gate just in time to see you take that shot from the ground. Outstanding young lady, and don't you ever forget it,' he chastised her playfully, but his tone said how proud he was of her and that the issue was closed.

'Did you see Rommel this morning?' she asked, slightly embarrassed by Hurley's commendation of her actions, but pleased nevertheless.

'I did. He looks like bloody Tin-Tin with that bandage around his head and his fair hair poking out the top.'

They both laughed and Maggie crossed her arms as the pain pulsed through her.

'Sorry,' he said quickly, putting a protective arm around her. 'But he'll be fine, providing he doesn't dwell on the little things that can't be changed. For Christ's sake, the mission objective was met, and no one died. It's a win.'

'That's very measured and a bit blasé from the man who nearly knocked Harry's block off on the day,' she teased, grinning wickedly.

'I did not,' he said quietly with a slight grin, just a little embarrassed.

'Well, that's not what Lucy told me,' Maggie said as she twisted the knife happily.

'Well,' Hurley yelled at the top of his voice, 'Lucy is a serial embellisher of the truth!'

They both laughed. And inside, Lucy laughed too.

'What small things with Rommel did you mean?' she asked, when they had both stopped laughing.

'Ah, he's all in a pickle about the fact that he didn't prop at the gate. It was poor close-quarter battle drills unfortunately, and he knows it. He's living it over and over in his head, poor bloke.'

'What did you say to him?'

'I told him to put his hand up for extra training, and then I thanked him.'

Maggie looked at him askew, her face questioning.

'Maggie,' he said seriously, facing her. 'You do realise if Rommel had done the *right* thing, you would be dead, don't you? That guy was distracted by Rommel's arrival at the gate and saw him as a new threat. That's why he shot him. If there was no new threat, he would have put another bullet into you, and at that range he would very likely have killed you. It's just one of life's little funnies — God at his computer. So, I told Rommel the options are; two of our people wounded and both recover, or one person dead. It's a no-brainer. Just quietly, I'm very happy with the result we got,' he said simply, in his matter of fact way.

'Me too, now that you put it like that,' she agreed, and leaned into him.

'He's also taking it badly that he called the house empty when it wasn't. But as I told him, which was supported by all the others, on the information available any one of us would have made the same call and he shouldn't beat himself up over it.'

'He'll settle I suppose, it's a big shock,' she conceded, perhaps speaking as much for herself as for Rommel, Hurley mused.

'Talking about shocks, Harry had one for me this morning. He wants me to talk to Borges.'

'Oh, Matt,' she said, her voice filled with dread for him. 'What for?'

'All for good reason, Maggie. Don't worry, it's just follow-up stuff from the op. A line of inquiry we think he might be able to tie off. Harry can't do it because he isn't with the UN, so I'm best placed to do it. He briefed me on all the background to do with the op, what a cracker it was, all things considered,' he summed up, the admiration evident in his voice.

'And I heard you sparkled bringing the team out,' she teased, but the pride was evident in her voice too. 'It's going to be one of your great stories isn't it?' She asked, smiling up at him.

Hurley just nodded, his gaze distant and a thin smile on his face.

'Have you seen Josefina?' he asked.

'Harry had to have Stan and Freon take her away from the hospital when I was there. It wasn't good for her security, but she wouldn't leave me. She's been up here a couple of times but Harry's keeping her well busy.'

'She was terrific that day with you, and then later bringing the guys out. I couldn't have asked for more,' he admitted. 'But I think you're going to have to brief me in here, Maggie. I mean, Josefina, she's not an *agent*, is she? Otherwise she would never be allowed within a bull's roar of Casa Dili, you know that just as much as I do.'

'That's something you'll have to speak to Harry about, Matt,' she said carefully, pretending to be officious and making light of it, but obviously guarding her hand. 'All I can say is she's absolutely amazing. Her tradecraft is unbelievable, and the way she reads people makes me think she might be a witch. She's the queen-piece on any operational chessboard I can tell you. I was lucky enough to get the job working with her, and I mean lucky. She saved my life Matt, and I owe her everything.'

'Yes, *we* do,' he emphasised. 'And you don't know how close she came to wasting that border guard the day you came over either.'

She sat forward slightly, her face attentive and searching. Her expression told Hurley this information was completely new to her.

'She carries her namesake in a special scabbard at the back of her waist, doesn't she?' Hurley quizzed, smiling, having put the little puzzle together.

'Yes, why? Tell me,' she urged.

'There was a moment when you were coming over. It was the longest moment of my life. I knew you were badly wounded, but I didn't know any more. It crossed my mind I might lose you when I'd just found you.'

She squeezed his hand tightly and put the back of her other hand to his cheek, running it down the line of his jaw. Her eyes glistened.

'That's why I got shitty with Harry, but that was stupid. Jack put me straight on that. It just is as it is. Anyway, when the guard got annoyed, I watched her hand go back to her waist and Harry told me to wait, because he knew what was going to happen. But it never did of course, she pulled it off. But I've no doubt she would have killed him in a heartbeat to get you over. You have that effect on people, I think,' he said, smiling and making light of it.

She nodded. 'One thing's for sure, all my guardian angels were there that day.'

She raised her face to his and kissed him long and lovingly on the cheek.

He turned his face and brought his lips to hers, kissing her with all the emotion he had stored up since they were last together. She held him, with her hand at the nape of his neck. Pausing, their faces close he could see her arousal too, and knew it was just for him.

'I love you, Matt Hurley,' she said softly, for his ears only.

'I know,' he answered, his grey eyes holding hers and smiling.

CHAPTER 42

UNITED NATIONS DETENTION FACILITY
DILI, UNITED NATIONS ADMINISTERED EAST TIMOR

....

February 2001

'*Bon dia*, Senhor Hurley,' the prisoner said formally, dipping his head slightly towards his visitor as the barred door slid closed with a loud clang and the guard walked away, his boots echoing on the cement floor. Hurley did not react, but the prisoner's greeting certainly gave him cause to think his visit might be even more interesting than he had anticipated.

Hurley was not in uniform and had not really anticipated that Borges would know him, know of him, or even remember his face from the airfield in Batugade. He shook Borges hand. It wasn't his choice but a cultural norm it was difficult to avoid without giving offence. He also knew the human contact created a sub-conscious connection which would advantage him, whether Borges realised it or not.

Borges skin was dry and cool, his hand thin and bony — *like a reptile*, thought Hurley.

'Hello Marcelino,' Hurley responded, using an informal tone which wasn't unfriendly, but deliberately choosing to abandon the cultural titles and affectations that Borges may have come to expect.

'You should know first of all, I cannot help you.' Borges opened unexpectantly in his thickly accented voice, establishing his red line as he saw it. 'I will not talk about the militia times. It tires me and I have a long, drawn out trial ahead of me, as you well know,' he said, in a way acknowledging Hurley's part in that process.

Hurly nodded slightly, *the militia times you would prefer to forget.* Hurley could see the person they had brought from West Timor at such great cost had changed markedly since the day of his arrest. Borges was not really a good-looking man, and there was a certain animal aura to him, but he was clean shaven and his hair had been cut and combed.

His clothes fitted him well, they were clean and light; linen shorts and a simple collared shirt worn loose, and leather sandals on his feet. His skin was a dark nut brown and glowed; he looked in far better health than the drugged war criminal he had been when Hurley had put the handcuffs on him in Batugade. He could have been on his way home from the beach.

'I don't want to know anything about those times,' Hurley said surprisingly as he sat down opposite Borges. He held Borges' gaze while he placed his hat and a vacuum flask he had brought onto the stained wooden table the UN Detention Centre had provided; the hat to the right, the flask to the left.

Borges watched him keenly, as prisoners always do. His eyes gave little away, though Hurley detected a glimmer of curiosity about his visit and his manner, which he thought might just be enough to play with.

Hurley pulled two small glasses, one from each pocket of his light jacket, and placed them on the table. He took his time to fill each of them from the flask. He pushed one across the table towards Borges and picked the other up and sipped from it. The aroma of the thick black coffee filled the cell, mixing with the odour of disinfectant and general damp.

'And you should also know that I can't offer you anything to help your situation.' Hurley further explained. 'I am not empowered to offer you any deal that would see you avoid your trial or reduce any sentence that might be applied.' *The trial you deserve, and the sentence you will rightfully get,* Hurley thought, but he didn't say it.

While he despised what the man opposite him had done, Hurley had long ago learned there is little point in antagonising someone just for sport, especially when you actually want something from them. He had supped with the devil for the greater good before, and as painful as it always was, he would do so again today.

'Then why have you come?' Borges challenged him, picking up the glass and drinking from it, his eyes watching Hurley, assessing, looking for the advantage like all predators do. And at the same time, he heralded his curiosity, and his weakness.

'Before we get to that, let's see if we can first determine the terms of trade,' Hurley suggested cryptically with a thin smile, taking another sip of his coffee and his eyes never leaving Borges.

'If you cannot help me, there is no basis for trade,' Borges stated flatly.

Hurley placed his glass on the table. 'Not necessarily,' he countered, as he reached into his shirt pocket and withdrew a photograph which he placed carefully, deliberately, on the table. He oriented it towards Borges and with one finger slid it slowly across the table for him to see.

Borges looked down at the photograph, as Hurley knew he would, and it captivated him. He did not look at Hurley for a long moment. Hurley knew he feared his eyes would be read, and he would be weaker because of it. He was right.

When he did look up, he had composed himself, but Hurley could see he was well on the path he had set himself.

'You don't come across to me as a person who would harm my wife and son,' Borges said sharply, his voice edged with emotion, his eyes moist.

'I'm not, and I never would,' Hurley said with conviction, and Borges knew it was the truth. 'But there is a world of difference between the life I can offer them, and the life they are leading now, which is the life they will surely continue to lead with you in prison for all of your son's life,' Hurley said, letting the last of it hang between them.

Borges shifted slightly on his chair, his gaze moved to the wall and he sat motionless, thinking. Hurley knew Borges was trying to work out just why he had come, he was trying to get ahead of the game to improve his own negotiating position. That wasn't going to happen.

Hurley took a packet of Indonesian *Kretek* cigarettes from his pocket and opened the foil top, exposing the dark cigarettes inside. He leaned over the table and offered Borges one, which he accepted. He laid the packet on the table near his hat, and with a cigarette lighter he lit Borges' cigarette.

'What exactly are you offering?' Borges finally asked, as he exhaled the blue smoke, and picked an errant piece of tobacco from between his yellowed teeth with a fingernail which was too long.

'I am prepared to offer your family a very reasonable sum of money, which will ensure their quality of life — living expenses, health care, education for your son — in return for your full cooperation on, shall we say, a matter of interest to me,' Hurley explained cryptically, laying the first of his cards on the table.

The small cell quickly filled with the pungent smoke from the *Kretek*, as it struggled to escape from the tiny barred windows high in the clean but unpainted cement walls. Hurley waited in the fug and showed no sign of impatience. It was actually one of his little quirks. He loved this part, and he could wait forever. He gave Borges all the time he needed and was never tempted to fill the silence.

'What sum are we talking about?' Borges asked finally, unwittingly signalling to Hurley that he cared less about the topic in question, than the spoils his family would enjoy.

'You can name the sum. But remember,' Hurley warned him, don't shit in your own bloody nest. We are talking about a reasonable sum for your family to live well in East Timor, not Hollywood; and for your son to be educated in the best schools in this country, not at Oxford.'

Borges laughed, and because the rhythm of interrogation dictated it, Hurley laughed with him. Hurley knew the power of it, and his message was passed too. Borges considered the offer. While he did, Hurley could see the wheels turning in his head and knew he was not in a position to baulk.

It was impossible to say what aspects Borges was weighing up, but in the end, it didn't matter.

'And in exchange for this you want my full cooperation about some… matter of interest to you, is that correct?'

'Yes.'

'And this matter is not connected to my militia activity or the militia activity of anyone else?'

'No.'

Borges considered this new information and nodded almost imperceptibly. Hurley reckoned he liked what he heard but was trying to work out exactly what it was he knew that might be so valuable.

'I have one condition too, and it is not negotiable,' Borges said gravely, shaking his head slightly.

Hurley did not blink but he thought this turn of events extraordinary. Borges was willing to forego a financial windfall for his family, as yet undefined, for something that was more important, but Hurley might reject. It could only be his life, or that of his family.

'I'm listening,' Hurley answered, nodding his encouragement.

'Nothing I say is to be traced to me, this discussion never happened. I won't put my family in a position where they might be killed in revenge for what I have said.'

'Agreed. Nothing you say will be attributed to you. We will do everything to exploit the information as having come from another source, otherwise it will not be used. We will not endanger you or your family,' Hurley promised, just as he had discussed with Harry when they had workshopped the possibility this might be raised.

Borges nodded slowly. Hurley saw in his eyes he had made his decision.

'One hundred thousand US dollars,' he said finally, holding Hurley's gaze.

'Agreed,' replied Hurley, without any hesitation. He smiled inwardly; not only were they well on track, he had won his bet with Harry who had counted on Borges being much greedier. Borges would never know how high Harry had been prepared to go, and it was much, much higher.

'So, do I just trust you to keep your word?' Borges said almost playfully, but still assessing Hurley as he did so.

'In part, yes,' Hurley began, as he reached into the internal pocket of his jacket and withdrew a package wrapped in white paper. He placed it on the table and pushed it across to Borges.

'Because of your situation this is a little complex, but I will make it work. You may count that if you wish. It contains ten thousand US dollars and it is a show of good faith on my part. Hide that and give it to your wife at her visit tomorrow. When we have completed our conversation, I will deliver the remaining amount personally to your wife in the next few days. Please tell her to be… careful… with such a large sum of money. We don't want to attract unwanted attention, and neither should you. There are no further strings attached.'

Borges thought this through and then picked up the package. He slit the paper with his long, discoloured thumbnail and opened it to see the used US notes inside. While he didn't count the contents, he flicked through the notes perfunctorily, probably noting the denominations, and then leaned back on his chair, stuffing the package securely down the front of his shorts.

Hurley thought on balance he may have adopted the dictum *one bird in the hand is worth two in the bush* and would probably be happy even if Hurley reneged on the remainder.

'Alright,' he said finally. 'What is it you want to know?'

Hurley took a sip from his coffee glass and slowly placed it down. He leaned slightly forward on his chair and rested his arms on the table. He held Borges' gaze and his own was open to the other's scrutiny. It was game time and he played his final card.

'Tell me everything you know about Roger Sanderson.'

~

Hurley leaned back on his chair and went over every aspect of Borges' story in his mind. He had already reviewed and questioned Borges' story in fine detail and satisfied himself that the line of inquiry was fully exploited.

In some respects, he was staggered at the extent of Borges' knowledge. His story certainly contained everything Harry had asked for, and more. Moreover, much of it confirmed other information Borges couldn't possibly have known, and his version of events and the murder of Urquhart was supported by the team's secret photography and the recording from Urquhart's watch.

On balance, Borges had been truthful with him, certainly within the bounds of his own knowledge. He had earned his money. Nevertheless, Hurley was both bitterly angry and deeply sad in equal measure that in some ways their worst suspicions had turned out to be true. Still, he sensed there might still be icing to be had on this cake.

'Can you prove any of that?' Hurley asked finally.

'Does the payment depend on proof?' Borges asked guardedly.

'No of course not, that wasn't the agreement. You've already earned your money, but it would help me all the same.'

Borges thought about this and Hurley sensed he had done enough to now get something for free. He sensed also that some form of proof might exist but there was something he needed to get around, a bridge he had to cross, to get to it.

He noted Borges did not immediately ask for more money in exchange for proof. If indeed it did exist, there was something at stake here that was more important than money, something he didn't want to part with. He took a punt.

'You took out insurance, didn't you Marcelino?' Hurley put to him, directly, but ever so gently.

Borges nodded, just once.

'Tell me about it,' Hurley coaxed.

The guard's approaching footsteps alerted them both. It seemed the precious time Harry had paid for with their celebrity prisoner had expired. The keys rattled in the lock.

'When you visit my wife, ask to borrow my family Bible,' Borges whispered urgently. 'I will tell her you will come for it. Make sure my wife is alone but do not alert her. What you want is pasted into the back cover. When you have finished with it, return everything. I may need it in the future.'

'What is it?' Hurley urged under his breath.

'Everything you need. And remember your promise to me.'

'The money will be paid.'

'No, that's not important. The promise that my family is not exposed.'

'Yes, you have my word,' Hurley acknowledged, as the guard placed the handcuffs on Borges' wrists.

He turned to face Hurley. He seemed taller and stood just a tad straighter than he had previously. His expression was of someone who had achieved something, someone who still had some element of control.

'I was like you once,' he said simply, his voice thick with emotion. 'My word was trusted, I was respected. Then all the madness came.'

He shook his head and his face dropped. Regret.

Hurley looked at him but kept his feelings in check. It was a common story he had heard before in places just like this, from people just like Borges.

'Then own your crimes, speak the truth, and accept your punishment,' he counselled. 'Most importantly, do not make those women face you in court. They will relive their pain, and it will bring shame on their families, and yours. Only when you give back the dignity you have stolen from them can you hope to win back what you have lost.'

Borges looked Hurley in the eye and in that instant, he thought Borges knew it was the truth and he might act on it. A faint hope perhaps, but it was the best Hurley could do. He watched as the guard led Borges away, their feet patting on the cement floor, just like his and Harry's had done that day in the Kissing House. He closed his eyes and pushed the memory away.

You were never like me, he thought, as he walked along the narrow corridor and heard the sliding door bang shut behind him.

43

Laulara
United Nations administered East Timor

March 2001

Hurley enjoyed the short drive to the little village of Laulara; for much of the journey the road was wide and in good condition, the vegetation low and lush by the roadside. The air was heavy with the threat of rain and overhead the low clouds were the colour of burnished iron.

Hurley eyed them carefully and reckoned he might just make the twenty kilometres back to Dili before the storm broke. Still, it was better to be safe than sorry and he had borrowed Harry's hard top Land Cruiser rather than be caught under the questionable tarp of the Land Rover.

As he drove into the village, his mood changed to reflect the sky above. Like many of the small satellite villages within touching distance of Dili, the wretchedness of the inhabitants was plain to see. Half a dozen barefoot children played without purpose in what was the main street, the larger dusty road around which most of the houses were set.

Their clothing was dirty and threadbare; grimy faces with matted hair looked up at him blankly. Thick yellow snot bubbled from their noses as they breathed. Here and there, mangy dogs ranged around the village sniffing for any morsel that might sustain their emaciated bodies. Like the children, they were sullen and lethargic, and their eyes were vacant and uncaring.

The house Hurley was looking for was near the end of the row on the left, and he easily identified it from the description the team had given him at Casa Dili. Harry had been in a right chirpy mood; over the moon with Hurley's interaction with Borges and what it might mean. In truth they all knew the lead had to be followed to the bitter end, but Hurley's agreement to visit Borges' wife burdened him even though he knew the importance of it.

Hurley parked outside the house that had once been green, although there were only scrapings of paint left on the dirty cement walls. The door and the window shutters, two of which could be seen from the street, had fared better; the thin wooden planks holding the green paint over time.

He knew the house belonged to a distant cousin of Borges; his wife Senhora Luisa had relocated from the border area to support her husband and more easily visit him in detention in Dili. Hurley walked to the door and took a deep breath as he knocked, stepping back from the raised doorstep as he did so, with his small backpack in hand.

When the door was answered Hurley was taken aback, but there was no hint of this in his demeanour. He knew from her photo that it was Borges' wife standing before him, but he had prepared himself for a difficult encounter; he sensed immediately it could be something entirely different.

'*Bon dia*, Senhora Borges,' he said formally.

She smiled politely and stepped to one side, allowing his entry as she held the door open.

'*Bon dia*, Senhor Hurley,' she replied as Hurley crossed the doorstep into the house.

She was clearly expecting him and had obviously been briefed by her husband. In some ways she was the epitome of everything the urchins playing outside in the street were not. Her floral dress was not new, but it was immaculate and in good repair. The light pattern projected a gaiety against the gloom of the storm's approach.

The light brown skin of her face and arms was smooth and shiny, and her black hair was sleek and pulled back in a small tight bun. It was carefully decorated with hairpins featuring old gold coins. Hurley knew such decorations were not worn to be showy or as a statement of wealth; they were hand crafted and common throughout the country, and often received as gifts by women prior to marriage.

She was an attractive woman with no need of make-up to highlight her beauty. Hurley noted the photo he had shown Borges had not done her justice at all. She carried herself with grace, but in her eyes, Hurley could see the pain and shame that had been visited on her by her husband.

She too came from a prominent East Timorese family, but instead of the position of privilege that was her right to enjoy, she was now damaged goods. Instead, she would forever be known as the wife of the war criminal Borges. She seemed to sense Hurley's thoughts and gestured awkwardly towards the wooden table, covered with a simple linen cloth.

Upon this she had set two ornate coffee glasses and a matching glass pot, as yet empty, but the aroma of coffee was in the air nevertheless, its origin in another room. Another matching bowl contained perfect white cubes of sugar and a small metal spoon, unusual for East Timor, Hurley thought, and probably provided for his benefit.

Also for his benefit on the table was the old family Bible, its black leather cover smooth and inviting to the touch, in fact, more inviting to Hurley than Senhora Borges knew.

The room was sparsely furnished but neat and clean, it was the main living room of the house. The other rooms, while unseen to Hurley, were off the main room or the single hallway he could see leading away. Hurley sat as he was beckoned, and she excused herself, taking the glass coffee pot away with her to what he presumed was the kitchen.

When she returned, she sat across from Hurley, just as her husband had done three days before. Her opening caught Hurley somewhat by surprise.

'Thank you Senhor Mateus for treating my husband as you have,' she said informally but in a matter of fact way, to which Hurley warmed immediately. 'He should not expect and is not deserving of the courtesy and respect you have shown towards him.'

Hurley looked into the eyes of the woman opposite him. Her life was all but destroyed, and she knew it. She and her son were among the collateral damage wrought by her husband and his crimes, and she clearly had her own thoughts about that, Hurley reflected. She didn't deserve to be reminded of it.

'There are a great many people who must answer for their crimes Senhora Luisa and your husband is one of them. It is not for me to decide their guilt, administer their punishment, or take revenge. The courts will do their job and bring the entire episode to a close. Unfortunately, the pain will never go away for any of the victims, which include you and your son. Until then, how I treat people reflects on me, not them.'

She considered this as she stood and poured their coffee, the steam rising from the glasses. Hurley thought by her look that she appreciated his acknowledgement of her situation. She nodded and smiled sadly as she sat down.

'It does you credit and is nothing less than I expected. Your reputation in Balibo and on both sides of the border is well known.

You are a good man, Senhor Mateus, in a world where too many men have lost their way,' she said bitterly as she sat down.

'I have something for you, Senhora Luisa,' Hurley said, a little embarrassed and taking the opportunity to change the subject as he reached for his backpack.

'And I you,' she replied, passing the Bible on the table to him. Hurley nodded and took the book from her. He placed it next to him on the table.

From his pack he took nine packages wrapped in white paper, just like the one he had passed to Borges in the cell in Dili, and placed them carefully, neatly on the table.

'Please assure yourself there is ninety thousand US dollars in total Senhora Luisa, as I promised your husband,' he said sincerely.

In response, she very deliberately ferried the packets from the table and placed them into the drawer of a heavy wooden cabinet sitting along the wall. When she had finished, she closed the drawer with a woody squeak and returned to the table. She took a sip from her coffee and looked at Hurley.

'Senhor Mateus, I have no doubt the amount is correct so please don't make me count it or you will make me feel like a drug dealer, or worse.'

They both laughed easily, and Hurley thought it a good moment, and she an extraordinary woman. She would have her dignity to the end, of that he had no doubt and his heart went out to her.

'Thank you,' Hurley replied, humbled, as he placed the bible away in his pack, but also for the compliment she had afforded him.

'Senhora Luisa, please allow me to provide you with some... security advice,' Hurley offered.

'Of course, Senhor Mateus.'

'Firstly, you now have a great deal of money, the purpose of which is to ensure the quality of life of you and your son, and his education, although you may do with it as you wish, of course.'

Hurley took a grey business card from his shirt pocket and placed it on the table.

'You can trust this person. She is a lawyer in Brisbane and I have advised her that you might call. If you do, she will come to Timor if you wish and provide you with advice on protecting the money so you can even draw on it from Australia as you require. It is very important people remain unaware of the money as it could cause difficult questions to be asked and compromise your husband. Indeed, in certain circumstances it could endanger you and your son.'

'I don't know what has been traded for this money, Senhor Mateus. My only hope is that it will not bring the suffering of another innocent.'

'I give you my solemn word Senhora Luisa, it won't. My concern is only for you and your son.'

She picked the card up from the table and looked at it, turning it over in her slim elegant fingers. 'You trust this person?' she asked finally, watching Hurley closely.

She had the look of someone who had been betrayed, but desperately wanted to trust again.

'Yes, she is my wife's sister,' Hurley said simply. 'And should you seek her help I have arranged the fees will be modest.'

'Thank you,' she said, and walked over to place the card with the money in the cabinet. Hurley almost wanted to correct her understanding; it wasn't for her own, or Borges' benefit that such an arrangement had been made, it was quite simply to enhance the security of the transaction and protect it over time.

But for some reason it seemed trite to explain this and so he remained silent. When she returned, they both drank from their coffee glasses before Hurley finally spoke again.

'Senhora Luisa, should anyone ask why I have come today you should say that your husband asked me to visit you, to check on your circumstances, and to take the family Bible back to him,' he explained earnestly, his eyes watching hers carefully and willing her understanding. It was the cover story that would protect her and her son, and he needed to be sure she understood the importance of it.

'And should anyone ask about the lawyer, the card was given to you by a nameless but helpful guard at the UN Detention Centre when you visited your husband, do you understand?' he asked cryptically, holding her gaze and smiling.

'Yes.' She nodded with a thin smile at her lips, their conspiracy understood and complete.

They finished their coffee in light and comfortable conversation, their business finalised. Hurley knew from his research that Senhora Luisa had spent time at boarding school in Australia, and she was certainly an engaging conversationalist. At one stage she laughed at something trivial Hurley said and in that instant, she filled the otherwise dim room with light.

At that moment he glimpsed the woman she had previously been, but then the light faded and she was gone, lost to a fate Hurley could not control. Hurley thought Senhora Luisa was a person he would very much like to have known in better times. He sensed she felt the same about him and for not the first time in his life he cursed the circumstances that oftentimes brought people across his path.

When they parted, Senhora Luisa kissed Hurley formally on alternate cheeks. Her embrace was warm, and strangely reassuring. Hurley felt himself unworthy to enjoy her embrace; as a person who hated, and had hunted her husband, and finally arrested him. He sensed she knew this and wanted to tell him that was not the case.

Thoughts of the meeting consumed him on the journey home and the miles passed quickly under the wheels, unnoticed. With just a few kilometres to go, the rain drops, large and heavy, began pelting onto the road and hammering on the roof overhead.

The windscreen wipers tried valiantly but struggled to cope as Hurley ploughed on through the torrent, the road now awash. He patted the small backpack by his side and drew it closer to him, for safety. He could feel the Borges' family Bible inside and knew that, one way or the other, whatever happened now would be linked to the secret it contained.

Chapter 44

Casa Dili

Dili, United Nations administered East Timor

. . . .

March 2001

By the time Hurley returned to Casa Dili, the capital was bearing the full force of the tropical storm he had been trying to outrun; sheets of lightning blitzed threateningly across the now inky-black sky, and these were interspersed with the deep rumble and sharp crack of thunder, reminiscent of massed artillery.

The roads were awash, and the wind blew the trees frantically, scattering debris everywhere. Inside the gates, Hurley sat marooned in the cab of the Land Cruiser looking for a break in the rain, but he knew in his heart the storm was settled in for the long haul. Reluctantly, he gripped his backpack and committed himself to the elements, making a mad dash for the house.

Walk or run, it made no difference and Hurley was literally soaked to the skin by the time he made the refuge of the house. The rain was falling in the inner courtyard too, but the impact was lessened due to the protection the house offered from the wind.

He headed straight upstairs to dry off and change before he sought Harry and the others out, knowing the weather had probably relegated those who were at home to the library or the ops room.

He went via the kitchen and made himself a cup of tea before he sought Harry out and cut a comical figure in running shorts and t-shirt with rubber thongs on his feet, the Borges family Bible in one hand and balancing a mug of tea in the other.

Harry was with Merlin and he beamed as Hurley entered the ops room.

'Where is everybody?' Hurley asked as he placed his mug on the table.

'Watching a movie in the library,' Merlin said.

Harry spied the Bible in Hurley's hand and knew they were another step closer.

'How did it go?' he quizzed.

'What an amazing woman,' Hurley began, struggling to adequately convey his impressions of Borges' wife in a single sentence. 'One thing's for sure, he has fucked her life completely, you know,' he said sadly.

'That's true mate, and far too common unfortunately,' Harry conceded.

'Aye, but her situation will now be somewhat improved,' Merlin said optimistically, as he raised his eyebrows and held his hand up, his index finger and thumb slowly rubbing together.

Hurley smiled glumly in reluctant agreement. It was true.

'Now, let's have a look at this book,' Harry said eagerly as he took the bible offered by Hurley and placed it on the table in front of them. He searched around for his half spectacles and placed them on, the lenses sitting part way down his nose. As Harry opened the back cover and inspected the lining, Merlin reached over and opened a nearby drawer. Hurley watched as he selected a razor-sharp blade with a long wooden handle.

'Careful mate, it all has to go back once we're finished, remember?' Hurley warned. 'I promised.'

'Aye, no problem Matt. We'll slit the edge of the inner sheet without touching the leather cover at all. Then we'll simply replace the item and refurbish the inner sheet when we're finished,' he explained as he picked up a steel rule from the table and lined the blade up carefully against it.

When he had made a neat slit a few inches long he picked up the Bible and carefully manipulated the malleable cover, easing out the contents until what looked like a white piece of paper slid onto the desktop. Harry turned it over.

It was a colour photograph which he straightened up as they all looked down at it. It was a good quality photo; clear and well taken. The people in the photo were easily identifiable and they all recognised each of the three faces. As clear to Hurley was the significance of them being together, and where the image had been taken.

'Well, that just about says it all, doesn't it?' Hurley challenged Harry as he sat down, the anger rising in him.

'Hard to see this being easily explained away,' Harry agreed coldly.

They were all silent as Harry took a magnifying glass Merlin provided and examined the photo more closely. Finally, he spoke.

'We shall have to get this authenticated as best we can; we need to confirm it's an original and not a fake, and then get a good copy made. Subsequent to that I need to talk to some people about this before we do anything more.'

'How long will that take do you reckon, Harry?' Hurley asked, knowing he would be heading back to the border as soon as the storm eased.

'Probably a week… possibly a bit more. I'll let you know as soon as we get word, don't worry.'

Hurley nodded and wondered distractedly where this might all finally end. He didn't need to be told how serious it had become and that the ramifications would be significant, to say the least.

'And thanks for all your good work, Matt,' Harry confided earnestly, 'we wouldn't be in a position to resolve this without you.'

45

CASA DILI

DILI, UNITED NATIONS ADMINISTERED EAST TIMOR

....

March 2001

Harry's estimate proved to be correct; it was ten days before Hurley received word and at the first opportunity, he took to the much-travelled road between Balibo and Dili. It was insecure and most definitely against procedures to have an AUSBATT Land Rover seen at Casa Dili, or for Hurley to go there in uniform, so he parked at HQ and changed into civilian clothes, knowing a vehicle would be sent to collect him.

He was pleasantly surprised when *Stiletto* arrived to pick him up.

'Hi Josefina, I see you got stuck with driving duties,' he joked as he climbed into the cab.

She smiled broadly. 'It's one of my many skills, *amigo*.'

They both laughed, comfortable in each other's company and their relationship forged by the events of the recent past.

When they arrived at Casa Dili, Hurley and *Stiletto* joined Harry in the library.

'Hello Matt,' he chirped as they came in, and made themselves comfortable on the Chesterfield setting.

Stiletto chose one of the matching chairs and wound her legs up underneath her like a swami.

'Matt, have you thought much about what you're going to do when you leave the army?' Harry queried him unexpectedly.

'Not really, do you know something I don't?' Hurley joked, looking from one to the other.

They both laughed. 'No, of course not,' he said. 'But the time comes to us all you know, and you've had a very good run, by any standard. In fact, I don't think there's anything more they could really offer you that you haven't already done, do you?'

Hurley wondered where this might be going. It was an odd discussion to be having, particularly with *Stiletto* present but he was nonplussed; he figured Harry must have a reason and his logic was certainly sound.

Indeed, it hadn't been lost on Hurley either and he had thought long and hard about just this issue over recent weeks, particularly when his mind turned to his future with Maggie, and how they could make it work.

'I hear what you're saying,' he said, nodding his agreement.

'What if I was to offer you an interesting role that is well paid, UK-based and involves doing the things you enjoy most?'

Hurley's brow wrinkled in curiosity. 'I would certainly be interested to hear more, Harry. But doing what exactly?'

'It can vary greatly depending on the requirement, some of which might be relevant to your special talents. Or it might be something completely different, in a unique scenario. In certain situations, you might be required to learn a new skill, specific to the job at hand. The resources for that would all be provided of course.'

'How would it work?' Hurley queried, intrigued by the idea.

'It would mean leaving the army sometime later this year, coming to the UK to live and working in some kind of cover employment. At the same time, you would make yourself available at short notice to go pretty much anywhere in the world, to do whatever job is needed.'

'That sounds right up my street actually Harry, but to be fair, I don't want to make that type of decision without talking to Maggie first, if I can,' Hurley said in his matter of fact way, watching Harry's reaction. He suspected it was something he was expected to keep to himself.

Harry and *Stiletto* both smiled. 'It's funny you should say that. Less than an hour ago we had a similar conversation with Maggie and she said exactly the same thing.'

Harry turned and nodded slightly to *Stiletto* and without a word she stood up and left the room.

'Is Maggie here?' Hurley asked, surprised.

'Yes, but don't worry, everything's fine and it will all become clear,' Harry soothed.

'So how did everything go with the photo Harry?' Hurley asked, changing the subject.

'It's all on track mate, we'll talk about that a bit later after–'

They heard the door open and Hurley turned around to see Maggie with *Stiletto*. She looked rested and strong, her convalescence had worked wonders and she had come along in leaps and bounds, beyond even where she was when he had seen her at the Jesuit house. When she saw Hurley, her face lit up and she went straight to him. They sat close together on the sofa.

'OK, so here we all are,' Harry started, rubbing his hands together and smiling wickedly as he always did when it was either an operational issue, or a conspiracy, or both. Hurley couldn't help but smile inwardly as he waited to see which way the wind was blowing.

Harry made eye contact with each of them. 'I have made each of you an offer — separately — if you would consider leaving the army and throwing in your lot with me and a group of like-minded individuals. You've both said independently that you want to involve the other in your decision. The offer stands, to you both, as a team.'

Hurley looked askew at Maggie as she did likewise to him. He could tell it meant a great deal to her he had held his decision for her. The reverse was also true, and she read it in his eyes.

'I should say at the outset though, there are some things you should know. This is not a traditional organisation we are talking about.' He let his words hang for effect. 'It is not an intelligence agency as such, but a small group that operates on behalf of all the allied intelligence services, civilian and military, and increasingly with law enforcement. But it operates from without, not from within.

'The existence of the Project, as we call it, is known only to a small number of people who work in the upper echelons of the agencies we support. It is these people who provide input to the executive, a panel of people who are the primary decision makers. These people take into account the national and agency interests so there is nothing done at cross purposes. We simply carry out the direction of the executive. Often, we are able to achieve things the individual services cannot, simply because we fly under the radar; we are not subject to the same scrutiny they are, from within their own services, from their own governments or by their adversaries. This also means we operate without the formal protection of those governments and services and are deniable if the circumstances require it. Importantly, it also means we are sometimes asked to carry out instructions that enhance operational outcomes but cannot be levied on those services because of legal or other constraints.'

'When you say allies, who does that include?' Hurley asked.

'As you'd expect, the big five predominantly — Australia, Canada, New Zealand, UK and the US — but we have provided support to other democratic and like minded countries in the past.'

'When you say we are not bound by legal constraints, you mean the work is extra-judicial?' Maggie asked carefully.

'Sometimes, yes,' Harry answered truthfully, but just as carefully. 'Having said that, I've never been asked to do anything that didn't make complete sense to me, all things considered.'

'Do we have any discretion on the jobs we accept?' asked Maggie.

'Yes and no,' Harry said. 'For a start, you will work to me and only to me, no one else will task you. Josefina is in a similar situation. If a job comes up, we will talk about it and if there are reasons against your involvement, we will work through them. We do have to remember that when we agree to join, the Project pays us well for our services, so in the end we are available for their tasking.'

'What if we agreed, and then changed our minds?' Hurley put to him.

'Then you leave with our blessing. If we have trusted you enough to ask you to join us, and we do, then we trust you enough to keep our offer and what we have told you secret, to protect us.'

Hurley and Maggie looked at each other, searching each other's faces for questions that needed to be asked.

'OK, I want you to go and talk this over with each other,' Harry interjected. 'And if there are any issues, we can discuss them.'

'So, what do you think Maggie?' Hurley asked as they crossed the courtyard to the kitchen.

'It sounds interesting Matt, but it's a big decision. What about you?'

'It certainly solves one problem. It's a way we could be together, and I trust Harry, just as you do. Having said that, my career is nearing a natural end, so I'm happy to think about moving on.

You still have much to look forward to. I don't expect you to just give it up if that's not what you want,' Hurley explained as he put a glass under the tap of the water cooler and filled it, big bubbles of air glugging upwards inside the glass canister as he did.

Hurley could see Maggie was thinking about what he had said. *Good*, he thought. He wanted her to make the right decision for herself. He threw his head back and drank the water.

'Harry did say if we don't like it, we can move on,' she said tentatively.

'In that situation we'd be in the same space we are now, looking for options for our future. Nothing ventured, nothing gained I reckon,' Hurley summed up.

'I suppose it makes me feel better about it knowing Josefina is involved,' she admitted.

'Yes, and Harry would have known that,' Hurley said with a grin. 'He's a cunning bugger after all.'

She laughed. It was so true.

'You look great,' he said, catching her gaze and offering her the glass he had refilled.

'I feel refreshed, and back to normal Matt,' she replied with a cheeky grin as she accepted the glass, 'if that's what you meant. Either way I'll take it as a compliment.'

'It was meant both ways,' he said smiling.

'Listen, I reckon we vote yes or no, and if we get one vote each way we agree now to respect the wishes of the one who doesn't want to go. What do you think?' Hurley suggested, watching her closely and not wanting to push her in one direction or the other. It was a big decision for both of them.

She nodded thoughtfully. 'But we need to write it down and then show our votes together, at the same time,' she implored. 'Otherwise we might be influenced to support the one who voted first. I know I would be,' she explained with a smile.

Hurley returned her smile in kind, reaching over to touch her hair. He pulled her to him and kissed her cheek softly. She was right, and it made complete sense. He went to a nearby drawer and after rummaging around he came back with a pen.

'Let's write yes or no on our hand and then show them to each other,' he suggested.

With this, Hurley wrote on the inside of his hand and passed the pen to Maggie. She did likewise hiding her response as she did so.

'OK, reveal on the count of three,' Hurley said playfully.

'One, two, three,' they counted together and then showed what they had written to the other.

They both seemed unsurprised at the outcome and Hurley hugged her, unsure where this all might go but sure that it might be a path for their life together.

'Let's go and tell Harry,' Maggie said.

~

'OK Harry, we're in,' Hurley reported on their behalf when they were again seated in the library.

'Alright, that's terrific,' Harry said enthusiastically. 'First of all, you both need to be aware that no one else at Casa Dili is aware of the Project. Only we four here,' he explained, circling his hand to encompass them all. 'For security reasons, you will only be exposed to others when the work requires it.'

They nodded in unison.

'Now, to the issue of your first job, which you don't have to accept I might add. Technically it has been allocated to me and Josefina. But due to the unique circumstances, and your already substantial investment, I am prepared to let you run with it, but only if you want to,' he finished.

Hurley sensed that recent events and his agreement to join the Project were not just on a collision course, but that the collision had already happened. Looking at him, Harry knew he had made the link.

'Go on,' Hurley said quietly. 'I'm listening.'

Harry drew a breath and watched the younger man, as did *Stiletto*. 'You asked me before about the photo. We have confirmed it is real and all the information regarding the events of the recent past have been briefed upwards to the Project executive. The Australians have made it clear they want the Sanderson problem to go away, Matt,' Harry said.

Hurley thought about this for a long time. 'When you say "go away", you mean go away permanently, don't you?'

Harry nodded, his face sombre.

'The simple fact is they cannot risk an inquiry, a court case or any type of public exposure of this case, and you can bet that would be Sanderson's tactic, to drag it through the courts and use public opinion. At the same time, it would put the emerging Australia-East Timor relationship to the sword and set the relationship with Indonesia back twenty years.

'It is absolutely critical the Indonesians remain unaware of our knowledge of this case, which, if I read between the lines correctly, is probably ongoing. Because of the unique circumstances, the role you have already played and the fact the victims were your own people, I want to offer this operation to you — in partnership with Josefina,' he explained as his head motioned towards her.

Hurley's eyes went immediately to *Stiletto*, as did Maggie's. *Stiletto* had beautiful eyes, of that there was no doubt. Her irises had the hue and flecking reminiscent of the richest mountain coffee, and they were framed in a perfect almond setting.

Hurley knew these were the same eyes in which he had

previously seen so much mischief and laughter, but today there was only care for him, and acknowledgement of the burden of making a decision that was right for him.

Hurley knew she was sending him a message, and that if he agreed he was walking down a road that would see him changed as well, but that she would walk with him as a friend.

'Josefina would be the lead,' Harry continued, bringing his attention back to the present, 'due to her expertise in this area, but you will do the interrogation. The Project executive would first of all like him to admit what he has done before any action is taken against him. It's a common theme in these cases and an opportunity to learn things they may not know.'

'What else do they still need to know?' Hurley quizzed, his mind moving to the puzzle.

'The meeting arrangements with the Indonesian, Hermanto, and whether any paperwork or records exist about the operation. If this information isn't forthcoming, however, it doesn't change the endgame. You understand?'

'Yeah, I get it.'

'You can take some time to think about it if you like, or even talk it over with Maggie if you want.'

'I just want you to know it's not revenge,' he said softly and then with finality, 'it's gone beyond that. It's just the way it has to end, and there's no normal way that can happen.'

'I know,' Harry smiled knowingly. 'I wouldn't have put this idea forward if I thought you were driven by revenge. We couldn't trust your actions if you were still in that mind set.'

Hurley looked at Maggie and could see she supported him, no matter what. He nodded.

'I'll do it Harry, I'll finish it. I'll do it for us, and I'll do it for all those who have been hurt by this.'

'Then we have a lot of work to do,' Harry replied simply. 'We have a window of opportunity to mount this operation in a few days, but there's a lot of thinking, planning and rehearsals to get you ready before then, and a lot you need to learn from Josefina.'

46

DILI

UNITED NATIONS ADMINISTERED EAST TIMOR

....

March 2001

Hurley and *Stiletto* walked together along the uneven footpath, shadowed by the overhanging trees. The gravel underfoot caused their footsteps to echo lightly in the warm night. It was dark, there was no street lighting, and all was quiet except for their footfall and the humming of the night insects.

They stopped in front of the large green security gates and Hurley pushed the buzzer on the adjacent pedestrian gate with the back of his hand. There was no answer. He pushed the buzzer again, knowing Sanderson was at home and expecting him. He also knew Sanderson's wife, Marjorie, was away in Australia and that there were no live-in domestic staff.

There was a loud click as the gate was unlocked remotely from inside the house. They looked at each other briefly and walked through. *Stiletto* leaned on the gate to close it. When they arrived at the house, the door was already held open for them.

'Hello Matt, who's this then?' he said jovially, turning to *Stiletto* and admiring her. 'I thought Harry might be with you too.'

'This is Josefina,' Hurley said, motioning towards her. 'She has been intimately involved in the case Harry mentioned to you. Unfortunately, Harry had a little accident and isn't walking around too well at the moment.'

Stiletto smiled engagingly and offered her hand, which he shook briefly.

'Roger Sanderson,' he smiled in return. 'Welcome.'

'Well, I hope he's not too poorly and back on his feet quick smart. Let's get a drink,' he suggested, turning to face Hurley, 'and then we can deal with this work stuff you and Harry want me to look at. Scotch OK?'

The house was quiet, and he guided them into his study. It was an agreeable room and without windows, Hurley noted. Sanderson made each of them a drink from his cabinet and Hurley placed his briefcase on the shiny redwood desk with the green leather inlay. He flicked the locks open with his thumbs.

Sanderson settled opposite him across the desk, his drink in hand. *Stiletto* hovered, appearing to inspect the displayed photographs and trinkets, and admire the books and artwork as she moved around the room, as any interested guest might do.

When Hurley opened the briefcase, he left the lid cocked open, so the contents were shielded from Sanderson's view.

'We wanted your perspective on this case, so I have a number of things to show you,' Hurley began casually. He took a small tape-recorder from the briefcase and placed it on the table in front of Sanderson.

'Please listen carefully,' he urged, and turned on the tape.

The two sat in silence while the tape played. *Stiletto* had taken up a position largely behind Sanderson, perched on the arm of a comfortable sofa chair. The tape was in English and although Sanderson couldn't know it was the recording of Urquhart's meeting at Borges' house, he easily recognised Urquhart's voice.

Hurley knew he recognised the others too, so his ability to

grasp the context was heightened even though he gave no overt indication. Sanderson was clearly gobsmacked and became more so as the tape progressed, his face showed he couldn't for the life of him work out how Hurley had acquired a tape of that meeting. Towards the end there was a gunshot, and then shortly after, another. It was clear from the conversation what had happened.

'What do you think about that?' Hurley asked lightly, as he clicked the recorder off.

'That's absolutely incredible,' Sanderson blurted out, animated. 'Where on God's earth did you get this? It's proof that Urquhart isn't just missing, he's probably been killed. Tell me all about this,' he urged, apparently fascinated.

He would play right until the end, Hurley thought, appraising Sanderson's performance. In response, he reached into the briefcase and pulled out a collection of photos. He placed the first one on the desk in front of Sanderson, positioning it neatly against the line of the leather inlay.

'This is Urquhart arriving at a house in West Timor two Sundays ago. Urquhart you recognise, do you know who the other man is?'

He scrutinised the photo. 'No.'

Keeping his cards close to his chest, but lying all the same, Hurley thought.

'Actually, it's Marcelino Borges, and this is Borges' house, the place where he has been in hiding.'

Sanderson stared, open-mouthed and nodded. 'Jesus, Matt, how did you and Harry get these?' And then something else fell into place for him. 'My God, it was Harry's crew who captured Borges! It was! This was the very day, wasn't it?' he pressed triumphantly, having cracked a little riddle in his own mind.

Hurley ignored him and placed another photo on the desk next to the first one.

'Do you know this man?' he asked, pointing to the image of a small, neat Indonesian man standing alongside a black Mercedes sedan.

Sanderson studied the photo, probably for too long, but Hurley indulged him nevertheless. He could well understand Sanderson had a lot to think about and it was growing by the minute. When he looked up he shook his head.

'Maybe,' he muttered vaguely, 'I think I've seen a photo of him before, he could be an Indonesian intelligence officer.'

Hurley nodded, seemingly impressed. 'He most certainly is a BAKIN officer. His name is Rio Hermanto and he is a senior counter-intelligence officer. He is the one on the tape Urquhart refers to as the sponsor. He is also the one who shot and killed Urquhart.'

'My God.' Sanderson gasped.

Hurley noted small beads of perspiration had begun to form on Sanderson's bald head, but the room was actually quite cool. He placed another photo on the desk. It wasn't pretty, and Sanderson visibly reacted, stiffening in his chair. His eyes were glued to the image nevertheless.

'This is the body of Simon Urquhart being loaded into the back of his hire vehicle. It was removed from the house by an associate of Borges. You will note from the blood stains he has been shot in the body, and in the head. The outcome of the two shots you heard on the tape.'

Sanderson was silent and sat shaking his head slowly in disbelief. Finally, he couldn't contain himself.

'How in God's name did you get all this? It's dynamite.'

This time Hurley chose to answer, because he wanted to show Sanderson their reach, and he knew it would burden him even further.

'Harry's people had an OP on the escarpment above the

house,' he explained simply, 'because we knew Urquhart was going there to meet Borges.'

'Christ! How did you know that?'

Hurley knew Sanderson needed to know as much as possible; he was thinking the more he knew, the better he might weave his lies and Hurley might make sense of them.

'Urquhart made a phone call to Borges the Monday following the interrogation, after you sent him and Tomms packing on gardening leave. He requested the presence of a person he named as the sponsor. Later we knew this to be Hermanto.'

'So how did you know Urquhart made that call, and how did you get the conversation at the house?' he asked carefully, realising the possibility Hurley was just getting started.

He had watched Hurley work on Urquhart, and now felt himself distinctly under the same spotlight. In the back of his mind was Harry's warning about Hurley's original intentions.

'When we took Urquhart and Tomms for interrogation, a listening device was placed into Urquhart's watch. We monitored every conversation he had from the time he left the interrogation site until the time he was murdered. We did try and use the device to find him, or at least the location of his body, but unfortunately the battery did not last.'

Sanderson processed this and his face visibly paled, but his first inclination was his own self-interest.

'Do you mean Urquhart was wearing this bugged watch when he was inside my station, recording what was going on there?' he asked angrily, offended.

'Yes. Actually, under the circumstances I thought you did a sterling job of dressing those two down and the sacking was first class, and just as well,' Hurley said sarcastically. 'All in keeping with your agreement with Harry of course.'

Sanderson glared at him. Hurley knew he had not seen

anything yet that he couldn't talk his way out of, but for the first time he had an uncertain look on his face and Hurley reckoned he could smell a very big rat. So be it, they had planned for it.

'Let's listen to the tape after Urquhart is killed, shall we?' Hurley asked rhetorically as he reached forward and switched the tape on again.

They listened again as the tape played, although this one was shorter in length than the first recording. It was in Indonesian, a language which only *Stiletto* spoke, but she said nothing. She had become a fixture outside Sanderson's attention, which was increasingly focussed on Hurley, and what he produced from his magic box, the briefcase.

But among what was otherwise gibberish to the two men, there were three recognisable English words used by Hermanto and Borges after the shooting of Urquhart. The same word, three times over. The word was *Sanderson* and they all heard it clearly as they listened.

At a certain point, Hurley reached over and stopped the tape. The sound of the vehicle driving away with Urquhart's body in the back was clearly audible before he did so.

'Now you and I don't speak Indonesian, so I have taken the liberty of getting us a transcript,' Hurley said helpfully.

He reached into the briefcase and removed a pink sheet of paper which he placed on the desk in front of Sanderson, neatly lined up with the photographs. It was the same pink piece of paper Harry had handed to him in the library at Casa Dili.

'Please read this if you will,' he asked politely, but it was a direction nevertheless.

Sanderson now looked extremely worried. He swallowed the last of his drink and picked up the pink sheet. He read through it quickly, his eyes darting along the lines of print. He then returned to the start and read it through more slowly. The more he read, the more his jaw tightened and the more he fought for control. When he finally looked up, he was defiant and ready for a fight, his eyes blazing.

'So just what are you implying?' he spat indignantly at Hurley, now fully aware of the entire strategy of the evening and that he had been duped into participating. He was also angry Harry had stroked his ego asking for his *advice* on a case. He had fallen headlong into that abyss and was nowhere near the bottom yet.

'Implying? I'm not implying anything,' Hurley said coldly. 'You've heard the tape and read the transcript. It's quite self-explanatory but just for clarity, allow me to read it out for us.'

Hurley reached over and retrieved the pink sheet from Sanderson, who shifted uncomfortably in his chair. Hurley read aloud:

'Hermanto:	*That ends that little problem. It seems Sanderson was right.*
Borges:	*What do you want me to do now?*
Hermanto:	*Clean up this mess. Take him up to the mountains and get rid of him.*
Borges:	*Silvestre! Get his car and bring it back inside the gates.*
Silvestre:	*Yes, boss.*
Borges:	*What about the plan?*
Hermanto:	*All might not be lost. Let's see if Sanderson might be able to bring it back on track. I'll contact him and let you know when I've spoken to him.*
Borges:	*Alright. Do you think that's possible?*
Hermanto:	*Sanderson has been creative to date, after all, it was his idea to introduce you to this one. There might be other options, we'll have to see.*

Hurley placed the sheet down on the desk.

'It sounds to me that Hermanto, a foreign counter-intelligence officer, and Borges, a wanted war criminal, clearly identified you as a conscious party to their operation. It's now up to you to comment. I concede it was exceptionally clever of you to go in with Hermanto and arrange for Borges to approach Urquhart. You knew all too well Urquhart would lap it up and think he was making the play. You must have laughed yourself stupid when he actually proposed the operation to you and you rejected it, of course, for all the right reasons. But you knew all the time through Hermanto he was running it unofficially so you could reap the benefits in the long term but keep your own hands clean. Perfect — almost.'

'I think you're reading a bit much into this,' Sanderson said pompously, fuelled with false bravado and the three glasses of scotch he had already consumed.

'Am I?' Hurley asked.

'You're very clever, Matt,' he began condescendingly, 'but just not cerebral enough for the more nuanced aspects of this game. Allow me to enlighten you. Just because an adversary intelligence officer and a militia thug implicate me, doesn't mean it's true. It's classic disinformation and nothing but, set up to put a stain against me and achieve exactly your response. And you've fallen right in. But there's no proof; I don't know Hermanto, I don't know Borges, and apart from the photos you've showed me tonight, I've never seen them before. End of story.'

He sat back, looking very pleased with himself and confident he had batted away the worst of it.

Hurley was quiet for just a moment while he sorted what he would like to say to Sanderson, from what he should say. His eyes held Sanderson's throughout, and in this game, Hurley had few equals. Sanderson was not one of them. Finally, Sanderson looked away. Hurley already knew that his talk of a lack of proof was just another indicator he was lying.

'Perhaps in another life you could explain to me how and why BAKIN, in league with a former militia leader, would even contemplate organising and providing complex disinformation about *you* through a channel they didn't even know existed, which was the bug in Urquhart's watch.'

He let the logic of his words speak for themselves.

'But that's possibly a discussion for another time,' Hurley ended coldly, his eyes still watching Sanderson closely.

He then reached into the briefcase and selected another photo which he instead placed face down on the table, again carefully lined up with the others and the pink sheet of paper, all now spread across the table. It had all been part of an interrogation strategy known as the *weight of knowledge*.

A case slowly built up, logically and piece by piece, with the visual impact of each piece of evidence growing on the person at each disclosure, wearing away their will to resist, the enormity of it all designed to bear down and finally break them.

But Hurley wasn't ready to play the final piece just yet. It would be worth far more at the end if Sanderson had lied about it first — multiple times.

'Have you ever been to West Timor, Roger?'

Sanderson looked at the blank back of the photo on the desk, trying to discern the threat that might linger beneath, but he had no knowledge, and few options. He was slightly distracted by the question, exactly as Hurley had planned.

'No,' he answered softly.

'To Kupang perhaps, in West Timor?' Hurley pushed, allowing him a second chance.

Sanderson appeared to contemplate this, as if he might have been there at some time and simply forgotten. It was what Hurley expected; he was buying all the time he could.

'No, not that I can recall,' he said finally, hedging his bets.

'Are you sure?' Hurley asked carefully, his emphasis on the last word. For the third and final call.

'Yes, I'm sure,' he said, too quickly, apparently annoyed about having his honesty questioned over a simple question.

In reality, his annoyance came from being painted into a corner he couldn't see but smelling the wet paint all around him. Hurley nodded and turned the photo over.

'This is a photo taken at the Celebes Cafe in Kupang just over a year ago,' he explained clinically, watching Sanderson's face carefully. 'The café is readily identifiable from the sign in the background. You will note the photo is date-stamped and this matches the date on the newspaper, which has been deliberately folded across the back of the chair in centre shot for that purpose. The war criminal Marcelino Borges is sitting on the left, the BAKIN counter-intelligence officer Rio Hermanto is sitting next to him. The third person at that table is you, isn't it Roger?'

47

Dili

United Nations administered East Timor

....

March 2001

Sanderson looked long and hard at the photo and seemed to be willing the image to blur and go away. His eyes said he was seeking salvation, but he knew there was none and instead he could have been staring into his own grave.

'It *is* you,' Hurley emphasised as he continued on mercilessly. 'And your service has confirmed to us you have never travelled to West Timor, never asked permission to go there, and never furnished a report of any operational activity conducted there. Indeed, it's not even within your station's area of responsibility, is it?' he asked rhetorically.

Sanderson remained silent and motionless, though Hurley knew it was defeat, not defence and he twisted the knife.

'So, we can safely assess that your travel there was deliberately under the radar — clandestine — and for the sole purpose of secretly meeting these two men. It was at this meeting the details of what became Operation FAJAR, or in English, Operation DAWN as you named it, were discussed. It was here that the plan of having Borges approach Urquhart was first suggested, by you.

It was also suggested by you that cleaning up Borges' background might be best done by Urquhart once he was unwittingly on board, again leaving your hands clean. And as to having no proof of this, apart from this photo, which I strongly encourage you to explain if you can, I have the sworn testimony of not only a witness who can verify everything I have said, but also that of the person who took the photograph,' he lied smoothly, driving the final nail home.

It was the last straw, as Hurley knew it would be. Sanderson's face suddenly became drawn and tired. It was the face of surrender and his eyes had lost their shine. He exhaled and placed his head in his hands.

When he looked up he had the look that all rats have when they are caught in a trap. He was desperate and seeking a way out. But Hurley marched on relentlessly; he had a lot of ground to cover.

'And it's the reason why you not only allowed, but actively supported, your two errant officers when the murder of my agents first came to light, because you wanted them to continue on if possible. It served your purpose to discredit Sergeant Campbell instead. And it was the reason you were so decidedly laid back about their venture into West Timor, where they were photographed at the refugee camp — something any Head of Station worth their salt would normally have been incandescent with rage about. And it's the reason Rio Hermanto knew you had sacked them when Urquhart went over, because we heard him say it on the earlier tape. And it was also the reason Hermanto was armed that day and had already planned to kill Urquhart — because you advised him of what had happened and Urquhart had outlived his usefulness.

'Borges,' Sanderson said simply, almost spitting it out. But in so doing he admitted every allegation levelled against him, without even realising it. It was the first part of Hurley's task complete.

'Does it matter?' Hurley put to him, without confirming anything.

'Not really, I suppose,' Sanderson said weakly, defeated.

'What was the reason, Roger? What was it all about?' Hurley asked with the tone of true curiosity, wanting to know but sensing Sanderson would be more compliant in response.

Sanderson was quiet and sat very still for a moment. He looked through Hurley and beyond. Hurley could see he was gathering his thoughts for a storm, a storm that would assuage his guilt, wash away his culpability and give reason to his actions. He needed the freedom of his catharsis and it was in this process Hurley might learn what he still needed to know.

'I should have damn well been a Head of Station fifteen years ago, you know,' he said bitterly, almost mumbling to himself but loosening the plug on the floodgates nevertheless. 'And what do I finally get? Almost as a charity card, Dili... *Dili*. And with it the sobriquet of being the oldest head in the history of the service. And with that the additional humiliation of having to promise the DG everything would be just tickety-fucking-boo on my watch, as if I actually couldn't be trusted with the job. And why would that be, do you think?'

His eyes blazed but Hurley was not the focus. These grievances were born long before Hurley entered the story. Hurley was now simply the medium through which they would all be brought to light.

'Because I didn't go to the right school, that's why. I didn't have the right family or the right connections, and all that meant I didn't have the money, and the means to put up the appearances I needed to,' he finished sadly.

'Was there money to be had through this?' Hurley pushed gently, but keeping to the theme Sanderson had set.

'Oh yes, and lots of it,' Sanderson answered, but without

apparent interest. 'I wasn't there for that specifically, but it would have proved a nice retirement bonus that's for sure. The way I planned it, Borges would have eventually been on the East Timor negotiating team for the Timor Gap Treaty as an Australian agent of influence. We would have had both sides covered and the Indonesian angle too. Our ability to play groups off against each other and manipulate the consultancy fees through some faceless third party — and ultimately the share prices — would have been unparalleled. Everyone would have been a winner and no one would have been any the wiser. The intelligence success would have been truly breathtaking, the coup of this century. *My* coup,' he stressed, but his tone said it was now a lost dream.

'What about Urquhart and Tomms?'

'He had some egotistical fantasy he was a spymaster of some repute, playing the Machiavellian game, and doing it better than anyone. He also saw a big paycheque, that's what reeled him in. He was very smart, but dangerous and delusional, perfect as the patsy for this job. God only knows what Tomms wanted from it all, it was Urquhart who brought her on, much to my surprise I have to say when Hermanto told me. She was harder to pick, excitement I think, and power over others. Little rich bitch looking for an adrenalin rush is all, I think. The whole thing would have worked too, you know, if it wasn't for you,' he said tiredly. 'I told them you and Harry were trouble, and I was right.'

'But surely it was you who failed, not us who triumphed,' Hurley corrected simply. 'You say Urquhart was the perfect patsy, but it was chasing him that eventually led us to you. It was simply ego and a poor operational decision on your part to have him involved, unwittingly or not. And it was you who covered up his initial transgressions and then facilitated his interrogation, even though it was for your own selfish purposes. It was this that started the chase, so you have no one to blame but yourself. But perhaps all that was Hermanto's doing,' he put to him gently, taking the risk he and Harry had talked about long and hard.

'No, those decisions were all mine,' Sanderson acknowledged firmly, without hesitation.

'You did maintain contact with him though,' Hurley suggested, avoiding the direct question for now but making it sound obvious.

'Yes of course,' Sanderson agreed, apparently irritated, as if he needed to prove his worth. 'He's old school is Hermanto, no technology or anything like that,' he admitted, somewhat admiringly.

'Oh?' Hurley prompted, professional curiosity the only motive on display.

Sanderson took another long swallow of scotch, the glass helpfully refilled by *Stiletto*.

'I don't suppose it matters, it will all come out anyway,' he started, keen to show a degree of cooperation, Hurley thought, but he was reasoning it would be revealed later in some type of formal debrief.

'There is a little tailor shop called Beni's in the alley at the back of Hotel Turismo here in Dili. I go there regularly to have suits and shirts made. It is a BAKIN front I suppose, although that was never specifically explained to me. I would simply leave a message addressed to the manager with Beni. Sometimes Beni would give me an envelope from him. If we needed to meet, he would be there on the date I picked up my order and we would speak briefly in the little workshop at the back. In an emergency, I would use the phone there to call the head office in Jakarta, a number that put me straight through to Hermanto. It was foolproof really,' he summed up regretfully.

His focus returned to the photo on the desk and his eyes hardened.

'That was the only bloody time we ever met out in the open,' he spat bitterly, jabbing his finger towards the offending photo on the table as if it were the source of all his troubles, which of course, it was.

'Did you keep any working papers to refer to, or to keep yourself on track of operational details?' Hurley asked unexpectedly.

For what seemed a fleeting second or even less, Sanderson's eyes seemed to flash to his left, to a point beyond Hurley's shoulder, and then they resettled on Hurley's face without emotion.

'No,' Sanderson said evenly, 'why would I do that?'

'I don't know that you would, I just thought I'd ask,' replied Hurley smoothly, knowing Sanderson had lied, but not knowing yet quite how that problem might be solved.

Hurley wanted to tell Sanderson a lot more. He wanted to tell him that he too, was delusional. That the Indonesians had played him as well, and that Sanderson was Hermanto's agent and any pretence of equality or cooperation in a joint venture to make them all rich was pure theatre to stroke his ego.

He wanted to tell him that his BAKIN code-name was *Gagak* — Crow — given to him in derision and laughed about by Hermanto and Borges behind his back, and that at the end there would have been nothing for him but either disgrace or a bullet, or both. Just like Urquhart.

He wanted to tell Sanderson all these things and more. He wanted to pay tribute to his dead agents and to his misguided sergeant, and he wanted Sanderson to face the personal cost, of lives lost. And of course, there was little Manuelito, who would never understand why he had become an orphan. But he checked himself.

He knew this need was an expression of his own frustration and emotional investment, and would not benefit Sanderson, or the outcome. Harry had predicted he would feel exactly like this and warned him accordingly. He was right, and Hurley saw this now.

Instead, Hurley slowly collected all the exhibits from the desk. Methodically, he placed them back into the briefcase like a tired magician packing up his box of tricks. When the desk was clear he took a handgun from inside the briefcase and placed it in on the desk, close to himself and out of Sanderson's reach, but in his direct line of sight.

Sanderson looked down at the sleek black form of the Colt .38 snub-nosed revolver in disbelief, although he wouldn't have known the model or even the calibre. He was also unaware it was the weapon used to shoot Maggie and Rommel, taken by Toby from the scene on that fateful day Borges was captured. Now, it was destined for a higher purpose.

He looked up at Hurley, incredulous, his eyes red-rimmed and wide, and his expression now tired and beaten. *Stiletto* had fixed Sanderson yet another drink, and she placed it conveniently at his elbow. He took a long swallow from the glass.

'There's no need to be so melodramatic. I'm quite happy to take my medicine, you know, even if that means going to gaol for a short time, although I don't think that's likely. I'll submit myself to a full debrief as I alluded to, all the details will be known and available for the service to benefit from operationally. My lawyers will facilitate everything,' he finished, almost tartly as if this was his due, and that all the wreckage left in his wake was incidental and unimportant.

The reference to his lawyers confirmed that Harry's worse fears, and those of the Project executive, were correct.

'This *is* your medicine, Roger,' Hurley said quietly, inclining his head briefly towards the revolver. 'It's been decreed by the people with the real power.'

'What people are you talking about?' he spat at Hurley, his face contorted with confusion, and a growing suspicion that his version of the end might not play out.

'Listen to me,' Hurley ordered coldly. 'The first concession I will allow you is a brief explanation as to how we got to this point. Firstly, you should understand that I represent a group of people who have decreed your fate — *this* fate. You can be assured it has been carefully weighed against what you have done, and the decision has not been taken lightly. You don't need to know who or where those people are, or what they do, but for our purposes tonight, they are the people who matter. It is their decision, and it will be carried out.'

Sanderson was rendered utterly speechless, and the blood visibly drained from his face. Hurley thought it the moment he realised he would die that night. Sanderson tried to stand on reflex, outraged and afraid, the fight or flight response clearly switching to flight, but *Stiletto* easily pushed him back down with firm pressure on each of his shoulders and held him there until he acquiesced, beaten.

'Please stay seated,' Hurley directed him, 'or this will be far less orderly and civilised than it needs to be. But it will still end the same way.'

Sanderson looked into Hurley's eyes just as Harry had predicted he would. He was seeking connection, compassion, and even some measure of forgiveness. But Hurley was prepared and there was no redemption to be found there.

Sanderson was an arch-traitor, and the collateral damage he had wrought, including the lives lost in the process, weighed heavily on the tally board. Accordingly, he would go the road of all traitors. There was no sympathy that Sanderson could see in Hurley's eyes and in his, Hurley could see only that Sanderson was now frightened.

'Matt, there must to be another way…,' he implored, desperate.

'Unfortunately, it is not in the interests of those people for your deeds to be made public, and for operational reasons there is an additional desire for the Indonesians to be none the wiser. That is the decision,' Hurley summed up.

From the desk drawer Hurley took a single piece of Sanderson's own notepaper and a pen. He pushed the piece of paper across the desk in front of Sanderson and placed the pen on top of it.

'I am prepared to allow you to leave a note for your wife. I'm sure under the circumstances you understand I shall have to read it. Of that, I am sorry.'

'A suicide note, I presume?'

Hurley nodded. 'It is the other concession I am prepared to offer you. It was insisted upon by Harry.'

'For old time's sake, eh?' he said sarcastically, his voice wavering.

'No. Actually, for Marjorie's sake,' Hurley corrected him simply, devoid of emotion.

Sanderson sat quietly staring at the paper for a few moments and finally looked up.

'I don't think I'm in the mood to compose a letter right now,' he said finally, folding his hands in front of him on the desk.

Hurley was irritated by Sanderson's petulance, and filled with sadness for his wife, who he felt might have taken some comfort from such a letter. But he pushed both thoughts from his mind. He simply nodded and pulled the paper and pen back towards himself. He placed both items away in the briefcase.

Sanderson was momentarily distracted as Hurley stopped and pulled a white, neatly folded handkerchief from his jacket pocket. Holding it by the corner, he flapped it once to open it. A second later and without warning, Sanderson was dead.

When everything had been packed away and the desk was clear, they knew he would watch the gun and take comfort from it being away from him, far away on the other side of the desk. He had thought, as anyone would, that death would come from the gun, but it was a deception to make the end easier for them all.

The handkerchief was a signal to *Stiletto*, and it brought the long blade soundlessly and at lightning speed from its hiding place, just as she and Hurley had rehearsed. She drove the long thin blade quickly and easily into Sanderson's brain through his right ear, at the same time bracing his head firmly, but gently with her left hand.

She held it there briefly as he tremored, and when the spasm finally ceased he was still. Hurley saw the fleeting look of shock in his eyes but it was all too late and the life went quickly from him, his eyes remaining glazed and open. As *Stiletto* slowly withdrew the blade, she used the handkerchief offered by Hurley to wipe and guard the underside of the blade as it was retracted.

There was very little blood on the thin blade, and it was returned from whence it came, the Toledo steel as clean and shiny as it had ever been. The bloodstained handkerchief was placed, like everything else, into the briefcase.

Hurley and *Stiletto* did not speak as they set to work. Hurley pulled a pair of blue rubber gloves from the briefcase and stretched them on with a tortured squeak. While *Stiletto* remained supporting Sanderson in his sitting position, Hurley took six bullets from the briefcase and carefully manipulated Sanderson's hands to produce partial fingerprints on each, placing them into the chambers of the revolver as he did so.

When he had finished loading the weapon, he screwed a silencer onto the barrel. This he pressed hard against Sanderson's right ear and fired. There was a softened metallic thud as the bullet travelled through Sanderson's brain in an instant, obliterating any sign the thin blade had preceded it.

At the same time, blood, bone and brain matter exploded from the left side of Sanderson's head and showered the rug and wall beyond. At Hurley's nod, *Stiletto* released Sanderson and he collapsed naturally, first into an awkward sitting position, and then onto the floor, the chair toppling over beside him. They let it happen, just as it would have done had Sanderson pulled the trigger himself.

Hurley placed the dead man's right hand around the weapon, including smudging a fingerprint on the trigger before he laid it next to the body, just where it might have fallen. *Stiletto* immediately donned her own rubber gloves and collected all the drinking glasses bar one; the first one Sanderson had used on which only his fingerprints remained.

She had quarantined this one as she had resupplied him during their visit. The others she took to the kitchen and washed, carefully drying them and placing them back into Sanderson's drink cabinet. Everything she or Hurley touched was wiped clean or disappeared into the briefcase.

Just before he closed the briefcase, Hurley's eye was caught by the glint of a metal chain on Sanderson's neck, which had fallen free as his body dropped to the floor. On impulse, he reached down and withdrew the chain from inside Sanderson's shirt.

On it was a single brass key, the type that no locksmith would duplicate without an authority. The type, Hurley knew, used for safes. He held the key in his hand as he crouched over the body, and his mind was immediately taken back to Sanderson's response to his question about the paperwork.

Hurley looked over his shoulder in the direction of Sanderson's surreptitious glance and his attention was drawn to the painting on the wall. It was Arthur Streeton's *Golden Summer, Eaglemont* painted well over a hundred years before.

Hurley walked over and examined the painting, taking a moment to admire the gum trees and the farmer with his sheep in the bleak Australian summer landscape. He knew for certain it wasn't the original which hung in the National Gallery of Australia, but it was an attractive, high quality reproduction.

Looking the part, but a fake nevertheless, Hurley thought, and providing an apt metaphor for Sanderson himself. Feeling around the light wooden frame, Hurley moved the painting from its hook and placed it gently down against the wall. The dull grey metal door of the wall safe was revealed and stared enticingly out at him.

Inserting the brass key, Hurley turned it and the safe unlocked with a rhythmic click, the door springing open on its hinges. Reaching inside, he withdrew the contents and laid them methodically on the floor. The contents were sparse. A few items of Marjorie's jewellery, some personal family papers, and a nondescript buff coloured file with nothing on the cover to indicate what might be inside.

Hurley opened the file and flipped through the contents. It was the substance of Sanderson's lie and at first blush contained much of the detail he was looking for. Certainly, all the material the Project did not want found by accident.

There would be time for closer scrutiny later on. Hurley closed the file and placed it into the briefcase, snapping the locks shut. He quickly refurbished the safe and locked it also, hiding it behind the painting once again. The chain he replaced carefully around Sanderson's neck and tucked it neatly into his shirt.

When they were finished, the pair walked back through the house, pulling the front door closed quietly behind them. When they arrived at the pedestrian gate, *Stiletto* looked through the grill to check the street beyond. Nothing but the darkness.

They closed the gate behind them soundlessly and walked together down the road, just as they had come. In the darkest shade of the trees lining the street, they each removed their rubber gloves and placed them into their pockets. They walked on into the night, the tired magician and his beautiful accomplice.

48

East Perth Railyard
Perth, Australia

....

April 2001

The carriage lurched as the slack was taken up and the powerful diesel locomotive moved off. The long train, stretching back more than thirty carriages and over half a kilometre, gleamed in the sunlight, and groaned as it came to life.

The platforms and railyards of East Perth were still visible from the compartment windows, but they would quickly disappear in a blur as the train gathered pace. For the excited travellers inside, Sydney lay four days and three nights to the east.

'Oops, nearly lost it,' Maggie giggled at the sudden, unexpected movement and almost spilled her champagne.

'Lucky there's plenty where that came from,' Hurley said as he took the bottle from the ice bucket and refilled their glasses.

Earlier he had watched amused as she had poked around into everything that Platinum Service on the Indian-Pacific Railway had to offer them; she was like a child finding wonder wherever she looked, bubbling with excitement at the prospect of what would be her first long distance train journey. For now, she reclined on the lounge with Hurley sitting alongside her, their feet resting on the leather ottoman.

'It's been a busy few months, hasn't it?' she reflected.

'Yeah, and interesting to say the least, some good, some not so good,' he summed up, nodding slowly to himself, trying not to think too much about the changes ahead, let alone all that was now behind them.

She seemed to read his thoughts. 'It's going to be a completely new life, isn't it?' she asked.

Hurley could tell watching her that thoughts of Harry's talk with them were going through her mind. His revelation and the subsequent offer had certainly been earth shattering, and they both knew their decision to accept it was life changing. It already had been for Hurley.

'Yep. But one we get to spend together, remember? You *are* happy with our decision, aren't you Maggie?' he asked tentatively, hoping there were no second thoughts.

'Absolutely,' she replied, 'and I know you are too. I just wonder where we might go and what we might get involved in.'

Hurley noted her voice was a mixture of excitement and trepidation, which probably matched his own thoughts. He watched as she sat quietly, staring out the window as the scenery flashed past, lost in her own thoughts. The noise of the wheels beneath them had risen in tempo and become urgent, part of the sound and movement around them.

'Who knows, and who cares?' Hurley said, upbeat for now and putting his arm around her shoulder. 'In the army we don't ever know what's coming next, do we? And that's a big part of what we like. And we trust Harry, don't we?' he asked rhetorically. 'For now, we have other fish to fry, madam. We have two weeks off during which time you will cross the island continent, travel on the longest stretch of straight railway anywhere in the world, do loads of other stuff, some of which is still a surprise to you, and drink champagne with one of the nicest blokes you will ever meet.'

Maggie knew it was all true and inside her she felt her heart skip a beat, though her face did not betray her. Instead she just smiled.

'Why? Is someone else joining us?' she asked nonchalantly, teasing him.

Hurley said nothing but his look mirrored hers. He angled his champagne flute slightly towards her in salute and nodded knowingly.

'Actually, I'm feeling quite tired,' she said, her voice completely lacking in any conviction, as she well knew.

'Are you now?' he played along, a sceptical grin on his face and eyes that said it all.

'Yes,' she said weakly, not wanting to look him in the eye in case she laughed.

'Well, it says here in the brochure the staff will prepare the cabins for night later, but I think I can muster enough technical knowhow so, please my lady, allow me to prepare your bedchamber for you.'

'That would be very nice, kind sir,' she purred demurely.

Hurley played with what looked like the obvious latches and handles and after some confusion managed to lower the double bed and fix it in place. When he had done so he stood back to admire his handiwork; she immediately jumped onto the bed playfully and moved up to the head, the pillows stacked imperiously behind her.

Hurley took in the scene as if he were taking a photo. Which of course he was, in his mind. Her hair had been trimmed just that morning, and the neat bob framed her face perfectly. Hurley didn't know the name of the colour, emerald maybe, or jade perhaps, but her soft summer dress was that shade of green worn so exquisitely by redheads.

It had ridden up her thighs which were now slightly parted, her legs crossed casually at the ankle. Her strappy sandals were discarded at Hurley's feet. He thought she was stunning and wanted her a great deal.

'I like your new dress, Maggie Redcap,' he said, his emotions in check, as he twirled the little handle and closed the thin venetian blinds inside the double glassed window.

'I wore it especially for you,' she said simply, the colour rising slightly in her neck. 'I know how you've been telling anyone who'll listen you've never seen me in a dress. Really Matt, you'll have them all thinking I don't own any at all,' she fussed.

He smiled and walked across to the compartment door and turned the lock. The audible metallic click made her jump and seemed so loud she worried it would be heard — and understood — by everyone on the train.

'Yes, I like it — a lot,' he said, his emotions now less in check as he sidled up next to her. 'But you do know I'm going to have to take it off, don't you?' he whispered as he gently slid the shoulder straps down revealing the sweep of her sun-kissed shoulders.

As he did, the line of the dress dropped to reveal the scars from the shooting; he knew she had chosen the dress partly because it hid both below the line. She closed her eyes and let him caress her. His touch was feather-light and his hand finished on her scar, his finger gently touching the smooth new skin.

'There's a lot of street cred here, you know,' he said playfully, trying to be positive, and at the same time let her know he didn't give a damn about the scars.

'I know why you changed our holiday plans too Matt Hurley, and it wasn't because you were tired of the heat, and I love you for it,' she said softly, holding his gaze.

He leaned down to kiss her neck and shoulders.

'But I'll be alright, you know,' she urged, 'I even put my swim-suit in.'

She smiled up at him. She wanted desperately to reassure him, wanted him to know she had put it all behind her and everything would be alright, and that he shouldn't worry.

'I know you will,' he acknowledged confidently.

'And you're wrong about one thing, you're not taking this dress off me at all,' she said, trying to look serious and steely eyed, but the smile breaking at the corner of her mouth.

'Oh, why not?' he challenged playfully.

She grinned cheekily. 'Because I'm going to do it for you.'

T H E   E N D